MU01073073

TED BELL'S
MONARCH

TITLES BY TED BELL

THE ALEX HAWKE SERIES

Ted Bell's Monarch (by Ryan Steck)

Sea Hawke

Dragonfire

Overkill

Patriot

Warriors

Phantom

Warlord

Tsar

Spy

Pirate

Assassin

Hawke

NOVELLAS

White Death

What Comes Around

Crash Dive

YOUNG ADULT NOVELS

The Time Pirate

Nick of Time

TED BELL'S
MONARCH

RYAN STECK

BERKLEY

NEW YORK

BERKLEY
An imprint of Penguin Random House LLC
1745 Broadway, New York, NY 10019
penguinrandomhouse.com

Copyright © 2025 by Evelyn Byrd Bell
Penguin Random House values and supports copyright. Copyright fuels creativity, encourages
diverse voices, promotes free speech, and creates a vibrant culture. Thank you for buying an
authorized edition of this book and for complying with copyright laws by not reproducing, scanning,
or distributing any part of it in any form without permission. You are supporting writers and allowing
Penguin Random House to continue to publish books for every reader. Please note that no part of
this book may be used or reproduced in any manner for the purpose of training
artificial intelligence technologies or systems.

BERKLEY and the BERKLEY & B colophon are registered trademarks of
Penguin Random House LLC.

Book design by George Towne

Library of Congress Cataloging-in-Publication Data

Names: Steck, Ryan, author.
Title: Ted Bell's monarch / Ryan Steck.
Other titles: Monarch
Description: New York: Berkley, 2025. | Series: Alex Hawke novel
Identifiers: LCCN 2024029858 (print) | LCCN 2024029859 (ebook) |
ISBN 9780593817230 (hardcover) | ISBN 9780593817247 (ebook)
Subjects: LCGFT: Spy fiction. | Thrillers (Fiction) | Novels.
Classification: LCC PS3619.T4325 T43 2025 (print) |
LCC PS3619.T4325 (ebook) | DDC 813/.6—dc23/eng/20240715
LC record available at https://lccn.loc.gov/2024029858
LC ebook record available at https://lccn.loc.gov/2024029859

Printed in the United States of America
1st Printing

The authorized representative in the EU for product safety and compliance is
Penguin Random House Ireland, Morrison Chambers, 32 Nassau Street,
Dublin D02 YH68, Ireland, https://eu-contact.penguin.ie.

For Theodore Augustus Bell III

The monarchy is so extraordinarily useful.
When Britain wins a battle she shouts,
God save the Queen; when she loses,
she votes down the prime minister.

Winston Churchill

TED BELL'S
MONARCH

PROLOGUE

UNFINISHED BUSINESS

Lord Alexander Hawke stood proud on the bridge of his magnificent flagship, *Sea Hawke*, as it sailed straight into hell.

It was time to finish what he had started.

Poised atop the crest of the sixty-foot wave it had climbed only moments before, the two-hundred-foot sailing yacht seemed to hover at the edge of an abyss. The howl and shriek of the wind tearing at the sails was barely audible over the sustained thunder of the Phalanx missile defense system, its Vulcan minigun hurling thousands of rounds into the sky, targeting a spread of incoming anti-ship missiles. Hawke had added the Phalanx system to augment *Sea Hawke*'s primary weapon during the last refit before leaving on the Antarctic expedition, a decision that now seemed nothing short of prescient. The missiles—Soviet-era P-15 "Termit" and the Chinese knockoff SY-1 "Shang You"—left bright ribbon trails across the night sky as they homed in on the *Sea Hawke* at supersonic speeds, only to erupt in fiery detonations as 20-millimeter shells from the Vulcan sought them out and, one by one, tore them apart.

Farther out, across the undulating ocean surface, bright flashes not only marked the location of the source of those missiles—four destroyer-type naval vessels—but also signaled the launch of a second wave.

"Steady on!" cried Hawke. "We've almost got them right where we want them!"

"And where is that exactly, boss?" asked Hawke's friend Stokely Jones Jr. "'Cause where *I* want them is about three thousand miles away. You know . . . approximately."

Stoke, as he was known to his friends, was a former US Navy SEAL who had spent more than his fair share of time getting pounded by high seas and weather aboard vessels far less robust than *Sea Hawke*, but he was nevertheless looking a little green about the gills.

"Where I want them," countered Hawke, "is at the bottom of the bloody Southern Ocean."

"Ah" was Stoke's thoughtful reply. "Well, it looks like the feeling may be mutual. And in case you hadn't noticed, there's a lot more of them than there are of us."

Hawke just laughed. "Never fear, Stoke. As Lord Nelson said, 'When the enemy is committed to a mistake, we must not interrupt him too soon.'"

Stoke wasn't exactly sure what mistake their enemy had committed to but decided now might not be the moment to explore the topic.

As a Navy man, albeit one who had never commanded one of His Majesty's warships, Hawke had long admired . . . No, *admired* was too plain a word. . . . He *idolized* Britain's greatest naval hero, Admiral Lord Horatio Nelson, who, despite being badly outnumbered, had led his small naval expeditionary force into battle and crushed Napoleon's navy at Trafalgar without the loss of a single ship. Nelson—who famously said, "A glorious death is to be envied"—was the very embodiment of the heroic ideal that a young Alex Hawke had aspired to and that he now, as a grown man of thirty-eight years, did his utmost to live by.

It was Nelson he strove to emulate as he drove *Sea Hawke* before the wind, headlong into the towering seas and straight down the throats of the enemy vessels who mistakenly believed that they were the hunters and not the hunted. Nelson, whose valor and spirit of sacrifice inspired him to boldly go on the offensive, even in the face of seemingly over-whelming odds.

And if, like Nelson, he did not live to see the ultimate victory, he would at least have the satisfaction of a glorious death.

To the extent that he had already accomplished his primary objective, the complete destruction of the ultrasecret Antarctic Dragon Base, that victory was already in hand. The only remaining question was whether he would live to celebrate it or if, like Nelson, he would receive his greatest honors posthumously.

The destruction of the Dragon Base, like the facility itself, had been a clandestine affair. International treaty forbade any sort of military activity on the continent, which meant that, despite the fact that the very existence of the base was a violation of international law, the aggrieved nations of the West could not take direct action against it. It had fallen to Hawke and his crew of modern privateers to rectify the situation, which they had done in spectacular fashion. Hawke and Stoke, leading a crack team of commandos—the legendary outfit known as Thunder and Lightning, so named for the call signs the two founders had used during their time serving as Navy SEALs—had gone ashore and traveled cross-country through the harsh polar environment in order to infiltrate the facility. Once there, they had planted enough explosives to destroy a small city and, once clear, had detonated the lot, collapsing the underground tunnels and chambers where the rogue nations of the Red Star Alliance had established a secret forward operating base from which to launch their bid to control the Southern Ocean in its entirety.

The mission had gone spectacularly. The Dragon Base had been completely destroyed without the loss of a single man from Hawke's team. All that had remained was to reunite with *Sea Hawke* for the long voyage home, a voyage that would take them once more into the most dangerous seas on the planet.

A belt of frigid water spanning more than twenty degrees of latitude—upward of fifteen hundred miles in places—and constantly circulating, unimpeded by continental landmasses, the Southern Ocean generated fierce winds and monstrous waves. Mariners called the region south of forty degrees latitude the "Roaring Forties." Below that was the "Furious Fifties," followed by the "Screaming Sixties."

To reach Antarctica, *Sea Hawke* had already braved the southern seas once. Getting home would require a second crossing, but this time, wind and waves were not the most immediate threat.

The destruction of the Dragon Base had not gone unnoticed. Even before the Zodiac rigid-hulled inflatable boats carrying the triumphant commandos reached the yacht, *Sea Hawke*'s radar had identified two naval vessels—the *Guangzhou*, a Chinese Type 052B destroyer, and the *Mariscal Sucre*, an Italian-made *Lupo*-class light frigate in service to the Bolivarian Navy of Venezuela—on an intercept course. Not long thereafter, two more military signatures were identified—the *Rio los Palacios*, a Cuban Revolutionary Navy *Rio Damuji*–class frigate, and the *Admiral Vinogradov*, an *Udaloy*-class frigate in the Pacific Fleet of the Russian Navy. Having failed to defend their Antarctic base, the Red Star Alliance forces now had a new objective.

Revenge.

Sea Hawke was a triple-masted sailing yacht, capable of speeds in excess of thirty knots depending on wind conditions—and there was no shortage of wind in the Screaming Sixties, which meant that it could easily outrun the military vessels now pursuing it. The supersonic anti-ship missiles those vessels were carrying were another matter, but this was of little concern to Hawke, who had no intention of running from this final battle. Retreating, to turn tail and run scared, was simply not in his blood.

What *was* in his blood, though, stretched back centuries. And now, as it came alive more than ever, Lord Alexander Hawke smiled.

Hawke, a direct descendant of the legendary English privateer Blackhawke, had always known that the blood of pirates flowed through him, but never had he felt so in touch with his ancestral calling as he did in this very moment.

When the hostile ships had begun appearing on the screen of the fire-control radar system, Hawke ordered the yacht to come about and set a course straight for the enemy.

Sea Hawke was going on the attack.

"Incoming!" Stoke shouted, pointing at the flare of a missile's rocket motor burning through the sky toward them. The Phalanx system had taken out most of the first wave, but *most* was not *all* of them. One missile had slipped through.

And one missile was enough to break *Sea Hawke*'s back.

"I see it," replied Hawke calmly. A former naval aviator, he'd been on the wrong end of an enemy missile before and knew that, at a certain point, it all came down to luck. And if this was to be the end, he would meet it in true British fashion. With almost casual indifference, he stabbed at the ship-wide public address and said, "All hands, brace for impact!"

At that very moment, *Sea Hawke* rolled over the lip of the wave and tipped downward, going almost vertical in the blink of an eye to plunge down the sheer face of the wave. At almost the same instant, the missile, armed with a proximity fuse, detonated in the air seventy-five feet above the yacht's mizzenmast.

The shock wave reverberated through the hull. From his station on the bridge, gripping a rail in a state of near free fall, Hawke couldn't tell how extensive the damage was, but none of the blast's fury had reached the bridge.

The yacht continued its swoop to the bottom of the wave trough like a surfer shooting the curl and then, with a suddenness that lifted Hawke's stomach into his throat, bottomed out. The bow plunged into the sea like the blade of a dagger but then just as quickly rose up again in an eruption of spray as the buoyant hull brought the vessel back to the surface, where *Sea Hawke*'s momentum hurtled it forward, plowing a furrow through the choppy waters.

Hawke slammed his palm down on the PA push-to-talk. "Damage report!"

For a long moment, there was only ominous silence over the line, but then the familiar, if breathless, voice of Tommy Quick, *Sea Hawke*'s chief of security, issued from the speaker. "We lost the mizzen skysail. Aside from that—"

The speaker went silent as the deck seemed to rise up underfoot. *Sea Hawke* was climbing the back of the next wave.

"Minor damage to the main deck," continued Quick. "No serious injuries."

The loss of the topmost sail on the mizzenmast was unfortunate, but if that was the extent of the damage from the shipkiller, Hawke considered it a lucky break.

Hawke's icy blue eyes flicked to the radar screen, which had momentarily gone blank, the radar beams unable to penetrate the wall of water separating the yacht from its enemies. Out on the deck, however, the Vulcan guns roared to life as the Phalanx system tracked incoming missiles in the sky high above.

"Fire control!" he called out. "I need a target!"

At the main weapons station, the gunnery officer, Edward Burton, was frantically reviewing the information displayed on his computer monitor. With the pitching seas, tracking targets manually would have been impossible, but *Sea Hawke*'s AI-enhanced targeting system overcame that limitation, predicting target locations with uncanny precision. All that was required of Hawke was to make sure that the yacht was pointing in the general direction of the target. "Come ten degrees starboard. The Venezuelan will be in range when we crest the wave top."

"Charge the laser," commanded Hawke, spinning the wheel to make the minor course adjustment. "And fire at will."

The laser cannon—on loan from Hawke's good friend, the eccentric billionaire innovator Elon Musk—was a 200-kilowatt free-electron laser (FEL) and *Sea Hawke*'s primary offensive weapon, which Hawke had dubbed the "Green Monster." Its energy beam could cut through armor-plated steel like a hot knife through butter and could, so its creator bragged, slice an aircraft carrier clean in two.

The weapon had already been used to great effect in previous engagements with Red Star Alliance forces, yet, for all its awesome power, the laser had its drawbacks. By its very nature, a directed-energy weapon required massive amounts of power. The energy needs of most weapons-grade high-yield lasers could not, in fact, be met with electricity alone but instead utilized chemical reactions that created toxic effluents as a by-product. Elon's innovation had not been the laser itself but rather a battery that could store enough electricity for multiple discharges.

Another limitation of the laser for naval use, and one of which Hawke was now acutely aware, was its linear nature. Focused light traveled in a straight line, meaning that the weapon—which was mounted at the yacht's bow—required an uninterrupted line of sight with the enemy. Unlike a missile or artillery shell, which could strike a target well beyond the horizon, the laser could reach only targets visible in a straight line, limiting its usefulness to about twelve miles on flat seas. It was wonderful for close engagements, but modern naval warfare was fought at a distance. The location of the gun turret also required *Sea Hawke* to be oriented head-on with its target, which was why the yacht was now racing *toward* the enemy vessels.

"Boss, you know I love you, man," Stoke rumbled, "and I'd follow you anywhere. But I just gotta ask. Are you sure this is how you want to do this?"

"The enemy chose this battle, Stoke. I'm simply obliging them."

As if responding to his verbal cue, *Sea Hawke* broke the crest of the wave, and as it teetered on the lip, Owen cried out, "Target acquired. Firing!"

When it had first been installed, the laser cannon had been operated manually from the gunnery turret on the bow, with target information relayed to the gunner over the ship's wireless communications network. During the retrofit for this mission, however, Elon's engineers had equipped the cannon for remote operation so that the weapon could be fired from the bridge. A good thing too, given the conditions.

In actuality, the Green Monster consisted of three lasers working in concert: an infrared targeting laser; a precursor beam that ionized the air between the emitter and the target, creating a vacuum tunnel through which the primary FEL could pass without simply turning the air itself into plasma; and of course, the FEL itself. Neither the targeting laser nor the FEL was in the visible spectrum, but the precursor beam shone like a shaft of pure emerald brilliance, describing a perfectly straight line out across the black nothingness of the chasm between the waves. And then, amidst the velvety nothingness, a blossom of orange fire marked the ray's terminus. The *Mariscal Sucre* had just been sliced in half.

"Hit!" shouted Burton. "Target destroyed, sir!"

And then, as if to punctuate that moment of triumph, *Sea Hawke* began plunging down the face of the wave.

High overhead, three missiles—all that remained of the eight that had been launched in the second wave—were beginning their final downward arc toward the yacht. One missile getting through was just bad luck, but three? Well, that was just unacceptable.

"Evans!" Hawke barked at the technician manning the Phalanx system. "Are you going to do something about those damn missiles flying our way?"

Evans, who was hanging on to his console for dear life as *Sea Hawke* sliced down the near vertical wave face, somehow managed both to answer, "On it!" and to manually retarget the Phalanx to splash first one, then another of the missiles. The remaining shipkiller, now less than a mile out, rocketed onward.

"Evans?" prompted Hawke. "The missile!"

"Yep" was all Evans said by way of reply.

At that moment, the pitch of the deck rose as the yacht curled into the base of the wave, going from near vertical to almost horizontal in the blink of an eye. The incoming missile was now almost directly overhead, beyond the elevation of the minigun.

Hawke, knowing that their luck had just run out, sent another warning over the PA. "All hands, brace—"

The next thing he knew, he was flat on the deck, his ears ringing and the smell of smoke in his nostrils. Stokely's face hovered above him in the gloom. The big man's lips were moving, but he didn't seem to be saying anything.

No, Hawke realized. *I just can't hear him.*

Even in his muddled state, the reason for this deficiency was obvious. The missile had struck *Sea Hawke.* The detonation had left him and everyone else on the bridge stunned.

There was no telling what it had done to the rest of the yacht.

"I'm all right," he murmured, or at least thought he did, and then, with more than a little help from Stokely, Hawke struggled to his feet. A haze of smoke hung in the air, but through it, Hawke could see warning lights flashing on consoles, and gradually, through the persistent ringing, he thought he could hear alarm Klaxons sounding. He staggered forward and might have stumbled if not for Stoke's firm grip on his arm. It wasn't just a failure of equilibrium; the deck was canted at an odd angle. *Sea Hawke* was climbing the back of another wave but doing so at a precarious angle and gradually turning broadside to the wave. If it did so before it went over the crest, the yacht would, in all likelihood, roll over and capsize.

Hawke lurched up the slope and seized the wheel, hauling it over until the bow was once more head-on with the wave. With that crisis averted, he turned his attention to the myriad other immediate problems.

"Stoke. Get a damage report. Find out if we're still intact."

"On it, boss!" answered the big man.

Hawke liked to say that Stokely Jones Jr. was about the size of your average armoire, a reference that always left Stoke scratching his head. Was there such a thing as an "average" armoire? How had that determination been made? Had some furniture designer collected the dimensions of all armoires in existence and done the math to find the mean? Why couldn't his friend have chosen a more relatable comparison? Like a refrigerator or maybe a Mack truck? That would have made a lot more sense since Stoke, unlike your average armoire, could *move.* He'd been a professional football player—a defensive lineman for the New York Jets—for about fifteen minutes until a late hit from a disgruntled opponent had taken him out of the game and ended his NFL career, but what a fifteen minutes it had been. Even now, decades later, Stoke was still as big and fast as any man alive.

He reached the control console in a single bound and sent out the request for a damage report. Then he scanned the board. "Fire alarms on the main deck. Automatic suppression systems have been activated. No damage to the hull."

Just then, Tom Quick's breathless voice came over the comms. "It's a mess out here. We've got multiple wounded. The aft mass is gone. The sails are burning."

"Do what you can," Hawke advised, knowing full well that Quick would already have begun tending to the wounded and rallying the able-bodied to begin the work of saving the ship. He directed his next question to Stokely. "What about our weapons systems?"

Stoke's gaze flitted over to the combat control center and the stations where Burton and Evans had been sitting only moments before. The two men were sprawled on the deck. Evans was stirring, but the gunnery officer did not move. Blood ran from his ear in a thin trickle. Stokely didn't try rousing the men but instead shifted over to Burton's abandoned chair and began studying the computer display.

"If I'm reading this right . . . and that's a mighty big *if* . . . then everything is still working."

"And the laser? We've got to hit them back."

Stoke's gaze flitted across the console. "Looks like the laser is still . . . Ah, shit."

Hawke's heart sank. "Talk to me, Stoke."

"Remote targeting is offline. The laser works—"

"But we can't fire it," finished Hawke. He immediately saw the solution to this problem. "Take the wheel, Stoke. Hold her steady and keep her pointed at the enemy."

"Aye, aye, boss." Stoke didn't hesitate. He left the weapons station and made his way down the tilting deck to relieve Hawke. As soon as the big man had his hands on the wheel, Hawke pivoted away and made a quick dash for the exit.

He was prepared to brave the full fury of the elements, but it was the state of his beloved *Sea Hawke* that nearly stopped him in his tracks. Tom Quick's hasty report had not prepared him for what he now beheld.

The beautiful teak deck had been blasted to splinters. One mast was completely gone. Twenty feet of another had broken off and now hung down, its spars and sails flapping impotently and wreathed in fire.

His beautiful yacht was dying, and he was helpless—

No, he told himself, thrusting the thought away. *Never helpless.*

He could still save *Sea Hawke,* but only if he dealt with her enemies first.

Holding on to the safety rail with both hands, he pulled himself toward the companionway that led down to the main deck, descended, and then reversed direction, pulling himself hand over hand up the sloping deck as the vessel climbed yet another wave. When he looked out past the bow, all he could see was the sky, and *Sea Hawke* appeared to be rising into it.

Then, all of a sudden, the yacht tipped forward, leveling out.

Hawke knew what was about to happen next. He heaved himself forward, crossing the rest of the distance to the cannon turret as the yacht began nosing over the edge. He was a heartbeat too slow. His fingers had just grazed the hatch when the deck began to fall away from beneath him. Desperate, he flung out a hand and caught the safety rail attached to the turret's exterior just before his feet slipped out from under him. Undaunted, he began hauling himself up the rail until he reached the turret hatch. Still fighting gravity, he wrestled the hatch open and pulled himself inside just as the yacht leveled out again at the bottom of the wave trough.

Quickly taking advantage of the reprieve, Hawke wriggled into the gunnery chair and put his hands on the laser's targeting joystick. "Stoke. I made it to the turret. Point me at a target!"

"Just hold your horses" came the reply in his earbud. Then, a moment later, Stoke said, "The Cuban ship will be off to port in ten seconds."

As the yacht began climbing the next wave, Hawke used the joystick to orient the laser in the indicated direction and then pressed his face against the eyecups of the aiming scope. The scope was tied into the AI-targeting system and utilized augmented reality to give not only a view of the outside world but enhanced targeting information, allowing Hawke to "see" the enemy ship even though it was presently hidden behind a wave crest, nearly half a mile away. He put the target reticle on the Cuban destroyer, making micro-adjustments to compensate for the yacht's chaotic motion, and waited for the electronic outline of the vessel to come into range. When it did, Hawke was ready. His finger tightened on the trigger, and a lance of pure emerald energy reached out across the chasm to touch the enemy.

The beam winked out in an instant, and in that same moment, *Sea Hawke* plunged down the sheer face of the wave, but the targeting scope treated Hawke to a computer-enhanced vision of the *Rio los Palacios* splitting down the length of its keel, the two halves immediately slipping below the waves.

Hawke did not pause to savor his victory but instead began scanning back and forth with the scope until he found his next target, the *Admiral Vinogradov*. The Russian destroyer was three miles away to the north, rising and falling with the waves as it tried to navigate toward the *Sea Hawke*.

Hawke understood now why the enemy had stopped firing missiles.

Sea Hawke was inside the minimum range for the shipkillers. The final battle would be fought up close and personal.

Exactly the way Hawke liked it.

"Stoke! As you crest the next wave, come twenty degrees to port."

There was a moment's hesitation before his friend's incredulous voice came over the comms. "Boss, you know what's going to happen if we're turned sideways when we go off the lip."

"I know, Stoke. I'm counting on you to make sure that doesn't happen."

He could hear Stokely grumbling over the line, but then the big man said, "All right, hold on to your socks."

And as the yacht rose toward the inevitable precipice, the bow began to swing to the left. In the scope, Alex saw the Russian destroyer as a yellow silhouette rising from behind the wave, then turning green as it was fully revealed. He depressed the trigger and sent a searing blast of coherent photons lancing out across the distance to drill a hole the diameter of a basketball clean through the Russian ship. The beam flickered out of existence as abruptly as it had appeared, but the fleeting contact was more than enough to trigger a secondary explosion, transforming the *Admiral Vinogradov* into a floating fireball.

Then something truly unexpected happened. Hawke's perspective on the world, revealed through the aiming scope, continued shifting to the left. *Sea Hawke* was still turning to port.

"Stoke! What the bloody hell—"

Hawke didn't get a chance to finish the question, for at that moment, the yacht began to tilt sternward, and he found himself staring straight up into the sky. As a naval aviator, Hawke had put fighter jets through turns and maneuvers that seemed almost impossible, but even he was gobsmacked by what his friend was attempting to do with the yacht. Rather than reversing course and bringing the bow back around to make the descent head-on—a move that would have required more time and maneuvering space than he had—Stokely instead chose to continue the turn, bringing the vessel into line but facing the wrong way.

A rare curse—one he did not often utter aloud—slipped past Hawke's lips as *Sea Hawke* plunged backward down the wave slope. The insane free fall lasted only a moment or two, and as the slope flattened near the bottom of the wave, the vessel continued its turn, carving across the face of the wave like a surfer performing some elaborate spin trick. Now breathing a relieved sigh, Hawke scanned the horizon for the last remaining enemy vessel.

Even with the scope's enhancements, the *Guangzhou* was a mere spot in the distance dipping in and out of view ten miles out and just coming abeam to port. "Stoke, if you can swing forty-five degrees to port, I'll nail this bastard."

"Forty-five degrees," replied Stoke dubiously. "Any other impossible things I can do to make your life easier?"

"I wouldn't say no to a celebratory tot of Goslings. . . ." He trailed off, spying a bright flash in the far distance. It had come from the general vicinity of the Chinese destroyer and could mean only one thing. The *Guangzhou* had just fired on them. "Stoke! Hard to port. Incom—"

There wasn't time to finish the hasty command. Both in the sky and in the enhanced objective of the scope, the projectile from the Chinese ship was a bright streak, incredibly fast, more like a plasma bolt from a science fiction blaster weapon than an artillery round. It reached *Sea Hawke* in less than a second, and when it hit, the effects were like nothing Hawke had ever experienced.

It felt, or so he imagined, like being hit by a lorry carrying a load of flaming napalm. The interior of the turret was suddenly as hot as a blast furnace, forcing Hawke to heave himself out onto the deck even as the entire yacht began rolling to starboard. Frantic, he threw his arms out, just managing to hook an elbow around a stanchion to keep from sliding down into the starboard gunwale. From the corner of his eye, he saw the shredded remnants of sails hanging from the two remaining masts, wreathed in fire as they dipped toward the ocean's surface, and realized what had happened. The enemy projectile had hit only the sails and likely passed right through them, but because of its tremendous velocity—given the distance it had traversed in the blink of an eye, its speed had to have been in the neighborhood of Mach 8—its kinetic energy had pushed a wall of compressed air as hard as steel ahead of it, a wall that had slammed into *Sea Hawke*, knocking it over sideways like a toy in a bathtub. Hawke knew of only one weapon that could produce such a devastating effect.

The Chinese had developed a working rail gun.

Hawke knew that the US Navy had experimented with rail guns in the early 2010s but ultimately found the technology unsuitable for combat applications because of the prodigious amount of electricity needed to power the weapon. Evidently, the Chinese had found a solution to that limitation. The rail gun utilized an electromagnetic field to propel projectiles to velocities well in excess of anything that could be achieved with gunpowder or rocket fuel. Unlike most naval artillery, the rail gun didn't fire an explosive warhead; it didn't need to. A simple tungsten slug accelerated to eight times the speed of sound—more than a hundred miles per second—produced the equivalent kinetic force of a school bus slamming into a target at five hundred miles per hour. The broadside shot that had knocked *Sea Hawke* over had actually been a graze, almost a near miss. A direct hit would have completely disintegrated the yacht.

For a fleeting moment, Hawke believed the yacht would roll completely over, but just as the starboard gunwale dipped into the frothing sea, the keel stabilized, and the vessel began to right itself. As the deck returned to something more or less level, Hawke climbed back into the turret and was relieved to see that the laser and its targeting system appeared to be functioning normally. He hoped that was the case, because *Sea Hawke* wouldn't survive another "near miss" from the rail gun, never mind a direct hit.

He scanned the horizon with the targeting system and located the *Guangzhou*, still several miles away but just outside the limits of the laser's traverse. "Stoke, are you still with me?"

There was a long delay—*Too long,* thought Hawke—but then his old friend's voice rumbled in his ear. "I'm here, boss. Shit, what the hell was that?"

"A rail gun, Stoke. If they hit us again, we're finished. You've got to turn us head-on into them."

"Turn," Stoke mumbled. "Yeah, I'll do that."

For several excruciatingly long seconds, however, *Sea Hawke* kept moving forward, riding the rolling waves. Hawke continued to monitor the enemy vessel, expecting at any moment to see the bright flash of a projectile bursting out of the magnetic weapon so fast that it set the air on fire. But then, as the yacht descended the face of yet another wave, the bow began angling to port as it rode across the wave. This new course kept the yacht hidden from the rail gun, but unfortunately it also meant the Chinese ship was hidden from the reach of the Green Monster. What's more, the enemy vessel was now falling *behind* them.

"Stoke, we're going to need to come around to get a shot. Can you manage that?"

"Boss, I don't know if you're aware of this, but the sails . . . Well, they're not exactly *there* anymore. If you know what I mean."

Hawke did know. *Sea Hawke* was primarily a wind-powered vessel, and while it was outfitted with twin diesel engines as a backup propulsion system, their top speed was seventeen knots. Riding with the wind and waves at their back as they were, that wasn't a problem, but he was asking Stokely to turn the vessel *into* the wind.

"Do what you can, Stoke. I just need one shot."

One shot.

And that was if they were all exceedingly lucky.

Up on the bridge, Stoke was pushing the diesels to all ahead full, and for a few seconds, *Sea Hawke* shot forward on a diagonal descent across the face of the rolling wave, building up a head of steam. Hawke kept his eye on the display of the targeting computer, which showed the yellow outline of the *Guangzhou* just below the virtual horizon. When Stokely began his turn, pushing the yacht back up the face of the wave, the yellow image swung abruptly toward *Sea Hawke*'s rising bow.

The yacht seemed to be clawing its way, inch by inch, up the wave. Hawke, with his eye to the scope and his finger on the trigger, kept the targeting reticle on the yellow image as it rose slowly like a bubble in a vat of molasses.

Just give me one bloody shot at this.

Indeed, that was all Hawke would get. Because the moment that the *Guangzhou* became visible to him, the *Sea Hawke* would be visible to the enemy. The two vessels would be facing off like a couple of gunfighters from the Wild West.

A yellow silhouette continued to rise steadily while just above it the black outline of the ocean's surface undulated, sometimes dipping almost low enough to reveal the Chinese destroyer, only then rising so high that the enemy ship almost disappeared completely.

"Wait for it," Hawke whispered to himself as the Chinese vessel began rising above the heaving ocean. "Wait for it. And . . . *now!*"

But as he said it . . . in the fraction of a second it took for his finger to depress the fire button, a yellow-orange flame blossomed from the *Guangzhou.*

The Chinese destroyer had gotten off the first shot.

Hawke pushed the button. A shaft of emerald-hued brilliance blinked into existence, instantly bridging the distance between the two vessels, and when it blinked out again, the *Guangzhou* was no more.

On the targeting screen, the projectile round from the rail gun shot toward *Sea Hawke* so quickly that there wasn't even time to shout a warning. Then a thunderclap split the air above the yacht as the tungsten slug ripped through the sky overhead and kept going. The yacht rocked a little from the hypersonic shock wave, but that was the extent of its effect.

The *Guangzhou*'s rail gun had shot high. It hadn't even been close.

Hawke allowed himself a delayed sigh of relief. He'd done it. He had won the day and, unlike Nelson, had survived the battle. Now all that remained was the far more arduous task of limping the battered *Sea Hawke* to the nearest port for repairs.

Stokely's voice sounded in his ear. "That was some nice-ass shooting, boss."

"We got lucky," Hawke admitted. "If our enemy had waited just half a second longer to take his shot, things might have ended very differently for us."

Stokely chuckled. "Well, as the man said, 'I'd rather be lucky than good.'"

"Hmm. Not familiar with that particular pearl of wisdom."

"Lefty Gomez. Pitched for the Yankees back in the thirties. Got hisself five championship rings."

"Ah" was all Hawke could think to say. With the adrenaline of battle draining away, he felt too spent for witty repartee. "Secure from general quarters. Bring us about, Stoke. And set course for somewhere warm and dry."

"Aye, aye, boss."

As the yacht began turning to starboard, running with the wind and waves instead of against them, Hawke exited the turret and stepped out onto the deck of his beloved yacht. What he saw then hit him like a gut punch.

Sea Hawke was barely recognizable. The decks were in shambles. Most of the safety rails were gone—only a few twisted stanchions remained, protruding from the ruin of the deck like modern-art sculptures. The fire in the rigging was spreading, consuming the tattered sails and creeping down the masts toward the deck. Worse than any of the damage to the vessel, however, were the screams of injured and dying crewmen as they emerged from the wreckage, some of them carried by their mates, others crawling on their bellies trying to get to the sick bay belowdecks. Still others were not moving at all.

Hawke stood there a moment, frozen, overcome with emotion.

These men . . . these brave sailors . . . had entrusted their lives to him, and he had let them down.

The rational part of him knew better. His crew had known the risk when they signed up. In fact, it was the inherent danger—the adventure—that had brought many of them aboard in the first place. And as every commander knew, victory was seldom achieved without losses—and this had been a victory—but standing amidst the wreckage and the carnage, it was hard to see it that way.

"Skipper? You okay?"

Hawke turned to find Tommy Quick, who was helping an injured crewman make his way along the deck. There was a smear of blood on Quick's forehead.

"Right as rain," Hawke replied, trying to sound upbeat. "Here, let me give you a hand."

"That's all right, sir. I've got this. Besides, you've got the hard job."

"What's that?"

"Getting us home."

Hawke nodded, knowing that the other man was right.

As if sensing Hawke's inner conflict, Quick added, "That was some fine shooting."

"Thanks, Tommy." Hawke managed a smile and started for the companionway. He hadn't gone five steps when the general quarters alarm sounded.

Hawke bounded up the stairs in three steps and burst onto the bridge. As soon as he entered the control room, he heard the rapid pinging sound of active sonar.

"Stoke! What's going on?"

"Got a fish chasing us," answered Stokely.

Fish was naval slang for a torpedo, and a torpedo launching *after* the destruction of the Red Star Alliance vessels could mean only one thing: There was one more enemy vessel hunting them from below. A submarine.

"Deploy the SeaSpider."

"Automatically launched one the second they started pinging us," replied Stoke.

"I guess we're finally going to find out if they're worth what I paid for them."

Modern naval torpedoes had little in common with the unguided, fire-and-forget weapons used in the World Wars of the twentieth century. The fish used by twenty-first-century navies were smart, utilizing a variety of guidance systems—from active sonar to acoustic wake tracking to detect and home in on a surface target. Usually connected to the submarine by a thin communications wire, a torpedo might make several passes in order to verify the target before finally detonating, not on contact but beneath the vessel, breaking its back with an undersea shock wave. Once a torpedo was in the water and tracking you, your chances of survival were slim. The Atlas Elektronik Sea-Spider, a next-generation anti-torpedo torpedo, had been designed to improve those odds by hunting down and destroying torpedoes before they could find their target. Whether they performed as advertised remained to be seen.

"Hope you saved the receipt," said Stoke. "You know, just in case you want a refund."

Hawke went to the combat center and bent over the console, watching a digital three-dimensional representation of what was unfolding in the depths below *Sea Hawke*.

The enemy torpedo was using active sonar, emitting a stream of intensely loud pings that bounced off the yacht's hull and returned to the source, fixing the yacht's location and reporting it back to an operator on the submarine. The SeaSpider was using passive sonar to fix the torpedo's location simply by orienting on the source of those pings.

For a few seconds, the only thing that happened was that the pings got louder as the torpedo closed in. Then the SeaSpider's onboard computer registered a positive target lock. Its solid propellant rocket propulsion system activated, sending it hurtling through the water like the shaft of a speargun to intercept the enemy torpedo six hundred yards from *Sea Hawke*'s position. The pinging ceased instantly, replaced by a sound like the roar of Niagara Falls. And then there was silence.

But a few seconds later, the pinging sound returned, almost as loud as before.

"Got a second fish," roared Stokely. "It's close!"

"That canny son of a bitch," said Hawke, both impressed and incensed. "He used the first one as a decoy while the second one was running silent."

"SeaSpider launched!"

Hawke glanced down at the screen, visually confirming the automatic deployment of the anti-torpedo torpedo. The device quickly acquired its target and, in seconds, was shooting through the depths, seeking out the enemy torpedo even as it closed with *Sea Hawke*.

Hawke held his breath, eyes fixed on the display, mentally calculating the time to intercept and watching in both fascination and horror as the estimated distance between the yacht and the incoming torpedo continued to diminish even as the pings grew louder.

Two hundred yards.

One hundred seventy-five.

One fifty.

"Too bloody close," he murmured.

Then, in a rush of noise, the pings ceased.

Suddenly, the deck heaved underfoot as the shock wave of the torpedo's premature detonation slammed into *Sea Hawke*'s hull, lifting it half out of the water. Hawke was thrown across the bridge like a rag doll, and for a chaotic moment, he couldn't tell up from down. Gravity brought the yacht crashing back down into the tumultuous sea, where it bobbed and shook for several more seconds before the violence of the explosion was finally spent.

As Hawke struggled to rise, the bridge was filled with a cacophony of alarms. He hauled himself to his feet and then staggered like a drunkard back toward the console. For a moment, he thought the difficulty was the result of having his bell rung by the close proximity of the detonation, but when he saw the multiple messages on the display, he realized the actual source of the problem. The yacht's automated monitoring systems were registering numerous hull breaches. *Sea Hawke* was taking on water, and despite the fact that the emergency pumps had been activated, the vessel was listing to starboard.

If that had been the full extent of the crisis, Hawke might have nurtured a slim hope of saving the yacht, but unfortunately, it wasn't. And worse yet, the enemy sub was still out there.

He turned slowly, looking about the bridge . . . saw Stokely still at the helm and clinging to the wheel . . . saw the few remaining crewmen still at their posts but looking to him for salvation.

Sorry, chaps, he thought with more than a little self-disgust. *Guess I wasn't so lucky after all.*

Hawke reached for the console, entered the command to silence the alarms, and then activated the public address system. He didn't know how many of the crew still had functioning comms, and this was a message everyone needed to hear. "All hands to the lifeboats. Prepare to abandon ship."

Stokely raised his eyes, looking at Hawke in absolute astonishment. "Boss? You sure?"

"The ship is lost, Stoke," replied Hawke, entering commands into the combat computer. "We have to do what we can for the crew."

"That sub is still out there."

"I know." Hawke entered a final command and then hit the return key. Then he looked up at his friend. "I said 'all hands,' Stoke. That includes *you.*"

"I'll leave when you do," replied Stokely. "You wouldn't be entertaining some foolish idea about going down with the ship, now, would you?"

Despite himself, Hawke smiled. "Never fear, Stoke. I fully intend to fight another day."

"Then why aren't we heading to get our asses on the lifeboats too?"

"Unfinished business. As you just pointed out, that submarine is still out there."

"And you have a plan for dealing with it?"

"I do. I've deployed all the remaining SeaSpiders. If that sub launches another—" He broke off as an alert message flashed on the screen. "Ah, here we go."

Five miles away and fifty fathoms down, the lurking submarine had just opened the outer doors to two of its torpedo tubes, a distinctive sound that did not escape the notice of the advanced detection suite utilized by the four SeaSpiders Hawke had just released. And as the torpedoes shot from their tubes, the cavitation of their gas-powered Otto turbines churning the water created an unmistakable acoustic signature that the SeaSpiders immediately homed in on. Almost as one, the rocket motors of the SeaSpiders ignited, propelling them into the depths. Yet the anti-torpedo torpedoes did not seek out the enemy weapons. Instead, they shot toward the spot where the cavitation noises had first been detected.

Hawke and Stoke stood on the bridge of the beleaguered *Sea Hawke*, watching the screen of the combat computer as it tracked both the enemy torpedo and the SeaSpiders. The torpedo—likely a Russian Futlyar or a Chinese Yu-6—cruised through the depths at a speed of about fifty knots, or almost sixty miles an hour, nearly twice as fast as *Sea Hawke* could go under full sail with a favorable wind. There would be no outrunning it. In another four minutes or so, it would reach the yacht and detonate. The SeaSpiders, on the other hand, were even faster, capable of speeds up to eighty knots.

A minute passed. Then another. *Sea Hawke*'s list had worsened slightly, but more alarming was the fact that the yacht was riding lower in the sea, weighed down by the accumulation of water pouring in the multiple fissures in the hull.

"Boss," said Stokely, "you know I like a good swim as much as the next guy, but if we don't launch those lifeboats soon . . ."

"I know, Stoke. I know."

Another minute passed. Passive sonar tracking the cavitation trail placed the enemy torpedo less than two miles away. If the torpedo reached them and detonated underneath the yacht, it wouldn't matter if the crew was in the lifeboats—they would all be killed.

Suddenly, a loud, prolonged rushing sound came over the passive sonar speakers. The SeaSpiders had reached their designated target and detonated in concert. Hawke held his breath, waiting . . . hoping . . . praying . . . to hear something more.

As the rushing noise began to fade, a different sound issued from the speaker—a shriek of tearing metal and the distinctive pop of implosions. Five miles away and fifty fathoms down, the enemy submarine, damaged by the close proximity of the SeaSpider detonations, was breaking apart. The torpedo, its guidance wires cut, continued to churn ahead mindlessly and would do so until its fuel supply was exhausted, whereupon it would sink into the depths.

"We got those bloody bastards, Stoke," said Hawke, pivoting away from the console.

"Good shit, boss. All things considered, you gave worse than you took. That's a win in my book."

Hawke nodded. "To the lifeboats. *Quickly.*"

"Ya think?"

The two men dashed from the bridge and raced down the companionway, then across a deck already awash in frigid seawater, to the starboard lifeboat davit, located amidships, where they climbed inside the enclosed escape craft. *Sea Hawke*'s lifeboats were more like space capsules than boats. Fully enclosed to protect their occupants from the elements, they would keep the survivors safe and warm for several days while they waited for rescue. Hawke and Stoke joined more than a dozen men—a mixture of crewmen and commandos from Thunder and Lightning—who had come through the hell of battle. Weary and wounded, they were a sorry-looking lot, but they were alive, and God willing, they would stay that way.

"Is everyone accounted for?" asked Hawke.

"You two are the last," answered a crewman. "Tom Quick got everybody else to the port lifeboat."

"Abandon ship," said Hawke, giving the formal order. "Away all boats."

He pulled the hatch shut and spun the flywheel to extend the latch bolts, sealing them all inside; then he hit the button to release the boat from its mooring. The escape vessel dropped only a few feet before splashing into the water, whereupon the crewman assigned to the helm activated the outboard and began motoring away from the now abandoned yacht.

Through a porthole, Hawke searched the dark water until he spied the other lifeboat, which looked like an enormous orange-colored bottle bobbing along in the tumultuous seas. Just behind it, *Sea Hawke*, abandoned and alone, water sloshing over her decks, her remaining masts blazing like torches, drifted away with the wind and waves. The sight evoked a storm of conflicting emotions in Hawke's breast. He felt relief that he and so many of those who had gone with him would live to fight another day, and sorrow for the fact that some of them had not. He savored the triumph of what had seemed like an impossible victory and smarted at the sting of what felt like a Pyrrhic one.

Slowly, almost gracefully, as if it might sail on forever, the yacht climbed the back of a wave, teetered on the crest for a long moment, and then plunged forward into oblivion.

"I'm sorry, boss," said Stokely with uncharacteristic solemnity. "I know how much she meant to you."

"She served us well," agreed Hawke. He sighed, then shook his head. "Life is too short to waste time mourning the loss of *things*, Stoke."

Stokely chuckled. "That's what I love about you, man. Nothing keeps you down."

Hawke shrugged. "What's the point?" After a pause, he said, "I can't believe I'm saying this *again*, but I do believe I'll need to build a new ship."

"Two things," said Stokely, rolling his eyes.

"Hmm? What's that, Stoke?"

"Next time, let's lose the laser. That thing was more trouble than it was worth."

"Yes, well, when Elon gets Twitter or whatever he's taken to calling it these days in order, I shall inform him that if he wants his weapon back, he's going to need a bloody submarine and a bit of luck to retrieve it." With *Sea Hawke* finally lost, Hawke turned to face his old friend. "What's the other thing, Stoke?"

"The next ship will have to wait. You got a wedding to get home for."

ONE

BALMORAL ESTATE, SCOTLAND

I t was the considered opinion of Chief Superintendent Tommy Fairbairn-Sykes that His Majesty the King was just a touch barmy.

How else to describe someone making an intentional, voluntary decision to venture out into the cold gray drizzle to tramp around in a bog for hours, literally beating the bushes in hopes of maybe having the satisfaction of shooting what was little more than a glorified wild chicken?

What sane person would do that? wondered the chief superintendent.

Coming up in the commandos, Fairbairn-Sykes had spent more than his share of days and nights tramping around in cold, damp, miserable places, but doing that had at least served a purpose. That had been military training, the *anvil* upon which he and his mates had been forged into the hardest, deadliest elite warriors on earth—the Royal Navy Special Boat Service.

What it was *not*, by any stretch of the imagination, was his idea of a holiday.

It wasn't as if the King's options were limited. The man could spend his leisure time almost anywhere—Corfu, Malta, Switzerland, the Caribbean, Transylvania . . . yes, even bloody Transylvania—and those were just the places with royal estates.

No, if this was the King's idea of a good time, then he had to be just a little bit touched in the head.

Chief Superintendent Tommy Fairbairn-Sykes, of course, wasn't going to say any of this aloud. Not if he wanted to keep his job. Because after all he wasn't the King's bloody travel agent. He *was* the King's personal bodyguard and senior commander of the Royalty and Specialist Protection branch of the Metropolitan Police.

Farther up the hill, he saw the King and the head gamekeeper, one Roderick McClanahan, stop in their tracks, and so he did too, maintaining a respectful distance of about 150 yards from his charge. Close enough that he could sprint to the King's defense or aid if needed, but not so close as to disrupt the hunt.

"We're holding," he said into the lip mic of his radio unit, letting the other five members of the protective detail, who were fanned out in a broad crescent trailing out behind the two-man hunting party, know to halt their advance as well.

In the hilly, fog-shrouded terrain, most of them didn't have a direct line of sight on the principal, and in fact, they were not required to. While they needed to know where he was, their real purpose was to mind the flanks, creating a barrier between the King and any would-be attacker. Fairbairn-Sykes's preference would have been to have the detail completely surrounding the King, but doing so would have risked spooking the game the King was so intent on killing, and thus ruined his sport.

It also would have put them in the direct path of his shotgun. Not a great concern given the limited range and effect of bird shot, but not something to be taken lightly either.

Ultimately, it didn't really matter, because Fairbairn-Sykes and his RaSP team—all veterans of the SBS and the SAS—had already taken steps to ensure that the entire estate, all fifty thousand acres of it, was locked down so tight that not even a weasel could slip inside the secure perimeter without their knowledge.

The King and the gamekeeper lingered on the spot for a good two minutes, presumably hoping to flush a hapless grouse out of hiding, but when nothing happened, they resumed their trek up the hill.

"We're moving," Fairbairn-Sykes said into his radio mic and then recommended his own ascent.

He supposed that there was a certain . . . not quite beauty, exactly . . . *appeal*? Yes, that was the word. A certain appeal to the Highlands. It was possible, at least theoretically, to have too much sunshine and golden sandy beaches or to get bored lounging by the pool with tall rum drinks.

It was like music. Sometimes, you wanted something with a beat that you could dance to, and sometimes you wanted a sad song.

Maybe it was the hunting that put him off, he admitted to himself. He was not opposed to hunting game per se. He just couldn't see the appeal of it as a recreational activity.

During survival training as a commando, he'd spent weeks in the Brecon Beacons living off whatever he could catch in snares, so he was intimately familiar with the primal satisfaction that came with killing your own food, but at the same time . . . why? In a civilized world where you could just nip out to the pub for bangers and mash or pick up a steak-and-kidney pie at Tesco, why would anyone want to spend their holiday trying to procure wild game?

Shooting was fun, sure, but there was more to hunting grouse than just blasting them out of the sky. After you pulled the trigger, you had to stomp around the moor to find where the bloody thing had fallen. Then you had to cut it open and—

"Tommy, I've lost visual. Do you see them?"

The radio call snapped Fairbairn-Sykes out of his reverie, and he was dismayed to see that he also had lost sight of his charge. The King and the gamekeeper had crested the hill, and now the foggy summit was blocking his view.

"No, the bloody hill is in the way," he replied, quickening his pace, not quite running but definitely moving with a purpose to reach the summit. "Jamie, do you have them?"

A different voice sounded in his earbud. "No, I don't. . . . Wait. Okay, I've got them. They've turned northeast, heading my way."

Even though there was no real crisis, Fairbairn-Sykes felt palpable relief that someone in the detail had eyes on the King. All the same, he hurried to the top of the rise, slowing only after he spotted the King, who stood only five feet ten inches with sloping shoulders in his favorite raggedy-looking Barbour jacket and his Lock & Co. wool flatcap. The King was moving along a narrow game trail off to Fairbairn-Sykes's right, perfectly oblivious to the fact that, for a period lasting about five seconds, he had been, at least technically speaking, missing.

"All right," Fairbairn-Sykes said into his mic. "I have them again."

And then, realizing that the King was taking another pause, he added, "Holding."

Downslope from his position, the gamekeeper was pointing into a particularly rugged-looking section of sedge as if something there had caught his eye. The King nodded enthusiastically, and then the two of them began moving in that direction.

"Moving again," said Fairbairn-Sykes.

The King and the gamekeeper strolled over to the patch of wild grass and then began carefully moving into it, gently pushing the long blades aside. Then both men knelt down, almost disappearing completely into the waist-high sedge.

A loud, mournful wail—the baying of a hound—filled the air. Fairbairn-Sykes turned, looking for the source of the sound. As loud as the howl had been, it had to have come from somewhere nearby, but that didn't make any sense. The King hadn't brought along any of the royal hunting dogs, and his favorite Jack Russell terriers certainly didn't have the pipes for a howl like the one he'd just heard.

"Do we have any dogs on the grounds?" he asked over the radio, hoping that one of the other protection agents would be able to fill this apparent knowledge gap.

"Just Beth and Bluebell" came the reply.

Fairbairn-Sykes felt a vague uneasiness in the pit of his stomach. He felt like he was staring at one of those visual puzzles in a magazine.

What's wrong with this bloody picture?

Then it hit him.

There aren't supposed to be any damned hounds on the estate right now.

He supposed that it might have been a feral dog that had wandered onto the property days or even weeks before the King's visit and that it had somehow managed to escape the notice of both the household staff and the RaSP team's security sweep. It was a plausible enough explanation, but it was still an anomaly, and anomalies are what happen when you don't do your job.

"I want to know where that dog came fr—" He stopped short as he realized that the King was no longer kneeling in the sedge. "Oh, bollocks, I've lost him again. Does anyone have an eye on?"

He didn't wait for the answers but jogged ahead to the sedge, turning this way and that, certain that the two men would, at any moment, materialize from out of the fog, but they did not.

Voices sounded in his ear like a Greek chorus.

"I don't have him."

"Nothing here."

"Where the hell did he go?"

Fairbairn-Sykes ignored them. He wasn't quite frantic, not yet, but his heart was definitely beating faster.

"Majesty!" he called out.

He waited for the King to answer, knowing that when the King finally did, he would feel like a ninny for having panicked. But the answer didn't come.

He turned ninety degrees and shouted, louder this time, "Majesty! Where are you?"

No reply.

"Bugger," he growled, then took out his Scotland Yard–issued mobile phone and opened a tracking app that was linked via Bluetooth to the King's Parmigiani Fleurier Toric Chronograph, which had been specially modified with a panic button and a location tag.

The phone display showed a topographic rendering of the surrounding area, along with two little dots closely spaced—one blue and one red. The blue dot, which also had a little arrow to show the direction of travel, marked the location and orientation of the phone. The red dot was the King.

Had the monarch pressed the panic button, the red dot would have begun flashing, and the phone itself would have sounded an alert. That neither had happened meant that the King at least didn't think he was in any trouble.

Fairbairn-Sykes turned until the blue arrow was pointing directly at the red dot and then began moving in that direction. "Majesty? Call out if you can hear me!"

Within just a few steps, the dots began to overlap.

He should be right here, thought the bodyguard. *I'm right on top of him.*

He looked away from the phone's display and saw that he had returned to the sedge, the last place he'd seen the King.

Before I got distracted by that infernal dog.

"Majesty?"

The red dot was there, right in front of him, but where was the . . .

Wait a minute. . . .

He knelt down, pushing aside the blades of grass, and saw, lying on the ground, the white face and gold bezel of the Parmigiani watch.

His heart stopped. He opened his mouth to speak but couldn't seem to form the words.

No. This can't be happening.

The white watch face transfixed him, held him captive like the gaze of a basilisk. The sweep second hand moved smoothly around the dial, ticking past the black Roman numerals.

III . . .

IIII . . .

V . . .

A dozen scenarios flashed through his mind.

Was the King putting one over on him? Playing a foolish prank?

VI . . .

He dismissed the notion, recognizing it for what it was.

Denial.

The Yanks had a name for it. Normalcy bias. The human tendency to want to disbelieve or minimize an impending crisis.

Better known as the "Ostrich Effect."

Pull your bleeding head out of the sand, he shouted to himself. *This* IS *the bleeding crisis!*

There was only one possible explanation for what was happening here.

VII . . .

He caught his breath and managed to gasp a command into his lip mic. "Close in."

He saw that the watch's black leather band had been unbuckled and was splayed out as if for presentation. There was no evidence that it had been forcibly removed, suggesting that the King himself had taken it off or had at least submitted to its removal by his . . .

His abductor.

Fairbairn-Sykes hesitated to even *think of* the word, but what other explanation could there be? And if that was what had happened, then he needed to act quickly.

VIII . . .

He tore his gaze away from the watch, took out his radio, and switched from the private channel used by the detail to the general frequency monitored by the entire contingent of RaSP officers present at the estate.

"Lock down the property," he said. "I say again: Lock. Down. Condition Black!"

Just then, he heard the pounding of approaching footsteps and raised his eyes to see Chief Inspector Jamie Faulkner, number two on the King's detail, running toward him, the first to answer the summons.

"Where is he?"

The question was not casually asked.

Fairbairn-Sykes held the other man's stare but did not answer until the rest of the team joined them. He didn't want to have to repeat himself.

It was a long twenty seconds.

"The King has been abducted," he said, surprised at how calm he sounded.

Well, he thought, *I've had a moment to process it all, haven't I?*

"I've given the order to lock down the property. Nobody in or out. Nowhere for them to go. I don't know who they are or how they did it, but they have to be close."

He did a quick mental calculation. How long had it been? A minute? Ninety seconds? Surely not longer than that. How far could they have gone in that time?

"No more than five hundred meters," he went on. "They didn't come back through our line, so they must be moving north. Fan out. Find him. *Now!*"

The RaSP officers moved without question or hesitation, wheeling around and sprinting out across the foggy moor.

Fairbairn-Sykes, however, remained where he was, his gaze drawn back to the King's designer chronograph and its sweep hand endlessly turning circles as it ticked away the seconds. Minutes went by.

And then hours.

And yet the King was still nowhere to be found.

TWO

It was said of Lord Alexander Hawke, on the eve of his birth, that he would be "a boy born with a heart for any fate."

Those prophetic words, uttered by his father, the late Lord Admiral Hawke, had manifested time and again in diverse ways over the course of Alex's nearly forty years, but never . . . not once . . . would he have interpreted fate in terms that could have been construed as synonymous with anything even remotely resembling happiness.

Surely, there could be no happy endings for a boy who, at the tender age of seven, had witnessed the brutal murders of his parents. Or for the husband who had held his dying wife as the life slowly drained from her body following an attack that occurred mere minutes after their wedding.

No peace for the man who it had also been said was "a creature of radiant violence" and "naturally good at war." And who had just proven that to be true yet again only days ago.

As a Royal Navy aviator, Hawke had flown sorties over Baghdad and been thrice decorated for valor. On his last outing, his Harrier had been shot down. He had been captured and endured the brutality of Saddam's torturers, but in the end, he had managed his own escape, killing many of his captors with his bare hands, because death at the hands of such men was not the fate for which his heart had been forged.

He had gone on to become his nation's foremost counterintelligence operative, carrying the war into the shadows, fighting, killing, and saving the world time and again.

Victorious?

Always.

But happy?

Ah, happy.

Oh, there had been moments, too brief in hindsight, when he had dared to let himself believe he had achieved that most ineffable of romantic ideals.

Moments that had always ended in blood and loss and sorrow.

How many friends had he buried? How many lovers?

Even the joy he had felt upon discovering that he was a father, that a woman he had loved and lost had, in fact, survived and borne him a son . . .

My beautiful Alexei.

Even that, which ought to have been a source of surpassing joy for any man, had instead arrived with an equal measure of heartache. Alexei's mother, Anastasia Korsakova, the love of Hawke's life, had already been given to another. And from that moment forward, Alexei himself had been in near constant danger, targeted by the enemies of both his mother and his father.

And yet . . .

And yet now, for the first time in as long as he could remember, as Lord Hawke sat in one of the old cast-off planter's chairs that furnished the whitewashed living room of his beloved Teakettle Cottage, perched fifty feet above the turquoise sea where he'd made as many memories as the ocean had waves, he felt nothing but happiness.

Or was it contentedness?

Anastasia had come back into his life, freed from the shackles that had held her in exile. There had been bumps along the way, to be sure,

as they both reacclimated and attempted to resume where their relationship had left off. It wasn't always easy, and there were still things
they were trying to work through, but they were a family at last.

"M'lord, before I retire for the evening, is there anything else I can
get for you?"

Hawke raised his eyes from the novel he had forgotten he was reading and met the kindly gaze of Pelham Grenville.

If asked, Pelham would have modestly described himself as Lord
Hawke's faithful butler. Hawke, however, considered the octogenarian
to be much more than a household retainer. Pelham was his oldest and
dearest friend. Along with Chief Inspector Ambrose Congreve, Pelham had raised the orphaned Lord Hawke, shaping and forging the
boy into the man he had become.

Hawke closed the book, not bothering to mark his place, and set it
aside. The novel, penned by one of his favorite authors—a man who
once held the esteemed title of Writer in Residence at Cambridge and
who, before that, had conquered the world of advertising—concerned
the machinations of a man who imagined himself the next Russian
Tsar. It was a gripping tale, one he had read many times, but for some
reason, on this night, the words eluded him, losing their way somewhere between his eyes and his brain.

It was not the fault of the author. Hawke was simply not in the right
mood to countenance tales of woe.

"Uh, no, Pelham, that'll be all for the night. Thank you kindly."

"Would you like me to wait with you, sir?"

Hawke smiled. "No, no, I shall offer a perfectly warm welcome on
my own, don't you think? Besides, I've Sniper to keep me company,
don't I?" He cast a glance to the magnificent black hyacinth macaw sitting on the cage stand in one corner of the room, looking deceptively
serene. The parrot, trained in the old pirate fashion to warn of danger
and possessed of a colorful vocabulary, had been, like Pelham, Alex's
companion since childhood. "Isn't that right, Sniper?"

Sniper merely regarded Hawke with a slow blink.

"Off with you now, old boy," Hawke went on, making a shooing gesture toward Pelham. "Get your rest. I daresay you are looking more tired by the day. Rest up now. We have a busy week ahead of us."

Anastasia and Alexei were due to arrive in port this very night, returning from a weeks-long cruise aboard the *Blackhawke*, Alex's other mega yacht.

Now my only bloody yacht.

He pushed the thought from his mind.

The voyage had been a chance for mother and son to reconnect after more than six years apart.

Alexei had gone the first three years of his life without knowing his father. Then, without any warning to either of them, he had been thrust into Hawke's arms while aboard a train en route to Saint Petersburg. From that moment forward, he had been without a mother.

Now, with Anastasia finally returned to them, the young lad had both parents in his life at last. Nevertheless, Hawke understood and respected Anastasia's desire to have but a few short weeks alone with Alexei at sea to reconnect as mother and son. So, despite knowing that he would miss both of them terribly, Hawke had given his blessing to the adventure. The mild sorrow of separation would be nothing to the joy of the eventual reunion. A reunion that would culminate with a too-long-postponed nuptial celebration.

Besides, he knew it would be better for them to remain occupied than to just sit around and wait for his return from Antarctica.

"Thank you, sir," Pelham was saying. "Don't stay up too late, now. I may be tiring by the day, but you're not getting any younger yourself. And those damned things aren't helping the cause, you know."

As he said the last bit, Pelham thrust his chin toward the end table upon which rested not only the discarded novel but also a crystal highball glass that, depending on one's philosophical inclination, was half-filled with or half-emptied of Hawke's second dark 'n' stormy of the night.

Interpreting the remark as a dare, Alex seized the glass and took a long sip, savoring the sizzle of Barritt's Ginger Beer, muddled lime, and Goslings Black Seal 151 rum on his tongue. He then raised the glass to Pelham as if offering it for inspection. "I do suppose you're right there, aren't you? But what can I say, Pelham? A drink or two shouldn't hurt, I would think. It's my only remaining vice, now that I've given up women and smoking."

This was, of course, manifestly untrue, but not a lie so much as an exaggeration. A shared joke between two men who knew better and one that had changed with the telling over the years.

Hawke was certainly no monk, but after too many years of wantonly indulging his carnal urges, he had come to understand that there was perhaps even greater pleasure in the love of a single woman.

As for the cigarettes, a secret tobacco blend Morland had created and dubbed Hawkeye just for him . . . Well, he was fast becoming an expert at kicking that habit, having forsworn it several times.

"Besides," he went on before Pelham could challenge the veracity of the claim, "how can anything that tastes so bloody perfect possibly be bad for one's body?"

He knew better, of course. In truth, there had been times when Alex hadn't had the healthiest relationship with alcohol or, well, with anyone, for that matter. Back then, alcohol had been his way of dealing with such profound unhappiness. A substitute for the joy that had proven so elusive, but now?

Now he *was* finding happiness.

Wasn't he?

Pelham regarded him with a tight-lipped smile. "Right, sir. Well, g'night."

"Sleep well, Pelham," said Hawke as he returned his glass to the coaster on the end table and picked up the novel again. He thumbed the pages until he found the last page that had made any kind of impression, and began reading, but almost immediately he felt his attention being pulled away. He had the unmistakable feeling that someone was watching him.

It was an awareness he'd developed and honed in damned near every corner of the planet, something that had saved his life more times than he could count. Yet he intuited no threat. He looked up and beheld Pelham's bony figure still standing in the doorway.

"Pelham? Are you all right, old boy?"

"Indeed, I am, sir."

Hawke detected just a touch of emotion in the man's voice, the faintest hint of a quaver.

"It's just that when you said you were retiring," said Hawke, "I assumed you meant to your chambers. Have you taken to sleeping in doorways now, or is there something else on your mind?"

"I was just thinking, sir, that . . . well . . . uh . . ."

"Well, get on with it, Pelham," Hawke said. He tried for a humorous effect to hide an unexpected twinge of irritation. "No secrets here these days, am I right? Spit it out, old boy. Whatever it is, I assure you I can take it."

"I was just thinking to myself that you . . ." An odd, proud smile stretched Pelham's face, erasing the leathery wrinkles and making his gaunt cheekbones seem rounder and fuller. "Uh, well, m'lord, it's just that you look the spitting image of your father."

Hawke received this with perhaps less enthusiasm than Pelham had no doubt expected.

He remembered his father well and knew the two of them shared the same jet-black hair, patrician nose, and arctic blue eyes—the sort of attributes one would reasonably expect father and son to have in common, features that Alex himself had passed down to his own son.

But there were other traits he had inherited from his father, traits that had nothing at all to do with physical appearance and yet were as plain as . . . well, the nose on his face.

There was a hard streak running through the Hawke line. A *cruel* streak. And why not? The blood of pirates ran in their veins. To survive, a warrior had to be cruel. But Hawke was not at all certain that cruelty and happiness could exist in the same vessel. Wine might sweeten poison, but the poison remained just as deadly.

Hawke's feelings for his father were complicated by memories of that seldom glimpsed but undeniably present Hawke cruelty. It was something he prayed he had not passed on to Alexei.

"I do hope that's a compliment, Pelham," Hawke said, forcing a laugh.

"Indeed, it is, sir. The highest I could ever offer." Then, as if sensing that perhaps he had erred in saying it, Pelham allowed his smile to slip away. "Well, g'night, m'lord."

Hawke watched as the old man turned and disappeared into the dark hallway, his frail frame hunched over as if he were folding in upon himself.

"G'night, Pelham!" he called belatedly, but his old friend was already gone, and Hawke was alone once more. He closed his eyes, muttering, "Damn it, Pelham. Why'd you have to bring him up anyway?"

But it was too late. Without intending it, Pelham had inadvertently summoned the nightmare that had played all too often in Hawke's mind throughout his life.

———

"It's going to be all right. We just have to hide you for a while, and you have to be very, very quiet. Not a single noise till Daddy comes to get you, understand? Not a peep, okay?"

"Yes, Father, it's going to be fun, isn't it?" Blissfully naive, young Alexander did not understand what was happening and thought it all a game. Why else would his father hide him away in a secret locker aboard their sailing yacht?

"Right you are. Here's the key. I'm going to stick it into the lock on your side of the door. I want you to lock the door from the inside. And don't open it for anybody but Daddy, all right? Now, three knocks, remember?"

"Three knocks," Alex replied. A secret code just between the two of them. *"Aye, aye, sir."*

But those three knocks had never come.

Instead, a seven-year-old boy had watched helplessly as his parents—first his mother and then his father—were brutally slain by savage drug traffickers who had spilled blood with no regard whatsoever for the lives they were stealing or the boy whose future would be forever altered.

"No," Hawke whispered, struggling to banish the memory. He reached for his dark 'n' stormy, his hand trembling as he brought the glass to his lips, then downed what remained in a single gulp.

"Bloody hell," he whispered to himself. "That was more than thirty years ago. Get ahold of yourself, will you?"

He let the rum dull the pain, slowly but surely soothing his nerves, and contemplated fetching another drink.

If two is good, three must be better, right?

But no, tonight he was drinking to celebrate, not medicate. The two people he cared most for were coming home. Alexei, his only child and all that was good in him, and Anastasia, the love of his life, twice taken from him but now restored.

He was done with cruelty, done with fighting. Especially now that he had finally made good on his promise to destroy the Dragon Base. If life had taught him anything, it was that there would always be evil men—terrorists, criminals, power-hungry madmen—and that hunting them all down was not the secret to happiness but was, in fact, its very antithesis.

Oh, to keep his family and friends safe, Hawke would surely fight and kill if necessary. Of that, there was no question at all. But he no longer cared to be a creature of radiant violence. The creature who'd once been referred to as the Warlord.

"Why, you're the 'lord,' Alex. The lord who's 'always off to war.'"

No, Hawke was ready to leave his old life behind for good.

He regarded the empty glass and decided that two drinks had probably been enough.

A good moment later, Hawke heard the crunch of tires rolling on the crushed seashell drive, a noise that grew louder before suddenly stopping, followed by the sound of doors opening and slamming shut. Then the front door burst open, and Alexei, who was far too awake for such a late hour, came bounding inside, running straight for Alex.

"Dad!"

Alex stood from his chair and lifted the child into his arms in one motion, hugging him tightly.

"Alexei, my boy. How delightful to see you. I missed you terribly, you know. Here, let me have a look at you." He held the boy at arm's length. "Ah, yes indeed, you have grown yet again. A giant you shall be, bigger than Hercules himself."

Alexei laughed. "I just want to be bigger than *you*."

Hawke, who was well north of six feet tall, had little doubt that Alexei would one day surpass him in stature. He hugged Alexei once more, then sat him down. "Where is your mother?"

"She's coming. Oh! And can you guess what I saw just as we were coming into port?"

Hawke shook his head. "I couldn't fathom a guess, my boy. Do tell me."

"Three hawks. They were circling overhead, almost as if they were following us. Beautiful birds, don't you think, Father? And not one, but *three*! One for me, one for you, and one for mother!"

Three.

That single word transported Hawke into another memory—to the time he'd learned that Anastasia had survived what he had long believed to be certain death. Even more astonishing was the unforeseen revelation that they had a son together.

Alexei had been a day shy of three years old when Hawke had met him in Siberia, kissing his warm pink cheeks for the first time, forever changing the course of both their lives. When Hawke had asked how old he was, Alexei, who was learning English but far more fluent in Russian, had held up three sweet, chubby little fingers and declared, *"Free!"*

"Three," Hawke had said, interpreting the childish mispronunciation. *"That's right!"* But as the memory played like a film in his mind, Hawke realized that they were now indeed finally *free.*

Free of the bounty once placed on the heads of Alexei and Anastasia. Free of the demands imposed by MI6 and His Majesty's secret service. Free to live their lives however they wanted. And with all the resources available to them—Hawke was the sixth-richest man in England after all, and Anastasia had inherited a staggering fortune from her late husband—there was no limit to what kind of life they could create for themselves.

Just then, Anastasia, attired in a fitted white sundress that clung to her body like a lover's caress, emerged from the hallway, radiating beauty.

Alex felt an overwhelming urge to take her into his arms, and that was exactly what he did. As they kissed passionately, Alex lifted her off the floor and spun her around. She laughed, delighted, until she was out of breath.

"Alex, my love. Oh, how I have missed you! How wonderful it is to be—"

The sudden, harsh ring of a telephone cut her off.

Part of the charm of Teakettle Cottage—indeed, the very thing that had attracted Hawke to the property in the first place—was its rustic simplicity. Aside from basic maintenance and repairs and a few modern concessions, the cottage, once a sugar mill, was in almost every way just as it had been when Errol Flynn had made it his temporary abode or when Hemingway had used it as a retreat in order to finish *The Sun Also Rises.* The furnishings were an eclectic accumulation of items supplied by its many residents over the years, and that suited Hawke just fine.

Except now, he found himself regretting his decision to hold on to the old Bakelite house phone. There was something to be said for a telephone that could be put on silent mode.

"Now, just who might be calling at this hour?" asked Anastasia, the thread of their earlier discussion already lost.

"I don't bloody care," said Alex. He cupped her face and brought it close to his. "Let it ring," he said, and kissed her again.

Then again.

Eventually, the ringing stopped, but only for a moment or two. Then the old relic was alive and shouting yet again, demanding an answer that, quite frankly, Alex was unwilling to give. But when it rang a third time, Anastasia pushed him away.

"My love, answer the phone please, or do unplug it. I fear whoever is trying to reach you won't stop until they do." She arched an eyebrow and gave him a stern look. "And, Alex, my dear, it had better not be another woman, or we will be having a rather unpleasant conversation."

He knew she was joking, of course, but also knew that such jokes often hid a grain of fear. "You've already made an honest man of me, Anastasia. The rest is just a formality. All the same, I cannot wait to see you walking down the aisle in that magnificent dress, looking like an angel. My heart thrills just to think of it."

"Nothing will stop us this time, my love."

"Nothing will stop us," Alex said, pulling her close for another kiss.

The phone rang again.

Anastasia pushed him back and turned away. "Alexei. Come. It is far past your bedtime, sweet boy."

"But, Mother," sighed the boy a touch too dramatically, "we just got in!"

"Off to bed, dear. No arguing." She turned back to Hawke. "It is your bedtime as well. Tend to whoever is calling, and then come find me so we can have a proper reunion, my dear Alex." Her voice became low and husky. "I have missed you fiercely . . . in more ways than one."

Alex grinned. "Then I shall deal with the caller forthwith."

As Anastasia took Alexei by the hand and led him away, Hawke strode over to the phone, silently cursing whoever was so hell-bent on reaching him at this ungodly hour.

Lifting the receiver from the cradle, Alex made no attempt to hide his annoyance at the intrusion. "Yes, hello?"

"Alex, where the devil have you been? I've been trying to ring you. It's an emergency—"

"Ambrose!" said Alex, pleasantly surprised to hear his old friend's voice. "It's been forever since I've heard from you." He stopped himself, recalling that the last time they had spoken had been at the funeral. Then, realizing that good news is never given late at night, he said, "I'm sure you didn't call just to catch up. So, what's the matter?"

"It's the King. . . ."

And even before Ambrose Congreve could finish his sentence, Hawke knew, his promises notwithstanding, that all of his plans were about to change.

A moment later, his intuition proved correct.

Congreve wasn't calling to catch up. He needed help. *Desperately.* And he needed someone he could trust. He needed Alexander Hawke.

He needed . . .

The Warlord.

THREE

There were, not surprisingly, more than a few benefits to being the sixth-wealthiest man in all of England, not the least of which was never having to fly commercially.

Less than an hour after taking Congreve's call, Alex Hawke was wheels up aboard his Gulfstream G800—a recent acquisition and a considerable upgrade from the smaller and somewhat slower G IV that had reliably met his needs for many years. Six hours after that, the jet was on the ground at Aberdeen International Airport.

Hawke spent most of that time asleep, for he possessed a soldier's gift for grabbing sleep whenever an opportunity presented itself.

The dark 'n' stormys probably helped a little as well.

What he did not do during the flight was speculate on the nature of the urgent summons that had taken him away from his beloved family. *"It's the King,"* Congreve had said. *"Come at once."* And that was enough.

Charles was Hawke's friend, though that word alone hardly captured the significance nor did justice to their long relationship. The Hawke family had been close to the Windsor family for generations, and Alex had known Charles since his schoolboy days. Following the tragic death of his beloved parents, Alex had taken comfort knowing that Charles, in particular, had looked out for him, even going as far as to invite young Hawke to spend many weekends at Sandringham and Windsor and even allowing him to partake in the summer holiday festivities with the Royal Family at Balmoral Castle in Scotland. But even beyond their personal relationship, Charles was *his* king. Hawke was bound by duty as both a loyal subject and an officer in His Majesty's Royal Navy. And while he no longer wore a uniform, when duty called, Hawke did not ask.

He *answered.*

The fact that Congreve had conspicuously neglected to offer even a hint of what might be going on was indeed a touch concerning, but if his old friend did not see fit to volunteer any information, Hawke knew there must have been good reason. No doubt Congreve would reveal the precise nature of the emergency to Hawke when he reached Balmoral Castle. No sense in losing sleep over something beyond his control.

Nor would he permit himself to expend his reserves of mental energy worrying over Anastasia's reaction to the news that he was leaving. At least, that was what he told himself as he dimmed the lights in the customized sleeping compartment and stretched out on the plush mattress.

His heart, however, had other plans.

When he closed his eyes and began the deep-breathing exercise that reliably put him in a state of total relaxation, that last conversation played like a movie in the theater of his mind.

"Anastasia, darling, something rather important has come up. I must go. Straightaway."

She had stared at him, the smile sliding from her lips when she realized that he wasn't having her on. *"You're serious, Alex? You're leaving now?"*

"Never more so."

"You told me you were done with that life."

"I know what I told you," he had said, striving to sound contrite. *"But this is a special circumstance. It's out of my hands, don't you see?"*

"Special circumstance," she'd echoed, her tone dubious. She'd looked as if she had more to say but then simply folded her arms over her chest and

sighed. *"You must be the man you are, Alex. If you were someone else, I would not have fallen in love with you. I only wish you would stop lying to yourself about it."*

"I'm not lying to anyone. I want to be with you and Alexei. You're my whole world now. It's just that this is a special—"

"Special circumstance. Yes, you said that already."

"Anastasia, I promise I'll make it up to you."

She'd raised her hand, palm out in a "stop" gesture. *"I never asked for promises, Alex."*

And then, as if to show that she forgave him, she'd taken him in her arms and kissed him tenderly. *"Go. Do what you must and come back to us. We will be here."*

"We will be here."

During the flight, Hawke had replayed those words over and over again in his head.

What the bloody hell did she mean by that?

"We will be here." What . . . this time?

Only, she hadn't said *that*. Hadn't given him any sort of ultimatum. No, what she had said was far more ominous.

"Be the man you are. Stop lying to yourself."

Is that what I'm doing? Hawke wondered.

He considered silencing his inner dialogue with a tot of Goslings but thought better of it. He wanted to greet the looming crisis with a clear head. So, he decided to watch television instead, hoping to find some hint regarding the dire emergency that had necessitated his abrupt departure.

Hawke tuned the onboard plasma screen to BBC News. He did not expect anything explicit. It was quite evident that information about the matter was under tight control. But Alex knew how to read between the lines, knew how to sift grains of truth from the chaff of "breaking news." However, none of the stories being reported had anything at all to do with the King or the Royal Family. He switched to Sky News, CNN, and Fox News. He even tried Al Jazeera, but nowhere was there even a whisper of trouble at Balmoral.

That was not to say it was a quiet news day. The big story out of the United Kingdom was the looming referendum for Scottish independence.

Because Teakettle Cottage's sole connection to the outside world was a single landline and an antiquated telephone—and that was the way Hawke liked it—he had only a passing familiarity with the issue, which is to say, he was aware of it but hadn't given it much thought.

The Scottish independence movement was nothing new. Indeed, it was a sentiment that went back to the days of William Wallace and the First War of Scottish Independence, but subsequently, the unification of the Kingdoms of Scotland and England had been a matter of strategic and economic alliance, not conquest.

In recent memory, there had been repeated efforts by factions within the Scottish populace and government to leave the Union, the most notable of which had been the 2014 referendum for Scottish independence. At that time, a majority of Scots had voted in favor of remaining a part of the UK, but much of the support for that position had arisen from the fact that critics of independence warned that admission to the European Union for an independent Scotland would by no means be automatic. Many of those voters felt betrayed when, less than two years later, the Brexit vote began the process of ending UK membership in the EU. Not surprisingly, supporters of Scottish independence began calling for another referendum on the question, and the time for that vote was nearly at hand.

Because he owned property in Scotland, in the form of a fine old castle in the Hebrides with a world-class golf course, Alex had something of a vested interest in the outcome, and indeed, had he cared to, he could have cast a vote. The problem was, he didn't have strong feelings one way or the other. While he admired the idea of independence, he also valued the strength that came with being part of something bigger.

Better, he supposed, to leave it up to the people who would be most affected by the outcome.

Eventually, the news broadcasts did what his relaxation techniques could not, and Hawke drifted into a deep slumber from which he did not awaken until the pilot announced their approach to Aberdeen International Airport. To get the blood flowing, he performed a somewhat truncated version of the Royal Navy aviators' daily physical fitness routine, which he did faithfully every morning, then toweled off and changed into attire more befitting a visit to a royal estate.

Given the urgency of Congreve's summons, he half expected to find a helicopter waiting on the tarmac, ready to whisk him off to Balmoral Estate, but there was only a lone Belgravia Green Range Rover parked just inside the general aviation hangar, and a single plainclothed figure standing beside it. Hawke's sharp eyes made out the face of the driver, and he felt a sudden surge of emotion.

"Ross!" he cried out, leaping from the jet's exit stairs and hastening to greet his old comrade in arms Ross Sutherland.

Many years before, Hawke and Sutherland had flown together in a Royal Navy Harrier Squadron. Their last mission together, a reconnaissance flight as part of a joint operation with the US Navy, had ended prematurely when a Russian-made surface-to-air missile the enemy wasn't supposed to possess knocked their F-14 "Tomcat" out of the sky. Hawke and a badly injured Sutherland had been forced to eject from their damaged aircraft and had subsequently been captured by enemy forces on the ground and subjected to brutal torture. Their lives would have been forfeit had Hawke not managed to overpower their guards and kill two men with his bare hands to win their freedom. Carrying Sutherland on his back and accompanied by another liberated prisoner, a US Army tank squadron commander named Patrick "Brickhouse" Kelly, Hawke had led a nighttime trek across the desert, navigating by the stars, to eventually link up with Kelly's command.

After recovering from his injuries, Sutherland went on to enjoy a successful career with the Special Branch of the London Metropolitan Police, in which capacity he and Hawke had had occasion to work together again. For several years, Detective Inspector Sutherland had been on permanent loan to Hawke, a trusted member of his cadre of counterterrorism experts conducting off-the-books missions on behalf of the governments of the United Kingdom and the United States. Later on, and in no particular order, Sutherland had accepted a promotion—to detective chief inspector—and had a proposal accepted—by the lovely Amelia Alcott. He was now a senior field officer with Special Branch and a proud husband and father of a beautiful two-year-old daughter.

As eager as he was to catch up with his old mate, however, Hawke was more interested in learning the details of the crisis. "So, what's this all about, old chap? The suspense is positively killing me."

Sutherland's smile slipped a little. "Sorry, Alex. I'm under orders to tell no one." The policeman was a strapping Scot, originally from the Highlands north of Inverness, and his brogue seemed unusually thick.

Hawke laughed, but it wasn't a humorous sound. "You're joking. It's me, Ross. How am I supposed to be of any bloody use if nobody will tell me what the devil's going on?"

Sutherland, however, stood his ground. "Orders from the PM. Not a word of this is to be spoken outside the security bubble at Balmoral. Too many listening ears. You'll be fully briefed just as soon as we reach the castle."

Hawke stared at his old friend in disbelief. "Well, then, you'd better let me drive."

Sutherland laughed for a moment until he saw that an unsmiling Alex was holding out his hand for the keys. "Oh, you're serious."

"Yes, Ross. Deadly serious, I might add. I was called upon and have been in the dark for the last six hours. I'm ready to find out what exactly it is that Ambrose needs from me." Hawke smiled. "Don't take this wrong, old friend, but you're not exactly known for your speed."

Ross laughed. "Well, then, let's not bring up what *you* are known for, Alex."

"I've no clue what you could possibly mean, and frankly, Ross, I no longer have the patience to guess."

"Fine," said Ross, tossing his keys to Hawke. "But not a scratch, Alex. And I needn't remind you that these seats don't eject."

Hawke climbed behind the wheel of the Range Rover.

"Then I suggest you strap in as tight as possible."

FOUR

Hawke, who had always believed driving at speed worked wonders for one's mood, was feeling surprisingly rejuvenated. "Nothing like a brisk drive in the country to get the blood pumping," he remarked, casting a glance over at his passenger. "I say, old boy, you're white as snow. Is something the matter?"

Their "drive in the country" had started off rather ploddingly, with the Rover bogged down in the congestion of early-morning rush hour, but as they left the Aberdeen hinterlands behind and climbed into the fabled and sparsely populated Scottish Highlands, Alex was finally able to make up for lost time. The Range Rover was not built for speed, and so required a deft touch in the corners, not a few of which he took on two wheels. Lord Hawke was a firm believer in testing the machines under his control to their utmost limit.

He was also a believer in testing himself.

Sutherland managed a tight-lipped smile. "Just, ah, recalling the last time we flew together."

Alex contemplated asking his passenger what he thought about the upcoming Scottish referendum as a way of distracting Sutherland from the white-knuckle ride, but decided it was probably best for *him* to keep his attention on the road.

It was fifty-odd miles to Balmoral, and Alex made the drive in fifty-odd minutes, which, given road conditions and traffic, was nothing short of extraordinary. The drive was indeed exhilarating—at least for Hawke, though less so for Ross—and the mental and physical effort required to maintain control throughout kept him from dwelling on less pleasant matters, but his primary motivation was simply to get to his destination as quickly as possible in order to learn the truth about what had happened to the King.

As they approached the turnoff to Balmoral Estate, Hawke saw no visible indication of a heightened security presence. If anything, there was a conspicuous absence of activity. The car parks, where visiting tourists could board shuttle buses to take them to the public areas on the grounds, were empty, blocked off with barricades and signs announcing that the estate was "temporarily closed" with "apologies for any inconvenience."

Hawke drove over the narrow single-lane bridge spanning the River Dee and pulled up to the gated main entrance. Only then did he see uniformed security personnel—four unsmiling men in full tactical kit—emerge from the gatehouse. One of them approached the Rover while three more covered the vehicle with their Heckler & Koch G36 assault rifles.

The officer looked in through the open window of the Rover and studied Hawke's features for a moment. "Identification, sir?"

"Well, I haven't got any bloody identification, have I?" replied Hawke good-naturedly.

Sutherland leaned across the center console. "This is Lord Hawke, Sergeant. You should have a security pass for him."

The sergeant leaned down to get a better look and, upon recognizing Sutherland, snapped to attention. "Right away, sir. Sorry."

The man scurried away to the gatehouse, returning a few moments later with a plastic card attached to a lanyard, which he passed over to Hawke. "Please keep this with you at all times, sir."

Hawke glanced down at the card, which featured a grainy likeness of his face taken, he presumed, from his military file, and then glanced over at Sutherland. "What's with all the rigmarole, Ross?"

"You'll understand once you're read in," said Sutherland as the sergeant stepped clear, waving them through.

"Well, we're here, aren't we? Inside the . . . What did you call it? 'The security bubble'? So, let's hear it. How bad is it?"

"Frankly, it's about as bad as you can imagine." Sutherland glanced back at the officers manning the gate. "Pull ahead a bit. Those lads don't know the whole story."

Hawke complied, letting the Range Rover roll forward in low gear, following the road into the woods that surrounded Balmoral Castle. When they were well out of the line of sight of the gate, Ross sighed. "The King's gone missing, Alex. And we haven't a clue who took him or where he might be.

"We don't know anything more than that," Sutherland went on. "Yesterday morning, he went out for a hunt and then simply"—he raised his shoulders in a helpless shrug—"vanished."

Although he had been prepared for the worst, the utter hopelessness in his old friend's voice chilled Hawke's blood. The last word wasn't the one Hawke had expected to hear, but somehow, it seemed even more ominous. "*Vanished?* You make it sound like some bloody magic trick or something."

"It *is* like a bloody magic trick. The protective detail lost sight of him for only a second or two, and as soon as they realized he was gone, they immediately locked down the entire estate. Whoever took him couldn't have gotten far in that time, but as of right now, we haven't turned up a single clue."

Hawke was still trying to wrap his head around the big-picture issue.

Charles is missing. . . . How is that even possible?

In some ways, that was even worse than death. While the King's fate was uncertain, the business of the monarchy was on hold. And while, as some critics of the Royal Family liked to argue, the King was little more than a figurehead, with very little real power or influence on the affairs of state, the institution remained a powerful symbol, uni-fying not just England or the United Kingdom, but all the nations of the Commonwealth. With the King's status unknown, faith in that institution would immediately begin to erode.

"Except for me coming to pick you up, not a soul has left the grounds since his disappearance. We're working under the assumption that his kidnappers are holding him somewhere on the property, but we've combed every inch. There's simply no trace of him."

"It has to be an inside job, then. I'd say you've got a traitor in your midst."

"That's our greatest fear, old boy. As his last order before turning jurisdiction over to me, Chief Superintendent Fairbairn-Sykes from RaSP placed the entire household staff, including himself and the rest of the protective detail, in custody. But if there's a rotten apple in the bunch, it may take a while to figure out who it is, and that, quite frankly, is time the King may not have."

They emerged from the woods, and Hawke beheld the turrets and gables of Balmoral Castle. It was a sight that he never tired of.

Acquired by the Royal Family in 1852, the estate had been a gift from Prince Albert to his bride, Queen Victoria. The castle, designed in the Scots baronial style and completed in 1856, had been the favorite summer residence of Queen Elizabeth II, and indeed, it was where her reign had ended in September of 2022, but it was not the only residence on the grounds. In addition to numerous lodges and cottages, stately Birkhall, formerly the abode of the Queen Mother, had become King Charles's preferred summer residence.

Hawke had visited Balmoral Estate on many occasions throughout his life, but his most recent had been particularly noteworthy. A few years earlier, when the Queen and several other members of the Royal Family, including Charles and his sons—the entire line of succession—had been taken hostage inside the castle by a band of international terrorists, Alex had personally led the successful commando raid to free them.

Hawke was beginning to wonder if perhaps there was some old Scottish curse on the land.

"Have you brought out dogs? Bloodhounds?"

"Almost the first thing we tried. They couldn't pick up the King's scent." Sutherland shook his head again. "It's a confounded mystery."

Hawke pulled the Rover to a stop at the end of a line of similar vehicles, some bearing the markings of the Metropolitan Police, others unmarked like Sutherland's. "Well, if I know Ambrose, he'll have it sorted before tea. Where is he anyway?"

"In the security command post. I'll take you there directly."

Sutherland led Hawke into the castle and down an unfamiliar corridor to a room that looked decidedly out of place in the elegant, if somewhat rustic, setting. The security command post was a strictly utilitarian affair, with a bank of flat-screen monitors displaying both CCTV images from all over the property and a GPS map of the surrounding area, which presently showed a number of markers with attached personal information.

Sutherland, noting Hawke's interest in the latter, explained, "Real-time location monitor. There's a chip in the security passes that shows the location of every person on the property."

"Did His Majesty have one of those?"

Sutherland gave a look of chagrin. "He had a locator beacon in his watch. Unfortunately, the watch was removed by whoever took him."

"Not a very bloody useful system, then, is it?"

Sutherland just shrugged.

"Alex?" boomed another familiar voice. "There you are! What the devil took you so long?"

Hawke spotted his dearest friend seated at a table in front of the monitors and hurried over to greet him with a warm embrace.

Hawke had first met Ambrose Congreve twenty years earlier, when Congreve was a detective inspector with Scotland Yard pursuing a jewel thief who had gone into hiding on Greybeard Island, the Hawke family's ancestral home in the Channel Islands. Young Alex Hawke had displayed not only a real fascination with police work but a genuine talent for investigations, which had ultimately led to the successful apprehension of the thief. More than that, however, Congreve had taken an avuncular interest in the orphaned Alex, who, aside from his somewhat aged grandfather and the already quite elderly Pelham, had very few role models. Over the years, that relationship had only grown deeper and stronger, with the two men working together on numerous occasions to thwart the designs of criminals and terrorists and to solve intractable mysteries. Congreve, a devotee of the writings of Conan Doyle and Dorothy Sayers, was himself a gifted investigator, often described by Alex as "Scotland Yard's very own demon of deduction." If anyone could cut through the fog and solve the mystery of the King's disappearance, it would be Ambrose Congreve.

"You're looking well, Alex," said Congreve as he stepped back from the embrace.

"And you, Constable, are looking . . . well, like there's less of you. I daresay, has Lady Mars stopped feeding you?"

It had been many years since Ambrose Congreve was a mere constable; that was Alex's playful nickname for him. Though officially retired, with the rank of detective chief inspector, Congreve continued to work as a consultant for the Crown, which was no doubt why *he* had been the one to summon Alex to Balmoral.

The fifty-something Congreve had never been what one would call a "prime physical specimen," and indeed, he was still quite . . . What's the word? *Round*. But Alex was not mistaken in thinking that he was just a bit less round than the last time they'd been in each other's company. Congreve had an abiding passion for fine food and drink and absolutely detested all physical activity—with the sole exception of golf, which he enjoyed with fanatical devotion—so to see him looking about half a stone lighter indicated some sort of change in his normal routine. His new wife, Lady Diana Mars, had not shown the slightest inclination toward slimming down her new husband, leaving Hawke to wonder exactly what was different in his old friend's life.

"No, no, nothing like that," Congreve said hastily. "It just, well, you see . . . I never thought that I would marry. I was quite content as a bachelor, as you know. But having Diana in my life, in truth, it's brought me such happiness. And you see, I want that feeling to last as bloody long as I can manage. So, I suppose I've found a new motive to take better care of myself." He looked down as if embarrassed by the admission.

Hawke clapped his friend on the shoulder. "Good for you, old chap. No longer starting every day with a heaping dollop of Tiptree's strawberry preserve on toast, I would guess? I do seem to remember a certain chief inspector describing such a meal as . . . What was it again? Ah, yes, 'pure, unadulterated bliss.'"

"I do miss that damned strawberry preserve, you know. Starting the day without it just isn't the same, but I will admit that I've taken to appreciating having dropped some weight. It's not all been glorious, I'm afraid, though. Having less to swing around," Congreve said, touching his still-plump gut, "has affected the path of my club. I keep slicing the damn ball, Alex. It's both peculiar and utterly frustrating."

"Well, then, perhaps it's finally my time to beat you on the golf links, Ambrose," Hawke said with a smile.

Yet Alex's smile hid a sudden pang. Without intending it, Congreve had struck a nerve. Quite unexpectedly, Hawke's dear friend had found love and the happiness that came with it, happiness so sublime that he felt compelled to take better care of himself in order to prolong that state of bliss. It wasn't all that long ago that Hawke remembered feeling quite the opposite. He'd spent months drowning his sorrows in booze and cigarettes, anything to numb the pain of losing the love of his life. Then Charles had called, needing him rather urgently. That had indeed been the wake-up call—*quite literally*—that Hawke needed to crawl from the depths of hell he'd been occupying prior to that.

Now, though, Alex knew he should have felt a similar happiness at the mere thought of being with Anastasia and Alexei, and yet . . . Well, here he was.

"Special circumstances," he had told Anastasia, and it was true.

The bloody King has managed to disappear.

Could there be a circumstance more special than that?

He simply could not have refused the call. And yet . . .

And yet Anastasia had accused him of lying to himself. Lying about giving up the life of adventure that had always been his first love. Lying about the sort of man he claimed to want to be.

Hawke shook his head, trying to silence his inner accuser. This wasn't the time or place for such ruminations.

Changing the subject, he said, "So, old friend, have you solved the mystery yet? I told Ross my money was on you to have things figured out by the time I arrived."

"Then I do hope you brought your checkbook, Alex." Congreve shook his head wearily. "It's a damned fiendish plot, I tell you. Makes no bloody sense at all." He gestured at one of the screens, which showed two hunters—one of them easily recognizable as His Majesty the King—making their way up a hill. "This is from yesterday. Just watch."

The men moved from one side of the frame to the other, and then the feed switched to another camera, following their movement.

"There are CCTV cameras all over the estate," Congreve explained. "And not many blind spots. So, we're able to track the King's movements right up until this happens."

On the screen, the two men entered an area of heavy vegetation and then knelt down, seeking temporary concealment. There was nothing particularly unusual about what they had done; a veteran of more than a few grouse hunts, Hawke knew that one of the men had probably heard a bird nearby, and they were trying to avoid spooking it before they had a shot. He expected one of two things to happen. Either one or both of them would shoot, or after an appropriate pause, they would resume stalking.

Except neither of those things happened.

A long moment passed, and then a different figure appeared in the frame, no doubt one of the King's protective detail rushing to discover why the men weren't moving. As the bodyguard waded into the sedge, the look of confusion on his face gradually turned to horror.

Congreve paused the playback. "That's all there is. They were there one moment, gone the next."

Hawke frowned. "Well, mystery solved. The villain you're looking for is David bloody Copperfield." When his half-hearted attempt at levity fell flat, Hawke went on. "Watch it again. There's got to be a clue we've missed."

"I've watched it several dozen times now," said Congreve miserably. "When I close my eyes, I can see every detail."

"Well, then . . ." Hawke groped for some thread to lead his old friend out of the darkness. "Cameras lie, don't they? What does this chap . . ." He pointed to the screen and the frozen image of the King's head bodyguard. "What does he have to say about it? Perhaps he saw something the camera didn't."

"I've spoken with Chief Superintendent Fairbairn-Sykes. It all happened just as you saw in the playback." A strange look came over Congreve's face. "Except . . ."

"Except, what?" prompted Hawke.

"Well, just before the protective detail lost visual contact with the King, they reported hearing the baying of a hound. This was unusual because there weren't supposed to be any hounds on the property."

"Well, which is it? Were they there or not?"

"There were no hounds on the property at the time," said Congreve. "But you see, it's the timing that's suspicious. The baying of the hound occurred exactly at the right moment to distract the protective detail."

"So now you've got a phantom dog on top of it all. I say, Ambrose, this is turning out to be just like one of your favorite Conan Doyle stories. *Hound of the Baskervilles*. The cursed dog that didn't bark. Only this time, the dog did bark."

"You're confusing *Baskervilles* with 'Silver Blaze,'" replied Congreve. "And I'll wager the 'dog' was actually a recording played on a loudspeaker. A bit of misdirection. A magician's trick."

"Then you've solved one mystery at least." Hawke looked at the frozen image on the screen again. "Have you been out there?"

"What?" Congreve raised an eyebrow. "Out where?"

"Where it happened. Visiting the scene of the crime, looking for clues. Isn't that what Holmes would do?"

Congreve seemed put off by the suggestion. "Briefly, yes. But the crime scene investigators have combed every inch of ground, along with just about everyone else from Special Branch. There's nothing there. No smoke and no bloody mirrors. Don't tell me you want to venture all the way back out there to see it yourself. It's a waste of time, Alex."

"It's a damned fiendish plot, I tell you."

Indeed, it is, thought Hawke.

"Come now, Ambrose," Hawke said, slapping Congreve on the back. "Wait until you see how much faster you'll whip yourself into shape when you start mixing diet changes with a little activity. I daresay, Constable, a walk in the countryside is just the thing for your new lease on life."

FIVE

Attired in a borrowed mackintosh and a pair of too large Wellingtons and armed with his trusty umbrella, Ambrose Congreve reluctantly left the relative comfort of the security office and set forth with Alex and Ross in Sutherland's Range Rover, with the DCI himself at the wheel, on an expedition into the darkest heart of Balmoral Estate. They followed the same two-tracked game road the King's party had traveled to the distant reaches of the estate set aside for hunting.

The road, which had now seen more traffic in a day than it usually saw all year, was a muddy mess. Sutherland parked with the other official vehicles at a staging area near the head of the same trail that the King had followed out into the hunting preserve.

"I say, Constable, I really don't think you'll be needing that umbrella," opined Hawke as they got out.

Congreve tapped the furled rain canopy to his forehead in a mock salute. "You should thank me," he said. "There's no better way to keep the rain away than preparedness."

Hawke raised a skeptical eye. "Well, there's a surprise, Ambrose. That sounds rather like magical thinking. Not something I'd expect coming from you."

Congreve laughed. "You're not wrong, old boy. But we all need our good-luck charms. Especially today."

Someone had thoughtfully marked the King's route with strips of bright orange engineer's tape tied to tree branches, but even without the markings, the well-trod—read: muddy—path would have been impossible to miss. Although their destination was only about a mile from the staging area, the uphill walk took the better part of an hour owing to Congreve's frequent stops to "look for clues," which the other men came to understand as a euphemism for catching his breath.

Although the view from the actual trail was somewhat different from what the cameras had shown, the change in perspective offered no more obvious insights. The patch of heather where the King and his head gamekeeper had knelt down and subsequently disappeared looked no more mysterious in three dimensions than it had in two.

Congreve lifted the cordon of tape around the spot and went in for a closer look, not so much interested in the exact place where the King had been standing as he was in all the possible lines of egress from that place.

"Well, Constable?" asked Alex. "Have your keen powers of deduction eliminated the impossible and brought you unerringly to an improbable but nonetheless accurate solution to this mystery?"

"They have not," replied Congreve, a touch more sternly than he intended. "The process of ratiocination requires a foundation of facts, which are at present in short supply." He stabbed the tip of his umbrella down the hill. "Two men cannot simply vanish; ergo, there must be some rational explanation for the observed phenomenon. However, without some mechanism to explain *how* it happened, I cannot even begin to establish a testable hypothesis."

"Well, perhaps you're looking at it all wrong," said Hawke. "Instead of looking at this like a policeman, put yourself in the villain's"—he glanced down at Congreve's mud-caked Wellies—"shoes, as it were. If you were going to abduct His Majesty, how would you go about it?"

"Well, I certainly wouldn't do it this way." Congreve shook his umbrella for emphasis. "This is far too elaborate. Too many variables. Too many pieces on the board. The more complicated the plan, the higher the likelihood of failure."

"Agreed. And yet our unnamed villain seems to have pulled it off."

"Indeed."

"I suppose the other question is, well . . ."

"As long as I've known you, Alex, you've never been at a loss for words. Don't tell me you've finally run out before finishing your thought now."

"Well, no. It's just such a bloody awful thing to say out loud, you know? But truly, Ambrose, the other variable that makes no damned sense isn't just why you would kidnap Charles here of all places. No, the *real* question is why they didn't just put a bullet in him and call it good. Unless, of course, whoever did it wants something else and has reason to keep him breathing."

In many regards, Hawke was speaking from experience on the matter, though he didn't want to voice that point aloud.

"We'll come back to that. At the moment, we must assume that because there is no body, they wanted the King alive, which means he's *still* alive. Why move him only to kill him elsewhere?"

It's a fine point, thought Hawke, *unless they plan to torture him in order to extract information.* He didn't have the heart to voice that reality either.

"To your point, I would agree we must assume he's alive." Hawke almost added, *"For now,"* but didn't. "So, back to the original question."

"You asked how I would—" Congreve stopped short, struck by inspiration. "I say, Alex. That's it!"

"Do go on, old boy."

Congreve turned and looked at the sedge again, then gazed back down the trail. "You asked *how* it was done, but the real question is *why* it was done."

"Why abduct the King? Well, I suppose there could be any number of motives—"

Congreve raised a hand. "That's not the *why* I'm talking about. Why do it *this* way?" He made an encompassing circle with his extended hand. "Why the distraction of the baying hound? Why the elaborate disappearing act? Why go to the trouble, not to mention the risk, of a complicated scheme?"

Hawke nodded. "Yes, Ambrose. Why? Do tell."

But Congreve just shook his head. "Let's return to the castle. I must speak with Chief Superintendent Fairbairn-Sykes immediately." Without waiting for a reply, he stuck his pipe between his teeth and started down the trail, moving with uncharacteristic speed and sure-footedness on the slippery path. After a dozen quick strides, he looked back and, seeing that neither of his companions had moved, shouted, "Well, come on, Alex. The bloody game is afoot!"

———————

Although nobody considered him to be a suspect in the King's abduction, Tommy Fairbairn-Sykes's career with the Yard was finished, and he knew it. There would be inquiries to determine exactly how it had happened, where the critical failures had occurred, and what procedural gaps had been exploited by the hostage takers, but even if every single one of them found him utterly blameless, nothing would change the simple fact that it had happened on his watch.

He would forever be known as "the man who lost the King."

Nevertheless, he remained a man of honor, bound by duty to do everything in his power to set things right, and so while he was officially suspended from his duties, he was only too eager to assist Scotland Yard's most esteemed criminologist, Ambrose Congreve, DCI retired, in reenacting the events of the day before.

As directed, he was waiting outside the carriage gate at the castle's main entrance when a mud-splattered Range Rover pulled up, bearing Congreve, along with DCI Sutherland and another familiar face in Lord Alexander Hawke. In his many years as first an officer and then the leader of the Royalty and Specialist Protection branch of the Metropolitan Police, Fairbairn-Sykes had seen Lord Hawke on numerous occasions during his many visits to the royal residences, though to the best of his recollection, they had never exchanged so much as a glance. When the royals were in public, their protectors—or, rather, a few of them—were always conspicuously visible, ready to step in front of their charges at the first whisper of trouble, but when they were in their homes, the ever-present bodyguards prided themselves on remaining unobtrusive as shadows.

Congreve bounded out of the Rover. "Chief Superintendent, thank you for joining us," Congreve said, and then got right to the point. "I want you to take me through everything that happened. Start from the beginning and leave nothing out."

Fairbairn-Sykes had done exactly that several times and didn't think he had anything new to offer, but he would tell the story a thousand times if he had to. Anything to see the safe return of His Majesty. "Right. Well, we left here just before sunrise."

Congreve raised a hand. "Forgive me. I did not make my meaning clear. I want you to walk me through it. Step by bloody step. Start when you first met with the King yesterday morning."

Fairbairn-Sykes nodded, then walked about twenty-five yards away. "I was right here," he said, raising his voice a little so that Congreve could hear, "waiting outside my Rover."

"And the rest of the detail?"

"We were all here."

"How many vehicles?"

"We had two Rovers between us. And the King had one as well."

"And did any of you ride with him?"

Fairbairn-Sykes shook his head. "No. That's not how it's done. The King has his vehicle, and we have ours."

"So, you were all waiting here? None of you were inside the castle?"

"No. It's their home. The Family. We don't go inside unless there's some specific reason to enter. That's how His Majesty prefers it."

"Yes, I thought as much." Congreve turned to his companions. "Alex, Ross, come over here. Now, Chief Superintendent—"

Fairbairn-Sykes forestalled him. "If it's all the same, Detective

Chief Inspector, I'd just as soon you called me Tommy. Might as well get used to it."

Congreve blinked at him uncomprehendingly, then went on. "Chief Superintendent, I want you to pretend that Alex and Ross here are His Majesty the King and the gamekeeper, Mr. McClanahan. Alex, Ross, I want you to go inside, then come back out."

Alex gave the criminologist a bemused smile but complied with the direction, stepping through the door to the carriage porch with Ross in tow. Congreve meanwhile walked over to stand beside Fairbairn-Sykes. A moment later, both Hawke and Sutherland stepped back out.

"Stop there," called Congreve, who then turned to the other man. "Just like that?"

Fairbairn-Sykes nodded. "More or less."

"And what happened next?"

"They got in the King's Rover. Roddy drove—"

"Did you speak to either of them?" Congreve interrupted.

Fairbairn-Sykes shook his head. "No. They got in, and we all took off."

"You said that Mr. McClanahan was driving. Was that typical behavior?"

Fairbairn-Sykes considered the question. "Now you mention it, that was a bit unusual. The King usually prefers to drive himself. I didn't think anything of it at the time, but . . ." He cocked his head to the side. "You don't think Roddy—"

"I don't care to speculate," replied Congreve quickly. "Not until I have all the facts." He paused a beat. "So, the King and Mr. McClanahan drove off, and you followed."

"That's right."

Congreve clapped his hands together. "To the car, gentlemen."

———

Little was said during the drive up to the hunting trail. Congreve seemed lost in his own thoughts. The esteemed investigator clearly had the scent in his nose, but Hawke knew from experience that Congreve would not share his suspicions prematurely.

When they reached the parking area, the former detective chief inspector fairly bounded out of the Rover and hastily resumed the reenactment. With guidance from Fairbairn-Sykes, he positioned Hawke and Sutherland farther up the trail and then walked alongside the bodyguard as he described the progression of the hunt. The thrill of his own hunt for the truth seemed to have energized Congreve. He did not have to stop even once to "look for clues."

As they neared the site of the King's disappearance, just half an hour later, Congreve was meticulous in positioning the men exactly as they had been in the moments leading up to the event. He sent Alex and Ross into the sedge and stood with Fairbairn-Sykes some fifty feet away.

"This is where you were standing?" he asked.

Fairbairn-Sykes looked around even though he knew the answer beyond a shadow of a doubt. "The very spot."

"And none of your men were any closer to the King?"

"We try to remain as unobtrusive as possible. Especially during a hunt."

Congreve nodded slowly. "Now, this is the moment when you heard the hound. Is that correct?"

"That's right. I turned to look. . . ." Fairbairn-Sykes approximated his original reaction. "I radioed to ask if there were any hounds on the property. There weren't. And that's when I realized I had lost visual on the King."

Congreve directed his attention up the hill. "Ross, Alex, duck down, would you?"

Hawke shared a grin with Sutherland, and then they both crouched down in the heather. For a few moments, the conversation between Congreve and Fairbairn-Sykes was muted but then grew louder as the two men drew closer.

"Majesty. Where are you?" The bodyguard hove into view above the two men but pretended not to notice them. "So, then I took out my mobile and brought up the tracker in the King's watch."

He pointed to the patch of ground where Alex knelt. "The watch was right there."

"And what did you do then?"

Fairbairn-Sykes hung his head. "I froze. I should have acted right away, but I hesitated."

"How long?"

"A minute, give or take."

"And you saw nothing? Nobody moving away from this spot?" Congreve's voice took on a sense of urgency. "Think, man. This is important."

"No. Except for us, there wasn't a soul to be seen anywhere."

Congreve looked down at the kneeling men. "Alex, Ross, I want you to move off. It doesn't matter which direction. Walk quickly, but don't run."

Alex, sensing that Congreve had very nearly reached the heart of the mystery, complied without question, striding off at a brisk pace with Ross at his side. After about half a minute, he heard the investigator cry out, "Stop there!"

Alex did so and then turned around to look back at the two men. He and Sutherland had gone about fifty yards, still well within visual range and close enough to see Congreve waving for them to return.

"Chief Superintendent," Congreve said as Alex and Sutherland rejoined the group, "would you say that we have been reasonably accurate in our reenactment of the events you witnessed?"

"I'd say so," replied Fairbairn-Sykes.

"Now, think about this next question very carefully. Did you or any of the men under your command speak personally with the King or Mr. McClanahan at any time?"

The answer was swift and unequivocal. "No, sir."

"Did you or any of the men under your command approach to within . . . say, thirty feet of the King or Mr. McClanahan at any time?"

"I'd say no closer than fifty feet."

"Fifty feet," echoed Congreve. He put his pipe between his teeth. It was, Hawke knew, a signal that his old friend had solved the mystery.

"Well, out with it, Ambrose. *How* was it done?"

Congreve gave Hawke a sidelong glance and then removed his pipe. "I told you, Alex. The question is not how, but *why*.

"From the very beginning, this crime . . . And make no mistake, that is what it is. . . . This crime has been described as something almost supernatural. A magic trick." As he spoke, Congreve gestured with the stem of his pipe. "That is exactly what it was. A conjurer's trick. An illusion. But *why?*"

"I know you quite fancy the spotlight in these moments, Ambrose, but we're all waiting for you to tell us why, old boy."

Congreve poked the pipe stem toward Hawke. "Why does a magician do anything?"

"To entertain the audience, I would imagine."

"Not merely to entertain. But to *fool* them. To deceive. And that is what has happened here." He turned to Fairbairn-Sykes. "You were deceived, Chief Superintendent. We were all deceived. Deceived into believing that the King vanished before our very eyes."

"But he did," protested Fairbairn-Sykes.

"No, sir. He did not," declared Congreve gravely. "The King was never here."

"That's bollocks!" exclaimed Fairbairn-Sykes. "I was here. I saw him!"

"You saw someone that you *believed* was the King."

"What are you saying, Ambrose?" asked Hawke.

Congreve faced his old friend. "Do you know, dear boy, how stage magicians perform the illusion of teleporting their assistants from one place to another in the blink of an eye?"

Hawke gave the question only cursory consideration. "Smoke and mirrors, I should say. Along with the gullibility of the audience."

"Not so. They use doubles. Often identical twins. One twin steps behind a curtain and then drops through a trapdoor, while the other twin steps out from behind another curtain on the opposite side of the stage. To the untrained eye, it is the same individual."

"I've served the King for twenty-six years," protested Fairbairn-Sykes. "It was him. I'd stake my life on it."

"No one is doubting your powers of observation, Chief Superintendent. But the villains behind this plot were meticulous in the preparation of the double. They chose someone with the same general build as the King, put him in the King's own clothes, and likely used theatrical makeup to perfect the illusion. From a distance of fifty feet, and with no reason to question your initial assumption that it was indeed the King, I'll wager you never even gave him a second look."

The chief bodyguard opened his mouth to issue yet another rebuttal but then seemed to think again and closed it with a frown. "I suppose I wasn't really looking at the King himself, but—"

"The illusion succeeds because the double is in on the trick. The King and Mr. McClanahan were indeed abducted, but the deed did not occur here. Rather, they were taken from the castle and quickly replaced by their doubles so that no one would be the wiser. The doubles then continued with the charade, leading you and your men out here, away from the castle, while the hostages were smuggled off the estate. The purpose of this elaborate deception was to give the villains time to make their escape."

"You've given us the *why*," said Alex. "But you still haven't explained the *how*. How did the two men simply disappear?"

Congreve strode forward into the sedge and began poking the ground with the tip of his umbrella. His first few stabs into the sodden earth yielded nothing of consequence, but then the metal tip struck something solid with a resounding *thunk*.

Congreve looked up, flashing a triumphant smile, and then resumed probing the area. After several more successful hits, he outlined a rectangular area about six feet wide and four feet across. A search of the outer perimeter soon yielded a rope handle attached to a large sheet of pressboard concealed beneath a six-inch layer of sod. Congreve made an unsuccessful attempt to lift it, then called Hawke over. "Alex, give me a hand with this."

Eager to see what lay beneath the trapdoor, Alex nudged his friend out of the way, gripped the rope handle, and raised it up. The plywood was seated in a wooden frame, hinged on the opposite side, and swung up and away to reveal a dark recess beneath.

"That," said Congreve, "is how the disappearing act was carried out. The doubles simply waited for the signal—the baying hound—and then lowered themselves down into the hole and closed the lid after. While you were looking everywhere for the King, Chief Inspector, the man who had been impersonating him was literally right under your feet."

Ross Sutherland immediately took out his radio and called in the discovery, along with the dire revelation that the King had almost certainly been taken off the property by his abductors.

"Pull all the CCTV footage from the main entrances for at least twenty-four hours prior to the report of the King's disappearance," Congreve recommended. "We need to trace every vehicle that left the estate during that time period. The King was almost certainly borne away in one of them."

Hawke held the trapdoor up with one hand and shone the light from his mobile down into the cavity. The space had roughly the same dimensions as the cover and was about four feet deep. More than enough room to hide two men.

"No one here now," observed Alex. "But it does look like they left something behind for us."

The beam of his light revealed a shapeless pile of clothing and something else, something that looked like a human face surgically removed from the skull of its owner.

"Latex mask," murmured Congreve. "Not a bad likeness of His Majesty."

"Where did the doubles go?" asked Fairbairn-Sykes.

"They very likely shed their disguises," surmised Congreve. "Then, as soon as the protective detail moved off to search for the King, they slipped out and made their escape."

Fairbairn-Sykes stared down into the hole. "I just can't believe it. How could anyone pull this off?"

Congreve folded his arms across his chest. "This plot has been a long time in the planning. Weeks, perhaps even months of preparation. The villains are likely members of the household staff who somehow slipped through the security vetting process or were suborned by the mastermind of this conspiracy. Fortunately for us, your order to lock down the estate will have prevented the doubles from making their escape."

The chief bodyguard's mood brightened a little upon hearing this revelation but then just as quickly fell. "Including my security team and the King's and Queen's personal entourage, there are over two hundred people on staff. How would one identify the culprits?"

"Not to mention," said Hawke, "we still need to identify the doubles."

"Well, there is that," replied Congreve. "We're looking for two males, roughly the same height and build as our missing King and gamekeeper. That should winnow our suspect pool. Besides, they've left us an abundance of physical evidence." He thrust the tip of his umbrella down into the recess, spearing the latex mask with the King's face, raising it as if displaying a war trophy. As the mask came away from the pile of discarded clothes, Alex heard a faint but distinct *twang*—the ominous sound of a thin wire going taut and then breaking.

"Down!" shouted Hawke, letting the door fall shut and tackling his friend to the ground.

Having encountered his fair share of booby traps, Hawke prepared himself for the expected detonation of a small explosive device by opening his mouth so that the sudden pressure change from the shock wave wouldn't rupture his eardrums.

But there was no shock wave. No detonation. Instead, he heard a hissing sound, as if water were sizzling on a hot stovetop nearby. The sound, faint at first, grew louder, and as it did, intense heat was radiating up from the ground. Hawke felt suddenly very warm.

Having instantly recognized his mistake, Hawke cursed himself. It was a booby trap, all right, just not one of the explosive variety. Seizing hold of Congreve's shoulders, he rolled both of them away from the trapdoor and out of the sedge, even as the wooden cover erupted in flames.

"I say!" exclaimed Congreve, picking himself up off the ground and brushing at the mud that now clung to his borrowed coat. "What the devil was that?"

"Incendiary device," replied Alex. "Willie Pete, I should think."

Willie Pete was military slang for white phosphorus, a nasty chemical compound that ignited on contact with air and burned at temperatures approaching 1,500 degrees Fahrenheit. The flame of burning phosphorus was so bright that it could blind anyone looking at it. White phosphorus grenades were often used by military units to destroy damaged vehicles and equipment on the battlefield to ensure that they would not be captured by the enemy. Evidently, the King's abductors had used it for a similar purpose, destroying the evidence that they had been forced to leave behind.

With one hand raised to shield his eyes from the light and heat, Hawke gazed into the heart of the inferno and spied the handle of Congreve's umbrella poking out of the sedge. Braving the heat, he dashed in and seized hold of it, only to discover that the rest of the umbrella was already in flames and that the mask of the King's face stuck to the metal tip was now a molten glob, dripping liquid fire. He cast it back into the blaze with a snarl of disgust.

"Sorry, Constable. I don't think you'll be pulling any fingerprints from that after all."

Congreve frowned. "Pity," he murmured. "I rather liked that umbrella."

SIX

By the time they returned to the castle, the review of the CCTV footage recorded in the hours leading up to the King's abduction had already borne fruit. Three vendors from Aberdeen had made early-morning deliveries to the castle, leaving well before the start of the King's hunt. When officers from Special Branch paid a visit to each, they discovered one of them—a baker—bound and gagged in a storeroom at his shop and his delivery van missing. The stolen vehicle—or rather its smoldering remains—was found shortly thereafter, not far from the village of Dinnet. With that discovery, the primary lead resulting from Congreve's adroit revelation of the kidnappers' diversionary tactic came to a most unsatisfying conclusion.

The identities and affiliations of the abductors remained unknown. The King had been taken beyond the secure borders of Balmoral Estate and now, almost twenty-four hours later, might have been anywhere on earth.

Congreve, however, staunchly refused to give in to despair. There was real police work to be done. At his direction, the household staff was brought to the castle ballroom in small groups, where they were further divided. All the men of roughly the same height and build as the King and the gamekeeper McClanahan were taken aside and sent to wait in the Grand Ballroom, while all the women and any men shorter than five feet and eight inches or taller than six feet and two inches were returned to the various rooms they had been occupying throughout their enforced sequester.

Although many of the men who met the target height criteria appeared, at a glance, to be too slight or too portly to impersonate either of the missing men, Congreve did not discount them out of hand.

"We are looking for a master of disguise," he reminded Sutherland when the latter inquired about this. "Don't trust your eyes."

"Well, then, old chap," countered Alex, "maybe we shouldn't exclude the women out of hand."

Congreve dismissed the suggestion with an airy wave of his pipe. "There are some things that even a master of disguise cannot conceal."

"Not from your keen powers of observation, at any rate."

"What's that?"

"Nothing, old boy."

Congreve merely harrumphed and planted the stem of his Briar between his teeth.

Because the details of the King's abduction had been kept under wraps even from the household staff, rumors of what had actually occurred were already rampant among the employees. Those conversations had been covertly monitored in hopes that one or more of the conspirators might let something incriminating slip. There was a general consensus that something had happened to His Majesty. But thus far, all that had been overheard were speculations ranging from bizarre to eerily accurate. The separation of staffers into seemingly arbitrary groups served only to intensify the rumors.

The winnowing process brought the number of possible suspects down by more than half, still a considerable number, but Congreve, ensconced once more in the security office, remained unperturbed. One of Sutherland's operatives, a delightful young lady named Mary Havilick, began pulling the personnel files for the men in the suspect pool and assembling them into a database that Congreve perused at length, committing names, faces, and salient details to memory. Meanwhile, the rest of Sutherland's Special Branch officers were sent to begin collecting fingerprints and DNA samples from the men in the ballroom while casually circulating a rumor that the samples would be compared against recently obtained forensic evidence. It was this last detail that brought Congreve's scheme into focus for Hawke.

"They're going to think you've got the evidence to identify them, even though you don't, and you're hoping that will provoke some kind of reaction."

"Just so," said Congreve, gesturing toward the screen that displayed the feed from one of the CCTV cameras in the ballroom. "We'll be watching them carefully to see who starts to sweat—"

The words weren't even out of his mouth when the low, constant hum of conversation issuing from speakers monitoring audio from the ballroom erupted into a tumult of shouts and cries. The display screen now showed a scene of general pandemonium, with dozens of men shoving and pushing away from a smaller, isolated group. Hawke recognized Sutherland and several of his officers closing in around a man of average appearance wearing the coveralls of a groundskeeper.

Suddenly, a loud *pop* crackled from the audio, and on the screen, one of the Special Branch men went down while the man in coveralls brandished a pistol.

"Good heavens!" exclaimed Congreve, rising from his chair and bolting for the door.

"Ambrose, wait!" Hawke shouted, but the investigator ran on, heedless. "We must take him alive at all costs."

But even before they reached the door to the security office, several more reports issued from the speaker in quick succession, and Hawke knew without looking that the Special Branch officers had just dealt with the threat expediently and permanently.

A couple of turns put Hawke and Congreve in the north corridor, and one more brought them to the passage, situated between the plateroom and the butler's pantry, that led away from the main castle and over to the ballroom in the north wing. As they emerged into the yard, they ran headlong into the human flood rising out of the ballroom, a stampede of panicked men fleeing the violent encounter in the ballroom.

Congreve was caught in the crush and would have gone down, but for Alex stepping around him to meet the horde head-on. The intervention kept Congreve on his feet, but the sheer mass of bodies pressing in the opposite direction bore both men backward into the now closed door to the passage leading back into the castle. They were pinned there for several seconds, unable to push back or even move, but then gradually, the pressure eased as the mob found the alternate exit through the public entrance that let out onto the garden walkway north of the main castle. Nevertheless, Congreve's insistent shouts of "Move!" and "Get out of the bloody way!" went largely unheeded, and it was nearly a full minute before the crush subsided enough to allow Alex, with Congreve in tow, to begin shoving through the crowd toward the steps leading down into the ballroom.

They were almost there when the sound of more gunfire cracked through the air—not a pistol this time, but the sharper report of an assault rifle, and coming not from the ballroom, but rather from somewhere outside the castle.

Hawke divined the significance of this even as Congreve exclaimed, "The other double. He's escaping!"

The rotund investigator then wheeled about and joined the rest of the throng, squeezing through the public exit. Alex, caught off guard by his old friend's abrupt change of priorities, was slow to react. By the time he got through the narrow doorway and stepped out onto the stone walkway that ran along the north wall of the castle, Congreve had a good twenty paces on him, and with so many people in between himself and Congreve, Hawke was unable to close the distance.

Although the second round of shooting had ended almost as quickly as it had begun, it triggered another panicked stampede, this time with the horde fleeing north across the lawn, moving away from the castle altogether. Evidently making the reasonable assumption that they were all running away from the shooting, Congreve, pushing against the flow, rounded a hedge wall and disappeared from Hawke's view.

In his best rugby fashion, although he hadn't played the sport in many years, Alex lowered his shoulder and began plowing forward, knocking men out of the way until he reached the turn that led down into the west garden. Congreve, still several steps ahead of him, was making a beeline for the castle's southwest corner, where a pair of Special Branch men, still clutching their smoking H&K G36 rifles, were shouting into their radios. Alex finally caught up to Congreve just as the latter, now completely winded after his sprint, wheezed out a question. "Where?"

"Bleedin' nutter stole one of our Rovers," replied one of the officers, pointing down the road leading away from the castle.

"Won't get far, though," supplied the other man. "They'll be waiting for him at the gate."

"You mustn't"—Congreve had to pause to suck in more air—"kill him."

"Up to him, i'n'it? He tries to leave, and we'll perforate him."

Congreve shook his head emphatically but didn't have the breath to argue, so Alex spoke up. "I think what the constable is saying is that it's imperative we take this man alive. You must relay that message to the men at the gate. *Alive.* As in still breathing."

"On whose bloody authority?"

"Mine," snapped Hawke. "Tell them Lord Alexander Hawke gave the order."

Congreve nodded vigorously and then, as if catching a second wind, turned and ran toward the row of parked Range Rovers, shouting, "Alex. Quickly!"

"Ambrose, wait—"

But Congreve had already slipped behind the wheel of a Rover and started the engine. Alex ran along the off side of the same vehicle and pulled open the driver's door. "I'll drive."

"There's no time," protested Congreve. "Just get in."

"You don't drive."

"Nonsense. I'm an excellent driver." Congreve's bold assertion was only slightly more accurate than Hawke's statement. Congreve had only lately taken up driving, motoring about in his restored 1962 canary-yellow Morgan Plus 4 Drophead Coupe, which he had taken to calling the "Yellow Peril."

Not very PC, but with Ambrose at the wheel, not entirely inaccurate.

"Besides," Congreve went on, "we're only going to the gate. Now, get in, would you? We're wasting precious time."

Alex bared his teeth, more grimace than grin, but conceded the point, running around to the near side and climbing into the passenger seat. Congreve already had the big SUV in gear, and as soon as Alex's door was shut, he let off the brake and mashed down on the go pedal. The Rover lurched forward, and Hawke was thrown back in his seat.

"Easy, Constable. This isn't your Morgan."

In fact, compared to the old roadster, the Range Rover, with its electronic enhancements and automatic gearbox, was a far simpler machine to operate. One merely needed to point it in the desired direction and apply gentle pressure to the pedal. The problem was that Congreve was accustomed to a more hands-on approach to driving.

He eased up on the accelerator, letting the rpm settle, but then, with the hum of the gearbox rising in pitch as it spun through first gear, Congreve dropped his hand to the gear lever and stomped down on the brake pedal with his back foot. The abrupt stop threw Hawke forward out of his seat and into the dashboard. His forehead smacked loudly against the windscreen.

"Bloody hell!" exclaimed Hawke as he pushed back into his seat, probing his forehead with his fingertips, expecting to find blood. Thankfully, there was none, but he could already feel a goose egg rising just above his right eyebrow.

Won't that look good in my wedding photos?

Congreve let off the brake and started the Rover moving forward again. "Sorry, old chap," he said, somewhat contrite. "Forgot there's no clutch. I've got it sorted now. Won't happen again."

"See that it doesn't, would you, please, Ambrose?" Hawke reached over his shoulder, found the safety belt, and pulled it across his chest, buckling it in place as the vehicle got up to speed once more. This time, Congreve kept his back foot well away from the pedals and let the automatic gearbox do its job.

They were just reaching top speed when Congreve was presented with a new challenge—a road junction. "Which way?"

It was a fair question. The intersection was a five-way convergence, and the fleeing suspect might have chosen a less obvious route. In addition to the road leading back to the main gate, which continued straight ahead after a slight dogleg, there were three other possibilities. One of the roads led back up to the tourist center and gift shop—not a likely choice—but on the opposite side, it continued along the edge of the estate, eventually joining the motorway near the Royal Lochnagar Distillery. Another road to their immediate right led south to other parts of the property. Alex, knowing nothing about the fleeing suspect or his intentions, had to make a snap judgment. "The main gate, I should think."

"Well, obviously," retorted Congreve. "But *which* way is that?"

The question left Hawke momentarily dumbfounded. It had not even occurred to him that Congreve might not know his way around the grounds. He made a serpentine motion with his hand. "Thataway!"

To his credit, Congreve made the dogleg smoothly, keeping all four wheels on the macadam without giving up too much momentum, and thirty seconds later, they rounded a slight bend and got a look at the main gate.

Or rather, what was left of it.

The wrought iron barrier had been knocked clean out of the stone gateposts and now lay flat on the macadam, fully fifty feet beyond the portal. The four Special Branch officers who had been set to guard it stood by, looking dazedly at the wreckage.

Congreve, looking similarly bewildered, let his foot off the accelerator, bringing the Rover to a halt. "Too bloody late," he moaned.

"Never say die, Constable." Hawke rolled his window down and leaned out, catching the eye of the nearest policeman. "Which way?"

The man stared back at him in confusion for a moment, then pointed south.

Hawke turned to Congreve. "You heard the man." He raised an imperious hand, pointing in the same direction, and then, sounding for all the world like his hero, Admiral Lord Nelson, ordering his flagship into battle, uttered a single word of command. "Pursue!"

SEVEN

Congreve reacted as if to an electric charge, bringing his attention to the fore and pressing down the go pedal. He threaded the narrow passage between ͜he broken gateposts, swerved around the mangled iron gate, and then accelerated forward onto the narrow two-lane road the fleeing suspect had taken.

Just north of the castle entrance, the road, designated the B976, branched off from the main trunk, which Alex and Ross Sutherland had driven on from Aberdeen, and it continued for a distance of more than forty miles, following the course of the River Dee for much of its length before diverging near Allancreich. Barely wide enough to accommodate two lanes of traffic, it was more of a scenic country lane than a motorway, ideal for sightseeing, less so for getting to distant points in a hurry.

"Steady on, old boy," advised Hawke as the Rover picked up speed and headed into a gentle curve. "Take it slow going into the turns. This brute won't take the corners like your Morgan."

Congreve glanced over with a look of disapproval. "We do want to catch the chap, Alex."

"Not bloody likely," countered Alex. "He's got at least a minute's head start on us, and since we're matched in horsepower and handling, there's not much chance that we'll close that gap." Hawke didn't add that even he would have been hard-pressed to close that distance. With Congreve at the wheel, it seemed an impossible ask.

"But the point isn't to catch him," Hawke went on. "I'm sure Ross has already sent word to the local constabulary to set up roadblocks. We just want to be there when they finally stop him to make sure he's able to answer our questions. And to accomplish that, you'll need to keep the vehicle in an upright position at all times. All four wheels on the bloody road."

Congreve grunted but eased off the accelerator a little as they rode into the turn. Off to the left, through a screen of ash, birch, and Scotch pine, the greens of the Balmoral golf course were visible, sandwiched between the road and the river, while to the right, long-horned Highland cattle grazed in the open pasturage. As the road bent into another, longer curve, Congreve slowed without being prompted, braking into the turn and then powering out of it.

"I think you're getting the hang of it, Constable."

"Quite right. It's not so difficult after all. I say, is that . . . *him?*"

Hawke looked ahead and saw the rear end of a vehicle farther down the road. Even with the distance, there was no mistaking the color and shape of a green Range Rover. Judging by the rapidity with which they were now closing on the vehicle, he estimated it was going no faster than about forty-five miles per hour, even in the straightaway. "Well, old chap, it seems I owe you an apology. It looks as if we are going to catch up to him after all."

"I rather thought he would be going faster," said Congreve. He pressed down a little harder, taking advantage of the straight stretch to further shrink the gap.

"Must have sustained some damage during the escape."

"What . . . ah, what do we do once we overtake him?"

"I hadn't really given it much thought," replied Alex. Indeed, had he been in the driver's seat, Alex would not have given the matter *any* thought at all. He simply would have acted. Flying fighter aircraft had taught him to trust his instincts. In the cockpit, there wasn't time to think things through—either you acted or you died. "I imagine we shall have to force him off the road."

"Force him off the road," echoed Congreve. "You make it sound so bloody simple. *How* do I force him off the road?"

"I'll talk you through it. Pull up behind him."

As Congreve continued narrowing the gap, Alex expected the driver of the other Rover to try to pull away, but if anything, the opposite occurred. The fleeing vehicle continued to lose speed.

"Try to get around him," said Hawke.

Congreve immediately swerved to the right, but the other driver, anticipating what he was about to do, steered into the middle of the road.

Now that they were well past the golf course, the road was little more than a slash across the riverbank, sloping down to the water on the left and rising to the right. An ancient stone retaining wall held the upslope soil in place just a few feet from the road's edge, leaving no room to pass on that side. Congreve muttered something unprintable. "Now what?"

Had he been at the wheel, Alex would have backed off just enough to get a running start, then charged ahead at high speed, and then, just before causing a rear-end collision, swung around on the near side, even though it would mean riding on the soft shoulder for a few seconds. Then, as soon as the front end drew even with the other Rover's rear wheels, he would have steered into the vehicle, executing what American police officers called a PIT—precision immobilization technique—maneuver, a method for disabling a fleeing suspect's car by causing it to spin out and stall in a relatively controlled fashion.

That's what he would have done if he had been driving. But trying to talk someone else through the steps, never mind someone without any kind of tactical driving instruction or experience, would not only have been futile but quite probably would have ended in disaster.

He would have to come up with a simpler solution for Congreve.

"Back away a few lengths. A hundred feet should do it."

Congreve eased his foot off the accelerator. The Range Rover immediately began to lose forward momentum and the fleeing vehicle began to pull away.

"That's good," said Hawke. "Keep this pace. In just a moment, when I give the word, you're going to accelerate hard, pedal to the floor, and ram him."

"*Ram* him?" Congreve's voice rose an octave. "You want me to crash our Rover into his?"

"It's an old race car driver's technique called the bump-and-run."

"I wasn't asking for the name of the bloody technique. I wanted to make sure I understood you correctly. You want me to intentionally collide with another speeding vehicle?"

"The difference in speed won't be more than about twenty miles per hour. Probably less than that. You'll barely feel the bump." This was a lie, of course, but it wasn't the time to burden Congreve with facts. "If done properly, you'll cause him to lose control, spin out, and crash off the road."

"And if done improperly?"

"Hard to say, really. The most likely outcome is simply that he doesn't lose control and we have to try it again. We'll find out soon enough." Hawke now pointed forward. "We're in a straightaway. Now's your chance. Go, go!"

Despite his obvious misgivings, Congreve stomped the throttle pedal, and the Rover surged forward. Even though the other vehicle was also in motion, its rear drew close with alarming swiftness. Alex half expected Congreve to let up on the throttle at the last instant, but to his credit, the old copper kept the pedal to the floor, and when contact was made, it surprised even Hawke.

The Rover jolted with the impact. Hawke knew there was a good chance that the airbags would deploy, a possibility that he had intentionally neglected to share with Congreve, reasoning that the good constable already had enough on his plate, but evidently, the force of the impact was insufficient to trigger the mechanism. Instead, Hawke was thrown forward against his seat belt but nevertheless managed to keep his eye on the other vehicle as the full effect of the bump from behind manifested.

The Rovers' bumpers bore the brunt of the collision and neither vehicle sustained any visible damage, but the lead Rover lurched forward, its rear end rising up and slamming back down. Then, because Congreve was still mashing the pedal, a second jolt followed almost immediately, and this time, the other Rover, trailing a fog of metal, plastic, and fiberglass fragments, veered lazily toward the right side of the road. It hit the stone wall nose first, then rebounded away, beginning a clockwise spin right in front of the Rover carrying Hawke and Congreve.

"Brakes, Ambrose!"

Hawke's shout jolted Congreve out of his fixed state, but there was no time for the investigator to act accordingly. He let off the throttle and reflexively steered to the right, trying to avoid another collision.

He almost succeeded.

The front end of their Rover clipped the mangled rear end of the other vehicle, hooking its bumper and tearing it off, along with the left-front fender and headlights of theirs. The impact knocked the other vehicle out of its spin while at the same time sending Hawke and Congreve caroming into the stone wall. Hawke, seeing that Congreve was about to lose control, reached over and grasped the steering wheel, holding it steady as the Rover scraped along the wall in a shower of sparks.

And then, as quickly as it had begun, it was over.

Congreve's steady foot on the brake and Alex's hand on the steering wheel kept the Rover on the road as it slowed to a full stop. Fifty yards behind them, the other Rover had also come to a halt, sitting diagonally across both lanes.

Hawke immediately unbuckled his seat belt, threw his door open, and leapt out. He sprinted back down the road to the stalled vehicle, reaching it in seconds. The air around the vehicle was thick with the smell of hot metal, tire rubber, and petrol vapors. The Rover's engine had stalled and was ticking furiously. Hawke ran around to the driver's door. Through the window glass, he could see the form of the driver slumped over the steering wheel, not moving. The man had pale white skin and a thatch of red hair, and just like the other man who had died in the shoot-out with Sutherland's men, he wore the coveralls of a castle groundskeeper. Aside from that, there wasn't much to distinguish him.

Alex tried the door handle. Locked. The sound, however, roused the driver. The man lifted his head groggily and began looking around. When his gaze met Hawke's, his startlingly green eyes went wide in alarm.

Hawke banged his fist against the glass. "Open up!"

For just a moment, he thought the man would comply, but then something changed in the man's expression. He brought his attention forward, looked down at the console, and then pressed the start button.

The Rover's engine struggled noisily but refused to turn over. If the strong smell of petrol was any indication, the engine was likely flooded—a rare occurrence for a vehicle with fuel injection but not unheard of following an accident.

Hawke banged on the window glass again, this time more forcefully. "Open the damn door!"

The driver continued ignoring him and tried the starter again. This time, his efforts paid off. The engine roared to life with an explosive backfire and then settled into a clamorous idle as if the supercharged 3.0-liter V-6 under the hood was about to self-destruct. Still, it was running, and Hawke saw his chance to detain the suspect slipping away.

He slammed the window glass with his fist again, hard enough to hurt his hand but to no better effect. Flesh and bone were no match for tempered glass. He needed something much harder—the butt of a pistol, a tire iron, or a spanner, but he had none of those things. What he did have were empty pockets and . . .

My wristwatch.

The watch, a black-dial stainless steel GMT-Master that had once belonged to his father, weighed in at just over five ounces—nowhere near the heft of a tire iron—but when it came to breaking glass, weight wasn't everything.

The Rover shuddered visibly as the suspect shifted the gearbox into drive. Hawke, all too aware that he had seconds at best to act, deftly popped the clasp of the watch's Oyster bracelet and slid it off into his right hand. Holding the clasp between thumb and forefinger, he whipped the watch against the window. The overhand strike supplied just enough momentum to accomplish the task. The window went instantly opaque. Hawke rammed his fist forward through the glass, dislodging a small shower of glittering pea-sized fragments, and seized hold of the steering wheel just as the vehicle began rolling forward.

The driver, surprised by the unexpected intrusion, swatted at Hawke's arm, trying to dislodge his stowaway, even as the vehicle began accelerating. Hawke maintained his grip, jogging, then running alongside the Rover as it picked up speed.

Despite Hawke's grip on the steering wheel, the driver fought for control, cranking the wheel half over to line the Rover up on the road, facing back the way they'd come. Hawke knew that if the vehicle got up to speed, there would be no good outcomes for him. He could not hope to run alongside the Rover; he was already having difficulty keeping up, and in a few more seconds, if he did not let go, he would be dragged along. Even if, by some superhuman display of strength, he managed to hang on to the steering wheel or the side of the Rover, all the driver would have to do to dislodge him would be to simply slam on the brakes, launching him forward like a stone from a medieval trebuchet, resulting in broken bones, friction burns, and, quite probably, death.

All of which meant he had to stop the Rover. *Right. Bloody. Now.*

If I die before saying, "I do," Anastasia will kill me herself.

With a mighty heave, he pulled himself, head and shoulders,

through the window frame, knocking down what remained of the tempered glass pane, and got his other hand on the steering wheel. His upper torso was now practically in the driver's lap, his head and neck dangerously exposed, and his abdomen pressed uncomfortably down against the frame, but at least his feet weren't dragging. That was the good news.

That was *all* of the good news.

The bad news was that the Rover had already broken thirty miles per hour.

Hawke saw only one course of action. He could not trigger the brakes or force the driver to let off the accelerator, nor could he reach the engine shutoff. The only thing he had even a limited ability to affect was the steering wheel. So, with another unrestrained heave, he yanked the wheel toward himself as if hauling in a hawser. The violence of the move caught the driver off guard. The steering wheel slipped through his fingers, and the Rover cut toward the right side of the road. The abruptness of the shift, coupled with the vehicle's forward momentum, subjected both the Rover and its one and a half occupants to a high-G turn, and in the next few milliseconds, two things happened simultaneously.

The first was that Alex was hurled *forward*—his lower torso and legs flying *into* the interior of the vehicle. But for his fierce grip on the steering wheel, he would have been thrown headfirst against the passenger's-side door. As it was, he was whipped around in the headspace so that it was his backside that hit first before the steering wheel was torn from his hands.

The second thing was that in the resulting conflict of opposing forces—forward momentum versus directional shift—the top-heavy SUV could not keep its wheels on the macadam.

A heartbeat later, the Rover went for a roll.

Inside the vehicle, Alex was tossed about like a shoe in a clothes dryer. Side and dashboard airbags burst open, softening some of the initial impact, but only a little. For Hawke, it was like being pummeled by a heavyweight fighter in their prime. The blows to his body were debilitating but not nearly as painful as they would be later on once the adrenaline finally wore off. Hawke's stomach lurched and his head spun with the too rapid changes in direction. Smoke burned his throat and nostrils. Glass and other debris flew in a storm around him, stinging any exposed flesh. Yet, amidst the tumult, he retained the wherewithal to tuck into a protective curl, shielding his head and body with his extremities.

He lost count of how many times the Rover tumbled and, with his head still spinning, was slow to realize that it had come to a rest. Tentatively, he opened one eye and raised his head to take in the situation.

Hawke lay in a crumpled ball atop the headliner. The Rover was now standing on its roof, the frame somewhat compacted by the crushing weight of the vehicle. All the window glass had shattered, and two of the doors were sprung. There was a hot smell in the enclosed space as if something was burning, and while Hawke neither saw nor felt any rising heat, he knew how quickly a wrecked vehicle could turn into a funeral pyre.

Unfolding his body awakened him to a myriad of aches and pains, but as he took inventory of his injuries, he felt nothing to indicate any of his bones were broken. Internal injuries were a bigger concern, but as far as Hawke could tell, he'd gone twelve rounds with the champ and lived to both tell the bloody tale *and* fight another day.

Convinced it was indeed safe to move, he began crawling toward the deformed opening that had once been the rear-door frame.

"Alex!" cried Congreve, his voice full of dread.

Hawke wriggled his head and shoulders through the gap. "Here, Constable. Just taking a quick break from the action, if you don't mind."

"There you are." Congreve's face was immediately suffused with relief. He knelt down, offering his hand to Hawke. "I say, Alex! Are you quite all right?"

"Never better," lied Hawke.

"You're injured."

"Nothing that a little Goslings Black Seal and six months of rest and recuperation on a beach in Bermuda won't fix." He managed to turn his grimace into a smile. "You know, Ambrose, it's times like this when I feel as though I've lived an extra twenty years."

Congreve lowered his head and peered inside the wreck. "Where's our suspect?"

In all the chaos of the rollover, Hawke had completely forgotten about the driver, and only now did it occur to him that he had not seen the redheaded man during his egress. He knelt beside Congreve and looked for himself. There was no sign of the man.

"Well, he's got to be around here somewhere," said Hawke. "I can't imagine he was in any condition to flee the scene."

"I should say not, judging by your condition. In any event, I didn't see anyone leaving the scene, so as you say, he must be around here. . . ." Congreve trailed off, his gaze fixing on something protruding from underneath the inverted Rover. "Oh, my."

Hawke followed his friend's line of sight and saw what Congreve was looking at. It was a booted foot, along with a few inches of the leg to which it was still attached. Dark red fluid oozed out from under the vehicle where, he could only assume, the rest of the leg, as well as the rest of the body, now lay sandwiched between the Rover and the road.

Hawke stared down at the appendage and the growing pool of blood, then looked over at Congreve. "Well, Constable, I don't think he's going to be answering any of our questions."

EIGHT

t was the better part of an hour before Hawke and Congreve were able to leave the scene and return to the castle. When they got back, one of Sutherland's Special Branch officers hurried them inside with the somewhat cryptic explanation "They're waiting for you in the library."

Balmoral's library, it turned out, had become an ad hoc command center where the Prime Minister herself, having arrived discreetly during their brief absence, had come to take charge of the crisis.

At first glance, Livia Steele seemed an unlikely choice to lead the United Kingdom's government. Only the fourth woman in history to hold the office—and the only one to come out of the Labour Party—she was often measured in the tabloid media against her female predecessors, particularly Margaret Thatcher, and found wanting. An editorial in the *Sun* had famously remarked that "Steele is no Iron Lady." At forty-three, she was considerably younger than Thatcher had been and, if one was being honest, objectively better-looking, though in the hard-bitten world of politics, this was not necessarily an advantage. She was not what anyone would have described as a great beauty, but her slight build, fair complexion, and strawberry blond locks lent her a distinctive girl-next-door aura that had, no doubt, attracted supporters from among the working class while also causing political rivals and adversaries to underestimate her.

Alex Hawke had seen many Prime Ministers come and go during his years as both a military officer and an agent working under the auspices of MI6. Unlike the Americans, who elected their leaders to serve terms of four years, the office of Prime Minister was as changeable as public opinion, and the powers associated with that office were often constrained by the division of votes within the House of Commons. He had no particular feelings whatsoever about Steele on a personal level and only a passing interest in her political positions, which, in keeping with her party, trended toward socialist reforms and decreased participation in military interventions abroad—she had indicated a desire to withdraw the UK from NATO—and an unapologetic dislike for the "outdated and obsolete institution of the monarchy." However, because he was an agent of His Majesty's government, Hawke understood that, for the moment at least, Prime Minister Livia Steele was his boss, so as he and Congreve entered the library to find Steele presiding at the head of a sturdy antique reading table, he inclined his head in a polite bow and, following Congreve's lead, said simply, "Prime Minister."

Steele looked up from the sheaf of papers she had been perusing and regarded him with a somewhat bemused smile. "Lord Hawke, I heard that you were lurking about."

The subtext was unmistakable, the unspoken question hanging in the air above the table.

"What the devil are you doing here?"

"Lord Hawke is here at my invitation, ma'am," supplied Congreve hastily. "He's been of enormous assistance to my investigations in the past and, I might add, is a close personal friend of His Majesty the King."

"I'm quite aware of Lord Hawke's reputation," replied Steele, her eyes never leaving the subject of the discussion, "and his relationship with the Crown."

Hawke wasn't sure how to interpret these remarks and so responded

.with silence. After a long moment, Steele turned her gaze to Congreve. "Chief Inspector, I understand that we have you to thank for cracking the case, as it were. If not for you, we'd still be laboring under the misapprehension that His Majesty was still here on the grounds."

Congreve made a dismissive gesture. "Child's play, really. I only wish I'd figured it out sooner."

"Quite." Steele gave a heavy sigh, then gestured toward the empty chairs arrayed down the length of the table. Congreve settled into a chair beside Ross Sutherland, and Hawke sat next to him. When the two men were seated, Steele went on. "As you are no doubt aware, we have cast a net over this affair. Absolute secrecy is of paramount importance. The fewer people that know what's going on, the better. Officially, gentlemen, I am not here, and this meeting never occurred. Is that understood?"

"Of course, ma'am," answered Congreve. "You can count on Lord Hawke and myself to be the very souls of discretion."

Hawke merely nodded his head in agreement with Congreve's assertion. Steele continued to regard Hawke with an appraising glance, then waved the documents she had been examining. "Chief Inspector Sutherland was just telling me about the two conspirators who were killed today."

There was an unmistakable note of judgment in Steele's tone as if the failure to take the two suspects into custody was solely the fault of the police.

Taking his cue, Sutherland slid a similar folder in front of Congreve. "Both of our suspects were employed as groundskeepers. Ian Clewen, Aberdeen native. Thirty-three years old. Had worked here for just over two and a half years. He's the chap who shot it out with my men in the ballroom. The other fellow, the one that tried to make a break for it, was Colm Keaney. Thirty-six. Originally from Londonderry. He's been here just six months. Neither man had a criminal record nor any known questionable activities or associations."

Congreve flipped open the folder and scanned the pages, instantly committing the details to memory. "Not much to go on here," he remarked, tossing the folder down.

"All members of the household staff undergo a thorough background investigation before employment," said Sutherland. "Somehow, these two slipped through the cracks."

"Sleeper agents?" asked Hawke.

Congreve answered first. "Not necessarily. There are any number of inducements which might be used to corrupt or coerce an ordinary citizen into committing the crime of treason. When the kidnappers reveal themselves and make their demands, we shall have a better understanding of how this conspiracy developed."

Steele now spoke up. "Then it's your belief that the kidnappers will make demands, Chief Inspector?"

"They wouldn't have gone to all this trouble otherwise. A scheme this elaborate would have required months of preparation. These villains will want something for their efforts, whether it's money or some political concession. They will make contact—of that, I am certain. It's just a matter of *when*. I'd give it some time, and—"

"Time," Steele echoed, cutting off Congreve while shaking her head sadly. "You've just hit upon the real problem, Chief Inspector."

"Beg pardon, ma'am?"

"Time. We're running out of it. In less than four days, the people of Scotland will cast their votes on the referendum for independence. The latest polls favor the 'Yes' vote, but the margin is narrow, with a significant number of voters indicating that they've yet to make up their minds. His Majesty the King chose this moment to visit Balmoral to remind the Scottish people that they are a fundamental part of our great Union. I don't believe it's a coincidence that, with the fate of the United Kingdom in the balance, the King has gone missing."

"Are you suggesting that separatists are behind the kidnapping?" asked Hawke.

"The list of enemies who would benefit from a broken Union is not a short one," remarked Congreve. "Scots nationalists have never shown the slightest inclination to use violence to advance their aims. What's more, even if the vote goes their way, Scotland would remain a part of the Commonwealth, and Charles would continue to be their King." He paused a beat. "That said, we cannot rule out the possibility that certain elements within the movement might have taken it upon themselves to do something precipitous."

He steepled his fingers together in front of his face, staring at the Prime Minister over their tips. "If you're correct, and this abduction was motivated by a desire to influence the outcome of the referendum, then I retract my previous statement. We cannot assume that the kidnappers will have any demands whatsoever. They may merely intend to keep His Majesty on ice, as it were, until the votes are in."

Steele nodded. "That is precisely my fear, Chief Inspector."

Congreve hummed thoughtfully, then lowered his hands and placed them on the folder with the personnel files of the two groundskeepers. "We shall have to dissect these men. Question everyone who knew them. Sift through their financial records. Put their social media accounts under a microscope. Somewhere, there is a thread that will lead us to the conspirators."

"Keaney was from Northern Ireland," Sutherland said. "Might be a connection to the New IRA or some other such group. A few years ago, that lot attacked the castle and took the Royal Family hostage."

"You needn't remind me," said Congreve. "I was there, and probably would have perished if not for Alex's timely intervention. But if you'll recall correctly, the Ulster boys were merely dupes in a scheme masterminded by Islamic fundamentalists."

"All the same," countered Steele, "the Irish Republican movement would gain considerable momentum if Scotland left the Union. In fact, I would put NIRA at the top of the list of suspects."

Congreve frowned. "It's certainly an avenue worth exploring. But I believe we will discover that these two men were mere hirelings. This plot required the sort of meticulous planning and resources that I would expect from a state-level actor. Russia, perhaps. Or China. Either nation would benefit greatly from a weakened United Kingdom. Prime Minister, I urge you to enlist the full resources of the government, both domestic and abroad, in this endeavor. Five and Six can cast a much wider net than Special Branch alone."

Steele gazed at the former policeman for a long moment, then turned to Sutherland. "Chief Inspector, do you share your colleague's opinion? Or can Special Branch handle this without outside assistance?"

Sutherland's eyes widened in surprise. He shot a glance at Congreve as if looking for advice or permission, then faced the Prime Minister. "Ma'am, under ordinary circumstances, my answer would be unequivocal in the affirmative. But it's the King's life we're talking about."

Steele pursed her lips together. "The more people that know of this crisis, the more likely it is that word of it will leak, and that, I believe, would do more to harm our cause than the mere fact of the King's abduction." She shook her head. "I'm sorry, gentlemen, but for the time being, we must limit the investigation to those who already know. I fear you shall have to bear this burden alone."

Then, borrowing a page from the playbook of Her Majesty Queen Elizabeth, Steele rose to her feet, signaling the end of the audience. The men seated about the table rose as well.

"I must away before the newsmen begin asking what I'm doing here," said Steele. "I leave it to you to pursue this investigation as you see fit, but I cannot stress enough how urgent it is that the King be found and returned safely to the throne. Officially, in accordance with the Regency Act, His Royal Highness Prince William now rules in his father's stead, but insofar as the public is concerned, the status quo remains unchanged. However, even if the kidnappers do not reveal themselves, we cannot perpetuate this illusion indefinitely. The Crown must weigh in ahead of the Scottish vote. That is our deadline. If the Ki   is not able to speak out in favor of the Union, it will fall to the

Prince-regent, and the jig, as the Americans say, will be up. You have seventy-two hours and not a minute more. Find the King."

———————

Hawke tagged along with Congreve as the latter, in true Holmesian fashion, went about meticulously examining the personal effects of the two deceased suspects with a rather large magnifying glass. Twice, he exclaimed, "Aha," only to dismiss Hawke's subsequent inquiries with the wave of a hand. Ultimately, it was not Congreve who provided the first meaningful clue but rather the team of tech specialists assigned to comb through the suspects' social media and browser histories.

Sutherland brought them the news. "Until about six months ago, Keaney was a regular visitor to a social media group frequented by members of the New IRA. Lots of likes in support of the cause. That's our thread, Ambrose."

"Six months," said Congreve. "Exactly the same time that he began working here at Balmoral. What happened after that?"

"Nothing. He stopped visiting the site. Mostly stopped using the internet altogether."

"Well, that doesn't seem very likely in this day and age," remarked Hawke.

"No," agreed Congreve. "I'll wager that was when he was recruited to be part of this operation. No doubt, his handler warned him against using his mobile and personal devices. Probably started using a burner phone to communicate with his coconspirators. That would explain the sudden drop-off in activity. Why wasn't this flagged during the background investigation?"

"Hard to say. Perhaps it wasn't considered relevant at the time."

"The New IRA," mused Hawke. "So, we have our villains, then. And the Troubles are come again."

"It certainly looks that way," said Sutherland. "I'll contact my opposite number at the PSNI in Belfast and see if we can identify some of the other participants on this forum."

"It's a lead," admitted Congreve, staring fixedly at the bowl of his Briar pipe. "But hardly what I would call a smoking gun. This operation was carried out with a level of sophistication that, dare I say, one doesn't normally see from the IRA or any of its subsequent manifestations."

"It's our *only* lead," Sutherland persisted. "We know for certain that this Keaney chap *was* part of the conspiracy to abduct the King, and we know where his sympathies lay. We don't have the luxury of time. We have to start beating the bushes and see what flies up."

"An apt metaphor given the setting," murmured Congreve. After a long moment, he sighed. "You're not wrong, Ross. We must follow the clues where they lead, and right now they lead to Ireland. We must go away to Belfast. Make the arrangements."

Sutherland already had his mobile phone out, and as the call connected, he moved away. Congreve watched him go, and Hawke watched Ambrose.

"You don't seem particularly enthused by this development, Constable."

Congreve jolted as if startled by the observation, then clamped the stem of his pipe between his teeth. "Nonsense. It's good police work."

"But your instincts are telling you this is a dead end, aren't they?"

"Instincts." Congreve tried to sound dismissive. "It's a copper's job to follow the clues wherever they lead."

"And if this is more misdirection?"

Congreve frowned. "It does all feel a bit . . . obvious, doesn't it? Almost as if the villain expected us to discover this connection."

"That was rather my first thought as well. Which begs the question 'What are we going to do about it?'"

"I don't see that there's anything we *can* do about it. Ross was right. This is our only viable lead. We have no choice but to follow it." Congreve then gave Hawke a sidelong look. "Or should I say, *I* have no choice but to follow it."

Hawke's eyes narrowed. "Meaning?"

Congreve took the pipe from his mouth. "Meaning, while Ross and I jet off to Belfast, there's an opportunity for you to pursue other possibilities."

"The other fellow? Clewen?"

Congreve shook his head. "If our villain is half as clever as I believe he is, that will only be another red herring. No, we need to get out ahead of him. Go on the offensive, as it were. Start with motive, and then work backward. If we are correct in our assumption that the purpose of the King's kidnapping is to influence the outcome of the Scottish vote, then we should look for him at the intersection of political interest and access to the resources necessary to carry out this plot."

"Thus your suggestion that a foreign power is behind it all."

"A possibility we cannot dismiss. Go to London, Alex. Talk to Sir David. You needn't reveal what's happened here. Simply inquire as to which of our enemies has taken an interest in the outcome of the Scottish referendum."

"The PM will have our bloody hides if she hears of it," said Hawke with a grin.

Congreve gave a sly smile. "Best see that she doesn't, then."

NINE

MAGICIAN TAKES KING

The man known to his confederates only as the "Magician" hid his smile as he contemplated the face of his captive. His Majesty Charles III, King of England and the fourteen nations of the Commonwealth, did not look nearly so regal now, slumped against the wall, head bowed in defeat.

Checkmate, thought the Magician.

There was no better word for it.

The word *checkmate*, like most of the conventions and rules of the modern game of chess, had entered into usage by way of Persia. Derived from the phrase *shah mat*, which translates to "the king is help-less," a checkmate has been the ultimate goal of the timeless game of strategy, which is often mistakenly referred to as a "war game." The greatest chess minds in the game's history have proven time and again that the game itself is not about removing all of an opponent's pieces from the "battlefield" in direct combat. That line of thinking is purely amateurish. The real goal is to manipulate the opponent's king into a place where it is completely powerless and unable to escape. In fact, it is possible, indeed a sign of mastery, to checkmate an opponent's king without either capturing or sacrificing a single piece from one's board. The nearly unthinkable feat, which bears no official name, is the most sought-after victory of any devoted student of the game. A group that included the Magician.

And that was precisely what he had just accomplished.

His real feat, the same as any victory in chess, had not been an easy thing to pull off. It had taken months of meticulous planning as he deliberately moved the various necessary "pieces" into place, laying false trails to conceal the endgame so that when the moment—when *this* moment—finally arrived, nobody would see it coming. Recruiting two agents from the household staff had been a delicate chore. He'd gone to great lengths to identify not only the right incentives but, just as important, which pressure points to push in order to ensure that the men would stick to the plan and remain loyal.

And now, much like as in a masterfully played game, his attention to detail had yielded spectacular results.

In the end, his execution had been flawless. He'd expected nothing less. Not even when a slight, seemingly innocuous change of plans at the last moment had moved the King into the trap—a room out of the view of the castle's security cameras where he had been given a fast-acting sedative, rendering him unconscious, whereupon the doubles had stepped in and assumed the roles of King and servant.

That had been the first step.

Check.

Getting the King away from the castle and off the grounds had been a little more involved, not to mention risky, but no one had paid much attention to a deliveryman wheeling a trolley through the castle, and really, why would they? There was no reason for vigilance. Everything had been as it was supposed to be.

The moment of greatest risk—the masterstroke, if you will—had been the disappearance itself. The doubles had led the security team well away from the castle and then, with a little bit of misdirection to cover their movements, had dropped down into a prepared foxhole, shed their disguises, and then simply waited for an opportune moment to blend back into the household staff. That bit of theater, adding a supernatural flair to the abduction, had further befogged the King's sworn protectors, causing them to limit their search to the castle grounds, never suspecting that their charge was already miles away.

And that's what led to him winning the game.

Checkmate, thought the Magician. *And he doesn't even know how helpless he is.*

But then the King, it was well-known, was not a chess player.

If he had been, he might have realized that the true endgame, the final act in a drama begun more than forty years ago, was just getting started. . . .

July 29, 1981

It was a day he would never forget. Even at his tender age, he knew that he was witnessing a historic moment, but that was not the thought foremost in his mind. What he was thinking was that this was a real, honest-to-God fairy tale come to life. Prince Charming was going to marry his Princess, and they were going to live happily ever after.

"Lookit there, lad," his father had said, gesturing with a calloused hand to the television set.

The family had been gathered around the old telly for hours now, watching with varying degrees of fascination as royals and dignitaries from all around the world gathered inside St. Paul's Cathedral to witness what the newsmen on BBC were rightly calling "the wedding of the century." Now, finally, the pace was picking up. Only a few minutes earlier, the carriage bearing Her Majesty the Queen and the Royal Consort, Prince Philip, had begun the journey from Buckingham Palace to the cathedral, and now the man himself, His Royal Highness Prince Charles, with his brother Prince Andrew sitting beside him, was beginning the two-and-a-half-mile journey through the streets of London.

The Prince, resplendent in his Royal Navy dress uniform, rode in the 1902 State Landau, drawn by four gray horses. Trailing along behind them were more than two dozen horsemen from the Household Cavalry regiment, their upraised sabers gleaming in the morning sun. To the young boy, they looked like the knights of old.

"That's the man you'll serve one day," his father went on. "Just as I do and my da before me. That's the man who'll be King."

A chill went down the boy's spine as he beheld the future Princess. The television cameras could catch only a glimpse of her veiled visage through the windows of the flat-roofed Glass Coach as it rolled out from Clarence House, where the Lady Diana had spent the night in the company of the Queen Mother. The television commentators remarked on how her wedding dress seemed to completely fill the interior of the coach, leaving barely enough room for her father, the Earl Spencer.

For nearly half an hour thereafter, the cameras followed the processions as they made their way along the sand-strewn streets to the steps of the cathedral and then moved inside. Last to arrive, and only a few minutes late, was the bride herself.

Accompanied by fanfare and trailing a twenty-five-foot-long train, Diana ascended the steps and entered the cathedral. The diamonds on her tiara sparkled like a halo, and her dazzling smile shone through the veil, which lent her face an almost ghostlike quality. Had he known the word, the boy would have said that she looked ethereal, but at that moment, the only word he knew that fit was . . . angel.

He watched in rapt fascination as she made her way down the aisle to stand beside the Prince. He hung on every word as the Archbishop of Canterbury recited the sacred wedding vows, even though he had only the barest understanding of their meaning. The boy had never attended a wedding, but he understood the sacredness of these promises made before God.

"Wilt thou have this woman to thy wedded wife, live together after God's ordinance in the holy state of matrimony? Wilt thou love and comfort her, honor and keep her in sickness and in health, and forsaking all others, keep thee only unto her, so long as you both shall live?"

"I will," said the Prince.

And in that moment, the boy's heart was filled with such love for the Prince and his Princess.

"I will serve them, just as my father serves them now. One day, they will be King and Queen, and I will serve them," he whispered to himself.

The thought sent a shiver down the boy's spine. And what, he wondered, might come of that?

PRESENT DAY

The King raised his head as a figure, face hidden beneath a black balaclava, entered the dungeon—there was no other word to describe the long stone vault where he'd spent uncounted hours in isolation. Two more masked men came in behind the first, bearing the dazed form of Roderick McClanahan between them.

Oh, Roddy, thought Charles with an inward groan. *They got you too.*

The first man stood back as the others lowered McClanahan to the bare stone floor at the King's feet. The gamekeeper, evidently still suffering the effects of the sedative that had been used by their abductors, was slow to stir. The two men who had carried McClanahan in now exited, but the third man remained, staring down at Charles. He spat a derisive laugh and then executed a mocking bow, sweeping his hand before him.

"Your Majesty, welcome to your new holiday residence." The man was using some sort of electronic voice modulator, which made him sound rather like one of the Cybermen from *Doctor Who*, but the device could not mask the undercurrent of sarcasm in his words. "Please, let me know if there's anything I can do to make your stay more enjoyable."

The King looked up, holding the other's gaze. "Well, for a start, you can tell me who the bloody hell you are and just what the bloody hell you want."

The man folded his arms across his chest. "Suppose I told you that what I want is for you to give up your crown?"

"Abdicate?" scoffed Charles. "Never. Certainly not under duress."

"I could just kill you. Same result."

"Then you'd best get on with it because it's the only way I'd ever give up the bloody crown." Charles stared hard into the man's steel-gray eyes. "But if you really wanted me dead, you would have done it already."

The man appeared to consider this comment for a moment, and then a cruel smile broke across his face. "True enough. You may call me Mr. Sten."

The name, an alias to be sure, hinted at a possible Scandinavian origin, but it might also have been a nod to the venerable STEN sub-machine gun, which had been a mainstay of British military forces during World War II and into the 1950s, suggesting a possible military affiliation. The man spoke with a distinctive accent and cadence, but with the electronic distortion, Charles couldn't pin it down. "Can't quite place the accent, old boy. Where are you from?"

"Where I'm from is not what you should be concerning yourself with, *Your Majesty*." The sarcasm slipped through the digitized voice loud and clear when he said "Your Majesty."

"Well, then, perhaps you'll be so good as to tell me what it is I should be concerned with. You haven't killed me, so obviously, you want something from me, so let's have it. I've never been one for the-ater and I'm far too old to change now. Get to the bloody point, man."

"Fact is, there's nothing you can do for me, *Majesty*. You are, to put it plainly, a royal hostage. Just how valuable you are as a hostage will be something for someone else to decide."

Exasperated, the King threw up his hands. "Then why the devil are you even talking to me?"

"Just wanted to explain how things are, *Majesty*." He paused a beat and then added, "And also to caution you about the consequences of any . . . Shall we say, failure to cooperate on your part?"

"I have absolutely no intention of cooperating with you," replied Charles. "Damn the consequences."

"I thought you might say something like that." Sten gestured to McClanahan, who had just managed to sit up. "See, it won't be you who feels the consequences. It'll be *him*."

Sten smiled again. "If his life means anything at all to you, you'll think twice before doing anything . . . foolish." And with that threat delivered, Sten turned on his heel and strode from the room.

Charles immediately went to McClanahan's side. "Roddy, old chap, are you injured?"

The gamekeeper gazed back at him with a slightly bewildered expression. "I don't think so, sir. Just a little groggy. Not sure what happened."

"What happened is that we've been shanghaied."

McClanahan's eyes widened in surprise, and he sat up a little straighter. "How'd that happen?"

"Your guess is as good as mine, I'm afraid."

McClanahan regarded him with a searching expression. "I heard what that bloke said to you. 'Bout giving up the crown. Don't do it, sir. Don't give him the satisfaction."

"The thought never even entered my mind." Charles clapped the Scotsman on the shoulder. "Chin up, Roddy. We'll get through this."

"As you say, sir," said McClanahan with a grateful smile.

Charles returned the smile, wishing that he felt half as confident about their situation.

TEN

Although more than a month had passed since his return from Antarctica and the last fateful voyage of the *Sea Hawke*, Stokely Jones Jr. still felt the chill in his bones. It wasn't that he couldn't handle the cold. It was just that the older he got, the longer it seemed to take him to warm up. He much preferred working in places where it wasn't necessary to dress in layers.

Places like Cuba.

The weather, a balmy 88 degrees, with seventy percent humidity and a mild breeze from out of the east, wasn't all that different from Key Biscayne, where Stokely Jones Jr. lived with Mrs. Stokely Jones Jr., the lovely and talented international singing sensation known to the rest of the world as Fancha—one name, like Cher or Madonna.

But Key Biscayne was home. This visit to Cuba . . . well, this was work.

Stokely was a freelance counterterrorism operator—in modern parlance, a private security contractor—and he was very good at his job. His company, Tactics International, which he co-owned with Alex Hawke, specialized in hostage rescues and other covert activities, primarily on behalf of US intelligence agencies and mostly in the

Caribbean and Latin America, though as Stoke's bones could testify, their jobs sometimes took them to chillier climes.

A broad smile came unbidden to Stoke's lips as he steered his boat, a pale blue Contender 34, between the red and green channel markers and throttled back on the triple Yamaha 300 outboards to make the final approach to Marina Hemingway, located on the north coast of Cuba, nine miles west of Havana. He'd borrowed the boat from his good friend and sometime employee, Luis "Sharkey" Gonzales-Gonzales, the dude so nice, they named him twice. Luis was Cuban, a stringy little former bone-fishing guide who had earned his nickname when he lost an argument with a bull shark over the question of which of them needed Luis's right arm more.

The view from the cockpit was one few Americans ever got a chance to appreciate, owing to more than sixty years of frosty relations between Cuba and the United States. Marina Hemingway, Cuba's largest marina, was one of the few ports on the island open to foreign vessels, but because of the ongoing travel ban prohibiting Americans from visiting Cuba except under specific circumstances, very few of those boats flew the Stars and Stripes. Stoke navigated the narrow channel through the reef—the entrance to the marina was just a hundred feet wide—and edged up to the concrete customs dock, where a rather attractive *cubana* in a somewhat less attractive khaki uniform came out to greet him.

The young woman did a double take when she saw him, her eyes going up and down as she took his measure. Stoke *was* a very large man. He often had that effect on people. But then she flashed a smile. *"Bienvenido a Cuba,"* she said brightly, and then repeated the message in deliciously accented English. "Welcome to Cuba, *señor.*"

"Well, *bienvenido* to you too, darling." Stoke held out his passport open to the page displaying the visa stamp granting him permission to enter the country. She took it, flipping to the page with his photograph and vital information.

Her eyes moved as she read; then her gaze came back to him. "Your name is Sheldon Levy?"

Stoke laughed. "I know. You were expecting someone a little more Jewish, right?"

Stoke often used the Sheldon Levy alias when traveling to places where the name Stokely Jones Jr. would have raised red flags. Places like Cuba. He had chosen the unlikely nom de guerre for the simple reason that it *was* unlikely. For some reason, the incongruity of that name attached to an enormous Black man was enough to keep people scratching their heads when they should have been digging into his cover story.

The young woman, however, shook her head. "It's not that, *señor*. It's just that you have the same name as a famous American advertising genius. A relative, perhaps?"

The question took Stoke aback. Advertising, or really anything that might have been construed as promoting capitalism, was illegal in Cuba, so how did this little *chica* know anything about American advertising? "Uh, probably not. It's a pretty common name."

He thought she looked a little disappointed. "What is the purpose of your visit?"

"Cultural exchange." Cultural exchange was one of the few exceptions under which Americans were allowed to visit Cuba. Stoke didn't *need* official permission. He was traveling with a forged passport under an assumed identity. You couldn't get much more unofficial than that. Nevertheless, he needed a plausible cover story to satisfy the curiosity of the customs agent. "My firm, Sun Coast Marketing, represents the singer Fancha. . . . Maybe you've heard of her?"

She blinked, uncomprehending.

"From Cabo Verde? Famous Fado performer? Sings these sad Portuguese love ballads?"

The young woman just shrugged.

Stoke shook his head. *She knows about Sheldon Levy but hasn't heard of Fancha? Gotta love Cuba.*

"Well, you should look her up on Spotify," he went on, "or whatever you folks have here. Anyway, I'm organizing Fancha's next world tour, and she's got her little heart set on performing in Havana. I'm just here scouting locations."

This explanation seemed to satisfy the customs official. She held up the passport. "Stamp?"

Stokely Jones Jr. had what could be described only as a love-hate relationship with the Caribbean island nation. He loved Cuban culture: the food, the music, the sheer passion for life that seemed to run in the blood of every *cubano*. . . . Hell, he even liked their shirts.

But he hated . . . *hated* their government.

He had nothing but admiration for the resourcefulness of the Cuban people, who, despite sixty years of crushing poverty under Communist rule, had found a way to simply keep going, just like the vintage automobiles, mostly converted to taxis, that still roamed the streets of Havana. But he was outraged by the oppressive system that had made such resourcefulness necessary.

It had taken him a while to realize that what he both loved and hated about Cuba and her people boiled down to the same thing: stubbornness.

It was stubbornness that kept a veritable fleet of '57 Chevys running strong despite an economic embargo that prevented the importation of replacement parts, and it was stubbornness that kept Cuba's Communist Party in power long after the rest of the world had realized that Marxism was a recipe for disaster. Most Cubans *knew* that Communism had failed them, but they were constitutionally incapable of admitting that they might have been wrong about something.

It was that same stubbornness that kept many in the Cuban American community—most of them second- and third-generation descendants of refugees who had fled the oppressive regime—from supporting various attempts by both the Cuban and American governments to "thaw" the decades-long freeze that kept American tourists out of Cuban beach resorts and Cuban cigars out of American humidors.

Stubbornness was something Stoke could appreciate, even if he didn't always agree with the results it produced. He had even developed a grudging admiration for Cuba's great revolutionary leader, Fidel Castro. Years before, he had actually rescued the man from the secret prison where he had been sent following an attempted coup d'état that would have put a trio of psychopathic Colombian drug lords in charge of the country. Subsequently, Castro had declared him a "Hero of the Revolution," an honor that Stoke remained strangely proud of.

He actually wasn't sure if his status as Cuban national hero remained in effect now that El Jefe was gone. Probably not, given the fact that Cuba had thrown in their lot with the Red Star Alliance. And there was that time he and Alex Hawke had spent a memorable fortnight as guests at a joint Cuban-Russian military facility in the jungle where they had been subjected to unimaginable tortures, but shit, as they say, happens. Get over it.

Stoke was over it.

When he'd gotten the call from his old buddy Harry Brock about a job in Havana, Stokely had replied, "Gimme a second to think about it." Because that was all the time he needed. *An all-expenses paid trip to Havana? Where do I sign?*

What good was it being a national hero if he didn't drop in for a visit now and then?

If there was any aspect of the offer that might have given him pause, it lay with the man making it—Harry Brock *was* a friend, but he was one of those friends you always seemed to be apologizing for. He wasn't a bad guy, especially considering that he'd come out of a gated golf community in Southern California. He just had a way of instantly getting under your skin.

As Stoke liked to say, there was politically incorrect, and then there was Harry Brock.

Yet, for all his social deficiencies, Brock was the guy you wanted to have on your side, especially in a fight. A former Marine currently working as a CIA spook, Harry was one hundred percent on the side of the angels.

He found Harry waiting for him at an open-air, quayside drinking establishment named, creatively, Papa's. The literary reference was probably lost on Harry, who Stoke knew read Danielle Steel and not much else. For his part, Stoke had never really seen the appeal of Hemingway. Not the man and not his writing. Stoke preferred the classic works of John D. MacDonald, but, he supposed, to each his own.

"Hey, Harry," he said as he settled onto a cane chair across the table from the American spy. "How's it hanging?"

"Stoke! My man. How the hell are you?" He raised his hand and began snapping his fingers, demanding attention from the pretty young thing working behind the bar. "Hey, my friend needs a mojito."

The barmaid smiled, but Stoke thought that if she could have shot laser beams from her eyes, Harry Brock would have been sliced neatly in two.

Stoke didn't drink. Never had. Harry Brock knew this, but like most people who drank religiously, Harry was sure he could convert his friend if he just kept bearing witness to the holy spirits.

"How in the hell did I not know about this drink?" Harry went on.

"Looks like you've already had enough for both of us," Stoke remarked, eyeing the assortment of empty collins glasses on the table between them.

"That's 'cause they're just that good. One of the few things they get right in this shithole country. That and cigars. Know what I mean?"

"I really don't, Harry. I'll just have a Diet Coke."

"Sorry, amigo. No can do. Can't get that here." Harry didn't really sound sorry at all.

"How 'bout a rum and Coke? Can I get that?"

The question seemed to confound the CIA operative. "Well, gee, I don't know." He glanced over at the server, who was busy muddling mint leaves in a glass, and shouted, "Can my friend get a rum and Coke?"

The barmaid gave Stoke a long, appraising look, and this time, her smile seemed a little more sincere. "For you, *señor, sí.*"

Stoke returned the smile. She really was very pretty.

Brock, however, didn't like that answer. "Wait a minute," he protested. "Real Coke? Not some Cuba cola knockoff."

"*Sí*, Coca-Cola *auténtico. Hecho en México.*"

"That's the good stuff," said Stoke. "Real cane sugar in the recipe, instead of that high-fructose corn syrup."

"Well, I'll be damned," said Harry as if this revelation was a personal insult.

"I'll have one of those," Stoke said, smiling at the barmaid again. Were all Cuban women gorgeous? "Hold the rum."

He then looked Brock in the eye. "Okay, Harry, enough small talk. Why the hell am I here? For that matter, why the hell are you here?"

Brock waited until the pretty bartender delivered their drinks—a tall glass for him, and a glass bottle of Coca-Cola for Stoke—then leaned in close enough to make his conspiratorial whisper audible. "What do you know about Novichok agents?"

Stoke, who didn't recognize the reference, shrugged. "Sounds Russian."

"Yeah, they are. The deadliest nerve agents ever developed."

"Nerve agents. So you're not talking about a spy ring?"

"No. *Nerve* agents. Try to keep up. They're binary chemical weapons developed for military use in the Soviet Union beginning in the 1970s. Similar to VX but eight times deadlier."

Stoke was big, but he wasn't dumb. He'd learned all about nerve agents during his time in the military and knew that they were some of the scariest weapons on the planet—so scary that nearly every nation on earth had agreed to abide by the Chemical Weapons Convention of 1993, a treaty barring the development or use of chemical weapons in warfare. But that hadn't stopped many of those nations, even the ones that had signed the CWC, from continuing research and development programs and maintaining secret stockpiles of chemical weapons.

Nerve agents were the deadliest of chemical weapons because they worked by inhibiting neurotransmitter activity in the body, which, among other things, had the effect of causing paralysis in the diaphragm, which in turn caused rapid, irreversible asphyxiation.

"Binary," murmured Stoke. "As in two parts?"

Harry nodded. "The Novichok agents are made from two compounds that are relatively safe and undetectable until mixed together. Once they're combined, though, watch out. They've never been used on the battlefield, but the KGB . . . or whatever they were calling themselves at the time—"

"They'll always be the KGB, Harry."

"Ain't that the truth. Well, they started using it for political assassinations. In 2018, they used it in an attempt to kill a former double agent living in England."

"I remember that," said Stoke. "Weren't a bunch of first responders affected too?"

"Yeah. That's the thing about this stuff. A little bit goes a long way. A gram of the stuff can kill five thousand people, and it doesn't break down."

Stoke nodded. "All right, it's scary stuff. Why are you telling me about it?"

"We got a tip that a rogue Russian ex-general is here in Cuba trying to move a large quantity of this shit."

"Large quantity?"

"Couple hundred pounds of it, if our intel is correct."

"Ah. And you want me to help you stop the sale."

Stoke wasn't sure how he felt about that. He definitely didn't like the idea of Russian WMDs being sold on the black market just a hundred miles from his home, but as much as he loved blowing shit up, his preferred method for doing that when chemical weapons were involved was to launch a cruise missile strike from a nice safe distance.

Brock shook his head. "No, man, nothing like that. This is strictly a surveillance op. We just want to identify the buyer. Figure out who might be up to no good in our neck of the woods. Maybe tag the weapons if we can get close enough. But that's it. No contact. Zero residue."

"You don't know who the buyer is?"

Brock shook his head. "No idea. Could be almost anyone, but given the fact that this is all happening on the down-low, we can assume it's going to a rogue outfit. Terrorists or revolutionaries. This stuff is bad news, and whoever's buying it probably has a plan to use it. We need to disrupt that plan. *Fast*."

Stoke nodded slowly. "So, you want to see where the nerve agent goes after the sale. Cut the head off the snake once it's back in its hole."

"Cut the head off the whole enchilada, amigo."

"Enchiladas are Tex-Mex, Harry. And that doesn't make any sense."

"Huh?"

"Never mind, man. So, when is this going down?"

"Midnight tonight. Little place west of here where they hold cockfights."

"Cockfights?" Stoke made a face. Maybe there were a few things about Cuban culture he didn't love.

"It's the perfect place for something like this," Brock went on. "People come from all over to watch the fights, so strangers don't really stand out. Not even foreigners. Which will work in our favor too. We'll be able to blend in with the crowd and scope the place out ahead of time. Maybe even ID the buyer."

Stoke, who had zero interest in watching chickens tear one another apart in gladiatorial combat, said, "Sounds like you could do this all by yourself. What do you need me for?"

"While I'm watching the sale, I want you to watch my back."

"That's all?"

"Simple as that."

Stoke contemplated the beads of condensation rolling down the painted Coca-Cola logo on his bottle. "Nothing's ever simple with you, Harry."

ELEVEN

I n the nearly forty-year history of the internecine conflict known internationally as the Northern Ireland conflict, but more often simply called the Troubles, no single official entity had come to symbolize the alleged oppressiveness of the British government as much as the police force of Northern Ireland, the Royal Ulster Constabulary. Although responsible for only a small percentage of the more than thirty-five hundred civilian deaths during the four decades of conflict—in fact, Republican and Loyalist paramilitary groups had been responsible for ninety percent of the deaths—the RUC's reputation for sectarian favoritism, unchecked violence and brutality, and particularly accusations of mistreatment of children in custody made them, quite literally in some cases, the international face of Protestant oppression.

The animus toward the RUC was so entrenched among the Irish Catholics that one of the terms of the Good Friday Agreement, which largely brought the conflict to an end, was the abolishment of the controversial constabulary and its replacement by a new organization, the Police Service of Northern Ireland, or PSNI. A key part of the reform plan was an affirmative-action recruitment policy designed to ensure that the ranks of the new constabulary would have equal representation of both Catholics and Protestants, but this policy proved ineffective due in no small part to persistent antipathy toward the police from the Catholic population. Very few young Catholics wanted to join the ranks of the hated police force, and those who did were often subject to ridicule and harassment. Ten years in, fewer than thirty percent of sworn PSNI officers were from Catholic backgrounds. To many Catholics in Northern Ireland, the only thing new about the PSNI was its name, and despite the official cessation of hostilities as set forth in the Good Friday Agreement, police officers continued to be the primary target of bomb attacks and assassination attempts by dissident Republican forces.

The headquarters of the PSNI, and of the RUC before it, was situated in a walled compound at 65 Knock Road in Belfast. A constable kitted up in full tactical gear, like a soldier heading into combat, came out to greet Sutherland and Congreve at the gated entrance. After a thorough inspection of their credentials, they moved inside and followed the constable's directions to the main headquarters building, where Chief Constable Anthony Aimes had his office.

Like nearly all of his predecessors, Northern Ireland's top cop was not a local but rather an outsider with years of experience working in the higher echelons of the Metropolitan Police. Aimes had, in fact, been a detective inspector at Scotland Yard during the period in which Congreve had been Number One at the force, though their interactions had been quite limited. Subsequently, Aimes had continued to advance through the ranks, eventually taking the reins of the Specialist Crime & Operations Directorate. He had been on the short list to take the Number One job, and when he'd been passed over, he accepted the offer to take over at PSNI.

Aimes welcomed his visitors and made the obligatory offer of a cup of tea, which Congreve accepted graciously and Sutherland declined politely.

As Ambrose sipped from his cup, Sutherland, as the ranking officer in the investigation, took the lead. "I'll come right to the point, Chief Constable—"

"Please, it's just Tony," said Aimes, smiling.

Sutherland accepted this with a slight nod. "We're here because we've received credible reports of a threat against a member of the Royal Family, a threat that appears to originate from the New IRA."

Insofar as they could not come right out and tell Aimes the whole truth, this cover story, not exactly a fiction if viewed from a certain point of view, was what Congreve and Sutherland had agreed upon during their hour-long flight to Belfast.

Aimes raised an eyebrow. "Is that a fact?"

"*Fact* is perhaps too generous a word," said Congreve, setting cup and saucer on a corner of Aimes's desk. "More of a rumor, really, but one we can't afford to ignore. But, ah . . . do I detect a hint of skepticism in your question?"

"More than a hint," admitted Aimes. His gaze flitted from Congreve to Sutherland and back again as if unsure which man he ought to be addressing. He finally settled on Congreve. "What do you know about the New IRA?"

"Quite a lot, actually," said Congreve with a sniff. "I had a bit of a tussle with them a few years back when they took over Balmoral and tried to murder the Royal Family."

Aimes held his gaze for a moment. "Then you'll also recall that the dissidents were little more than hired muscle for that operation. They're hooligans, Ambrose. Always have been."

"So, you don't believe them capable of going after the royals?" interjected Sutherland.

"Capable? Frankly, no. They haven't the numbers or the resources to mount any kind of serious campaign, much less defend against the sort of reprisals that would follow if they targeted a royal or an MP. But it's not a question of capabilities. It's a matter of ambition. Or should I say, the lack thereof? They're not much interested in anything but low-hanging fruit. Think of them as little more than a street gang these days, dealing mostly in drugs and protection. Sure, they'll cause a bit of trouble now and again. But there's no grand vision behind it all."

"What if something's changed?" said Congreve.

"Like what?"

"The Scottish vote. If Scotland leaves the Union, might that not embolden some to take action?"

Aimes pursed his lips together. "There has been some talk of that," Aimes admitted. "But attacking the royals would be the last thing the Republicans would want to do. The Catholics don't want more violence. If anything, the Scottish vote is proof that ballots can accomplish more than bullets."

"And if the vote goes the wrong way? Might that not send exactly the opposite message?"

Aimes shook his head. "You still haven't made a case for why the dissidents would choose to go after the royals."

"We don't need to make a case," Sutherland cut in. "We didn't come here for your bloody opinion. The threat to the royals is credible. Special Branch has jurisdiction. We have to follow up on it, and we need your help to do it. It's as simple as that."

Aimes's stare suddenly became hard as diamonds. "And what exactly is it you expect from me?" And then, with more than a little acid, he added, "Chief Inspector."

Sutherland, unruffled by the senior copper's tone, replied, "We have a suspect in custody. A fellow named Colm Keaney from Londonderry. He was active on a New IRA social media page up until six months ago. That was when he managed to get a job working at one of the royal residences. We caught him in a random security review, but he's not cooperating, so we need to interview his family and any known associates."

"That's your 'credible threat'? Someone liked a tweet and then got a job with the Royal Family?"

"There's more, but at present, I'm not at liberty to share the details."

Aimes snorted in derision. "Anything else?"

"I will need to interview any informants you have working inside the dissident groups," said Congreve.

Aimes stiffened. "You're joking?"

"Not at all. We must know who's behind this threat."

"The only reason we've been able to keep a lid on things here is because we have informants who are willing to risk their lives to give us critical information to minimize loss of life. But they come to us. Not the other way around. If we pull them in for questioning, not only will you jeopardize our operations. You'll put targets on their backs."

"These are extraordinary circumstances," countered Congreve. "They demand extraordinary measures. The threat—"

"Yes, the threat is credible. You keep saying it. Only you won't tell me what the bloody threat is. Cooperation is a two-way street. If you're asking me to put lives in jeopardy, the least you can do is be honest with me."

"I'm sorry," said Sutherland, "but we can't—"

"The King's been abducted, Tony," said Congreve.

Aimes's eyes went wide in astonishment. Sutherland gaped at Congreve. "Ambrose."

"I'm sorry, Ross, but the chief constable needs to know what's at stake. Extraordinary circumstances." He turned to Aimes. "It goes without saying that this must be kept in the strictest confidence."

Aimes sat very still for a long moment. "The King? Abducted?"

Sutherland frowned but then nodded. "The PM wants to keep this under wraps for as long as possible, but yes, I'm afraid that's the situation."

"And the IRA have him?"

"We don't know who has him," said Congreve. "That's the problem. But this wasn't some snatch and grab in a back alley. The operation was far too sophisticated for a bunch of . . . What was the word you used? Hooligans? But this Keaney chap *was* part of it."

"And he won't talk."

"Can't talk. He's dead. His connection to the IRA, tenuous though it may be, is the only thread we have to pull on. And pull on it, we shall."

A pensive Aimes began drumming his fingers on the desk. "Gentlemen, I appreciate your forthrightness. The PSNI is at your disposal. Whatever you need. That said, I maintain my belief that you're looking in the wrong place, and I think I know of a way to prove it."

"I'm listening."

"There's someone you should talk to. A chap named Duggan. Padraig Duggan. Joined the Provos when he was sixteen years old, back in '67. A true believer. Killed a UVF paramilitary fighter a couple years later and was sentenced to life in Maze prison. He was released in 2000 under the terms of the agreement, but by then, he'd spent the best years of his life locked away, so as you might imagine, he wasn't exactly overflowing with gratitude."

"No, I don't suppose so."

"After flailing about for a few years, he eventually assumed a leadership position in the Saoirse, a far-left fringe political party that is still demanding independence. They're the public face of the New IRA, even if they deny it. Duggan is sort of an elder statesman in the dissident movement. If NIRA is involved in any way with this plot, he'll know it."

"Hmm. And what makes you think he'll talk to us?"

Aimes grinned like the devil. "Because Padraig Duggan works for me."

TWELVE

ir David Trulove's eyes rose from the book of poetry he'd been reading and settled on the unexpected visitor who was being shown into his private study on the fourth floor of 85 Albert Embankment, Vauxhall Cross—the modern ziggurat-style structure known variously as Babylon on Thames, Legoland, and HQ of the Secret Intelligence Service. As a general rule, Sir David did not like surprises, and as the head of the British Secret Service, he rarely encountered them. It was his job after all to get out ahead of the surprises, to know things before anyone else, and if necessary, to take the appropriate measures to ensure that the surprises never happened. To be surprised was to be caught off guard, and that was a position in which Sir David, a decorated naval warrior long before getting into the spy game, did not like to find himself. Which was why an unscheduled late-afternoon visit, even from someone whom he thought of as the son he had never had—a sentiment he would never have uttered aloud—filled him with grave foreboding.

"Alex," he murmured, trying to hide his discomfiture, "this is rather unexpected."

From the open doorway, Lord Alexander Hawke offered what he

no doubt intended to be a disarming smile. "Sorry to drop in un-announced, Trulove. Something has . . . ah, come up."

Trulove narrowed his eyes into a piercing gaze. His feelings for the other man notwithstanding, so long as Alex Hawke remained in service to the Crown, a secret agent working for MI6, their relationship would remain strictly professional, which meant that Sir David, who, like his predecessors, utilized the single-letter designation "C" for official business, was Alex's commanding officer, and Alex, despite being given a great deal of latitude in how to go about executing Trulove's orders, remained subordinate. As a subordinate, it was Alex's role to come to Sir David when summoned—not to drop in whenever he bloody well felt like it. C most definitely did not have an open-door policy. Alex Hawke understood this better than almost any man alive. Which meant that if Alex felt it necessary to violate that unspoken protocol, it could only be because he had good reason. And *good reason* could mean only something very bad indeed.

Sir David set aside his book. "Well, don't just stand there," he said, affecting a tone that was a good deal gruffer than usual. "Come in. Help yourself to a drink. I'm afraid I haven't got any of that awful rum you favor. Pour me one while you're at it."

Hawke glided through the office to the antique sideboard upon which rested a crystal decanter and four matching glasses.

"Scotch," he murmured as if this was somehow consequential. He splashed a couple fingers into two of the glasses and then carried them over, placing both glasses on the small table positioned between a pair of matching reading chairs, one of which was presently occupied by Sir David. Once Hawke was seated in the other chair, Trulove took up his glass and raised it to Alex. "To your health."

"And yours," said Hawke.

As he savored a mouthful of the whisky, Trulove did not fail to notice that Alex took only a sip. "Excellent work down south," Trulove said. "We might not have completely sunk the Red Star Alliance, but this is a blow from which they won't quickly recover. Rotten business about your boat, though."

"I'll build another," Hawke answered somewhat distractedly.

Trulove chuckled. "Of course you will." He set his glass down and regarded Hawke with an imperious stare. "All right, let's have it. Why are you here, Alex? What is this 'something' that, as you say, 'came up'?"

"It's a rather tricky matter that Ambrose Congreve asked me to look into for him."

"Ah, Congreve. How is the old chap?"

"Doing quite well, sir. Strange as it sounds, marriage agrees with him."

Trulove resisted the impulse to chuckle at the observation. His visitor, he knew, was presently contemplating his own upcoming nuptials, a decision that Sir David felt certain Alex would come to regret. Marriage, most certainly, did not agree with Lord Hawke. "And yet one wonders why he keeps coming out of retirement."

"A sense of duty, I imagine."

"Ha. Yes." Trulove took another sip. "So, Congreve asks *you* to look into something, and your immediate response is to ask me." He tried to inject a note of disapproval into his voice. "I'm not Google, Alex."

"No, sir." If Hawke was chastened by the mild rebuke, it didn't show.

"You do have an office here, you know," Trulove went on, "though God only knows why, since you hardly ever make use of it."

"Yes, sir. And I certainly could have undertaken this search on my own. Had I done so, you would have immediately been notified, and wondering what on earth I was up to, you would have called me up here to explain myself. I thought I'd just skip all the preamble and come here forthwith to get that inquiry out of the way."

Now Trulove did laugh. "Touché, Alex. Very well. What bee is currently buzzing about in Congreve's bonnet?"

"Well, it's this Scottish vote."

"Ah, yes. History repeats itself."

"Special Branch has brought Ambrose in to consult on an investigation concerning an attempt to . . . ah, influence the outcome of the referendum."

"A waste of his talent. You don't need to look any farther than the World Wide Web to find proof of it. Russian and Chinese hackers have launched a full-scale invasion. Bots everywhere, stirring up anti-government sentiment and pushing nationalist narratives. Imagine what Hitler could have done if he'd had the internet."

"Yes, well, Special Branch is concerned that someone might be planning to do something more . . . should we say, *provocative* than merely attempting to sway public opinion."

"Hmm. Blowing up the House of Lords, for instance?"

Hawke laughed, but the humor did not reach his eyes. "Something like that."

"Scotland Yard hasn't shared these concerns with us."

"I can't really speak to that, sir. I believe they see this as a domestic issue."

Trulove's eyes narrowed again. "And yet here you are."

"At Ambrose's behest."

"I see." Trulove leaned back in his chair. "And what is it he wants you to find out for him?"

"He's trying to put together a . . . Well, I guess you could call it a watch list. Who would benefit most from Scotland leaving the UK? Who might be willing to carry out some kind of terror attack to influence the outcome? And who would have the resources to make it happen?"

"As to the first question, it would be a long list. But I would say the rest of it depends on what sort of terrorist attack you're talking about."

"I should say something on the order of what happened at Balmoral a few years back."

Hawke did not need to elaborate. Sir David Trulove had been among the guests at Balmoral during the attack on the Royal Family. He'd taken two bullets for his troubles and nearly died.

"I see." Trulove leaned forward and took up the receiver of the phone on the tabletop. "Miss Guinness," he said, "be a dear and join me in my *salon privé.*"

Trulove noted Hawke's reaction, a mixture of surprise, pleasure, and bemusement. "Pippa's here?"

"Hmm. Yes." Sir David took advantage of the pause to take a slim black cheroot from the inside pocket of his suit jacket. He fired it up, filling the room with whorls of smoke, savoring the taste almost as much as he did the look of mild irritation that now joined the stew of emotions on Hawke's visage.

THIRTEEN

awke recognized C's seemingly abrupt decision to light up one of his poisonous black cheroots for exactly what it was—a none too subtle reminder of who held the real power in the room. For all his wealth and aristocratic standing, Hawke was the subordinate, the employee. C was the boss, and he wasn't about to let Hawke forget it.

Nevertheless, it was the revelation that Pippa Guinness was on her way in that had left Hawke more than a little unsettled.

Pippa?

It had been ages since he'd even thought about her.

Gwendolyn "Pippa" Guinness had gotten her start in government service as a "garden girl"—Churchill's pet name for the secretarial staff—at Number 10 Downing Street, which was where she had, quite literally, first crossed the path of Lord Alexander Hawke. He had quite enjoyed following her up the stairs on the occasion of that long-ago visit. Subsequently, she had gone to uni, gotten her degree in Latin American studies, and joined MI6, working her way up through the ranks of analysts to eventually head up Red Banner, C's brainchild, an ad hoc OPINTEL shop tasked with curbing the empire-building impulses of a resurgent Russia under Vladimir Putin. Hawke had led the OPS side of Red Banner, while Pippa, as acting chief of station, coordinated the INTEL. Somewhere along the way, she and Hawke had spent a rum-soaked night together in Key West, and it was that memory, more than any other, that now flooded Hawke's thoughts.

The recollection was not an altogether unpleasant one, and he struggled to remember why they had never reconnected.

The door opened, and Pippa strode into the room. Blond, stunningly attractive, attired in a bright red sleeveless sheath dress and matching heels, she was even more beautiful than he remembered.

Ever the gentleman, Hawke rose from his chair. Pippa did a barely noticeable double take upon seeing him but recovered smoothly, addressing a still-seated C as if he were the only person present. "Good afternoon, sir. You wished to see me?"

"Indeed," said C, puffing furiously on his cheroot. "I believe you already know Commander Hawke."

This, of course, was Trulove's idea of a joke.

"Hullo, Pippa," said Hawke, still standing.

She regarded him coolly. "My *friends* call me Pippa, Commander."

Ah, yes, thought Hawke. *Now I remember.*

He had been a bit of a cad that night in Key West, allowing the baser instincts and infamous cruelty of his pirate ancestors to take charge when his conscience knew damn well better than to mix work with pleasure. He regretted it now. . . . Hell, he'd regretted it then, but when a beautiful, naked woman invited herself into one's shower, the lower parts of one's anatomy tended to take the reins.

The next morning, when he'd dismissed her in order to take an important call from another former lover—a call that was most definitely work related—she'd hastened from his bed under a cloud of shame, and although they had subsequently worked together again, there had never been a return to intimacy.

Probably for the best, he thought. He had Anastasia now. He had real love.

Without acknowledging the rebuke, he gestured to the chair he'd occupied only a moment before. "Won't you have a seat, Miss Guinness?"

It occurred to him only then that she was still Miss Guinness, but he resisted the impulse to glance down at the fingers of her left hand in search of a ring.

She then smiled and laughed. "I'm joking, Alex."

Except, he didn't think she was. There was something behind that smile, a lingering hurt or . . . was it something else?

"It is good to see you again," she went on. "You look well."

Hawke was spared having to respond in kind by Sir David's intervention. "Yes, yes. We're all happy to see each other. Do sit down, dear girl. This isn't a social call. Commander Hawke was just about to tell me why he's come calling."

Hawke dragged another chair from a corner of the room, and when they were all seated, C resumed speaking. "Alex was just telling me about a possible terror attack relating to the Scottish vote."

Pippa raised a perfect eyebrow. "We haven't picked up any chatter to indicate something like that in the works."

"Hmm," continued C. "Targeting the Royal Family, no less."

Pippa turned to Alex. "This is credible?"

Hawke managed a half smile. "Just running down a possibility," he lied, "as a favor for Ambrose Congreve. He asked me to come up with a list of . . . I guess you could call them 'bad actors' on the international level who might be willing and able to pull off something like that."

The blond woman nodded thoughtfully. "Well, at first blush, I would say the usual suspects."

"And at second blush?"

Pippa straightened in her chair. "The truth of the matter is that losing Scotland or keeping it, for that matter, won't make much of a difference on the international stage. The most significant impacts will be mainly social and economic, both here and in Scotland, but even those will be marginal in the long term. In the near term, an independent Scotland would likely seek to preserve the status quo with respect to trade and travel."

"What about NATO membership? I've heard that the Scottish

National Party is antinuclear. If they banned nuclear weapons, it would be a strategic disadvantage."

"That's a concern but not likely an immediate one. The SNP is antinuclear as a matter of principle, but it would be in their best interests to maintain a strategic partnership both with the UK and NATO. I might add the SNP is pro-monarchy. Under their plan, Scotland would remain in the Commonwealth and continue to recognize King Charles as the head of state."

"Would a terror attack against the royals change that?"

Pippa considered this for a moment. "I can't imagine that it would. If anything, a sympathy vote might move the needle in favor of the 'No' vote."

"So, there's no plausible scenario where a terrorist attack on the Royal Family, ahead of the Scottish vote, really works to anyone's advantage."

"Not one that's readily apparent," Pippa said. She paused a beat before adding, "Contingent on the SNP holding the majority in the creation of an independent Scotland, that is."

The caveat surprised Hawke. "It's not a foregone conclusion?"

Pippa glanced at C as if looking for permission, then said, "I hesitate to mention this because it's rather . . . well, outlandish, but since you asked . . . The SNP is the most prominent pro-independence party in Scotland, but they aren't the only one. There are a few fringe parties to reckon with. They are mostly leftists, and one or two favor abolishing the monarchy. One of them—the Stewards of Alba Party—is unique in that they call for placing a Scottish monarch on the throne."

"I wasn't aware that there was a Scottish monarch," said Hawke. "Or do they plan to hold an election for that position?"

"They support the Jacobite succession."

"I'm sorry, the what?"

Pippa returned a smug smile, evidently delighted by the fact that she possessed information that the illustrious Lord Hawke did not. She glanced over at C. "Is there time for a short history lecture?"

C frowned in disapproval but then nodded. "If you think it's relevant."

She looked to Hawke, who, having no idea of the relevance of her information, could only shrug.

"If you paid attention in history class," Pippa began, "you'll recall that in 1603, when Queen Elizabeth I died without issue, the crown passed to her nearest living relative, James VI, the King of Scotland, who by virtue of an earlier political marriage was the great-grandson of Margaret Tudor. His ascension effectively unified the Kingdoms of Scotland, England, and Ireland under a single political dynasty—the House of Stuart—but because he and his line were Catholics, there was never anything remotely like a united kingdom. James's heir, Charles I, was eventually deposed and executed in 1649 following the Wars of the Three Kingdoms."

Hawke began to recall a few of these details. "Ah, yes. Cromwell's bloody revolution."

"Charles's son Charles II was named to the Scottish Throne but lived in exile in the Netherlands until Parliament voted to restore the monarchy in 1660 and put him back on the throne of the three kingdoms. When Charles died in 1685, his brother James—he's called James VII and II because he was James VII, King of Scotland, and James II, King of England and Ireland—took the throne but was deposed three years later and replaced by Queen Mary II, who co-reigned with her husband, William of Orange."

Hawke nodded. "William and Mary. It's all coming back to me now."

"After William's death, Anne, the Anglican daughter of James VII, ascended to the throne, and under her reign, the Acts of Union officially fused the Kingdoms of Scotland and England. Following Anne's death, the throne passed to her second cousin George of Hanover, the great-grandson of James VI—"

"I think we get the idea," murmured C. "It's all a bloody mess if you look at it too closely."

Pippa pursed her lips in a mild show of irritation, then went on. "The salient point is that when James VII lost the crown, by primogeniture, it should have passed to his son James Francis Edward Stuart. However, because he was a Catholic, he was held as ineligible, and instead, the throne went to Mary II. James Francis Edward and his son Charles Edward—Bonnie Prince Charlie—fought to reclaim the throne. Their supporters, known as Jacobites, held to the principle of the divine right of kings and argued that the removal of James VII was illegal and that all subsequent monarchs were pretenders. They hold that the legitimate line of succession continues through the Stuart dynasty."

"You don't mean to say that people today still care about that rubbish," said Hawke. "I mean, wasn't this all settled three hundred years ago?"

"In 2012, polling indicated that four percent of Scots would favor a Scottish monarch as head of state for an independent Scotland. I grant that's a small percentage, but that poll was taken when the Queen was still on the throne. Dare I say it, but King Charles is not as universally loved as was Her Majesty. I can only imagine the percentage has increased somewhat."

Hawke considered the relevance of this information as it pertained to the matter at hand. It seemed inconceivable that, in the twenty-first century, a fringe political movement inspired by an all-but-forgotten historical footnote might engineer the kidnapping of the monarch in order to advance their aims, but was that any more ludicrous than religious extremists crashing planes into skyscrapers over disagreements in the interpretation of their holy books?

"This Jacobite succession . . ." he said tentatively. "Is there an actual Stuart heir, or is this just hypothetical?"

"There is. According to the Royal Stuart Society, Franz von König, Duke of Bavaria, is a direct descendant of Charles II, making him the legitimate heir to the throne, not only of Scotland but of all of the

United Kingdom. Of course, he hasn't shown the least interest in making a claim to the throne. In fact, no Stuart heir has contested the monarchy in well over two hundred years. But if the Stewards of Alba Party were to put forward a name, he would be it." Her lips quirked in a sly smile. "He's ninety years old, never married, and openly gay, but he would be their king."

Alex returned the smile. "One supposes when he kicks off, they'll just pick another fruit off the family tree."

"One does suppose."

Hawke sat back in his chair, mulling over these revelations. He wondered what Congreve would make of it all. Would the criminalist dismiss the whole notion as a lot of balderdash, or would he insist on looking under every stone, if only to ensure that none were left unturned?

Recalling his friend's favorite Holmesian precept—*when you have eliminated the impossible, whatever remains, however improbable, must be the truth*—Hawke knew exactly what Congreve would want him to do.

"Well, this has been an interesting diversion," he said at length. "I doubt it will have any bearing on the investigation, but all the same, I think I should like to have a talk with the leader of this political party. Stewards of Alba, you said?"

"That's right. They're headquartered in Edinburgh."

"Edinburgh," echoed Alex as he gathered himself in preparation to depart. "I'll take the Locomotive. Make a day of it."

C, who had been watching him intently, now turned to Pippa. "Miss Guinness, why don't you accompany Commander Hawke? I'm sure he'd benefit from your expertise. To say nothing of your company."

Alex spoke before Pippa could give a reply. "There's really no need for that, sir," he said a little more hastily than he'd intended. He turned to Pippa apologetically. "It's not that I don't value your insights as an analyst. Quite the opposite. It's just that this is all probably much ado about nothing."

Something he said caused her lips to curl in a defiant smile, but it was C who spoke up on her behalf. "Miss Guinness isn't an analyst anymore, Alex. She's my Number Two."

Alex couldn't hide his look of absolute astonishment.

Number Two, as in deputy chief of the service?

There were four directors general in the SIS, all of whom reported directly to C, each specializing in a specific area of responsibility, such as operations or technology. The deputy chief, tasked with developing strategy for the service, also served as C's chief of staff and, as such, was his designated interim successor.

Wow, Pip, thought Hawke. *Good for you.*

It was all too obvious now. Pippa had always been ambitious. Charming as well, not to mention whip-smart and eager to climb the career ladder.

Whether she had once enchanted Alex and engaged in a heated, yet very short, love affair to advance her career or out of pure desire remained unknown.

An unknown that, to this very day, bothered Hawke.

Yet, even as these emotions filled his head, he knew he was being completely irrational. Not only did Alex know Pippa to be intelligent and highly capable, but he had witnessed her administrative expertise as Red Banner chief of station, and that had been many years ago. It was the height of arrogance to imagine that her career would have plateaued with that assignment. Indeed, Alex now saw clearly that Sir David had, in all likelihood, been grooming Pippa Guinness for this role all along. And that meant that their brief but passionate relationship had been *real* after all. That reality, however, only made their forthcoming reunion more awkward for Alex.

Hawke faced her. "Congratulations on a well-deserved promotion."

Pippa, who had not failed to observe his initial reaction, took a moment to weigh the sincerity of his expression before replying with a simple "Thank you."

Hawke then turned back to C. "But as I said, this is probably a lot of fuss over nothing. Just scratching an itch, you might say. I should hardly think it merits any attention at all, much less the direct involvement of the deputy chief of the service."

"Regardless of what *you* think it merits, Alex, when you brought this to my attention, you made it my business. And my decision is that Miss Guinness will accompany you."

Hawke still did not quite understand why C thought the matter warranted further investigation, but he knew better than to argue. "As you say, sir." He turned to Pippa. "It's a bit late to make a start of it today. What say we set out first thing in the morning? Where shall I collect you?"

He thought he detected something like disappointment in her gaze and wondered if it had been something he'd said or perhaps something he had failed to say. Was he supposed to have invited her to dinner? Was she, even now, contemplating another visit to his bed?

Or was she as displeased by C's decision to throw them together as he was?

"You may collect me here," she said after a moment's consideration. "I always come in early. Just call up to my office when you arrive." She then pivoted to face C. "If there's nothing else, sir . . ."

C made a humming noise and waved her off with the hand holding his cheroot.

Alex rose to his feet as she departed, watching her go with nothing even remotely resembling lust. He was not at all looking forward to spending several hours in close company with her.

He turned to C. "Well, I suppose I shall be off as well."

C hummed again, but as Alex reached the door, he called out, "Oh, Alex, one thing more."

Hawke glanced back. "Yes, sir?"

"As this is now official business, please, try to remember that Miss Guinness is in charge."

FOURTEEN

S hortly after sunset, Stoke and Harry rode out to the rural location where, according to Harry, the Russian ex-general would be conducting the sale of his stolen nerve agents. They rode in a lovingly restored pale blue '57 Chevy Bel Air, the car and its driver hired by Harry for way more money than it would have cost to simply rent a Kia or Hyundai from one of the local car rental services, but as Harry was quick to point out, hiring a vintage automobile was just the sort of thing ordinary tourists would have done, and besides, he could just expense it when he got back to the office. Anywhere else in the world, the Chevy would have turned heads, but this was Cuba, so nobody gave them or the car a second look.

Their driver was a wiry little guy named Alonso, who kind of reminded Stoke of Sharkey, but with both arms. And a pulse. Stoke wasn't sure if Alonso was his given name or a surname; Harry just called him Al. To Stoke's surprise, Al spoke more than just passable English, and he let the man play tour guide as they rolled through downtown Havana on their way out into the surrounding countryside.

Forty minutes later, Al pulled off into the grass at the roadside near the dirt track leading out to the farmhouse where, if Harry's intel was on the mark, everything was supposed to go down. As they got out, Harry turned to Al. "You're gonna be here when we come out, right?"

"*Sí, sí,*" replied Al. "Right here."

"'Cause that's the deal. We own your ass until morning."

"Ah, jeez, Harry," complained Stoke. "Really?"

Harry glanced back at him. His brow furrowed in confusion. "What?"

Stoke just shook his head.

Harry Brock, ladies and gentlemen. Mr. Sensitivity.

"Never mind, Harry. It would take too long to explain."

The move from the marina to the interior brought two noteworthy changes. Higher temperatures, as they were too far inland to benefit from the cooling effect of a Caribbean breeze, and, despite no longer being in close proximity to the sea, higher humidity. The combination reminded Stoke of his jungle warfare SEAL training in the Florida Keys, lovingly nicknamed "Heat 'n' Skeet," except for the facts that this wasn't the jungle and that he wasn't armed.

Plenty of heat and skeet, though.

Dusk brought little relief, the humidity holding in the heat of the sun long after it had slipped below the horizon, but the absence of the sun from the sky did have the effect of creating a friendlier environment for the mosquitoes, which, thankfully, seemed to prefer Harry's blood to Stoke's.

"Maybe they prefer the taste of mojitos," quipped Stoke when Harry complained about his seeming immunity. "Mojitos for mosquitoes. It even rhymes."

"I could really go for one of those right now," replied Harry with another futile swat at the swarm buzzing about his head. "I need something to deaden the pain."

Stoke was pretty sure the spy was only joking about wanting a drink but felt compelled to remind Harry to stay focused on the mission. It had taken hours and about a gallon of coffee to bring him down off his earlier buzz. "Maybe when we're finished here. Right now you just need to keep your head in the game."

The game was definitely going to require their full attention now that they had arrived at the so-called farmhouse—so-called because while the structure did meet the basic definition of a house, with four ratty walls and an even rattier roof, the piece of property upon which it had been built did not appear to be capable of sustaining an agricultural enterprise.

"Doesn't look like any farm I've ever seen," Stoke remarked.

"Maybe it's a chicken farm," suggested Harry. "That would make sense, right?"

"Chicken farmers are in the business of keeping their birds alive so they can either lay eggs or become dinner. They don't make them rip each other to shreds for entertainment. Either way, you need a lot of chickens if you're gonna be a chicken farmer. Do you see a lot of chickens, Harry?"

"Nah, but maybe they're not free-range birds, you know? Maybe they're all in that barn out behind the house."

The barn, like the house, was so dilapidated that it probably ought to have been condemned, but it did contain a quantity of chickens— specifically, roosters penned up in a variety of homespun cages stacked up along the interior walls and covered with blankets, presumably to keep them from trying to tear their way through the wire-and-wood structures in order to demonstrate superiority and, it could only be assumed, take control of a nonexistent brood. Despite not being able to see their rivals, the roosters raised a din that was audible, even over the low roar of human conversation. The barn, it turned out, was also the site of an improvised fighting arena where select cocks were already engaging in mortal combat to the delight of the assembled throng.

Cockfighting was not only legal in Cuba but wildly popular. And while gambling on the outcome was technically prohibited, it was not something the government seemed interested in policing, which meant that even informal—mainly underground—events like this could draw quite a gathering.

Despite his reservations, Stoke followed Harry inside. A few bare light bulbs hung down from the rafters, shining down through air that was thick with dust and tobacco smoke. As Harry had earlier intimated, there were more than a few obviously foreign faces in the crowd, and while Stoke earned one or two wide-eyed looks from locals, clearly in awe of his great size, nobody paid them much attention.

With Stoke in tow, Harry pushed his way closer to the big wood-walled ring in the center of the barn, where two roosters, coached by their handlers, were tearing at each other. Stoke, having already seen enough of the blood sport to last a lifetime, turned his gaze instead to the faces of the cheering spectators assembled around the ring.

"See the chubby guy at nine o'clock?" said Harry.

Stoke easily located the man, not only by his girth—his belly strained the buttons of his blue-and-white guayabera—but by his pale complexion and thinning light brown hair.

Definitely not a local, thought Stoke.

"That's General Osipov. He's the seller."

"Doesn't look like he's got the stuff with him."

"It's around here somewhere. You can bet on that."

"You see any other familiar faces?"

"Not yet, but it's still early."

Stoke shot a look at his watch, which was just ticking past eight p.m. "Well, it's past my bedtime."

"When did you get so old?"

Stoke ignored the gibe. "I'm gonna get some air. Text me if something interesting happens."

Brock mumbled an affirmative and resumed surreptitiously scanning the faces of the spectators. Stoke turned and began pushing through the assembled masses, which continued to increase with each passing minute. Once outside and able to move a little more freely, he meandered toward the farmhouse, where he spied a group of men, locals one and all by the look of them, sitting around a folding table on the porch, playing dominoes under the glow of a hanging shop light, and smoking fat cigars. Stoke had picked up a Montecristo No. 4 earlier and decided this was as good a time and place as any to enjoy it. Leaning against one of the upright posts supporting the porch roof, he snicked the end with a pocket guillotine and lit the cigar up with a wooden match, puffing until the tip was a bright red cherry, savoring the earthy taste of the tobacco as he watched the men slamming down their tiles.

From this vantage, he was able to keep an eye on new arrivals coming up the drive. As the Montecristo gradually turned to ash, he counted more than two dozen—all men, and mostly Cuban of either Latino or African ancestry. Because Brock had been unable to reveal anything about the buyer or what plans he might have for the nerve agent, he couldn't discount anyone. The buyer might conceivably be Cuban or Venezuelan or a middleman purchasing the chemical agent on behalf of another party.

One man, however, stood out from all the others.

It wasn't just his appearance, though his copper-orange hair, pale skin, and expensive, if understated, attire were all remarkable enough to set him apart from the locals. What grabbed Stoke's interest was something else, more a gut feeling than anything he could put into words. It was something in the way he walked, effortlessly dominating every aspect of his environment, maintaining three-sixty awareness almost without turning his head, all the while radiating a don't-even-think-about-fucking-with-me energy.

He moved like Alexander Hawke.

Stoke watched the man's progress from the corner of his eye, and when the latter disappeared inside the barn, he took out his phone and texted Harry.

Redheaded dude coming in.

———————

Harry Brock knew that Stokely Jones Jr. thought he was a fuckup. Hell, most people thought he was a fuckup.

He didn't *try* to be a fuckup. It just came naturally.

His fuckups were usually of the interpersonal variety. It seemed like no matter what he said, somebody got butt hurt. Was it his fault that people didn't get his sense of humor?

I mean, jeez, can't anyone take a joke anymore? Whatever.

But when shit went down and the chips hit the fan, Harry Brock was one switched-on motherfucker, and at the end of the day, that was the only thing that mattered. It was why, after years of getting his ass wrung out for saying the wrong thing at the wrong time to the wrong person, he was still in the fight, still at the tip of the spear.

Or pretty close to it anyway.

So, when he got Stoke's text about the redheaded dude, his inner early-warning system instantly went to high alert. Stoke wasn't the sort of guy to cry wolf. If he saw something, he said something, and he was usually right.

Casually, so as not to give himself away to anyone who might have been paying more than the usual attention to him, he turned and began making his way through the crowd.

Pay no attention, folks. Just an ordinary guy looking for someplace to drain the lizard.

The timing was perfect. Someone had just rung the bell, signaling the end of what had turned out to be a pretty unsatisfying battle. Despite a lot of cajoling from their handlers and a fair amount of rancorous jeering from the onlookers, the two roosters hadn't exactly gone at it. There had been a couple of charges, the roosters scrabbling at each other in a flurry of talons and feathers, but when one or the other beat a hasty retreat, his opponent didn't press the advantage.

Evidently, these cocks were the undercard fight. The undercocks.

He chuckled. *Undercocks. I don't care who you are. That's funny right there.*

But if that was all there was to cockfighting, Harry didn't see the appeal. He'd take an MMA cage match over this any day. But maybe this was all they could afford in—

Shit, there he is.

There was no mistaking the guy and not just because he was the only copper top in the place. This guy moved like an alpha predator. He was a redheaded lion sauntering through the antelope herd on his way to the watering hole.

Yeah, that's gotta be him.

With the crowd between them, Harry could catch only an occasional glimpse of the guy's face, his head bobbing in and out of view, but it didn't look like anyone Harry recognized. He'd need to get a pic of the guy and send it to Langley to get an ID, but that could wait. Right now he needed to see how this was going to play out.

He made a couple of random turns to reorient himself and headed back toward the fighting ring, this time so he was almost directly opposite General Osipov. The Russian was having an animated discussion with a well-dressed Cuban, someone Harry *did* recognize. Colonel Hector Diaz of the Dirección de Inteligencia Nacional—Cuba's spy agency. But whether Diaz's presence indicated that the sale of the Novichok agent was sanctioned by the DNI and, by extension, the Cuban government wasn't a foregone conclusion. It wasn't unheard of for even high-level officials in the regime to run a side hustle now and then.

Harry wasn't an expert in reading body language, but it looked to him like the two men were arguing about something, an argument the Russian appeared to be losing. After a couple minutes of angry gesticulations, Osipov threw up his hands and started pushing through the crowd. Diaz then leaned over the top of the arena wall and said something to one of the rooster wranglers; then he turned and followed after the Russian.

Their abrupt departure surprised Harry. He casually glanced back in the direction where he'd last seen the redhead, but the man wasn't there anymore. He did a more thorough—and obvious—scan of the crowd, but there was no sign of the guy.

"Now where the hell did he go?"

FIFTEEN

After reading the frantic text from Harry—just one word: *Now*—Stokely contemplated the last couple inches of the Montecristo and wondered what he was supposed to do.

"Now"—what the hell did that mean?

Was Harry trying to say that the sale was happening *inside* the barn? If so, was he supposed to rush in there? And do what?

Stoke thought about texting back and asking for clarification but decided that would be a waste of time. Harry wasn't very good at providing clarification, and given the apparent urgency of the situation, there probably wasn't time for it anyway.

The decision was ultimately taken out of his hands when, about fifteen seconds later, the Russian general emerged from the barn. Stoke didn't move, didn't even look in the man's direction. His caution was unnecessary; Osipov seemed oblivious to everything around him as he stomped across the open ground, charting a straight-line course toward the rear of the farmhouse.

Stoke let out a breath he hadn't even realized he'd been holding. He nonchalantly stubbed out the cigar and, after tossing a friendly wave to the domino players, melted away, walking along the front of the house, heading in the opposite direction from the course the Russian had taken. After rounding the corner and making a quick check to ensure that nobody was observing him, he moved in close to the side of the house and crept toward the rear corner. As big as he was, Stoke could be stealthy when the situation called for it.

And this was one time when the situation definitely called for it.

At the corner, he edged out and saw, illuminated in the glow of an overhead light extending out from the roof of the farmhouse, Osipov standing with two Latino men near the back of a parked newer-model crossover SUV. From his vantage, Stoke could see the ornament at the center of the vehicle's grille—it was the logo of the Geely automotive company, the Chinese outfit that was slowly but steadily taking the car world by storm and picking off legacy brands like Lotus, Aston Martin, and Volvo along the way. Stoke wasn't surprised that Geely would be selling their cars in Cuba; he just wondered who in the country could afford to buy one.

Osipov and the other men weren't talking or doing much of anything. They were just looking at one another, regarding one another with naked suspicion. Whatever else this was, it wasn't a reunion of old friends.

Of that, Stokely Jones was absolutely certain.

He used his phone to snap a picture of the meeting, which he sent to Harry, along with the message *Behind the house*. After about thirty seconds, he received a notification that the attachment had not been delivered.

"Cheap-ass Cuban data network," he muttered under his breath, edging up to the corner to resume his surveillance.

In the brief interim, another man had joined the group, approaching from the barn and carrying in his arms what appeared to be a large, slightly oblong glass cube—about twelve inches high and wide and eighteen inches long. It was, he realized, an aquarium. Except instead of holding fish and water, all it contained was a single rooster. The bird, which Stoke surmised was probably the loser from the latest cockfight, was bloody. The transparent walls of its enclosure were streaked red, but it was still very much alive, pecking at the glass and squawking furiously. Stoke felt a flash of anger at the animal's continued mistreatment, but this emotion was quickly overwhelmed by curiosity about how the chicken figured into this meeting.

The man with the chicken said something to Osipov in Russian as he set the aquarium on the ground between them and the other two men. Then he addressed the latter in Spanish.

Stoke had picked up quite a bit of Spanish over the years, and so had no trouble understanding him. *"You say I must prove it really works? I will give you a demonstration."*

Stoke suddenly had a very bad feeling. Nevertheless, he switched his phone to video mode, positioned it so that the camera was able to mostly capture what was happening, and then started recording.

The guy who had brought out the rooster—Stoke dubbed him Chicken Dude; Harry would probably have come up with something obscene—now said something to the Russian general in his own language. After a little back-and-forth, Osipov opened the back hatch of the Geely and leaned inside. Stoke couldn't see what he was doing; the angle was wrong, but the facial expressions of the first two Latinos grew increasingly tense as the minutes passed.

When the Russian finally stepped back into full view, he was wearing latex gloves and holding a small glass test tube, which he held out to the men. Both recoiled as if the glass contained a deadly poison, which Stoke guessed it probably did.

Or half of a deadly poison, he amended.

Osipov laughed at their discomfort and then proceeded to dump the contents of the test tube into what looked to Stoke like a large balloon. It was, in fact, a condom.

After shaking the substance to ensure that it rested at the end of the prophylactic, the Russian gave it several twists to isolate the substance at the receptacle tip. He then returned to the SUV's hatchback and resumed working, eventually coming up with a second test tube. This time, he didn't bother offering the two prospective buyers a sniff but simply dumped the test tube into the condom. He put a few more twists in it to isolate the second substance and then, without the least hesitation, put his lips on the open end and began to blow into it like it was a party balloon. After a few puffs—just enough to inflate the condom to the size of a baguette—he tied the open end off. Then he loosened the twists at the end, releasing the captive substances and allowing them to mix in the sealed chamber.

Stoke felt a chill go down his spine. If this was what it looked like, then Osipov had just mixed up a batch of Novichok nerve agent as calmly as if it were a cake mix. What had Harry said earlier? *"A gram of the stuff can kill five thousand people."*

How many grams were in that condom?

Talk about unsafe sex.

The Russian gave the improvised balloon a few shakes to mix the contents, then nodded to Chicken Dude. The latter knelt down next to the aquarium and carefully opened the lid.

Until that moment, Stoke had not realized that, unlike an ordinary aquarium, the glass enclosure holding the rooster was fully enclosed, with a hinged, gasketed lid and a latch to hold it shut. Chicken Dude raised the lid a few inches and, when the rooster inside made no attempt to fly at the opening, said something to the Russian. The latter jammed the semi-inflated condom into the small gap, whereupon Chicken Dude quickly slammed the lid shut.

Stoke couldn't bring himself to watch what happened next. It wasn't as easy to avoid hearing it, but for what seemed like a few minutes thereafter, the only sound was the distant roar of activity drifting out of the barn. Stoke almost dared to believe that the demonstration had somehow failed, that the binary nerve agent had proven ineffective, but then he heard Chicken Dude asking the buyers if they were satisfied with the demonstration.

A glance down at the screen of the phone, which was still recording the whole affair, showed the four men standing around the aquarium. The two buyers were staring down at the container with a mixture of horror, awe, and greedy anticipation.

Although Stoke didn't have an unrestricted view of the glass enclosure, there was not a doubt in his mind that the animal inside was stone-dead. The rooster had probably torn the condom open with its beak and talons, releasing the now active Novichok nerve agent to lethal effect.

There was no longer any doubt that the nerve agent was the real deal. Stoke was more concerned with what the buyers might have planned for it. He was now regretting not pushing back on Harry's plan to simply observe the transaction, identify the buyers, and let someone else figure out what to do about it. Novichok was bad shit. Period. Full stop. Do not pass go. Et cetera. Better to destroy it now than let it get out into the wild.

He was trying to figure out the best way to do that without getting himself killed when, from somewhere outside the frame of the video, a voice called out. In English.

"Very impressive."

Just two words, but it was enough for Stoke to know that it wasn't Harry. In fact, the guy sounded kind of like . . . well, like James Bond. Or, more accurately, Sean Connery's iconic portrayal of Bond.

Stoke didn't have much of an ear for accents, but he liked the Bond movies, some more than others, and as far as he was concerned, Sean Connery *was* Bond. He often joked with his friend Alex Hawke—an actual British secret agent—about how he didn't sound anything like James Bond. Truth be told, Hawke sometimes sounded a little prissy. Hawke, of course, had informed Stoke that Sean Connery was Scottish, not English, so, in fact, *he* probably sounded more like Ian Fleming's Bond than Sean Connery ever had.

The stranger, whoever he was, had some kind of accent that was more like Connery's than Hawke's.

Startled by the voice, the four men standing around the aquarium with the dead chicken whipped their heads toward the source. Chicken Dude's hand went for the handgun tucked in his waistband, hidden under his shirttail, but before he could clear the weapon, the distinctive *whump* of a suppressed pistol sounded, and his head snapped back in a spray of red mist.

It took a moment for the three remaining men to shake off the shock of what had just happened, a moment in which the suppressed weapon coughed again, dropping one of the two prospective buyers with another head shot. That was enough to jolt the second buyer and Osipov into action. The former spun around and made a break for the open country out beyond the reach of the overhead light, but Osipov turned the other way and ran straight toward the corner of the house, right at Stoke's hiding place.

Stoke, who was also still trying to get over his surprise at what he had just witnessed, realized that the Russian was about to trip over him, and worse, if he got that far and the killer gave chase, Stoke would probably be next on his hit list. He was about to turn and run, but before he could move a muscle, the suppressed pistol coughed twice, and the front of Osipov's guayabera burst open in a spray of blood. The Russian's momentum carried him forward a few more yards before he face-planted mere inches from the corner of the house, his dying face a dark blur that almost completely filled the camera frame.

There followed two more shots, which presumably took out the remaining buyer, and then all was silent again. Stoke, crouching down at the corner of the house, didn't move, didn't even breathe.

What the hell just happened?

Well, the answer to that was pretty obvious. Some uninvited guest had just crashed the Russian general's party, which, Stoke realized, was exactly what he had been thinking about doing. . . . Only this uninvited guest had shown up ready to dance.

Whoever it was had known about the sale, known about the Novichok agents.

Harry had known about them too, so it evidently hadn't been as secret as Osipov had probably thought. It wasn't a stretch to think that another intelligence agency might have obtained the same information

and made the decision to deal with the threat directly and permanently. The guy had spoken English, so it probably wasn't the Russians
running down their missing WMD. And that accent, that not-quite-
British, almost Scottish Sean Connery brogue?

Maybe this dude's from Alex's outfit.

Stoke would have taken comfort from the thought if not for the fact
that the as-yet-unseen assassin had just coldly wasted four men and
probably wouldn't have been too keen on leaving any witnesses alive,
even witnesses who occasionally did contract work for the British Secret Intelligence Service. Stoke had done his share of wet work and
knew that once you went kinetic, positive target ID pretty much went
out the window. Shoot first, and screw the questions.

So, popping out to say howdy? Probably not a good idea.

But there was something else about this whole scenario that just
didn't sit well with him. His instincts told him that it was too soon to
declare *mission accomplished.*

His curiosity burning, he slowly eased his hand out, picked up the
phone, and raised it up a few inches . . . just high enough for the camera
lens to look past the dead Russian. Framed in the display, kneeling
down beside the unmoving body of Chicken Dude, was the assassin.
Stoke recognized him instantly. It was the redheaded man he'd passed
going into the barn.

The man raised his hand. He was holding something between his
fingers, and while Stoke couldn't see what the object was, it was pretty
easy to figure out when the lights of the Geely flashed twice.

Keys.

The man stood up, moved to the open back hatch, and shut it, then
walked to the driver's-side door, opened it, and got in. A moment later,
the SUV's engine turned over. The running lights came on, and then
the car was moving. It cut a sharp U-turn and then rolled away from
Stoke's corner of the house and turned onto the drive leading back to
the highway.

As the car disappeared from his view, Stoke stopped the video recording on his phone and rose from his hiding place. Without the car, the yard behind the house looked strangely empty . . . if you didn't count the four bodies and the dead chicken in the aquarium full of nerve agent. No one in the house or the barn seemed aware of what had just happened, but Stoke knew that eventually someone would trip over a body, and when that happened, all bets were off.

He was about to text Harry to let him know it was time to move, but as he was composing the text, the CIA spook called out to him in a stage whisper from the opposite corner of the house. "Stoke! Man, did you see that? Who was that guy?"

"I was hoping you'd know."

"Not a fucking clue."

"That's too bad. Because he's got the nerve agent now."

"Well, shit." Harry turned his head, looking down the driveway at the rapidly disappearing taillights of the Geely. "What do we do now?"

Stoke glanced down at the bodies and the dead chicken in the aquarium and then thought about the cargo in the back of the SUV. "Well, Harry, I guess we'd better go after him."

Harry smiled, then, with a wink, said, "And here I thought it was past your bedtime."

He started to turn away, but Stoke called out to him. "Hey, Harry."

Harry turned. "Yeah?"

"This Novichok shit . . . it hangs around awhile, right? I mean, once it's mixed together."

"Yeah. A couple kids in England found a bottle of it the Russians had mixed up like a week earlier and got themselves killed. Why?"

Stoke nodded at the aquarium. "That thing's full of the stuff."

Harry shifted from foot to foot. "So? That guy's getting away with a hundred pounds of the shit."

"Yeah, I know, but what's gonna happen when some poor chicken farmer comes out here and opens this thing up?"

"Aw, jeez, Stoke—"

"Is there any way to neutralize it?"

"Yeah. Water should dissolve it."

"So, if we drop this thing in the bay, problem solved, right?"

"Well, yeah, but . . ." Harry stared at the aquarium. "I mean, we'd have to bring it with us, wouldn't we?"

"Unless you know of some other way to get it down to the water."

"I don't want to get within ten feet of that thing."

Stoke rolled his eyes and then scooped up the aquarium, tucking it under his arm. "Don't be such a baby, Harry. Now let's get this shit over with."

But even then, some part of Stokely Jones knew that whatever *this* was . . . it was far from over.

SIXTEEN

Because he did not think he would sleep, the King was surprised to awaken. Consciousness came gradually, sleep receding like a fog slowly burning away with the sun's rising, though, in fact, there was no daylight in the little cell.

The previous day—he assumed this to be true, though it was impossible to say for certain—he and McClanahan had been provided with mattresses and blankets, but these were the barest of creature comforts. They had also been given a five-gallon bucket, no explanation given, none needed. A meal had been offered in the form of a bowl of thick stew, almost certainly from a tin, and slightly stale bread. The King's first impulse had been to reject the fare on principle, but McClanahan had urged him to eat. "You've got to keep your strength up, sir."

The gamekeeper had even offered to take the first bite just to ensure that the meal had not been poisoned, an offer that the King had declined. "No need, Roddy. If they wanted to kill me, they would have just done it."

But now, as he struggled to throw off the lethargy of what had been an unusually deep slumber, he had cause to wonder if the food might not, in fact, have been drugged.

"Roddy?" he said, his voice just a hoarse croak.

The gamekeeper was kneeling at his side almost immediately. "Right here, sir. What can I do for you?"

"Help me . . . help me up. Feeling . . . bloody awful."

"It's disgusting how they're treating you, sir. I'll give that bastard Sten a piece of my mind if he shows his in here again."

Despite the fog hanging about his head, the King managed a laugh. "Good old Roddy, I can always count on you, can't I?"

"That you can, sir."

McClanahan helped him to a sitting position on the edge of the mattress, but before he could even think about standing, the door opened, and Sten came in, pushing a small cart upon which rested two covered dishes along with a cheap teapot and a stack of paper cups. The smell of cooked bacon and toasted bread wafted into the room.

"Breakfast is served, Majesty," Sten said, his voice dripping with sarcasm.

McClanahan rose to his feet and, without asking permission, lifted the covers, revealing rashers of bacon, poached eggs, and slices of toasted bread. The gamekeeper shook his head. "His Majesty always has fresh fruit and muesli for breakfast."

Sten recoiled in an exaggerated mockery of embarrassment. "Oh, dear, I shall sack the cook straightaway."

"It's all right, Roddy," said the King, still a little groggily. "I won't be eating any of their food again anyway."

Sten shrugged. "Your choice, of course. But if it's your intention to mount some sort of hunger strike, you needn't go to the trouble. You won't be with us long enough for it to matter."

"Is that some kind of threat?" challenged McClanahan.

"Not at all. His Majesty will be released just as soon as he agrees to our terms."

"And if I don't agree to these terms?" asked the King.

Sten held his gaze. "Then there will be consequences."

"Sounds like a threat to me," muttered the gamekeeper.

"What sort of consequences?"

Sten waved the question away. "We'll speak of it later. After you've had your breakfast."

"I told you, I won't be eating any more of your food. You drugged my supper yesterday."

Sten stared at him for a long moment. "A mild sedative. Just to help you get through your first night with us. It won't happen again. I need you to have a clear head."

"And why is that?"

Sten folded his arms. "As I said, there are terms that you must agree to in order to secure your release."

"And what, pray tell, are these terms?"

"Are you sure you wouldn't like to eat first?"

"Your terms," the King said sharply.

Sten nodded slowly. "Very well."

He reached down to the cart and took up and passed over a large envelope, which had rested unnoticed alongside the meal. Charles opened the envelope and took out the single sheet of vellum inside. It was, he realized, a piece of official stationery. Across the top was a bold heading that read: "Instrument of Abdication."

Beneath that, it read: "I, Charles III, of the United Kingdom of Great Britain and Northern Ireland and of His other Realms and Territories King, do hereby declare My irrevocable determination to renounce the Throne for Myself, and My desire is that effect should be given to this Instrument of Abdication immediately."

The King raised his eyes to Sten. "You don't actually believe that I will sign this?"

The other man seemed to be smiling behind his mask. "Oh, you will sign. The only question is how hard you're going to make it for yourself before you do."

Charles crumpled the document into a ball, then walked over to the corner of the room with the privy bucket, opened the lid, and dropped it in. "That's what I think of your demands."

"Good show, Your Majesty!" McClanahan cheered.

Sten continued staring at the King. "Are you sure you won't have some breakfast?"

"Need I tell you what you can do with your sodding breakfast?"

Sten nodded slowly. "So that's how it's going to be, then." He glanced over his shoulder and called out, "Now!"

Three more masked men swept into the room. McClanahan, misinterpreting their intent, threw himself in front of the King, shouting, "Keep your bloody mitts off him!"

Almost in perfect unison, two of the men seized hold of the game-keeper's arms, expertly bracing him, while the third came in close and dropped a blackout hood over McClanahan's head. It was only then that Charles realized they'd been honest about their intentions. Mc-Clanahan had indeed been their target all along.

"Roddy!" He stepped forward, intent on breaking the hold of Mc-Clanahan's captors, but Sten, anticipating this display of resistance, met the charge and deflected Charles backward. Off-balance, the King toppled back onto his mattress.

"That's enough of that, Majesty," said Sten. "It should be clear to you by now that you will not be the one to suffer the consequences of your resistance."

Before the King could answer, McClanahan shouted, "Don't give in, sire. Stand fa—"

A fist to the gamekeeper's gut silenced the exhortation and doubled him over, after which the men dragged him from the room.

"Keep faith, Roddy!" shouted the King after the departing group. Then he whirled to face Sten. "The throne is a sacred, God-given trust. I'll die before I'll relinquish it."

"But will you let others die for you?" asked Sten. He held the King's stare for another long moment. "I'll just leave you to think about that," he said, then turned and left, taking the cart with him.

In a nearby room, the Magician watched the feed from a small surveillance camera hidden in the King's cell with grudging admiration.

The initial show of resistance was not unexpected. Indeed, the scene had played out almost exactly as he had expected, as if Charles were reading from the script. What he had not expected was for the King to let the gamekeeper be dragged off like a lamb to the slaughter. He had believed Charles too squeamish to permit one of his faithful retainers to suffer unknown torments. He hadn't thought for a second that Charles would cave, agreeing to sign the worthless abdication, but he had expected the King to beg and plead or even offer himself up in McClanahan's place.

It would have been a noble gesture, to be sure, but not a kingly one. For a true king would know that his life was of greater value than that of any one of his subjects or indeed those of the lot of them.

Perhaps his spine is stiffer than I thought. If only he could have shown that kind of resolve as a younger man.

June 30, 1994

I'LL NEVER GIVE UP CAMILLA

The headline on the front page of the Sun, white letters against a black background, fairly jumped off the newsstand. Surrounding it were photographs of the three most talked-about, most controversial figures in the entire kingdom. The photos of Diana and Camilla, wearing almost identical black cocktail dresses and pearl chokers, seemed to be competing for the attention of prospective readers, though the full-length shot of the Princess with her radiant smile and the caption title REVENGE IN CHIC *left little doubt as to the bias of the reportage. The picture of the Prince, a candid shot, likely taken in midsentence, was the least flattering, but the smaller caption just above it,* CROWN IN CRISIS, *was even more disturbing.*

The fairy tale, the shining dream that had inspired the young man all those years ago, was dead.

It had not happened all at once, of course. The slow-motion disintegration of the royal marriage had been parceled out in tabloid headlines, stolen conversations, paparazzi photographs, and dueling accusations of infidelity. Rumors of discontent had begun filtering out of the palace almost from the beginning, but young and naive as the man was, he had not wanted to believe any of it. As he grew into adolescence, however, gaining experience in matters of the heart and, perhaps more important, a better understanding of human frailty, his disillusionment, not only with the Royal Family but with the very idea of serving the Crown, had grown. Shortly before departing for university, he'd raged at his father—"How can you serve that man? He's unworthy of you!" *And while they were not completely estranged, there was a barrier between them now that seemed insurmountable. That had been two years ago, and in that time the disintegration of the royal marriage had accelerated. The Prince and Princess had separated, and there seemed little chance of a reconciliation now, especially with the Prince proclaiming his undying love for another woman—a married woman at that.*

It was a train wreck, and even though it filled him with quiet rage, the young man could not look away.

"It's a right mess, isn't it?"

The voice, female, was not one the young man recognized, and it took him a moment to realize that the words were meant for his ears. He tore his eyes from the tabloid and glanced sidelong at the young woman who had come up alongside him to read the headlines over his shoulder. She was quite pretty, with long blond tresses and a pert nose. He couldn't quite place her posh accent, definitely not Scottish. He was sure he'd seen her in passing but did not know her name.

While he was, by any measure, handsome and confident, an unexpected conversation with a pretty girl was not something that happened every day. Ordinarily, he would not have wasted such an opportunity to give vent to his anger over this particular subject, but she had after all given him the opening.

"*It's disgusting, is what it is,*" *he said.* "*He's unfit to be King. If he had any decency, he'd renounce his claim to the throne.*"

"*I think the question of his decency has already been settled,*" *remarked the girl.* "*But what do you expect from the royals? When they don't like the rules, they just make up new ones. Bloody Henry VIII created a whole new religion when he didn't get his way.*"

The young man shook his head. "*We're supposedly more enlightened now. I mean, King Edward gave up the throne to marry a divorcée. She was at least single at the time. This . . .*" *He gestured at the tabloid.* "*This is happening in front of the whole world. They're making a laughingstock of us all.*"

The corner of her mouth quirked up in a smile. "*Well, I'm not sure it's as bad as all that.*"

"*Oh, it's worse. We're taught from the cradle to believe that the monarchy is special. A divine institution that has endured for centuries by the grace of God.*" *He spat these last words out. His belief in God had gone the way of his belief in the monarchy.*

The smile lingered on her face as she gazed up at him for a long moment. Then she stuck out her hand. "*I'm Liv.*"

Her surprising forthrightness quenched his ardor. "*Um . . . I . . . uh, Rick.*"

He'd taken the name when he'd come to uni, not just because he'd long since grown tired of being teased about his given name, but also because it was his father's given name as well. He thought Rick sounded American, like Humphrey Bogart's character in Casablanca.

"*I know,*" *she said with a sly gleam in her eyes.*

"*You know?*"

How does she know?

His head began to spin with all the possibilities, many of them wildly erotic. She'd noticed him, taken an interest, asked after him . . . desired him?

"You were at the meeting a couple nights ago. The Republicans Club. I saw you there and asked about you."

It was true; he had been at the meeting. His growing disillusionment with the monarchy had aroused a curiosity concerning the alternatives, and of them all, republicanism seemed like the logical choice. Yet he remained wary. Having lost faith in one institution, he was in no hurry to put his trust in another.

"I was there," he admitted. "I don't recall seeing you, though." Then, with what he hoped was a charming smile, he added, "I'd like to think I'd remember you."

She didn't respond to that directly but instead took a long, slow look around before meeting his gaze again. "Go for a pint?"

Rick felt his heart quicken. This was almost too good to be true, but how could he refuse? "Yeah, I could go for that."

She took his arm and steered him away from the newsstand and along the familiar cobbled streets that radiated away from the student union. They talked as they walked. Liv took the lead, but to Rick's surprise, she avoided the subject that had brought them into each other's orbit, focusing instead on topics of a quotidian nature. Later, he would reflect that she had asked more questions than she had answered and listened far more attentively than most girls of his acquaintance, but in the moment, he barely noticed.

It was only when they were seated in a quiet corner of a pub a few blocks west of the campus, however, with pints of bitter and a plate of chips on the table before them, that she returned to that earlier discussion. "Was that your first time at the Republicans Club?"

Sensing that she already knew the answer, he simply nodded.

"What made you decide to attend?"

"Well, you know, kings and queens. It's all kind of old-fashioned, isn't it? There's a new millennium coming. It's time for a change, right?"

She seemed to hang on his every word. "Do you really think it will happen? People fear change more than anything else. They cling to old traditions like a lifeline."

"True," he admitted, thinking about his father. "They don't realize that lifeline is an anchor dragging them down."

"It sounds like you're committed to the cause."

"The cause?"

"Republicanism. The end of the monarchy."

Rick shrugged. "I don't know if I'd go so far as to say committed. I mean, I'm not for storming the Bastille."

She appeared to consider this. "Short of that, how far would you be willing to go?" Then, hastily, she added, "Hypothetically speaking."

He laughed, then realized she was serious. "Well . . . as I see it, there are two paths forward. Either the people will vote to abolish the monarchy or the Queen—or I suppose it will be the next King—will voluntarily set aside the crown. I should imagine either path will require some . . . pressure. Protests and such."

"And you'd do that? Put yourself out there? In harm's way, so to speak?"

"Hypothetically," he said with a grin.

She gazed across the table at him for another long moment, then reached out and put her hand on his arm. "There's someone I think you should talk to. He's a lecturer in the sociology department."

For the first time since their meeting, Rick felt a twinge of uneasiness. This was an unexpected and not altogether welcome turn in the conversation. "Sure," he said with an indifferent shrug.

Perhaps sensing his ambivalence, she gave his arm a squeeze. "He's got some brilliant ideas. Not just the same old hash, but a real path to change."

"Yeah. All right."

She rewarded him with a smile. "Listen, I want you to do something for me."

His sense of uneasiness multiplied. Where was this going? He didn't answer.

"Don't go back to any more club meetings."

Although he didn't know what he had expected her to ask of him, this most definitely was not it. "Why not?"

"*The simple answer? If you keep going to the meetings, people will notice.*"

"*People? Who do you mean?*"

"*Just people. You might get labeled as a radical. A troublemaker.*"

"*You're joking,*" he scoffed. "*The Republicans Club aren't radicals.*"

"*All the same, an association like that can follow you long after you finish uni.*"

"*Why should that matter?*"

She regarded him for a moment. "*In a political movement like ours, everybody has a role to play. Some will be leaders. Some will be speakers. Some . . .*" She shrugged. "*Some will just be brute force. Foot soldiers. Bodies in the streets carrying protest signs, chaining themselves to the palace gates. But some . . . some are in a position to do so much more, behind the scenes, as it were.*"

Rick's blood went cold in his veins. Is she saying what I think she's saying?

"*I told you that I asked around about you,*" Liv went on. "*I know about your father . . . that he works for the royals. You could have a job like that too. They like to keep it in the family, as it were.*"

"*I don't want to work for the royals,*" he snapped. "*Weren't you listening?*"

She ignored his protest. "*But even with a family recommendation, you'd still have to pass a background check. You come up on the rolls of the Republicans Club, and they'll think twice about letting you come anywhere close to the Family.*"

"*I told you, I don't want to—*"

She gripped his arm. "*Rick, listen to me. Anybody can march in the streets or run for a council seat . . . whatever. But not everyone can get close to the Royal Family.*"

"*You want me to be some kind of spy—is that it?*"

"*Not a spy,*" she said. "*A time bomb.*"

PRESENT DAY

A time bomb with a very long delay.

He had been skeptical at the beginning, fearful that his new associates were setting him up for martyrdom. They assured him that was not the case, that when the time was right, his contribution to the great cause would be nothing so banal as mere violence.

Later on, after he had swallowed his pride, made a show of reconciliation with his father, and begged for an apprenticeship, he had begun to wonder if it was not all some colossal joke.

Liv had shared his bed during that last year at uni, and that had made the pill easier to swallow, but she was out of his life now, following a different path to the same eventual goal. He understood that what they had had together was never love, but in the long years that had passed, with only limited contact from anyone in the cause, and no one with whom to share his secret mission, never mind his rage at having to endure the humiliation of his servile existence, he couldn't help but wonder if he was being put on. Had he really set aside his personal ambitions, his hopes and dreams, for this?

Every interaction, every humble bow, every instance where he was obliged to treat the royals like they were somehow deserving of worship was like swallowing poison, and that, oddly enough, was what had kept him from simply walking away. Whenever despair threatened to overcome him, he only had to remember that he was the ticking time bomb that would, one day, utterly destroy the abomination that was the monarchy.

Now, at last, seeing the King himself brought low, he could believe that it had all been worth it.

He turned to the now unmasked figure of Mr. Sten. "I think he needs a little persuasion. Don't you?"

Sten smiled like the devil and then turned and left the room.

A few minutes later, Roddy McClanahan's screams echoed in the halls.

SEVENTEEN

Despite her senior position in the ministry, Pippa Guinness received no special treatment. She did not have a driver or a bodyguard. She did not drive an officially issued car; nor, in fact, did she even own a personal vehicle. The reason for this paucity of preferential treatment was simple. Like most international spy agencies, the British Secret Intelligence Service prized secrecy above all else. Indeed, the motto of the service was *Semper Occultus*—Always Secret. Outside the walls of Vauxhall Cross, the identities of the directors general of the service were unknown. In the rare instances when it was necessary to append a name to some external memorandum, an alias was always employed to prevent anyone outside—whether foreign spies or muckraking journalists—from learning the names of senior leaders. To any outside observer, Pippa Guinness was merely one of more than three thousand employees of the Ministry of Intelligence.

She awoke, as she did every day, at 0430 because that was the time when Bastet, her Egyptian mau, was accustomed to having her breakfast. With that duty attended to, she would spend the better part of an hour catching up on the latest news dispatches and reading any unclassified briefs generated during the night while she had her own breakfast.

Then it was off to work. Pippa liked this routine. She took comfort in it—the comfort that most people took from having a family.

Pippa, ever ambitious, had never really wanted a husband or a family. Oh, she had taken lovers through the years. Some of them had even aroused in her a desire for domestic stability, but either she had never given in to the temptation, or the desire had not been reciprocated.

She still wasn't sure which category Alex Hawke fell into. She told herself that it didn't matter, that she had the life she wanted. Most of the time, she even believed it.

On a typical day, she walked four blocks to South Kensington Underground Station, rode the Tube to Vauxhall Underground Station, and then made the short walk to Vauxhall Cross. Upon arriving, she would pass through security and then head directly to one of the exercise rooms for a forty-five-minute workout, alternating between aerobic routines and resistance training, and then return to her office for a shower—an office with en suite washroom was one of the few perquisites of her senior position—and a change of clothing. Then, after spending just a few minutes to check in, via email or text, with the two most important people in her life, her workday would begin.

This day had been a typical day, save perhaps for the fact that she chose a trouser suit—a bespoke number from Huntsman of Savile Row—instead of her customary work attire. She was going to be stuck sitting beside Lord Alexander Hawke on a long automobile ride and was aware that her legs might prove distracting to the driver. She certainly didn't want him getting the wrong impression.

When she finally sat down at her desk, she was surprised to discover a voicemail message waiting on her internal line, time-stamped at 0501. It was Hawke informing her that he was waiting for her in the underground car park.

———————

It was not a sense of urgency that had prompted Hawke to make an early start. Nor was he motivated by a desire to one-up Pippa by showing up well ahead of her. In truth, the real reason for his predawn arrival at 85 Albert Embankment was that he had nowhere else to be.

He'd spent a mostly sleepless night at his stately manse in Mayfair, just north of Buckingham Palace, trying in vain to think about anything besides the fact that he was alone.

Not so many years ago, he had spent quite a lot of time at the Mayfair residence. Back then, he'd been far more interested in nightlife and the diversions of the London scene. Of late, however, it had become merely a place to stay when some crisis or another required him to meet with C in person. He longed to be back at Teakettle Cottage, with Anastasia in his arms, and this made him feel acutely the emptiness of his bed.

It doesn't have to be empty.

The unwelcome thought, like a dandelion seed, took root in his subconscious before he could pluck it out, and try as he might, it lingered there, blooming again and again throughout the long, sleepless night.

Alex Hawke had had many loves and many lovers throughout his adventurous life. The loves he had loved deeply, with every fiber of his being. He'd buried many of them, and the losses always left him broken. When he had believed Anastasia dead, it had nearly killed him.

With the lovers, he had given rein to his carnal urges, making love—though that hardly seemed the right word—with unbridled passion but never deep emotion.

Had he been reckless with the feelings of his lovers? Cruel, even? Probably. But he had never lied to any of them, never promised his heart simply to get a woman into his bed.

Pippa Guinness had only ever been a lover. In fact, he hadn't really even liked her very much. As an intelligence analyst, she had discounted his warnings of a secret terrorist base in the Amazon jungle—a base where he had been held captive for months, forced into slave labor. In effect, she had accused him of either being delusional or exaggerating the threat. Yet, despite what amounted to an egregious error in judgment, Sir David had thrown them together, first in delivering an address to an international anti-terrorism conference in Key West and later in the creation of Red Banner. And yes, even though Hawke had been frustrated with her, he had not refused her when she'd offered herself. But that was just sex. Never love.

Anastasia was the great love of his life. He would never betray her, never give in to temptation. And yet temptation was a physical reality and one that, thanks to Sir David, he would have to suffer.

Damn him anyway.

Under any other circumstances, he would have prescribed himself a tot of Goslings Black Seal, but in addition to inducing drowsiness, the strong drink also had a tendency to lower his inhibitions, and given his present state of mind, he needed to keep his inhibitions intact. He tried reading himself to sleep, but the words on the page bounced off his brain like errant sleet on a tin roof. When sleep would not come, and he ran out of other things to think about, he left his lonely bed, showered, dressed, and then went down to the garage to unleash the Locomotive.

Of all the cars Hawke owned, and he owned quite a few, the Locomotive—that was his name for the elephant's-breath-gray Bentley R-type Continental—was far and away his favorite. One of just 208 produced between 1952 and 1955, the streamlined, fastback coupe, coach-built by H. J. Mulliner & Co., made extensive use of aluminum to reduce its weight. That was a critical consideration since its impressive large-bore six-cylinder engine with 4,887-cubic-centimeter capacity pushed the upper-weight rating of its Dunlop Medium Distance Track tires, and in that day gave the automobile an unheard-of practical top speed of 115 miles per hour and a comfortable cruising speed of 100 miles per hour. Built for speed, the Locomotive was a beast on the road. Hawke drove her hard, and she had never let him down.

He usually kept the Locomotive at Hawkesmoor, the family manor in the Cotswolds and his official home of residence, but anticipating a chance to do some driving in his search for the King, he'd had his primary mechanic, Young Ian Burns, bring the car to London. Of course, that had been before he'd known he would have a passenger. While elegant for its day, the coupe possessed few of the creature comforts of a modern luxury car—no cup holders or heated seats, though its cigar lighter could accommodate a mobile phone charger.

Pippa would be in for a wild ride, but not an especially comfortable one. The thought brought him some satisfaction.

He wheeled the Locomotive into the secure underground car park at a quarter of five but waited an excruciating fifteen minutes before making the call up to Pippa's office. She was either not in or not answering.

He spent the next hour trying to decide whether he ought not simply leave her behind. It would, he felt certain, be the course of wisdom, and not just for himself but for Pippa as well. Only his sense of loyalty to Sir David prevented him from driving off. While he could not fathom the old man's reasons for throwing them together yet again, his almost filial devotion to the Chief kept him from acting on the impulse.

When Pippa strode into view, however, he regretted not following his instincts.

––––––––––––

Pippa Guinness knew exactly why C had decided to send her off on this errand with Alexander Hawke, and it had very little to do with a possible threat against the royals. He was certainly curious about that matter but well knew that Hawke was quite capable of handling the crisis, if crisis it was, without being micromanaged.

No, C was concerned with what he perceived to be a much greater threat to England, to the service, and particularly to Hawke himself, namely Hawke's impending marriage to Anastasia Korsakova.

Sir David was not opposed to the institution of marriage. Indeed, he and his wife, Grace, had been happily married for nearly forty years until her untimely passing from cancer, a loss that he was still grieving.

It was just that he didn't believe marriage was right for everyone, and in particular, men like Alexander Hawke.

"Hawke was married once," C had once remarked in passing. "It ended badly, but not perhaps as badly as if it had lasted."

Marriage was worse than a distraction for someone like Hawke. Trying to live a dichotomous existence—one day a loving family man, and the next a lethal killing machine—almost invariably led to moral confusion, profound dissatisfaction with both halves of the divided life, and, worst of all, a potentially fatal loss of focus when operational. Some men were able to find balance, successfully walking that razor's edge. Alexander Hawke was not one of them. He might believe it possible, but in a year or five years, his wedding band would begin to feel like an iron fetter.

Better, or so Sir David believed, to nip this mating urge in the bud.

C's diabolical scheme to save Alex Hawke from himself was blatantly transparent. He would never say it aloud, never make it an explicit order. There was no need. All he had to do was put Alex Hawke and Pippa Guinness together and let nature take its course.

Well, thought Pippa, *we'll see about that, you wily old bastard.*

Pippa had her own reasons for not wanting to see Hawke marry the Russian woman, but she was not about to cast herself in the role of home-wrecker. If Hawke wanted to shackle himself to some Slavic ice queen, the daughter, no less, of a madman who had nearly plunged the world into an apocalyptic war, then bully for him. Nor, despite what Trulove might have believed, was she carrying a torch for Hawke. Was he desirable? Hell yes. But she had eaten the fruit of that tree once and had felt the prick of its thorns. The sting of the latter still lingered, even after so many years.

No, she would not offer herself to him as she had that night so long ago in Key West. In language that both Hawke and Sir David—former Navy men—would understand, that ship had, most assuredly, sailed.

But what if Hawke made the first move?

After the initial halting pleasantries, there was very little conversation between them as Hawke aggressively negotiated the congested streets until finally reaching the M1, where he was able to let the old Bentley run free. Hawke did not drive so much as fly the old car, sliding around slower vehicles with the adroitness of a Grand Prix racer.

Watching from the left side, Pippa saw such a look of pure delight on Hawke's face that she was hesitant to distract him with conversation.

Finally, it was Hawke who broke the silence between them. "So, you're Sir David's Number Two now. When did that happen?"

"A little over a year ago. While you were off chasing glory aboard that yacht of yours." She regretted her choice of words almost as soon as they were spoken.

"Ah, yes. That would explain how I missed the memo."

"You know how Sir David is about internal security. The right hand must never know what the left is doing and vice versa."

Alex hummed thoughtfully. "Perhaps one day, you'll be running the show?"

"That's not how things work at the top. The chief of the service is appointed by the foreign secretary. I'm afraid I've risen as high as I can at MI6. When the day comes that, God forbid, Sir David retires, the job will go to an ambassador or a military flag officer." She glanced at him sidelong. "You could have the job, you know."

"Me?" He shook his head. "I wouldn't want it."

That was, she thought, a young man's answer, and she almost told him as much. Wasn't he getting married after all? Wouldn't settling down be the responsible thing to do?

But that was none of her business.

EIGHTEEN

The headquarters of the Stewards of Alba Party was located in a squalid Leith office block just west of the Port of Edinburgh. As he pulled the Bentley to the curb, Hawke observed that the mere presence of the classic car would probably double the value of the property.

The interior of the SoAP office was about what one would have expected from looking at the outside. The carpets, wall coverings, and furnishings were 1970s chic and looked rather like they had been scrounged from a rubbish tip. Hawke supposed they would make for excellent barricades in the unlikely event of a revolution. The only things that appeared vaguely new were the framed posters, variations on the classic World War II–era "Keep Calm" placards, only instead of "and Carry On," these bore proclamations like "and Restore the True Heir!" and "and Await the Return of the King."

The front office was staffed by a handful of weary-looking men and women, most of them busy tapping away on computer keyboards, generating social media content. A few raised their heads when Hawke and Pippa walked in, but none moved to acknowledge their presence. Hawke waited exactly thirty seconds before loudly declaring, "I say, who do I need to talk to about buying this bloody place?"

The challenge raised heads again, but none of the workers seemed to know what to do. Finally, one middle-aged woman got up the courage to approach them. "I'm sorry?"

"Yes, you certainly are," said Hawke, affecting his haughtiest tone.

"Beg pardon?"

"I said, 'You are.' Sorry, that is. I was agreeing with you."

Nonplussed, the woman just stared back at him.

"Is there somebody in charge here?" pressed Hawke. "Somebody who actually possesses the power of speech?"

The woman blinked. "That would be Mr. MacAlpin."

After a long pause, in which the woman resumed staring at him like a deer transfixed by a spotlight, Hawke said, "May I speak to Mr. MacAlpin?"

That seemed to break the spell. The woman nodded. "Of course." She turned away, then just as quickly reversed and said, "Who shall I say is—"

"Lord Hawke, if you please."

"Lord Hawke," the woman repeated, looking even more nervous than before. "Yes, right away, m'lord."

As the woman scurried through the maze of desks to a door at the rear of the open office, Pippa leaned in close. "This is a rather different side of you."

"Yes. Well, contrary to what you might believe, there are sides of me you haven't seen."

Pippa reddened.

"As you are no doubt aware," Hawke went on, speaking in a low whisper for her ears alone, "I detest the use of my title. But there are some instances where it comes in handy. This, I suspect, may be one of them."

As if to confirm this assertion, a voice boomed out across the office. "Lord Hawke!"

The voice belonged to a fleshy, balding, middle-aged man who had just emerged from the doorway through which the woman had earlier passed. The man, attired in a rumpled suit, his unfashionable tie slightly askew, hurried across the office to greet them.

"Lord Hawke," he repeated a little breathlessly when he reached them. He spoke with only a mild burr, as if long years of practice had smoothed away his accent. He stuck out his hand but then, as if fearing that he had committed some breach of etiquette, pulled it back and inclined his head in a quite unnecessary bow. "This is an unexpected honor. Ewan MacAlpin. At your service, sir. I'm the executive chairman of the Stewards of Alba Party. What . . . ah . . . what can I do for you, m'lord?"

Hawke hid his customary irritation behind a smile and affected a supercilious tone. "Well, I was hoping you could tell me just what the devil this is all about." He waved an airy hand toward the office.

"Beg pardon, m'lord?"

"We're just up from London on a day trip, and Pippa here was telling me about this true-heir rubbish. I simply couldn't believe my ears. I had to see it for myself."

The man bristled visibly at the assertion that his mission in life was rubbish, but he held his tongue and instead gestured to the door from which he had just emerged. "Please, will ya na step into my office? I'll tell you all about it."

Hawke looked over at Pippa as if to get her opinion. "What do you say, Pip? Shall we hear him out?"

Pippa, dutifully playing her part, chirped, "Whatever you think best, m'lord."

"Jolly good," said Hawke, beaming. He turned back to MacAlpin. "Well, lay on, MacDuff."

A nerve in MacAlpin's cheek twitched, but he quickly turned away and began moving toward his office.

The little enclosure was stuffy and smelled of air freshener and sweat. Hawke, who had spent more than his share of days in fetid prison camps, was not put off in the slightest but, in keeping with his new lordly persona, wrinkled his nose in distaste before settling into one of the well-worn guest chairs.

"As you may well imagine," said MacAlpin, "we're quite busy here, what with the referendum just two days away."

"Ah, yes," said Hawke. "That independence business. Terrible idea. We're a *united* kingdom. Stronger together and all that."

MacAlpin coughed. "With respect, m'lord, not everyone shares that opinion. The people of Scotland remember a time when we got along just fine on our own."

Hawke flicked his hand as if brushing away a crumb. "Ah, yes. The good old days. Painting yourselves blue and all that rot."

MacAlpin stiffened, clearly approaching the limit of how much abuse he was willing to take from this English lord. Hawke decided to push that limit.

"You've rather a lot of cheek thinking you can speak for all the people of Scotland. You know, I own a bit of property up here. Castle Skye, up on Scarp Island in the Hebrides. Lovely place. I'm thinking about turning it into a golf resort. My domestic staff is not at all happy about the prospect of waking up in a whole new country."

"With respect, m'lord," MacAlpin said again, this time through clenched teeth, his brogue thickening, "has it occurred to you that the people in your employ may say one thing to your face for the sake of their jobs but hold a different view in their hearts? Buying up our land and drinking our whisky does na make ye an honorary Scot." Then, with a healthy dose of sarcasm, he added, "M'lord."

"I rather prefer rum, actually," replied Hawke. "But I suppose it's all academic. From what I've heard, you're no more likely to win this time round."

"I suppose we shall have to see what happens, won't we, m'lord?"

"Hmm. Quite." Hawke paused a beat, then shifted gears. "But what's all this rot about restoring the true heir? Even if the vote goes the wrong way, Scotland will still be part of the Commonwealth of Nations, and Charles will still be your King."

MacAlpin's demeanor abruptly changed. His ire, which had been steadily rising like a wave crest, suddenly dissipated and in its place was the confidence of a chess master who knows the game is already won. "History does not agree with you, m'lord."

"History? History is the very foundation upon which the monarchy is built."

"Indeed, it is. Why, your own title and hereditary holdings exist only because they have been handed down through the centuries. The rules of succession are clear. The right of primogeniture is absolute. When James VII, King of Scotland, was deposed, losing both the crown of England and of Scotland, rule should have passed to his son. That it did not is an egregious error which we intend to set right."

Hawke waved his hand again. "Yes, yes, Pippa's told me all about that. Utter rubbish. Nobody's cared about it in more than three hundred years."

"Some of us did na ever stop caring. The independence of Scotland is an opportunity to redress this historic mistake. When our nation is free again, the true heir will be welcomed to the Throne of the Kingdom of Scotland."

"And just who is this bloody true heir anyway?" countered Hawke. "Pip tells me it's a German bloke? You'd make a bloody German the King of Scotland?"

A hungry smile broke across MacAlpin's fleshy face. "The Duke is Bavarian, actually. But to your point, m'lord, perhaps you'd do well to review the ancestry of the British monarchy over the last two centuries."

Pippa chose that moment to break in. "Mr. MacAlpin, it's my understanding that the Duke of Bavaria has indicated that he has no interest in putting forward a claim to the throne."

MacAlpin's smile did not diminish. If anything, it grew. "The throne *is* his birthright. If he refuses to take it, he would, in effect, be abdicating his responsibility. I believe you will find that was exactly the argument put forth to steal the crown from King James, so there's a precedent. If he refuses to take the throne, it would pass to the next heir in line."

"And who might that be?" said Hawke. "I only ask because I've heard the Duke has no issue."

"In point of fact," added Pippa, "not one member of the House of

Wittelsbach—Bavaria's royal family—has shown the least inclination to claim any throne. Their own monarchy was abolished in 1918, and they've all been quite happy to accept the decisions of history."

"Perhaps not all of them."

Hawke raised an eyebrow. "You've found a man who would be King? Does this sucker have a name?"

MacAlpin's smile slipped, but only for a second. "Heinrich Prinz von Konigstahl, sixth in the line of succession if strict primogeniture is observed, has signaled his willingness to explore a formal claim. The Stewards of Alba are confident that the people of Scotland will rally behind him. Enough of them in any case for Parliament to vote to restore the Kingdom of Scotland."

Hawke glanced over at Pippa to see if the name meant anything to her. She gave an imperceptible shake of the head to signal that it did not. Hawke now returned his stare to MacAlpin.

The man had given them something they didn't have: a name. But did it really mean anything in the grand scheme of things? He didn't believe for a moment that the man sitting before him possessed the willingness, never mind the capacity, to carry out the kidnapping of the monarch in order to advance his pretender, but that didn't mean someone else might not possess both.

Hawke jumped to his feet, eager to be out of the shabby little office and away from their miserable host. "Thank you so much for your time," he said without a trace of his earlier haughtiness, and then turned to Pippa, offering her a hand up. She stared at it for a moment as if trying to decide whether or not she wanted to take it, then did.

MacAlpin also rose, though clearly uncertain what had just happened.

Hawke started for the door but then, implementing an old investigative technique he'd learned, from of all places an American detective television series, paused and turned back as if suddenly remembering something. "Oh, one more thing, old chap."

"Yes?"

"If I understand this succession business correctly, your pretender would have a claim not only to the Throne of Scotland but of the entire United Kingdom."

"Yes. That's correct. The crown rightfully belongs to the line of James Francis Edward Stuart."

"Hmm. And yet you're only interested in putting this Bavarian chap on the Throne of Scotland."

"The Stuarts were originally Kings of Scotland. It's a place to start."

"I see. And if your pretender were to decide to extend his claim, how might he go about doing that? Hypothetically, of course."

"Nothing hypothetical about it. The only legal basis for rejecting the Stuart claim was the Act of Settlement passed by Parliament in 1701, which forbade Catholics from taking the throne. The Succession to the Crown Act of 2013 has repealed that bit of religious intolerance. Were he to pursue a claim to the Throne of the United Kingdom, it would be for the courts to decide."

And now MacAlpin smiled again. "I suppose the people might have something to say about it as well. The Queen, God rest her soul, was far too beloved a monarch to oppose, but I think even you'll agree the same cannot be said of her children."

When they were back inside the snug confines of the Locomotive, Pippa said, "Well, that was a waste of time."

"Oh, I don't think so," replied Hawke.

She gave him a sidelong look. "Surely, you don't think this political party would engage in terrorism to advance their ridiculous notions of the succession."

"Hmm, no. Not them."

"Who, then? This Bavarian prince? Him?"

Hawke smiled. "What say we ask him?"

NINETEEN

Without the GPS to guide them, Congreve and Sutherland would likely never have found their destination. Even with the device, they were hard-pressed to identify the establishment, which seemed to hide amidst the brick council estates like a brick needle in a brick haystack.

According to Anthony Aimes, Padraig Duggan could regularly be found at a semiprivate little pub in the Bogside neighborhood of Londonderry. Bogside, a majority-Catholic neighborhood, had previously been a flashpoint of violence during the Troubles between the Catholic majority and the British-backed Protestant minority.

Half a century on, Bogside had not forgotten.

Following directions from the GPS, Sutherland circled the block several times, first in an effort to reconnoiter the area and then to find a car park, and each circuit took them past unvarnished examples of the locals' lingering discontent with English rule. Enormous wall murals celebrated famous heroes of the Civil Rights Movement—King, Mandela, Mother Teresa—and martyrs of Free Derry, the Troubles, and Bloody Sunday. The Bogside Murals, as they were sometimes called, were something of a historic artifact and popular with tourists, but Congreve got the impression that the sentiment that had originally led to their creation still smoldered beneath the surface. In addition to the murals, some walls were bedecked with paper posters, recently printed by the look of them, that demanded an end to British rule.

Congreve and Sutherland left their unmarked but nevertheless official-looking Rover in a car park on William Street and trekked back into the maze of brick buildings to find the door they had identified as the entrance to the pub where Duggan allegedly held court. There was no signage to indicate the place was anything but a private residence. It was only when they observed a number of men passing freely through the door that they concluded it was definitely the right place.

Padraig Duggan, Aimes had explained, was neither a confidential informant nor an undercover asset for the police. In fact, he remained unswervingly committed to the nationalist cause. His reasons for co-operating with Aimes were purely political. Duggan did not want to see a return to the violence of the Troubles, not because of a concern for the lives that might be ruined by wanton acts of destruction, but because he feared any escalation might be used as a pretext for loyalists to roll back any political gains that Saoirse, the political arm of the New IRA, had made. Whenever the more rambunctious NIRA lads, or some radical splinter group, decided it was time to blow something up, Duggan found a way to surreptitiously alert Anthony Aimes in order to make sure that the miscreants were rolled up without harming anyone. This arrangement posed no small risk to Padraig Duggan's long-term health. His motivations notwithstanding, if any of the lads in the movement learned or even suspected that he had a cozy relationship with the chief constable, he would be a dead man.

Setting up a clandestine meeting with Duggan was out of the question. Duggan had been quite clear about the terms of his cooperation: *"You don't call me. I call you."*

But there was a way to contact Duggan without arousing the suspicion of his cohorts. Congreve and Sutherland could, in their official capacity, pay him a visit at his usual afternoon hangout and question him, just as if they were interviewing witnesses in a crime. Duggan would not appreciate being roasted in front of his mates, but a seemingly hostile confrontation would not only preserve but possibly burnish his reputation in the dissident movement. And if he knew something about the King's abduction, he would find a way to let them know without giving himself away.

That was the plan at least.

Sutherland tried the door and, finding it unlocked, opened it tentatively. The interior was dark and close, with a long bar and just a few café tables arranged in front of a small fireplace. The tables were unoccupied, but several men—ages ranging from twenties to sixties—sat at the bar, hunched over pints of foamy dark ale. For a few seconds, nobody seemed to pay them any attention, but then, as if alerted by some invisible signal, heads began to turn their way.

Congreve felt the weight of their stares upon him, the unspoken message coming through loud and clear: *You don't belong here.* But he'd been a copper longer than most of the fellows in the establishment had been alive and he had walked boldly into dens of iniquity far more perilous than this.

"I've got this, Ross," he announced, and then strode up to the bar and addressed the bartender. "Pint of Guinness, my good man."

The bartender, a stout, older fellow with hair and beard the color and texture of steel wool, regarded him coolly. "I think you lads may be in the wrong place."

Congreve held the man's gaze. "You do serve Guinness, don't you? I hear it's quite popular in these parts."

"I serve Guinness. What I don't serve is bloody peelers."

"Ah. Well, that's unfortunate." Congreve shuffled his bulk onto a barstool. "But as it happens, we've nowhere else to be just now, so my friend and I will just sit here awhile. Just in case you change your mind. I'm sure your . . . regular clientele . . . won't mind."

The barman seethed quietly for a moment, then broke out in a disingenuous smile. "All right, then. One pint of Guinness coming right up."

He took a recently emptied glass from under the bar and spat a copious gob of saliva into it. Then he moved over to the tap, pulled the pint, and slammed it down on the bar in front of Congreve. "That'll be a tenner."

"Hmm," replied Congreve mildly. "And the local flavor is gratis, I take it?"

"Pay up. Drink up . . . or don't. And shove off."

Congreve folded his hands on the bar. "If it's all the same to you, I think I'll sip at it awhile. You see, I'm looking for a chap that I was told frequents this establishment."

Above his mustache, the bartender's nostrils flared angrily. "Look somewhere else. I know my rights. If you're not showing me a warrant, you can bloody well sod off."

Congreve pressed on. "His name is Padraig Duggan. Is he about? No? Well, then, my associate and I will just sit awhile—"

"Ambrose!"

Congreve turned toward Sutherland, the source of the hissed warning, and immediately saw the reason for it. Though it had escaped his notice, the other patrons of the establishment had slid from their barstools and were now stalking toward the two of them, fists balled menacingly.

With the alert now sounded, Sutherland squared off against the nearest threat. "Think on it, lads," he said. "Right now it's just a conversation. Raise a hand, and this won't end well."

"Not for you, peeler," replied the man.

Congreve felt his pulse quicken but managed to maintain his calm demeanor. "Gentlemen, you don't seriously think we would walk in here, just the two of us, without some backup, as the Americans like to say?"

This prompted an exchange of nervous glances among the men, and then one of them moved over to the door, opened it a crack, and peered out. "Don't see anyone," he called out.

"Well, of course you don't," answered Congreve, throwing himself fully into the fiction. "That's the whole point of covert surveillance. Now, be good chaps and sit down."

Another round of nervous glances followed, and then the self-appointed ringleader narrowed his gaze at Sutherland. "Bollocks. You two aren't with the local guard. I don't think anyone even knows you're here. And that means nobody is going to miss you."

Sutherland, sensing that the situation was about to escalate, moved his hand toward his holstered sidearm.

But just then a new voice rang out in the close confines of the pub. "Seamus! What the bloody fuck is going on out here?"

The bartender jolted as if he'd stepped on a live wire and swung around to face an older, bearded man standing in the doorway behind the bar. "These peelers came in looking for trouble. Thought we'd oblige."

The older man squinted at the bartender. "Are you touched in the head, Seamus? You want to stir the shit up, do it somewhere else. Not here."

Seamus the bartender dropped his stare. "I asked them politely to leave. We're just standing up for our rights."

The bearded man now swung his gaze toward Congreve. "Is that right? Did he ask you to leave?"

Congreve hesitated. "Well, in point of fact, he did, but as I tried to explain to—"

"If the man told you to get out, that's the end of it. We've got rights, you know."

"As I tried to explain," Congreve pressed, "I'd like to have a word with Mr. Padraig Duggan. My preference would be to keep it informal, but I am quite willing to return with a warrant if that's what it takes."

"And what do you want with Padraig Duggan?" asked the man.

Congreve, having seen photos of Duggan, knew that he was, in fact, already addressing him. "I have it on good authority that nothing happens in the . . . ah, community . . . without Mr. Duggan's approval. You see, Chief Inspector Sutherland and I are counterterrorism investigators looking into a threat against the Royal Family."

"Oh, sure." Duggan snorted. "You found us out. We're to blow up Buckingham Palace next Thursday. Seamus built the bomb right there behind the bar. Are you goin' to arrest us all now?"

Congreve stared into Duggan's eyes as if looking into his soul. Then he straightened. "No, I don't think that will be necessary. Good day."

He slid off his barstool, tossed a twenty-pound note onto the bar, and then turned for the exit.

Duggan called after him. "What? That's it, then?"

Congreve stopped but didn't look back. "I've looked you in the eye, Mr. Duggan, and I am satisfied that you have no knowledge whatsoever of any plot against the royals." He nodded to Sutherland. "Ross, let's go."

Sutherland waited until they were back in their Rover heading toward the nearby Bishop's Gate Hotel, where they intended to pass the night. Then he asked the question that had been burning in his brain from the moment they left the pub.

"Well?"

Congreve, in the passenger seat, began packing his Briar. "Now we wait and see. Duggan will wonder if something is happening behind his back. He'll do the investigative work for us. I suspect we shan't have to wait long for an answer."

He was not wrong.

Before they even got a chance to check into their rooms, Chief Constable Aimes texted to let them know that Padraig Duggan was requesting a meeting.

TWENTY

Stoke and Harry found the Geely abandoned on the side of the road just a couple miles from the farmhouse. The fastback hatch was open, revealing an empty cargo bay.

"That ginger dude must have had another vehicle waiting here," observed Brock. "Transferred the nerve agent components to it."

"No shit, Harry," Stoke snarled. "You're a regular Sherlock Holmes figuring that out."

"Yeah? Well, how are we going to track him now?"

"We're on an island, Harry. Ain't a lot of places for him to go. And he's not exactly going to blend in with the locals."

Brock scratched his chin. "Yeah, that's a good point."

"You got contacts here, right? Have them ask around about this guy. He's gonna need to get off the island somehow, and he's probably not going to be flying out. We can keep an eye on the ports. And maybe you can have your pals at Langley get an ID from this."

Stoke handed over his phone, which was cued up to play the video he'd taken earlier. While Alonso drove them back into Havana, Harry watched as the now deceased Russian general Osipov demonstrated the lethal effectiveness of the Novichok binary nerve agent.

"Is that a condom?" he asked.

"Yeah. He uses it to keep the components of the nerve agent separate until he's ready to mix them."

"Man, put that on your jimmy and knocking up some skank will be the least of your worries."

"You've got a real way with words, Harry," said Stoke. "Just keep watching."

Brock did, interspersing the viewing with more of his witty color commentary until the mysterious redhead entered the frame. "There he is," he murmured. "Hmm. That accent."

"Yeah," said Stoke. "Sounds kind of like Sean Connery."

"Yeah. Maybe he's . . . Oh, shit!"

Harry had just come to the part of the replay where the redhead ruthlessly dispatched Osipov and the others. Stokely took the phone and backed the video up to the best shot of the redhead; then he took a screenshot and sent it to Harry as a message attachment. "Send this to your friends at Langley. Maybe they can give us a name."

―――――――――

Harry Brock woke up the next morning with a pounding headache from one mojito too many at the hotel bar and an email from one of his "pals at Langley" supplying a name to the face of the redheaded assassin.

"His name is Sean Fahey," Harry told Stoke over breakfast at Buffet Miramar, one of the many eateries at the Hotel Meliá Habana, located in the Vedado District—the newer, upscale section of the city, west of Old Havana.

After the previous night's adventure, the two men had opted to take lodgings at one of the top-rated hotels in the city. Meliá Habana's five-star rating was, Stoke decided, adjusted for Cuba. It would have been a three-star joint anywhere else in the world, but three stars anywhere else was swank by Havana standards. Sometimes, you just had to take what you could get. The location was nice enough, though surrounded as it was by modern high-rise buildings, it lacked the unique charm of the Old Town. The hotel was beach adjacent, and the upper-story rooms on the north side had ocean views, but as Stoke and Harry were there on business, these considerations didn't count for much. The breakfast fare, however—which consisted of an assortment of *pastelitos de guayaba*, pastries filled with guava paste, and steaming cups of *cortadito*, espresso with a dash of steamed milk and a touch of sugar—was decent. Above average even.

Supplying the assassin's name seemed to momentarily exceed the limit of Hangover Harry's ability to communicate, so he pushed his phone with the open email across to Stokely.

"That's him," Stoke said, studying the attached image—a standard military ID picture. The photograph was more than a decade old, but the face was unquestionably that of the killer. "Ex–Royal Navy commando, Special Boat Service. So he *is* a Brit."

"I think he's actually Irish," Harry managed to say.

Stoke scanned down until he found the line where Fahey's birthplace was listed.

Belfast. Northern Ireland.

"Ireland. I guess that explains the accent." Stoke looked back up to the man's service record. "SBS. Those guys are the real deal, Harry. Almost as badass as the SEALs."

Harry, contemplating whether his stomach could handle one of the pastries and ultimately deciding it could not, just mumbled, "You snake-eaters are all the same to me."

"Snake-eaters," scoffed Stokely. "You're thinking of the Green Berets, Harry. They ain't shit compared to SEALs."

"Whatever, dude."

Chuckling, Stoke read on. "Demolitions expert. Three combat tours in Afghanistan. Mustered out in 2019. Now working as a private military contractor. Guy like this, that could be cover, right? Maybe he's British intelligence?"

"If he is, they aren't saying."

"They don't call it the 'Secret Intelligence Service' for nothing."

"True, but as a matter of professional courtesy, friendly services usually let each other know about assets that are in play. That way, the good guys don't shoot each other in a case of mistaken identity."

"So, he's probably not working for the good guys."

"I'm thinking not."

"So, we've got an English merc—"

"Irish. Call him English, and he'll probably kick your ass."

"He can try."

"I'm serious, Stoke. Calling a Scotsman or an Irishman 'English' is a serious insult."

Stoke waved dismissively. "You white boys are all the same to me." He winked and paused a beat, then resumed. "An *Irish* merc in the open with a couple hundred pounds of binary nerve agent. What do we think he's got planned for it? Does he have a buyer? Or is he going to use it against a target?"

"It would have to be a pretty big target. With that much nerve agent, he could take out an entire city."

"That's what I'm thinking," agreed Stoke. "Either way, we need to find this guy."

"Oh. Forgot the best part." Harry reached out, hand open. "Let me see it."

He took the phone, tapped the screen a few times, and then handed it back. Stoke now saw what appeared to be a photo capture of a passport page. The image showed Fahey's photo, but the name under it read "Sean Ferris."

"That's the cover he's traveling under," explained Harry.

"How'd you get this?"

Harry affected a hurt expression. "Do you have to ask? We're the CIA, Stoke. We're everywhere. Specifically, we're inside the Cuban customs computer system. Sean Fahey, aka Sean Ferris, arrived in Havana two days ago from Dublin by way of Paris. And are you ready for the best part?"

Stoke thought it was a rhetorical question, but when Harry didn't resume talking, he growled, "Jeez, Harry, just spit it out."

"Wait for it." Harry grinned and then held out a few more seconds. "He's staying here."

"Here?" Stoke started. "You mean at *this* hotel?"

"Yeah. Can you believe it? I mean, what are the odds?"

"Seriously? You didn't lead with that?" Stoke jumped up, threw down two fifty-peso notes, and then grabbed Harry by the arm, dragging him from the restaurant.

"What the hell?" protested Harry.

"We want to tail this guy," Stoke said in a low voice. "We're not going to be able to do that very well if he walks in here or passes us in the lobby."

"This place has like five hundred rooms," complained Harry. "What are the odds of that happening? Besides, he doesn't know what we look like."

"You serious right now, Harry? Look at me. He sees my face more than once, and he's gonna know we're onto him." He pushed through an exit leading out to the pool deck, where only a handful of tourists were lazily sunning themselves. Stoke doubted Fahey would be among them, so it was a good place to sit down and figure out what to do next.

"You still got Alonso on speed dial?" he asked.

"Yeah. Want me to call him?"

"Yeah. Gotta think Fahey's going to drive out of here with the nerve agent. We'll set up surveillance on the parking lot, figure out what he's driving, and then tail him to see where he's going with the stuff. We're gonna need a couple rental cars. Think you can swing that?"

"If we've got Alonso, what do we need rental cars for?"

"C'mon, Harry, just how hungover are you? We're gonna need 'em to shadow our subject." Stokely should not have had to explain this to Harry—running a tail was Tradecraft 101.

It was all but impossible to tail someone with a single vehicle. People, especially those with counterintelligence training, tended to notice when the same vehicle stayed behind them for any meaningful length of time. Ideally, surveillance in motion was a team operation, with five or more vehicles handing off the lead position so that the subject never saw the same vehicle twice. Stoke and Harry didn't have a team, but with a little help from Alonso, there was a chance they could pull it off.

Feeling somewhat chastened after having screwed the proverbial pooch, Harry rallied and managed to get several necessary things done in a very short period of time. The cars—a silver Malaysian-manufactured Proton Saga economy sedan and a white Chinese-made Aeolus Yixuan Max midsized—were rented from two different car rental services using Harry's bogus Canadian passport and international driver's license; they were delivered to the hotel about the same time that Alonso pulled up in his vintage Chevy. When Stoke explained what they needed him to do, the little Cuban driver was thrilled at the prospect of injecting some excitement into his otherwise dull routine of driving tourists around the city. The bonus promised at the end of the operation just sweetened the deal.

They quickly got into position, with Alonso parked on the street across from the hotel's main entrance and Stoke and Harry watching the parking lot through binoculars from the balcony of Stoke's room.

"Got him," announced Stoke less than half an hour after the surveillance began. With his copper-red hair, Fahey was easy to spot as he emerged from the hotel and headed toward the secure parking area. "Harry, get down there and be ready to take the handoff."

Harry was already moving. Stoke spoke into his phone, which was dialed into a three-way call with Harry and Alonso. "Alonso, get ready. He's on the move."

In the parking lot below, Fahey went to a coal-gray midsized SUV. He moved with the casual confidence of a seasoned operator, keeping his head on a swivel without looking like he had a care in the world.

When he reached the car, he did not immediately get in but instead did a complete circuit around the vehicle, surreptitiously checking for any signs of tampering. Evidently satisfied that nothing was amiss, he opened the rear cargo area, where, Stoke surmised, the nerve agent was being kept; then he closed it and went to the driver's door.

"Okay, Alonso," Stoke said into the phone. "He'll be coming out soon. Dark gray SUV. *Una camioneta gris.*"

"*Sí, señor*" came the reply in Stoke's earbud. "*Claro.*"

Stoke kept watching as the SUV backed out of its slot, then rolled to the exit and pulled out, turning left to head northeast on Avenida Tercera—Third Avenue. As soon as he made the turn, Stoke was on the move, passing through the hotel room and into the hall on his way down to the exit.

Alonso's voice came over the line. "I have him, *señor.*"

"Don't get too close," warned Stoke. "We don't want him to know he's being followed. Harry, you keeping up?"

"Almost there," said Harry, sounding a little out of breath.

"He's heading east. Gray SUV about a block ahead of Alonso." Stoke reached the stairs and bounded down with catlike grace. With his long strides, Stoke was able to walk faster than most people could jog, and while he didn't want to attract any attention, he knew that everything depended on his being able to reach his rental car and join the pursuit before Fahey put too much distance between them.

"All right, I'm on the move," Harry reported.

Stoke, who was just exiting the lobby, saw Brock's rental car—the Proton Saga—leaving the parking lot and turning onto the avenue. Alonso and Fahey were already too far down the road to be seen. Stoke now quickened his pace, reaching the Aeolus in just a few long strides. Thirty seconds later, he too was pulling out of the parking lot and onto the avenue.

So far so good, thought Stoke, mentally crossing his fingers, hoping that their luck would hold.

He accelerated quickly to reach the posted speed limit but then eased off the gas pedal, taking care not to do anything that might attract the notice of the traffic police.

Decades of restrictive economic policies had largely made private ownership of automobiles something of a rarity in Cuba. While that trend had changed somewhat in the twenty-first century, the number of cars on the road was still well below what one might have expected. As a result, traffic was relatively light, even in the heart of Havana. While this allowed Stoke and his shadow team to maintain a decent standoff distance with their quarry, it also reduced their ability to blend into the crowd.

Alonso now came over the line. "*Señores*, he is turning."

"Which way?" asked Stoke.

"*Izquierda*. Left. Onto Calle Sesenta."

Stoke checked the open map app on his phone and saw the street Alonso had just identified. The intersection was just a few blocks away, and a left turn onto that street would take Fahey back to the tourist-focused beachfront.

Where the hell is he going? Stoke wondered. He had expected Fahey to take his lethal cargo out of the city to some clandestine moorage or smugglers' airstrip.

"Should I follow, *señor*?"

"No, let him go, Alonso. Harry, can you pick him up?"

"Coming up on the turn now."

"Alonso, get yourself turned around. I'll let you know where to go next."

"I see him," Harry called out. "Uh, looks like he's making a right turn. Heading east."

"Shit," muttered Stoke. He hadn't anticipated Fahey making two turns in quick succession. "Harry, you're going to have to stay on him until I can catch up."

"Got it. Making the turn now . . . Hey, it looks like he's making another right turn."

Stoke glanced down at the map display on his phone. If he was reading Harry correctly, Fahey had just turned onto the outer ring of a road pattern that looked remarkably like a wagon wheel, with several roads slicing in like spokes toward a smaller inner ring. The spokes divided the neighborhood inside the wheel into several wedge-shaped blocks. Only one road—Third Avenue—passed all the way through the center to continue out the other side. Stoke, who had not yet reached the original turn, now saw an opportunity to close the distance with Fahey.

But something about Fahey's course was nagging at him. If it had been the Irishman's intention to turn onto the ring road, why hadn't he just kept going straight one more block to make the turn from Third Avenue? Then it hit him.

"Shit," he muttered. "He's running an SDR."

The SDR—surveillance detection route—was another basic tradecraft technique used by spies to identify possible tails. Rather than travel directly to a destination, a canny spy would choose a meandering route, with lots of turns and with lots of opportunities to observe what was happening behind him. If a person or vehicle kept showing up in the rearview, no matter how many times you doubled back, odds were good that they were a tail. The fact that Fahey was running an SDR did not necessarily mean that he was aware that he was being followed. Intelligence operatives were taught from day one to always expect trouble, to avoid routines that might be exploited by an enemy, and to always use surveillance detection routes when moving from place to place.

The SDR technique was not foolproof. A well-organized pursuit with multiple agents in constant radio contact could successfully maintain visual contact with a subject through even the most labyrinthine series of turns, but Stoke and Harry, with their limited resources, would be vulnerable to exposure.

"Okay, Harry," said Stoke. "Break off. Let him go. Turn west on the main avenue and find somewhere to pull over."

"Roger that," chirped Harry.

Stoke thought about chiding him for using the hackneyed expression. This wasn't a goddamned Tom Clancy novel after all. But he decided it wasn't the time. He continued on Third Avenue, crossing the outer rim of the wheel just as Fahey's gray SUV was coming to a stop, waiting for the cross traffic to clear so that he could continue on his way. Stoke kept going, but he kept an eye on the rearview, watching as Fahey's vehicle resumed traveling along the outer rim of the wagon wheel.

Stoke knew he was taking a big chance by temporarily breaking off the pursuit. There were several more roads intersecting the ring along its southern sweep, and if Fahey took any of them and exited the ring road, he would be gone for good. But Stoke's gut told him the better play was to hang back and avoid detection.

He continued through the center of the wheel and then made a right turn onto the outer rim, heading in the opposite direction from the one that Fahey had been traveling. If he didn't pass the gray SUV, he would know that the Irishman had turned off....

But no, there he was, moving with traffic in the oncoming lane. Stoke caught just a glimpse of the man's distinctive copper mane through the window as the two vehicles passed, and he breathed a sigh of relief. He angled his mirror to follow Fahey as he continued north, passing through the Third Avenue intersection before disappearing from view. Stoke made the next right turn, cutting back toward the center of the wheel. With a little luck and a heavy foot, he might just be able to circle around and pick up the tail before Fahey left the ring.

"Alonso, get up to Avenida Primera and head east. Harry, watch for him to come your way on Third Avenue."

"*Sí, señor,*" replied Alonso, almost simultaneously with Harry's second "Roger that." Stoke rolled his eyes.

He reached the inner ring, skidding into the turn and blowing through the Third Avenue intersection, weaving through the cross traffic without slowing to the accompaniment of screeching brakes and honking horns. He passed by the first right—the angle of the turn was too sharp to take at speed—and slewed into the next, heading due north toward the outer rim of the wheel. Directly ahead, the gray SUV passed by.

"Yes!" Stoke cried, pounding the steering wheel triumphantly. He slowed, approaching the intersection and making the turn with a little more caution now that his quarry was once more in sight. Fahey continued along the ring until he reached the west intersection with Third Avenue, whereupon he turned right onto that thoroughfare.

"He's coming your way, Harry," warned Stoke.

"I'm ready for him."

Stoke made the turn a few seconds later, just as Fahey, one block ahead, made a left turn onto Calle Sesenta. "What's this asshole up to now?" he wondered aloud. "Harry, Alonso, he's heading south now."

He made the turn and fell in behind the gray SUV, but no sooner had he done so than Fahey made another right turn, heading west again on Avenida Quinta—Fifth Avenue.

Fifth Avenue was the main east-west artery of the Vedado, a four-lane divided highway that bisected the entirety of new Havana. To the east, it continued through Miramar to a tunnel passing under the Rio Almendares, where it became the scenic Avenida Malecón, following along the water's edge all the way to the harbor entrance. To the west, it ran all the way to the outskirts of the city, where it became the Carretera Panamericana, linking Havana to the port town of Mariel sixteen miles away.

This was what Stoke had been expecting all along. Having completed his SDR, Fahey would take his prize out into the rural countryside, where he would presumably link up with a clandestine transport element.

As he contemplated this revelation, it occurred to Stokely Jones Jr. that it wouldn't be enough to simply tail Fahey to that meeting, because if the Irishman succeeded in handing off his deadly cargo and transporting it out of Cuba, the chances of figuring out where it was bound would fall somewhere between slim and none, while the odds of a city-killing weapon of mass destruction being used against a populated area would approach absolute certainty.

Orders or not, shadowing Fahey to see what he did with the nerve agent wasn't going to be enough. The Irishman had to be stopped.

TWENTY-ONE

Stoke managed the shadow pursuit like a street hustler playing a game of three-card monte, maneuvering their assets—the three vehicles driven by himself, Harry, and Alonso—up and down the highway, changing their position relative to Fahey's SUV every few minutes to ensure that the view in the man's mirrors never stayed the same. And while he was doing all of that, part of his mind was occupied with the business of planning exactly how he was going to interdict the steely-eyed assassin and separate him from his deadly cargo, all without bringing down the wrath of the Cuban authorities.

It was this last point that had him stuck. There wasn't a lot of traffic on the highway, but there was enough that if he tried to run Fahey off the road, it wouldn't take long at all for someone to alert the highway police. If he was going to pull this off, he would have to find a more secluded location, and that probably meant waiting until the Irishman reached his eventual destination.

It would happen in two stages, he knew. First, he would have to bring Fahey's vehicle to a full stop. That might require some fancy tactical driving techniques, but then again, depending on where he made his move, it might be as simple as boxing the SUV in between their vehicles and cutting the road. The second part, the actual takedown, would be the real challenge.

Fahey was armed and had already proven himself to be exceptionally dangerous. Stoke had only the pistol he'd taken off the body of Chicken Dude—aka Colonel Hector Diaz—the previous night, an old Soviet-era Makarov semiauto. The Makarov was a terrible handgun in Stoke's professional opinion—too small, especially for his big hands, with low-profile iron sights that made it damn near impossible to line up a shot, and a surprising amount of recoil for a pistol with such a small and underpowered 9-millimeter cartridge. Still, it was better than nothing. He didn't know if Harry was armed—getting caught with a handgun in Cuba was probably a lot more dangerous than getting caught without one, especially for a foreigner—but it probably didn't matter anyway. If things got so bad that he needed Harry Brock to save his ass, well, then it was probably already too late.

He had not yet shared his intent with Harry. If forewarned, the CIA man would probably balk, falling back on his orders from Langley to observe and report, but once things went kinetic, Stoke knew he could count on Harry to have his back. So, he wasn't going to give Harry a chance to refuse.

When they had gone about ten miles, Stoke called Alonso off and sent him home. Out beyond the city limits, the vintage Chevy was a lot more conspicuous. Stoke also didn't want the Cuban around when the situation escalated.

Harry took the lead, hanging back a couple hundred yards and pacing Fahey. Stoke kept a similar interval, which meant he could just barely make out the Irishman's SUV. A few minutes later, Harry, his voice tense with anticipation, reported, "He's slowing down. I think he might be getting ready to turn off."

Stoke glanced down at the open map application on his phone. "There aren't any roads on the map."

"Roads?" quipped Harry in a fair imitation of Doc Brown from *Back to the Future*. "Maybe where he's going, they don't need roads."

"That's funny, Harry," Stoke said with a chuckle, hiding the fact that his adrenaline was spiking. This was it. This was the opportunity he'd been waiting for.

His fingers tightened involuntarily on the wheel, squeezing it as if gripping an anchor line. "Okay, here's what we're gonna do. Maintain your speed, and when he pulls off, you just roll right on past like you've got somewhere to be. But when you see me make the turn and follow him, you're gonna flip a one-eighty and come back to join the party."

"Sounds kinda risky," opined Harry. "He's gonna notice you riding his ..." Harry trailed off a moment, then came back. "He's stopping. . . . No, he's turning off onto a dirt road."

"Keep going," urged Stoke. "Then get your ass back here and back me up."

Ahead, he could see the SUV moving perpendicular to the highway, trailing a cloud of dust behind it as it crossed a grassy meadow that rose to a wooded hillside. From the map, Stoke knew that the coastline and the Straits of Florida lay just over that hill.

"He's got a boat waiting for him," Stoke surmised. "I'm going after him."

"You're what?" Harry's voice had risen an octave. "Hold on."

Stoke ignored the protest, bearing down on the accelerator and closing the distance to the turnoff in a matter of seconds. Stoke braked hard, coming almost to a full stop, then made the turn.

To call the track Fahey had taken a road was generous in the extreme. It looked like an old jeep trail, a deeply eroded two track that probably hadn't been used since the early days of the revolution. Stoke knew that if he put his wheels in the parallel ruts, his rental would immediately high-center, so instead, he steered to the left, putting the right wheels on the center hump and the left wheels on the edge of the road.

It was slow going. So slow, in fact, that he considered abandoning the vehicle and continuing the pursuit on foot. But as he got farther from the highway and began climbing the hillside, the surface smoothed out, allowing him to not only travel on the two track but to actually increase his speed. Ahead, masked by the cloud of dust raised in his wake, Fahey charged on. The road wove through a stand of pine trees, rising up and over the crest of the hill, and then continued down the other side another fifty yards to where a shingle beach met the azure waters of the Straits of Florida.

As he broke over the summit, Stoke saw a boat—an old but still serviceable sport fisher in the forty-foot range—bobbing in the blue water a couple hundred yards offshore. He also saw Fahey's SUV sitting idle near the water's edge with the back hatch open. Right in front of it, tied to a beach anchor just out of reach of the outgoing tide, was an eight-foot inflatable tender, its outboard motor tilted up to keep the screw from scraping the rocks. Then Fahey appeared, rising up from a kneeling position at the front of the little inflatable, where he had just deposited one of the canisters he'd off-loaded from the SUV. Another just like it, containing the other half of the binary Novichok nerve agent, was visible in the vehicle's rear cargo area.

Stoke read the situation on the field and called an audible. Although Fahey's SUV was literally a stone's throw away, in the time it would take Stoke to negotiate the rugged track in his rented sedan, the Irishman would easily be able to off-load the second canister and shove off for the waiting fishing boat. So, instead of wasting his time trying to drive the remaining distance, Stoke slammed on the brakes, threw the shift lever into park, and leapt from the car, brandishing his captured Makarov.

His arrival had not gone unnoticed. Down at the water's edge, Fahey's head snapped up in alarm. Stoke took a measure of satisfaction in the look of surprise on the Irishman's face; their tail had gone undetected. But whatever advantage Stoke might have gained from the element of surprise was short-lived. Fahey quickly grasped that this unexpected visitor posed a threat and reacted accordingly, drawing his pistol and ducking down behind the front end of his SUV on the passenger's side, even as Stoke got off the first shot.

The little Makarov bucked in Stoke's big hand, and the 9-millimeter round whizzed downrange to splash in the water behind and a few feet to the right of where Fahey had been standing a moment before. Stoke hadn't expected to score a hit, not at that distance and not with an unfamiliar weapon. A lucky shot would have been welcome, but Stoke's real purpose had been to disrupt the transfer of the nerve agent and keep Fahey pinned down long enough to close the intervening distance and make the next shot count. Or maybe the one after that.

But as retired USMC general James "Mad Dog" Mattis was fond of saying, "The enemy gets a vote," and Fahey cast his by leaning out from behind his cover and snapping off a pair of shots that would have perforated Stoke, had he not, almost presciently, thrown himself flat a fraction of a second before the Irishman pulled the trigger.

Stoke didn't stay down. As soon as he hit the ground, he rolled to the right and then bounded up and squeezed off another shot in Fahey's direction before doing it all over again.

Wash. Rinse. Repeat.

Gaining ground with each repetition.

There were just a couple of problems with Stoke's clever assault plan.

First and most obvious was the fact that while shortening the intervening distance would improve Stoke's accuracy, it would do the same for Fahey. And Fahey had the added benefit of being behind cover, which meant there was a lot less of him for Stoke to target.

The second and more critical problem was that there were now just three rounds left in the Makarov's magazine, plus one in the chamber.

Four shots, and then he would be reduced to throwing rocks.

He needed a new plan.

When he was just fifty feet from the SUV, close enough to hear the sound of surf crashing on the shore, Stoke rolled behind a pine tree that wasn't quite broad enough to provide the sort of cover he really needed. He lingered there for just a moment, then risked a quick peek to reassess the situation. Almost right away, Fahey's pistol cracked twice more, and as Stoke pulled back, he both felt and heard the thunk of bullets slamming into the bough right above him. Splinters and bark chips rained down on him, and the air was filled with the aroma of woodsmoke. Nevertheless, that hasty glimpse of Fahey's vehicle had given him an idea.

He had been going about this all wrong. The gun battle with the Irishman had distracted him from the primary objective. His goal wasn't to eliminate Fahey but rather to prevent him from getting away with the nerve agent. Killing the man was certainly the preferred option, but as Stoke was no longer certain he could accomplish that, he decided to put his remaining ammunition to better use.

After another quick peek to fix the exact location of his new target, he rolled into the open and fired from the prone position. Two shots in rapid succession, aimed not at the corner of the SUV where Fahey crouched, but at the lone aluminum canister resting inside the open rear cargo bay of the vehicle. One shot missed, passing through the vehicle's interior and striking the windshield from the inside, but the other round hit the canister, the impact punching through its metal skin. Stoke allowed himself a smile of triumph, even as Fahey, evidently realizing what Stoke was now attempting, answered with a withering volume of return fire, driving Stoke back behind his tree. Judging by the intensity of the counterattack, Stoke figured Fahey had probably shot out his entire magazine, so as soon as the fusillade ended, he rolled back out into the open, intent on making his last two rounds count. One hole in the nerve agent canister was good, but three would be better.

But when he tried to find the canister over the front sight of the Makarov, he realized the purpose behind Fahey's profligate return fire. The Irishman had used the brief firestorm to break from cover, run to the rear of the vehicle, and slam the hatch closed, denying Stoke another chance to perforate the container.

So much for plan B, thought Stoke, bounding up to charge the last few yards to the SUV. He moved in a shooter's stance, with the little Makarov braced in his massive hands, finger on the trigger, sweeping the business end of the pistol back and forth, ready to fire at the first glimpse of copper. He was betting everything—literally betting his life—on the fact that Fahey would need a second or two more to swap out the spent magazine in his pistol, but even if he was wrong . . . even if the Irishman was ready for him, Stoke felt certain he would be able to get a shot off.

And one shot was all he needed.

He reached the rear of the SUV and hooked left, sweeping around the driver's side, dropping into a crouch to reduce his profile—no easy feat for someone of Stoke's mountainous dimensions—and continued around to the front end, where he expected to find Fahey crouching down.

But the Irishman wasn't there.

Stoke pivoted to check his six o'clock, just in case Fahey had tried to do a runaround, but no, the redheaded assassin wasn't there either, so he whirled back around and kept going, clearing the front end and moving to the passenger side.

Fahey wasn't there either.

Then Stoke glimpsed motion from the corner of his eye, something moving on the beach right behind him. He spun around, pistol at the ready, half expecting to catch a bullet but determined to give as good as he got.

It *was* Fahey, but the Irishman wasn't pointing his pistol at Stoke. He wasn't even holding a weapon.

Fahey was out in the water, up to his knees in the surf and shoving the inflatable tender toward open water. Just visible over the curve of the vulcanized rubber float tube were two identical metal canisters. Somehow, while Stoke had been busy trying to sneak up on Fahey, the other man had succeeded in retrieving the second container and carrying it to the tender.

Stoke took aim, putting the Makarov's sights squarely on Fahey's retreating back. He had no moral reservations about shooting an enemy in the back, especially not an enemy who was presently absconding with a weapon of mass destruction, but he did have some practical concerns.

He had only two rounds left. If he missed . . .

Don't miss, he told himself, and squeezed the trigger.

The little pistol bucked, and bright red blood sprayed across the tender's float tube.

Fahey staggered, fell forward, and disappeared beneath the surface. Stoke kept the pistol trained on the spot a moment longer, but when Fahey did not reappear, he started forward, running toward the beach, intent on intercepting the inflatable before the tide could carry it away. But before he could reach the water's edge, the crack of a bullet piercing the air much too close for comfort, followed almost instantaneously by the report of a rifle, caused him to once more seek the relative safety of a horizontal aspect.

The shot had come from the boat. And that meant Fahey wasn't working alone.

Even prone, Stoke was still more exposed than he would have liked, but with scant cover on the shingle beach, there was really only one place to go—into the water. Besides, he still had to get to the drifting inflatable and either secure or destroy the nerve agent.

Still gripping the Makarov, he high-crawled forward, scuttling on knees and elbows to reach the surf, even as more bullets sizzled through the air above his head. A moment later, he was face down in the salty brine, propelling himself forward down the sloping beach until the water was deep enough to allow him to swim. But as his head dipped under the water, he heard a low roar vibrating through the water. It was the sound of an outboard motor.

He risked lifting his head above the surface and saw the tender, now oriented with the bow facing out to sea, churning up a frothy wake as it motored away from the shore. Just visible over the hump of the outboard was the hunched figure of Sean Fahey. His head was down and all Stoke could really see was his back, but even from his questionable vantage, the red stain darkening the man's left shoulder was unmistakable.

Stoke swore through a mouthful of seawater. He'd hit the bastard, but it hadn't been a kill shot, and somehow, even though he was probably bleeding out, Fahey had found the inner fortitude to pull himself aboard the tender, fire up the outboard, and drive on with his mission.

Stoke couldn't help but feel grudging admiration for the man, along with more than a little self-reproach at his poor marksmanship.

"Damn useless Makarov," Stoke muttered as he dragged the little Soviet pistol out of the water, aimed for the tender's starboard float tube, and fired his last round. The shot was more of a symbolic gesture. Although the bullet struck true, puncturing the inflated cell, the damage was hardly catastrophic. Inflatable boats like the tender were designed to stay afloat even in the event of a rupture, and as Stoke looked on helplessly, Fahey piloted the little dinghy toward the distant sport fishing boat, carrying with him the deadly cargo.

Stoke resigned himself to the fact that the nerve agent was now beyond reach, but he was not ready to give up completely. Tossing the now useless Makarov aside, he rolled over and began swimming for the beach. He stayed horizontal, pulling himself through the water with long, powerful strokes until he felt his thighs dragging across the shingle. Then he sprang to his feet and began zigzagging across the beach, using the standard infantry tactic of three-to-five-second bounds interspersed with combat rolls—*I'm up, he sees me, I'm down*—just in case the sniper on the fishing boat was still targeting him. Evidently, the shooter was otherwise occupied with bringing Fahey aboard, because no shots followed, but Stoke remained on his guard until reaching the relative safety of cover behind the abandoned SUV. Only then did he gaze back out across the water to the sport fisher.

In his original haste to interdict Fahey, Stoke had not given the vessel more than a cursory glance, but now he studied it carefully, looking for telltale identifying marks that he could pass along to somebody with the authority to blow the boat out of the water. The registration numbers displayed just behind the bow would have been perfect, but he couldn't quite make them out.

"Stoke!"

Stoke turned his head toward the source of the shout and saw Harry Brock ambling down the hill on foot. "Hey, man," Harry called out. "Did I just hear someone shooting?"

"Harry! Get your ass down here! And keep your head down. There's a sniper out there."

Harry evinced only mild surprise at this revelation but did quicken his pace. A few seconds later, he knelt down beside Stoke. "What's going on?"

"Fahey got away with the nerve agent. He's on that boat out there."

"Shit." Harry raised his head and took a quick look, then dropped back down. "Okay. So now what?"

"So now we have to figure out where that boat is headed next." Stoke paused to consider exactly how they might be able to do that; then inspiration dawned. "You got your phone?"

"Of course. I've been trying like hell to reach you on it."

"I left mine in the car. Never mind that. Take a picture of that boat and then zoom in on the registration numbers."

"Good idea." He took out his phone and opened the camera app, then rose up again to take the picture. He stood like that for several seconds, long enough that Stoke started worrying that his friend might be making himself an easy target. "Huh," Harry muttered. "Smoke."

"Smoke?" Stoke lifted his head as well and immediately saw a finger of black smoke rising from the sport fishing boat. "It's on fire." He shook his head. "There's no way I hit it. I wonder—"

Out on the water, there was a flash, and then the boat was gone, disintegrating in an expanding cloud of smoke and debris. A second later, the sound of the explosion reached them, as did the shock wave.

"Holy shit!" said Harry, gaping in disbelief. "I did not see that coming." Then he shrugged. "Well, I guess problem solved."

Stoke shook his head. "That's what we're supposed to think."

"What do you mean?"

"They torched the boat to cover their real escape. Another boat we didn't see or . . ." He trailed off for a moment as the truth dawned on him. "A submarine."

"A sub? No way a sub could operate this close to shore."

"Not a military boat," Stoke clarified. "A minisub. Smugglers have been using them to move drugs and other bad shit into the States since the late nineties. That boat was just out there to give them cover while they transferred the nerve agent to the sub."

Harry stared back at him for several seconds as if trying to process what Stoke was telling him. "Yeah, I'll bet that's exactly what they did." He activated his phone and initiated a call. "I'll pass this along to Langley. Tell them to have the Coast Guard start searching for them." And then, as the call went out, he added, "We'll find them."

Stoke nodded, but as he watched the smoke rising from the burning oil slick offshore, he couldn't bring himself to share his friend's optimism.

TWENTY-TWO

At the dawn of the twentieth century, the map of Europe was a tapestry of monarchies. Only two nation-states—France and Switzerland—were ruled by democratically elected representatives, the former having ousted its monarch a century earlier. The rest of the continent, extending into Asia by way of Russian and Ottoman landholdings, as well as innumerable colonies, was ruled by emperors, kings, queens, princes, dukes, duchesses, and sultans, all of whom had inherited their divinely established thrones, and many of whom, thanks to nearly a thousand years of marriage alliances, were cousins. The British monarch Queen Victoria, who passed away mere days after the end of the nineteenth century, was the last British ruler of the Hanoverian Dynasty—the Hanovers being the Germanic royal family who had, through intermarriage with the Stuart line, become inextricably interwoven into the British royal tradition. Edward VII, the son of Victoria and Prince Albert of Saxe-Coburg and Gotha—another Germanic royal family—added still more threads with his marriage to the Princess of Denmark, and a new dynasty was established with the ascension of their son, George V, first monarch of the House of Windsor.

This European royal tapestry did not long endure in an age of increasing industrialization and economic discontent. The Kingdom of Portugal was the first to fall; the monarchy was ended by a coup d'état in 1910 and replaced by a republican government. But it was the Great War that wrought the greatest change, both directly, with the dissolution of the Empires of Austria-Hungary and Germany at the end of the war, along with the abolishment of the many constituent monarchies throughout the region, and indirectly, with the economic and human cost of the war playing a decisive role in the Russian Revolution and the Turkish War of Independence.

Subsequent political, social, and economic instability saw several more European monarchies abolished, more than one of them in lands that fell under Soviet influence at the end of World War II. Though a few European monarchies remain extant in the twenty-first century, their power is greatly diminished, and the tapestry of royal influence and intrigue that once bound them all together has unraveled. Only seven major European nations—Belgium, Denmark, Sweden, Norway, the Netherlands, Spain, and, of course, the United Kingdom—and a handful of lesser principalities—Monaco, Liechtenstein, Andorra, and the Grand Duchy of Luxembourg—are ruled by monarchs of royal lineage, and none of these play the real-world equivalent of a game of thrones for control of the continent as their ancestors once did.

Some of these historic monarchies ended violently—the annihilation of the Romanov line in Russia being perhaps the most dramatic example—but many more ended with peaceful resignations. This was particularly true of the many kingdoms that had composed the German Empire. Often, the deposed monarchs and their families remained influential, serving as statesmen and diplomats for the democratically elected governments that had replaced them, or leveraging their remaining assets into new fortunes, often with an eye to someday regaining royal power. Of these, none did quite as well as the former ruling family of Bavaria—the House of Wittelsbach.

The Wittelsbach family's saga began in 1092, when Otto II, Count of Scheyern, acquired Wittelsbach Castle in the *Bundesland* of Bavaria, eventually making it the seat of power for his dynasty. In the century that followed, House Wittelsbach was invested with the Duchy of

Bavaria and the Electorate of the Palatinate—the electoral body with the power to choose the Holy Roman Emperor. In the centuries that followed, Wittelsbach descendants ruled both in Germanic kingdoms and abroad. King George I, founder of the Hanoverian Dynasty ruling the British Empire, was descended from the House of Wittelsbach by way of his mother, Sophia of Hanover, as were the heirs and pretenders of the Stuart line.

In 1806, after throwing in his lot with an ascendant Napoleon to resist the machinations of neighboring Austria, Duke Maximilian Joseph declared himself King of the newly established Kingdom of Bavaria, a kingdom that would endure until 1918, ending with the defeat of the German Empire and the dissolution of all its constituent monarchies. Yet despite losing their kingdom, the House of Wittelsbach fared far better than the other noble houses of Germany. Rather than stripping them of their titles and holdings, the Parliament of the newly formed Bavarian Free State—part of the Weimar Republic federation—ruled that the landholdings of the Wittelsbach family, including the many castles built over the nearly eight hundred years in which they held power, were private rather than state property. This led to an agreement in which the House of Wittelsbach, through a real estate foundation known as the Wittelsbacher Ausgleichsfonds, or Wittelsbach Compensation Fund, managed by the Duke himself, retained possession of several of their castles, along with a substantial agricultural land grant. This foundation assured that the Wittelsbach heirs would want for nothing in perpetuity.

This golden parachute did not, however, insulate the family from the storm gathering on the horizon. Because of his open opposition to the rising power of the National Socialist German Workers' Party, former crown prince Rupprecht and his family were forced into exile abroad. His wife and children—including his son Albrecht and grandsons, Franz and Max, all heirs to the royal title Duke of Bavaria—were arrested in Nazi-occupied Hungary and sent to a series of different concentration camps, eventually landing in Dachau, where they remained until the camp was liberated by American forces.

Despite, or perhaps because of, these humbling reversals of fortune, the Wittelsbach heirs—Albrecht, who died in 1996 at the age of ninety-one; Franz, also a nonagenarian and current Duke; and his younger brother, Prince Max, the heir presumptive—remain beloved in the hearts of the Bavarian people.

The same could not be said for Prinz Heinrich Konigstahl von Bayern.

———————

A thousand miles separated Edinburgh and Munich, capital of the Free State of Bavaria in the Federal Republic of Germany. While Hawke was not averse to long drives in the country, he was less than enthused at the prospect of spending twenty hours on the open road and in the company of Pippa Guinness. Not that Pippa had, thus far, proven disagreeable. Quite the opposite, actually. Hawke and Pippa were getting along famously, and therein lay the source of his apprehension. He was acutely aware of how an offhand comment or a moment of shared laughter might be misinterpreted as flirtation or, worse, erode his resolve to maintain a completely professional relationship. He had enough to worry about right now without adding temptation to the mix.

Add in the urgency of the PM's deadline, and the necessity of finding a more expeditious mode of travel was self-evident.

That posed no problem to the sixth-wealthiest man in the United Kingdom. His G800 was still on the tarmac in London, its flight crew refreshed and awaiting his summons. It could be in Scotland in an hour's time and wheels down in Germany two and a half hours after that.

And yet the thought of taking the Locomotive out for a spin on the *Autobahn* was too enticing to pass up. There had to be a way, he thought, to do both.

Hawke put in a call to Young Ian Burns, who, in addition to overseeing the maintenance of Alex's automobile collection, also made sure that the cars got to wherever the Lord of the Manor needed them. "Ian, I'm traveling to Germany. Munich, in point of fact. And I'd like to have the Locomotive available when I arrive. Think you can make that happen?"

"Shouldn't be a problem, sir," replied Burns. "We can ship it by rail. Have it there by this time tomorrow."

"Ah, yes, well, the thing is, I was hoping to get it there a little sooner than that."

"Sooner, sir? How much sooner?"

"This afternoon."

There was a long silence on the line.

"I say, old chap. Are you still there?"

"Ah, yes, sir. Just . . . ah . . . considering our options."

"Can't we just fly the bloody thing over?"

"Shipping the car by air would be the quickest method, but it would depend on the availability of a carrier."

"Hmm. Yes, well, I've found that sometimes throwing money at a problem like this can have a most salubrious effect."

"Ah . . . yes, sir. I think it may require rather quite a lot of money, actually. You'd do better to just buy yourself a new car."

Hawke felt certain this was an exaggeration. He had, in fact, considered purchasing a car from a dealer in Munich, going so far as to inquire about the availability of a BMW Alpina B8 Gran Coupe, which he had been thinking about adding to his collection anyway. The sticker price was in the neighborhood of a hundred forty thousand euros. While he was no expert on air freight costs, he didn't think shipping the old Bentley would run to six figures. "My mind is made up," he told Ian. "And my heart is set on having the Locomotive. Find a way."

Young Ian sighed. "Aye, sir. I know a bloke who might be able to make it happen, but you'll need to open your checkbook."

"Never go anywhere without it," replied Hawke.

Young Ian did not disappoint. The promise of an extra zero added to the already hefty standard air freight hauling rate convinced the "bloke" at the Suffolk-based automobile air transport company to move Lord Alexander Hawke's shipment to the head of the list.

While Hawke was busy throwing money at his logistical problems, Pippa occupied herself with researching the subject of their hasty itinerary, turning the resources of the intelligence section loose on Prince Heinrich Konigstahl. When they were settled in aboard the Gulfstream, en route to Munich, she presented her findings to Hawke.

"Heinrich Konigstahl is the living embodiment of the spoiled-princeling stereotype," she began, casting the first of several photographs of the Bavarian royal onto the jet's large plasma screen.

Konigstahl was surprisingly handsome for a blue blood. With black hair swept back from a high forehead, a strong jaw, and an athletic physique, he looked more like the animated Disney ideal of Prince Charming than the flesh-and-blood scion of an ancient royal family.

"He's forty-two," Pippa went on. "Unmarried and, by all reports, uninterested in settling down."

"Might be that he's just not interested in women?" suggested Hawke, thinking about what Pippa had earlier revealed about the elderly Duke.

"He's not gay, if that's what you're thinking. Rumor has it that his tastes run more to the . . . exotic."

Hawke raised an eyebrow. "Leather? Whips and chains? I wouldn't have taken him for the type."

"Hmm. You're on the right track but with rather a touch more of the Marquis de Sade." She tapped the screen of her phone, changing the image on the plasma to one of the same man but in a different setting. Konigstahl, attired in khakis and a safari jacket, stood triumphantly alongside an enormous gray lump, which, Hawke realized upon closer inspection, was the carcass of a rhinoceros. "Among other things, he's a notorious big-game hunter with a penchant for bagging the rarest animals on the planet. That's him in Kenya, 2013, with a male northern white rhinoceros."

"Northern white," murmured Hawke. "I thought they'd gone extinct."

"They have. There are two left. Both female. Once they're gone..." She let the thought hang unfinished, the image on the screen making the point far more eloquently.

"Heinrich is sixth in the line of succession," she went on after a moment. "A great-grandson of King Ludwig III through his third son, Prince Franz. The line of succession is hereditary among male descendants of the royal house, and since neither the current Duke, also named Franz, nor the heir presumptive, Prince Max, have male offspring, the line of succession jumps to the other branch of the family tree. That said, his chances of ever leading House Wittelsbach are remote in the extreme. As his older brother's sons mature and sire offspring of their own, his position in the succession will diminish to the point of irrelevance."

"You called him a spoiled princeling," prompted Hawke. "What did you mean by that?"

"The usual antics. In his formative years, he careened from one scandal to the next. Some of his actions bordered on criminal, and once or twice, he crossed over that border, but he rarely faced any meaningful consequences. Between the family paying off accusers to keep things quiet and the tendency of school administrators and law enforcement agencies to safeguard the reputation of a prestigious family, no formal charges were ever made.

"In his third year at university, however, something happened that must have crossed a line. As before, there was no official record, but rumors range from sexual assault to involvement in a suspicious death. Whatever it was, Prince Heinrich abruptly withdrew from his classes and returned to Munich, where he was put to work in the offices of the Wittelsbach Compensation Fund. That seems to be when he adopted the surname Konigstahl—from a matrilineal grandfather—perhaps as a way of putting some distance between himself and the family.

"Since then, he's managed to largely avoid the spotlight, though rumors still occasionally surface. The word *sociopath* has been whispered, though never by anyone willing to go on record. Because he is so far removed from the succession, there's little concern about the impact his indiscretions might have on the public image of House Wittelsbach and seemingly little interest in trying to reform him."

Hawke stared at the lingering image of Heinrich Konigstahl with his trophy kill. "This is the man the Stewards of Alba would put on the throne? Not exactly a shining beacon of moral character."

"Sadly, there's no morals clause attached to the crown. That said, I can't imagine the people of Scotland, even those who support independence, would overturn centuries of tradition to put him on the throne. Never mind the fact that his claim would be contingent not only on the refusal of all those ahead of him in the Jacobite succession but also on making the legal case that such refusal constitutes abdication." She looked sidelong at Hawke. "You said that you were looking into rumors of a threat against the Royal Family. While I can certainly see Prince Heinrich cast in the role of villain, I can't fathom how perpetrating an act of terrorism against the Crown would advance his aims."

"Hmm. Nor can I. But, as Congreve might say, this is a thread we've plucked, and now we must follow it where it goes and hope that it leads us out of the labyrinth."

Pippa stared at him, clearly dissatisfied with this rationale. "And how exactly do you plan to start pulling on this particular thread?"

Hawke could not resist flashing a mischievous grin. "Why, I thought I'd invite myself to dinner."

TWENTY-THREE

BAVARIA

Hawke had no cause to regret his decision to fast-ship the Locomotive to Munich. The inconvenience of a nearly two-hour wait for the arrival of the plane carrying the Bentley was more than offset by the sheer exhilaration of driving the old coupe the way its builders had intended. Unlike the cramped and curvy motorways of Great Britain, the German Federal Motorway—better known by its name in the original language as the *Autobahn*—with its broad, multiple lanes and virtually no speed limit for ordinary passenger vehicles, was a playground for drivers with high-performance cars. Within minutes of taking delivery of the car on the tarmac at the Munich airport, he pulled onto the A92 and simply drove.

Their assignation with Prince Heinrich Konigstahl von Bayern was to take place not at the latter's apartment in Munich but rather at Schloss Wolkenheim, one of more than six hundred castles dotting the Bavarian landscape that, thanks to the agreement made with House Wittelsbach at the end of the Great War, were held in permanent trust on behalf of the Royal Family. Many of the castles had been lovingly restored and were open to the public and were visited by thousands of tourists. Many others were crumbling ruins, but a few, like Wolkenheim Castle, were apportioned to the family for use as holiday residences. Wolkenheim—the name translated to "Cloud Home"—sitting high atop an Alpine crag in the southern border region of Swabia, a good two hours' drive from Munich, was the favorite getaway of Prince Heinrich.

Hawke's cold call to the Prince had been well received, much to Pippa's surprise. She had anticipated the request for a private meeting to be turned aside by the Prince's staff. Hawke, though, had never for a moment doubted his ability to slip past Konigstahl's gatekeepers. He was after all a member of the exclusive club that was the European aristocracy—a peer of the realm and, in fact, a distant, albeit somewhat removed, cousin of the Prince. And while Hawke's title—Lord of Hawkesmoor—was of lesser rank than the Prince's, Hawke's noble status, unlike that of Konigstahl, was not merely a courtesy title. Moreover, he was considerably wealthier than the Bavarian, and wealth, particularly in the hands of the aristocracy, was a powerful equalizer.

Hawke believed, however, that there was an even more compelling reason for Prince Heinrich to grant him an audience—curiosity. From what Pippa had told him of Konigstahl's character, Hawke felt certain that the Prince would be unable to resist taking the meeting, if only to discover why Lord Alexander Hawke had elected to make his acquaintance, seemingly from out of the blue and especially if Konigstahl was involved in the abduction of King Charles.

The sun had just begun to graze the treetops of the hills rising in the west when the A92, which they had been following since Munich, became the two-lane European Route 533, which continued on to the village of Oberau. From there, with the shadows of impending dusk falling upon them, Hawke followed a maze of increasingly narrow roads up into the Ammergau Alps until finally arriving at the foot of Wolkenheim, the 5,445-foot peak that was the namesake of the mountain redoubt built upon its summit.

Commissioned in the late 1800s by "mad" King Ludwig II—who remained notorious for his excessive and expensive castle-building projects during his long and tragic reign—Wolkenheim Castle was built upon the foundation of an earlier fortress that had once guarded the pass through which ran an ancient Roman road. Similar in style to the larger and considerably more ambitious Neuschwanstein Castle, begun only a decade later and never completed, Wolkenheim possessed one trait unique among Bavarian castles. Aside from a treacherous mountain footpath that wended across the southern face of Wolkenheim Mountain—more a scramble than a hike—the only way to reach the summit and thus the palace itself was by cable car.

Even though Pippa had informed Hawke of this detail during her research into Schloss Wolkenheim, he nevertheless felt a mixture of excitement and apprehension as he pulled into the car park of the Wolkenheim cable car station and visually tracked the mile-long cable that snaked up the flanks of the mountain, suspended from concrete-and-steel pylons. Beholding it, he could not help but think of an incident a few years earlier involving a similar conveyance—a ski-lift gondola in Switzerland—that had been bombed by KGB agents intent on kidnapping his beloved son, Alexei.

To hide his anxiety, he glanced over at Pippa. "Rather reminds me of one of my favorite movies."

"One of the Bond films?"

"Close. *Where Eagles Dare*. Richard Burton and a young Clint Eastwood kill Nazis with reckless abandon in a German mountaintop fortress accessible only by cable car."

Pippa gazed up at the spires of the castle high above and gave a thoughtful hum. "Well, hopefully, we won't have to ride up on the outside of the cable car like they did."

Hawke raised an eyebrow. "You've seen it?"

"Of course," she replied, beaming playfully. "I love the old classics."

Her smile reminded Hawke that there were more dangerous things in the world than cable cars.

After gathering their luggage—a pair of garment bags containing formal dinner attire and toilet cases with sundry other items; in addition to aftershave and a change of socks, Hawke's included a Glock 17

concealed in a false bottom—they made their way to the open platform, where a red sky-tram cabin hung idly from one of the overhead
cables.

Two men waited on the platform. One was a slight, middle-aged,
balding man attired in a bland gray summer suit. The other, straining
the seams of his black chauffeur's uniform, looked like someone sent
over from central casting to play the role of castle ogre. Close to seven
feet tall, as big and broad as Hawke's friend Stokely Jones Jr. but with
none of the latter's wit or intellect, the man had a dull, listless affect
and a face that looked like a lump of clay that had been used as a
punching bag.

The smaller man stepped forward and seemed almost to come to
attention. "Good afternoon," he said in thickly accented English. "I am
Rudolf, private secretary to His Royal Highness Prinz Heinrich." And
then he added curtly, "You are expected. Come with me."

Unbidden, the ogre approached Hawke and reached out a massive
hand. It took a moment for Hawke to realize that the man was offering
to take his luggage. When both he and Pippa had passed off their bags,
Rudolf spun on his heel and stepped inside the cabin. Hawke and Pippa
exchanged looks and shrugs and then followed, with the ogre trailing
a few steps behind them.

The car was small by the standards of most skyway trams. Hawke
judged it might hold, at best, a dozen people if they squeezed in like
sardines. There were no seats or any other creature comforts. The only
concessions to riders were the grab handles hanging from metal rails
that ran the length of the cabin on either side. Rudolf slid the door
closed behind them and took hold of one of the handles.

"You should hang on," he advised.

No sooner had Hawke and Pippa grasped their loops than the cabin
lurched and then, rocking gently fore and aft, began to rise. There
were no controls inside the car; evidently, it was operated from one of
the stations or possibly automated like an ordinary lift. Once it was
moving, the car rose smoothly, the motion barely noticeable. Without

the visual reference of the ground falling away beneath them, Hawke would have questioned whether they were moving at all.

Despite the waning daylight, the view was magnificent. The forested hills resembled nothing less than an undulating sea of green, with the lesser peaks of the Ammergau Alps jutting up from their midst like islands. Soon, they were high enough to glimpse the sun, now visible behind those distant summits, shining up at them and illuminating the beautiful medieval spires of Castle Wolkenheim, high above them.

The cable car utilized a system known as a jig-back, in which the two cabins hung off of dedicated suspension lines but were tied into a continuous haul loop, assisted by an electric motor at the bottom station. Much as with a funicular railway, the cabins served as counterweights for each other. When active, the motor would pull one or the other cabin down, which in turn raised the other. When, not quite five minutes after the ascent began, the empty cabin moving in the opposite direction on the neighboring cable passed them by, it served to mark the halfway point in the journey. In the film *Where Eagles Dare*, Richard Burton's character, Major John Smith, had made good use of that moment of passing to leap from one cabin, which he had wired with explosives, to the safety of the other.

Gazing over at the descending car, across a gap of at least twelve feet, Hawke decided the stunt, exciting though it was, could have been accomplished only with movie magic.

Four minutes later, the cabin came to a smooth stop at a station that was a near duplicate of the one at the bottom, some three thousand vertical feet below, save for the fact that, instead of adjoining a car park and being surrounded by forested hills, the platform and operator's shack appeared to be clinging to nearly sheer rock face.

Rudolf slid the cabin door open and with another terse "Come with me" exited the car and strode down the platform to a broad stone staircase cut into the mountain rock that ascended another thirty feet to the threshold of a broad medieval-style fortress gate, complete with an iron portcullis in the raised position. As the fortress was about as ancient as the Eiffel Tower and had never been the site of a battle or held any strategic value, Hawke surmised that the palisade gate was purely a decorative accent, but the effect was nonetheless quite imposing. Between the cable car and the gate, Hawke felt a growing sense of unease. If Konigstahl was the villain Hawke feared he might be, escape would be difficult, if not impossible. With the simple act of boarding the tram car, he and Pippa had surrendered themselves utterly into the Prince's hands.

Too late to turn back now.

Beyond the gate lay an open courtyard about half the length of a football pitch, enfolded on three sides by what appeared to be the residential wings of the castle, and at the far end, another stone staircase ascended to the main porch. Rudolf set a brisk pace as he crossed the courtyard, never once looking back to see if the Prince's guests were keeping up.

Like the portcullis, the heavy ironbound wooden entrance door seemed like an unnecessary affectation, but there was no doubting its sturdiness. Hawke heard the Prince's secretary grunting with the effort of pushing the door open. He then stepped to the side and gestured for Hawke and Pippa to enter. "Prinz Heinrich welcomes you to Schloss Wolkenheim."

"Thanks, old chap," Hawke said, pushing inside with his best show of British aplomb.

Unlike nearby Neuschwanstein and Hohenschwangau Castles, which favored the baroque and rococo styles of interior decoration and elaborate murals depicting scenes from German history and Wagnerian opera, the interior of Wolkenheim was every bit as medieval as its exterior. The walls were bare stone adorned only with weapon displays and mounted trophy heads gazing down at the visitors with fixed glass eyes.

Stairs ascended the walls to either side, meeting at a balcony landing. There was no furniture and only one other door in the center of the far wall, under the balcony. The elaborate chandelier hanging above the center of the room cast onto the floor a circle of electric light that did not quite reach the corners, and despite the fact that they were well above ground level, the space seemed more like the entrance to a dungeon.

As soon as they were inside, a young woman, attired in a gunmetal-gray maid's uniform complete with matching lace choker and bonnet, emerged from the gloom and came over to meet them. She was brunette, with a waifish figure and a rather plain face without any makeup. When she got within a few feet of them, she stopped and curtsied, but her head remained bowed, her eyes downcast as if she were fearful of looking directly at them.

"Good evening, m'lord," said the maid, "and m'lady."

The accent wasn't German.

French maybe? Hawke wondered.

"I'm not a lady," Pippa said quickly, then added, "Well, not a m'lady anyway."

The maid lifted her head just a little and looked in Pippa's direction. "Please excuse, ma'am. Will you and m'lord require separate quarters?"

Pippa started to answer in the affirmative, but Hawke overrode her. "No need for that. We shan't be staying the night. Just take us somewhere we can change for dinner, please."

"As you wish, m'lord. Please, follow me." As she turned and headed for the stairs to the right, Hawke realized that Rudolf seemed to have melted away. The ogre was still there holding their luggage, but there was no sign of the Prince's private secretary.

The maid ascended the steps in a series of rapid little strides that reminded Hawke of the mechanical figurines of an automaton clock and then led them into a maze of corridors and stairs, eventually arriving at a heavy door on what Hawke guessed was the third or fourth floor of the west wing of the castle.

The maid led the way into the room, which was, like everything else in the castle, minimally decorated. There was a bed almost large enough for two; it was topped with a decidedly homespun quilt. In the room, there were also a couple of old wingback chairs that probably dated to the castle's initial construction and an armoire that, like the ogre, was also roughly the size of Stokely Jones Jr. There was a door on one wall that Hawke initially assumed must lead to the lavatory, but the maid disabused him of this notion by throwing the door open to reveal a balcony overlooking the courtyard.

The ogre followed them into the room and, with an efficiency that belied his dull expression, opened the garment bags and hung their contents on the rod in the armoire. Then, without so much as a look in Hawke's direction, he turned and left the room.

"Would you like me to show you the toilet?" asked the maid. With her accent, the word sounded like the French equivalent: *toilette.*

Pippa, nonplussed, managed a tentative "Yes, please," making it sound almost like a question.

"This way." The young woman turned and passed through the still-open door, moving down the hall to another door, upon which someone had helpfully posted a plaque inscribed, in Gothic letters, with the words *die Toilette.*

As she reached for the door handle, Hawke broke in. "I think we can figure the rest out. Thank you."

"Of course, m'lord. Please, make yourselves comfortable. We have cocktails at eight o'clock, with dinner served after. Someone will come to collect you." She executed another curtsy, then scurried away like a windup toy mouse.

Hawke shot a glance at his GMT-Master, mentally adjusting one hour forward for the time zone. It was seven twenty. "I can hardly wait," he murmured.

TWENTY-FOUR

At seven fifty-five, a heavy knock rattled the door in its frame. Hawke did not need psychic powers or X-ray vision to know who was standing on the other side. He opened it and found, as expected, the ogre, still attired in his chauffeur's uniform. "Ah," said Hawke, affecting disappointment, "it's you."

The ogre said nothing, did not even seem to have heard, but simply turned and began walking away, an automaton ponderously following a mechanically programmed directive. Hawke leaned out into the corridor to see if the big man would wait for them but instead saw the man's broad back disappearing around a corner. Fearing that they might lose their only guide through the castle, Hawke called out. "Pip, do come along."

Pippa, looking magnificent in a red satin calf-length Dolce & Gabbana sleeveless dress, hurried as best she could in her Jimmy Choo heels, catching up to Hawke, who had advanced to the corner to maintain a visual fix on the ogre. Moving together, they quickly closed on their unresponsive guide.

The man's behavior . . . his very presence, for that matter, and the simple fact that he, of all the Prince's retainers, had been sent to retrieve them spoke volumes to Hawke about their host. Konigstahl, it seemed, had a penchant for theater. The dramatic locale, the air of mystery about something even as simple as the location of their guest room, the brutish, unspeaking heavy . . . they all felt like something torn from the pages of a pulp spy thriller, with Konigstahl willfully casting himself in the role of megalomaniacal antagonist.

The ogre led them a merry chase through the halls of the castle, choosing a route that was different from the one the maid had taken them on earlier but that nonetheless brought them back in the direction of their original starting point, if Hawke's mental map was not mistaken. The journey finally ended on a south-facing open-air balcony.

In full daylight, the balcony would have commanded a spectacular view of the Ammergau Alps, but with the fall of dusk, the peaks were merely a silhouette against the velvet tapestry of night. The balcony itself was lit, almost predictably, with literal torches—six of them in wrought iron sconces affixed to the wall. The blue-yellow hue of the flames and the absence of smoke or soot stains on the stone suggested that the torches were burning propane or some other gaseous fuel. A similar fire burned from a medieval-looking brazier positioned in the center of the balcony, radiating warmth against the night's chill.

Hawke saw gooseflesh spring up on Pippa's bare arms and, almost without thinking, shrugged out of his silk tuxedo jacket and draped it across her shoulders, an act of chivalry that might have exposed his Glock had he chosen to carry it in a low-profile waistband holster at the small of his back. Fortunately, he had elected instead to wear it up front, concealed by his cummerbund.

The damn thing occasionally had its uses.

He turned to the ogre, ready to demand that he take them back inside, but the man had already departed, disappearing back through the doorway that they had just exited. Without the additional layer of fabric to provide insulation, Hawke felt the cold biting through the thin fabric of his shirt. Almost as a reflex, he put his arm around Pippa and steered her toward the brazier, only then realizing that they were not alone on the balcony.

"Lord Hawke." The voice, a man's with only a hint of an accent, came from behind them and to the left. "Welcome to my humble abode."

Turning, Hawke recognized the man from the photos Pippa had earlier shown him: Prince Heinrich Konigstahl.

If it was the Prince's intent to cosplay as a Bond villain, he failed utterly with respect to physical appearance. He was not maimed, grotesquely obese, or otherwise disfigured. In fact, in his immaculate dinner jacket, he looked more like Bond himself—as described by Ian Fleming—than one of the fictional spy's legendary foils. Yet behind his eyes, there was a glimmer of wanton malice that seemed to confirm Hawke's worst suspicions about the man. There was not a doubt in Hawke's mind that Konigstahl was a sociopath. The only question was whether he was the sociopath Hawke was looking for, the one who had masterminded the abduction of King Charles.

Konigstahl stood in front of a small but well-provisioned bar erected between two of the torch sconces. Alongside him was a willowy figure who looked as though she might have just been plucked off a runway in Milan or perhaps from the set of a music video. Platinum hair styled in a short bob framed a face that appeared angular, exotic even, though a closer look revealed the effect to be a contrivance achieved with makeup. There was something elusively familiar about the woman's face—perhaps it had graced the cover of a fashion magazine Hawke had glimpsed in passing. She wore a glossy black number—patent leather or latex—so tight that it might have been sprayed onto her torso and hips. The garment only just covered her bosom, which, in keeping with her almost gaunt physique, could not even charitably have been described as ample, but her arms and shoulders were left bare. Her exposed skin showed the effects of the chill wind and her nipples were visibly hard and erect beneath the material of her dress, but she did not shiver or give any other outward sign of being cold. Around her throat was a thin leather choker held together with what appeared to be a small heart-shaped padlock.

Hawke brought his gaze back to the Prince. "I'm not sure *humble* is the right word," he said, and then, allowing just enough of a delay to be almost insulting, added, "Highness."

Konigstahl's mouth twitched into a smile. "You're too kind, Lord Hawke. Or shall I just call you Alex?"

"I'd rather prefer it," answered Hawke. "Never had much use for the title anyway."

Konigstahl returned a quizzical gaze as if unable to comprehend Hawke's disdain for his own birthright, then shrugged. "Alex it is. And you must call me Heinrich. Would you care for a drink?"

Without waiting for a reply, he turned to the woman and made a shooing gesture. "Tildy, make my friend Alex whatever he wants."

The blonde tilted her head in a show of submission. "Right away, Your Royal Highness." She then turned to Hawke. "What would you like, m'lord?"

It was only when Hawke heard the voice, with the lilting accent, that he finally placed her. Tildy, Konigstahl's female companion, and the plain-looking maid who had escorted them to their room less than an hour before were one and the same. The transformation, achieved with the use of a wig and the artful application of cosmetics, was nothing short of startling.

More theater, thought Hawke.

Hiding his astonishment, he answered, "Something warm, I should think. Unless you'd care to continue this reception somewhere more agreeable."

A look of mild surprise crossed Konigstahl's face. "I always take my aperitif out here. I find the night air quite bracing. Just the thing before a meal. But if it's too cold for you," he added with a condescending grin, "we can move closer to the fire."

"I was only thinking of the women," replied Hawke, glancing over at Pippa.

She arched an eyebrow in annoyance at his generalization but then addressed Konigstahl. "I'm afraid I didn't dress for the weather, Your Highness."

Konigstahl looked back at her as if only now becoming aware of her presence. After a very obvious and uncomfortably thorough head-to-toe appraisal, he met her gaze. "I don't believe I've had the pleasure, Miss . . ."

"Guinness. Gwendolyn Guinness."

"Gwendolyn." Konigstahl gave a perfunctory bow. "Yes, how very thoughtless of me. We shall move inside. Tildy, we'll take our drinks in the dining room."

"If it pleases Your Highness," replied Tildy. "What shall I bring you?"

"My usual." Konigstahl turned to Hawke. "Laphroaig. Twenty-two-year-old single malt. I've developed quite a fondness for Scotch whisky."

"Never cared much for it myself," lied Hawke. "I'll take a Goslings Black Seal rum if you have it. Neat."

Tildy's already downcast eyes widened in a look of alarm as if the request had exposed some private shame. She turned to gaze at the Prince, a silent plea for him to come to the rescue.

"Alas," sighed Konigstahl, "I'm afraid I don't have anything quite so . . . ah, plebeian. Tildy, I believe there's a bottle of thirty-three-year-old Enmore Demerara single-still dark back there. That should do nicely."

Ignoring the obvious slight, Hawke smiled and addressed Tildy. "Thanks, but if it's all the same, I'll just have a vodka martini. Shaken, not stirred."

"You heard the man," said Konigstahl, seemingly oblivious to the reference.

Tildy curtsied again and started to move away, but Pippa called after her. "I'll have one as well." And then, coyly, added, "Dirty, please."

As they moved inside, Pippa slipped out from under Hawke's jacket and handed it back to him. "Tildy is the maid who showed us to our room," she whispered.

"Noticed that, did you?"

She gave him a hard stare. "I also noticed something else. Her choker."

"What about it?"

"It's a slave collar. They're used in the BDSM lifestyle to signify ownership. She isn't just his employee. She's his slave. He's her master."

Hawke considered this revelation and how it played into his impression of the Prince. "I don't know much about the . . . lifestyle, did you call it? But what two consenting adults do in the privacy of their own . . . well, castle . . . is their business. We didn't come here to kink-shame them."

"I'm not so sure it is consensual," she countered. "And you haven't actually told me *why* we're here."

"Of course I have."

"A vague threat to the Royal Family?" She waved away his denial. "Please. You haven't been straight with me, Alex. I've gone along with this in the hopes that you would trust me with the truth." She cocked a defiant hip. "It seems the Prince and his maid aren't the only ones playing power games here."

Before Hawke could offer further protest, Konigstahl called out, "Do come along, Alex."

Pippa glowered at Hawke a moment longer, then pivoted and started walking in the direction Konigstahl had gone.

They followed their host down a short passage into a vast hall filled with animals or, more accurately, the skins of animals now stuffed as taxidermy mounts. Unlike the trophy heads in the reception hall, these subjects were complete and displayed in lifelike poses. There was a male lion frozen midroar. A snarling jaguar with one paw lifted. An African elephant with its trunk and tusks raised defiantly. Hawke counted more than a dozen specimens in all—including a Cape buffalo, a polar bear, and, in pride of place, the northern white rhinoceros Konigstahl had killed more than a decade before. In the center of the room, surrounded by the lifeless menagerie, were a long oaken dining table and chairs.

Konigstahl moved to the head of the table and the only high-backed chair. "This used to be the Grand Ballroom," he explained. "But as I haven't any use for a ballroom, I decided to house my collection here."

"This is your dining room?" asked Hawke. "Seems a bit crowded."

A thin smile stretched Konigstahl's lips. "You disapprove?"

Hawke shrugged. "It wouldn't be my first choice of decor for a formal dining room." He made a show of surveying the stuffed animals. "You seem to have eclectic tastes."

The offhand remark had the desired effect. Konigstahl's brows came together in a look of bemusement. "Tastes? I don't follow."

Hawke gestured to the animals. "Lions. Bears. Elephants. I believe they call it bushmeat in Africa. I imagine it's an acquired taste. Particularly the carnivores."

The Prince's confusion deepened. "You don't think . . . You don't actually imagine that I eat these animals?"

Hawke, of course, did not, but he was curious to see how Konigstahl would rationalize his hobby. "Don't you? Where I come from, we eat the game we hunt. My good friend King Charles and his family put game on the table at Balmoral Castle. Actually, I've just come from there."

Hawke watched for any sign of a reaction at the mention of the King and Balmoral. Konigstahl, however, threw back his head in a peal of laughter. "My dear Alex, I do not hunt to eat. That is what animals do."

"No? Then why do it at all? Just for sport?"

The Prince's humor ebbed as quickly as it had risen, and his expression hardened. He leaned forward as if sharing a secret. "Power. It's as simple as that. These animals are the deadliest creatures on earth. By hunting and killing them, I demonstrate my superiority."

"I thought man was the deadliest animal," interjected Pippa.

Konigstahl regarded her with poorly concealed contempt. "What would you know of it? A woman?"

Pippa did not relent. "Quite a lot, actually. You see, women are the wives and mothers of all those men who go out to kill each other. Or get killed."

The Prince dismissed her with a sniff and then returned his attention to Hawke. "It requires hardly any skill at all to kill a man. Ask any soldier."

Hawke thought it sounded as though Konigstahl was speaking from experience. "You don't think man's intelligence and cunning make him a more dangerous foe?"

"You are perhaps thinking of that ridiculous short story 'The Most Dangerous Game'? Pure fiction. Most men, in fact, have utterly lost their survival instinct. Hunting them would pose no challenge whatsoever. One might as well shoot sheep in a pasture."

"Good to know that you draw the line somewhere," said Hawke with a forced chuckle.

Konigstahl smiled without humor. "I did say *most* men. Not all men are created equal after all." He narrowed his gaze at Hawke. "You and I are the living proof, are we not?" Then, without missing a beat, he looked past Hawke. "Ah, here's Tildy with our drinks."

Right on cue, Tildy stepped out from the midst of the trophy collection, carrying a tray upon which rested two cocktail glasses and an old-fashioned glass. She went first to Konigstahl, who took the latter, then to Hawke, and only then to Pippa.

The Prince raised his glass. "To the hunt."

"To the hunt," echoed Hawke, meaning something entirely different.

TWENTY-FIVE

No more was said on the subject of hunting or anything else of substance during the dinner service, which consisted of five courses beginning with an appetizer of *Obatzda*—a creamy cheese spread made with Camembert, onions, and paprika—and soft pretzels for dipping. This was followed by a hearty potato soup with leeks, smoked bacon, and soft bread dumplings.

The main course was *Schweinshaxe*—slow-roasted pork knuckle with crispy skin served with mustard and sauerkraut and a side of fluffy bread dumplings. This was followed by the cheese course—*Allgäuer Bergkäse*, a semihard cheese procured locally and served with crusty bread—and the dessert—*Apfelstrudel* drizzled with warm vanilla custard.

Konigstahl attacked the meal with gusto, supplying commentary on each course as it was delivered by, of all people, the ogre, now attired in kitchen whites. The Prince was quite proud of the fare. "Good traditional Bavarian food prepared by Chef Gustav from Königliche Brauerei in Munich."

Konigstahl, Hawke suspected, was a man who confused expense with quality. He had clearly spared none of the former in commissioning the repast, but his chef had somehow missed the mark. The potatoes in the *Kartoffelsuppe* were undercooked, the pork knuckle was both greasy and gristly, and the strudel had almost the same consistency as the soup. The cheese was at least passable. Hawke ate sparingly, and not just because he found the cuisine somewhat less than appetizing. His instincts told him that he would need his wits about him. He couldn't afford to have his mind or body rendered sluggish by excess.

As the silent ogre bore the dessert dishes away, Konigstahl turned to Tildy. "Bring the schnapps." Then, before Hawke could decline the digestif, the Prince fixed him with his stare. "Now, down to business. Why are you here, friend Alex?"

If the abruptness of the transition had been meant to catch Hawke off guard, it failed utterly. He'd spent the better part of the evening considering how to broach the subject, and with Konigstahl effectively opening the door, he charged through.

"Well, it's this Scottish business . . . the referendum for independence. Perhaps you've heard about it?"

Konigstahl brought his fingers together beneath his chin in a thoughtful pose. "I have been following the news quite closely." He paused a beat before adding, "I'm sure you realize why or else you wouldn't be here."

Hawke decided to just yank off the plaster. "Then the rumors I've been hearing are true. You intend to lay claim to the Throne of Scotland?"

"You cut right to the heart of the matter, Alex. I admire that. But I'll admit, I'm a bit surprised. Your countrymen are not usually so forthright."

"I find it saves time."

The Prince nodded slowly. "This matter of the succession is a delicate business. I have no standing whatsoever to lay claim to any throne. My great-uncle His Royal Highness Duke Franz is the true heir to the Scottish Throne. And the Throne of the United Kingdom as well. He has, of course, shown no interest in claiming his birthright, but if the Scottish people were to ask him to take it"—he shrugged—"who can say if he might change his mind?"

"Hmm, yes, but I think you're betting that he won't. And that none

of the other names ahead of you in the line of succession will. I've spoken with Ewan MacAlpin of the Stewards of Alba. He says you've all
but made a formal declaration."

Konigstahl's only reaction was a slight narrowing of the eyes. "And
what is your interest in all of this, Lord Hawke?"

Hawke did not fail to notice the switch back to formal address and
the sudden frostiness of Konigstahl's tone. "Oh, just doing a favor for
my friend the King. The *actual* King."

"A favor?"

"Well, yes. You see, he's heard about this succession business, and
he wants to know just how serious you are about it all, how far you'd be
willing to go."

Hawke was peripherally aware of Pippa sitting up a little straighter.

Konigstahl stared at Hawke for a long moment, a moment that was
interrupted when Tildy returned bearing a tray with three cordial
glasses and a frosted bottle with a label that Hawke didn't recognize.
Yet, even then, the Prince's stare did not break.

"The throne belongs to the House of Wittelsbach," he said. "I am
very serious about restoring my family's rightful legacy."

"Even if you're not the one sitting on that throne?"

"Without question."

"And you would do anything to make that happen?"

"Anything?" Konigstahl leaned back in his chair and shrugged. "Now
that covers a broad range of possibilities."

"Then, since I know you appreciate a direct approach," said Hawke,
"let me put it to you this way: Would you take the throne by violence?"

Beside him, Pippa sucked in a breath through her teeth. Konigstahl, however, seemed unruffled by the question. "What an interesting
idea. I suppose the answer to that would be an emphatic *yes.*" He smiled
and added, "But, lest your friend get the wrong idea, neither I nor anyone else in House Wittelsbach is raising an army. And I do not imagine
one will be at all necessary."

Hawke parsed the Prince's statement and studied the man's face for some indication of duplicity. He was no closer to having an answer to his question than when he began, and yet, short of coming right out and asking, he could think of no way to determine if Konigstahl was involved in the King's abduction.

Konigstahl did not give him the chance. He rose and began taking the glasses from the tray held by a still-standing Tildy. He placed one each in front of Hawke and Pippa and retained the last for himself. "To the King," he said, raising his glass. "Long may he reign, whoever he is."

From the corner of his eye, Hawke saw Pippa's questioning glance, but he held Konigstahl's gaze. "As much as I appreciate the offer, to say nothing of the sentiment, I'm afraid I will have to abstain. It's gotten rather late, and we've a bit of a drive."

"A *drive?*" That seemed to surprise Konigstahl. "Surely, you're not serious."

"Deadly, in fact," said Hawke. "I'm afraid we must. Other plans, you see."

"You misunderstand. You *cannot* leave. It is impossible."

"Look, old chap, you can't keep us here."

A hint of a smile touched Konigstahl's lips. "You misunderstand, Alex."

So, we're back to Alex again, thought Hawke.

"The cable car operator has gone home for the night. There is no other way off the mountain."

This revelation sent a chill down Hawke's spine. His apprehension when boarding the tram now seemed wholly justified. He and Pippa were indeed trapped in Wolkenheim Castle.

"I apologize for any inconvenience," the Prince went on. "If I had known that it was not your intention to spend the night, I would have made arrangements to keep the cable car open."

Hawke recalled that he had, in fact, told Tildy the maid that they wouldn't be staying but saw no benefit to pointing this out. It had always been Konigstahl's plan to keep them here, completely under his control.

Well, he thought, *we'll just see about that.*

Hawke managed a smile. "Well, if it can't be helped, then it can't be helped. We shall just have to make the most of it." He picked up the cordial glasses, handed one to Pippa, then raised his own. "To King Charles III. Long may he reign."

Konigstahl did not contest Hawke's modification of the toast but simply tipped back his glass and downed the contents in a single gulp. Hawke took only a small sip of the liqueur—berry flavored and overly sweet. He did not care for schnapps under the best of circumstances, and this certainly wasn't that.

"Speaking of your friend Charles," said Konigstahl, "did I hear you say that you had just come from Balmoral Castle?"

Hawke felt a fresh wave of apprehension wash over him. *So, he was paying attention.* "You did," he replied. "And I did."

The Prince gave a slow nod. "And you saw him? Charles, I mean. You spoke to him?"

The questions set Hawke's blood roaring in his ears.

He bloody knows.

"It's just that there's been talk," the Prince went on, "that nobody has seen him in quite some time. There are rumors that he may be . . . indisposed." He held Hawke's gaze. "But if you've just come from Balmoral, then you must already know what's going on."

Hawke did his best to affect an expression of mild surprise. "Where on earth are you hearing this rubbish?"

Konigstahl waved his hand in the air as if shooing away a fly. "Where I heard doesn't matter. What matters is whether there is any truth to the rumor. The monarch's place is on the throne, especially when the fate of the kingdom hangs in the balance. In 1689, my ancestor King James escaped to Europe, fleeing for his life in the face of an insurrection. Parliament decided that this amounted to an abdication of the throne and, in violation of the rule of primogeniture, illegally awarded the crown to Mary."

Standing, Konigstahl placed his empty cordial glass on the table. "Now it seems history has repeated itself. At the hour of greatest need, King Charles is nowhere to be found. If House Windsor is not up to the task of leading the kingdom, perhaps it's time to return the throne to the rightful heir.

"That is all I have to say on the matter. Klaus will show you to your room." He extended a hand, which Tildy dutifully took in her own. "Good night, Alex," he said, and then turned and strode away, half dragging Tildy, who moved with her mincing, mechanical steps. No sooner had he departed than the ogre—Klaus, presumably—materialized, made a come-along gesture, then turned and began lurching away.

"Alex!" hissed Pippa. "What the hell was he talking about?"

"Not here," Hawke said, raising a finger to his lips. He took Pippa's arm and steered her through the lifeless menagerie in pursuit of their guide. Pippa continued glowering at him but waited until they were back in the room and alone to vent her ire.

"Just what the hell is going on?" she demanded again. "You said there was a threat against the Family, but the way the Prince was talking, something's already happened to the King. Alex, what aren't you telling me?"

"Keep your voice down," Hawke warned. "No telling who might be listening in."

"I think it hardly matters at this point. Konigstahl already seems to know everything, which is certainly more than I can say for myself. Now, talk, Alex."

Hawke sighed. "The King has been abducted."

Even though the answer could not have come as much of a surprise, Pippa pressed a hand to her mouth. "Oh, my. By whom?"

"We don't know, and that's the problem. The PM put Ambrose Congreve on the case, and he brought me into the fold."

"When did this happen?"

"Two mornings ago. At Balmoral Castle. There were at least two members of the household staff involved in the caper. Unfortunately, both were killed before they could answer any questions."

"Why hasn't Six been read in on this?"

Hawke sighed. "The PM insisted on absolute secrecy. It wasn't my call."

"She had no right to make that decision. The monarchy is at stake." She narrowed her gaze at him. "You think Prince Heinrich is behind it?"

"He knows about it. Whether that makes him the mastermind or merely part of the conspiracy, I can't say."

"You must have had your suspicions already. Otherwise, why come here?"

"It was Congreve's idea, really. He's following a different angle. Northern Ireland. One of the chaps we flushed out into the open had ties to the New IRA. But Ambrose didn't want to put all our eggs in that basket, so he asked me to inquire discreetly of Sir David about other possible bad actors who might want to influence the Scottish vote by taking Charles out of play. You were the one who pointed me at the Stewards of Alba Party. That's why we're here."

"What could he possibly hope to gain? It's not like he can force Charles to set aside the crown."

"Can't he?"

"An abdication made under duress would have no merit. Even if it did, the crown would simply pass to William. Even Charles can't cede the crown to a Stuart heir. That would require an act of Parliament."

"The PM believes that the purpose of the abduction is to weaken the position of the remain vote in the Scottish referendum. She believes that by silencing Charles at the eleventh hour, as it were, Scottish voters might lose faith in the monarchy. That would play into Konigstahl's larger plan to make a claim to the Throne of Scotland."

Pippa appeared to consider this for a moment. She went to her toiletry case and took out her phone. "I'm calling Sir David. Don't try to stop me."

"Wouldn't dream of it," replied Hawke.

Then she froze in place, staring at the screen. "No signal."

Hawke retrieved his own mobile and saw the same indication. "Try it from the balcony," he suggested.

Pippa opened the door and stepped out, holding her phone high and staring at the screen, but no bars appeared. "Wonderful. There must be a landline here somewhere."

"I would actually be surprised if there was. Prince Heinrich doesn't seem like the sort of chap who would permit unrestricted communication with the outside world."

Pippa just looked at him, concern dawning in her expression. "Do you think Charles is being kept *here?*"

Hawke had been wondering that very thing ever since Konigstahl's tacit admission of involvement. "If he is, I'm not sure there's anything the two of us can do about it."

"Then what can we do?"

"The first thing we're going to do is get the hell out of here."

"You heard the Prince, Alex. The cable car is shut down for the night. There's no other way off the mountain."

"That is what he told us." Hawke smiled. "Now, let's see if he was telling the truth."

TWENTY-SIX

The King sat on the mattress in his cell, head bowed, forehead pressed against his knees, which he hugged close to his chest as if attempting to occupy as little space as possible. It was all he could think to do. He was holding on for dear life—barely—but with no end in sight, no light at the end of the tunnel, his will to endure was flagging.

Roddy's screams had torn his heart in two, but when they had abruptly stopped, the silence was even worse.

"Bastards!" he had raged. "Bloody bastards, you killed him!"

But then, after maybe half an hour, the wailing resumed, and he understood that McClanahan had simply passed out, only to be revived by their captors to endure another round of torture.

When silence fell again, Charles did not cry out, did not even lift his head. Though he was ashamed to think it, part of him hoped that McClanahan *had* died because then at least he would suffer no more. But after another interval of quiet, Roddy's torments resumed.

How many times this cycle repeated, Charles could not say. He tried covering his ears to shut out the screams. He shouted himself hoarse, cursing the villains for their cruelty, but never once did he consider giving them what they wanted. He would die first.

Then, after what seemed like several hours and an unusually long period of silence, the door opened. Charles looked up from his huddle to see Mr. Sten entering.

"Bastard," rasped Charles.

"Majesty," replied Sten sardonically. He held up a sheet of parchment—a duplicate copy of the Instrument of Abdication. "Have you reconsidered your position?"

"Go to hell."

Sten tilted his head to the side. "Not even to spare your loyal retainer further suffering?"

"How dare you put that on me?" snarled the King. "You're the one using torture, not me."

"You could end his torment with the stroke of a pen."

"And you could end it by simply showing some human decency."

Sten spat a derisive laugh. "What would you know of human decency? Raised in a palace. Your every whim catered to." He laughed again. "You don't even put the toothpaste on your own toothbrush. You're a spoiled child who never had to work for anything in his life."

Charles felt his cheeks flush with the heat of the accusations.

Sten wasn't finished. "And now, holding the fate of another man in your hands, is it any wonder you lack the spine to make the right decision? The *only* decision."

Charles wiped a hand across his face. "Even if . . . even if I signed that, it wouldn't mean anything. Not if you forced me to do it."

"Then there's no reason not to sign."

For just a moment, his resolve began to falter. *It's just a piece of paper. Words on a piece of paper. It won't mean anything. I'll still be the King, and Roddy . . .*

The gamekeeper's defiant shout echoed in his memory. *"Don't give in, sire."*

And his own exhortation, *"Keep faith, Roddy!"*

If he gave in, even if only symbolically, then all of Roddy's suffering would be in vain. He had to stand fast.

"I told you, I'll die before I give up the crown."

Sten nodded slowly, then turned and gestured with one hand. Two more masked men appeared in the doorway, bracing the groggy form of Roderick McClanahan between them. Charles's heart sank. Roddy was barely recognizable. His face was puffy and dark with bruises. His lips were encrusted with dried blood. His left eye was swollen shut, but his right found Charles and his split lips managed something almost like a smile.

"Majesty," he croaked.

"I've no doubt that you would rather die than give up your life of privilege," said Sten. "But would you give it up to save his life?"

Charles thrust his jaw forward in a show of defiance. "This man is willing to die for me. The least I can do to honor his sacrifice is to hold faith."

"If that's your decision . . ."

At a nod from Sten, the masked men dropped McClanahan to his knees. Then one of them slipped a heavy black cloth sack over McClanahan's head. Sten produced a pistol, which he pressed to the back of the hooded head.

"Last chance, Your Majesty."

Charles let silence be his final answer. He didn't really believe that Sten would go through with it, so when the air in the small room suddenly rang with a report and a gout of blood burst from the hood to spray directly in his face, Charles let out a yelp of surprise.

Oh, God! He did it. He actually did it.

As if in slow motion, he saw McClanahan tilt forward and collapse face down on the floor. Then Sten's men scooped up the lifeless body and dragged it from the room, trailing a long stripe of red.

"This is on your head, Majesty," Sten said gravely, and then he too was gone.

———

Sitting in his control room, the Magician replayed the video of the execution and savored the look of absolute shock on the face of the British monarch as Sten carried out his threat.

Still, as much as he enjoyed inflicting such psychic injuries upon the unworthy King, he couldn't help but feel a sense of failure. The Magician had not believed Charles would be so dogged in his determination to keep the crown. But then again, he supposed, the man had lived his entire life waiting to assume the throne. If he didn't have that, what did he have?

September 8, 2022
Balmoral Estate, Scotland

The Queen is dead!

Word spread quickly throughout the household staff, though the news hardly came as a surprise. She was after all an old woman—ninety-six, the longest-lived monarch ever to hold the throne.

When she had come to Balmoral, her favorite residence, it was understood that she had come there to die. And yet, because she had always been the Queen, the only one most of her subjects had ever known, it was difficult to imagine the world without her in it. Indeed, even at her advanced age, she rejected the notion of retirement and continued to carry out her royal duties. Why, just two days earlier, she had accepted the resignation of Prime Minister Boris Johnson and met personally with his successor, inviting Conservative MP Liz Truss to establish a new government in her name. A photograph taken shortly before that meeting showed her looking surprisingly robust for a woman of her age and smiling as if expecting to see many more sunrises.

And yet those closest to her knew that the end was nigh. Following the meeting with the new Prime Minister, she had taken a turn for the worse. The Family had been summoned. Princess Anne had been staying with her. Prince Charles had arrived earlier that morning. The rest of the children and grandchildren would not arrive in time to bear witness to her passing at three ten that afternoon. The rest of the world would receive official notice some three hours later.

For the man who would one day assume the nom de guerre the Magician, the Queen's passing reignited the coals of rage that had smoldered for years, cooling but never extinguished. Despite his antipathy for the institution of the monarchy, he, like many of his fellow citizens—he misliked the term subjects—*had felt for Elizabeth the same sort of affection they had for their grandmothers. If she had a flaw, it was that she had failed to raise upright, moral children and failed to keep her own house in order, but experience had taught him that there was only so much a parent could do.*

With her death and the automatic succession of Charles to the throne, those coals had been uncovered to blaze once more.

When he had returned home after completing his university studies, he had done exactly what he had been expected to do and had gone into what his father often referred to as "the Family business." It had not been an easy thing to do. He had gone to uni for the express purpose of breaking free of that life and earning his own way in the world, but Liv had assured him that he could do far more to change the trajectory of the world by returning home than by striking out on his own. So, he had swallowed his pride, buried his true feelings deep, and begun working as an apprentice to his father.

For the most part, he actually enjoyed the work, which kept him occupied both physically and mentally. He could almost forget why his job even existed. But then the Family would come to visit, all those suppressed feelings would rise to the surface, and it would require every ounce of self-control on his part to keep a look of contempt off his face when in their presence. Fortunately, because it was considered unseemly to look any of them in the eye, his disdain went unnoticed even when his self-discipline slipped.

Year by year, his responsibilities increased, and while the rage never went away, the idea that he was doing all of this in pursuit of some secret, world-changing ideal began to fade. And yet, inevitably, just when he would begin to wonder if maybe none of it mattered that much anyway, a new scandal would emerge and bring that distant objective back into focus.

There was the dissolution of the marriage of Prince Charles and Princess Diana, and then, just a year later, Diana's death, along with that of her Egyptian lover, and the ensuing rumors of foul play, perhaps orchestrated by the royals themselves.

Then there was Prince Andrew's association with the notorious pedophile Jeffrey Epstein and accusations of sex with underage women at Epstein's private pleasure island.

The next generation of royals was no better. Persistent rumors of infidelity hovered around Prince William. Prince Harry moved from one scandal to the next. Accusations of alcohol and drug abuse and even cheating followed him from Eton to Sandhurst. Even more egregious was his marriage to an American actress who was of mixed race, no less.

Still, while the Queen lived, the Magician's animus toward the House of Windsor had never approached critical mass, and the people to whom he had once pledged to serve as a time bomb did not contact him.

With her death, that changed.

When he returned to his cottage that evening, he found a large envelope on his doorstep. Thinking it to be some piece of correspondence relating to his duties, he almost tossed it aside, but an odd premonition made him take a second look. The absence of a return address intrigued him, as did the heft of the parcel, so he tore it open and found a cheap mobile phone—the first of many he would have occasion to use—and a small piece of paper containing instructions on how to activate the device.

His curiosity was now fully piqued, and he followed the instructions after entering the generic password as directed. Next, he saw that there was a text message waiting in the inbox.

Two words.

Call me.

He did and was not at all surprised to hear a familiar voice on the other end of the line ask, "Do you still want to change the world?"

PRESENT DAY

Exactly what that change would look like was not immediately apparent. At the beginning, there was talk—always in carefully indirect terms when speaking over the phone, which was the only way they communicated—of a possible assassination or a bomb attack aimed at the Family during one of their regular hunting holidays. The abduction of one of the heirs was proposed. The problem wasn't *what* to do but rather *when* to do it.

It was all about the timing. Simply attacking the Family often backfired, generating sympathy for them, at least in the short term. That was what had happened after the terrorist attack a few years earlier. No, for maximum effect, the action—whatever shape it would take—would have to coincide with some major domestic crisis.

The Magician's partners in crime, so to speak, did not desire one particular outcome over another. All they really wanted was to send ripples of chaos throughout the Western world in order to advance a global political agenda.

He had long since outgrown their socialist worldview. Years of enduring the haughtiness of the Royal Family had made it personal. He switched the screen back to the live feed from the camera hidden in the King's cell. Charles had not moved an inch, had not even made an attempt to wipe away the blood from his face. "My goodness, Mr. Sten," he said, "I think we may have actually broken him."

Sten—his real name was Pieter van der Berg—delighted in his role as the King's tormentor. The scion of a wealthy Afrikaner industrialist, he had as a young boy watched his family's wealth and status, to say nothing of his prospects for a secure future, evaporate when the nations of the West, chiefly led by Prime Minister Margaret Thatcher with the full support of Queen Elizabeth II, turned on white South Africa and feted the terrorist Mandela as some sort of messianic savior. The reversal of fortune had played no small part in van der Berg's subsequent decision to become a military officer and then, later, the founder of Strategic Vanguard Services. Although he had found monetary success in these endeavors, it had come at a cost—a broken family, children who wanted nothing to do with him, and, though he was a relatively young forty-eight, a warrior's body racked with chronic pain. His suffering had engendered a deep hatred for the British, especially the King.

His hard face and light blond hair now visible with his mask removed, Sten stared down at the monitor and sneered. "He didn't think I'd really do it, did he?"

"No, I don't believe he did."

"So now that we've given up our only leverage, what do we do?"

"We press ahead. A signed abdication would have been a nice prop, but it was never essential to the plan."

Sten shrugged. "Seems like a lot of wasted effort, then."

"Believe me, it was worth it if only to see that look on his face." The Magician might have expounded further on this topic, for he knew that antipathy toward the institution of the monarchy was something Sten and he shared, but at that moment, his phone began vibrating in his pocket.

The phone was a disposable, no-contract mobile—what the Americans called a burner; its number was known by only a handful of people under strict instructions not to call unless it was an emergency of the highest order. Phone conversations were not nearly as secure as the general public believed, and the devices themselves were like homing beacons that could be used by law enforcement to pinpoint one's location. If one of his associates was calling, it could only mean dire news.

He tapped the screen icon to accept the call. "Yes?"

"Sean is dead."

The Magician grimaced, and not just because the man on the other end of the line—Dylan Fahey—had indiscreetly spoken his brother's Christian name and the word *dead* over an unsecured line. "I'm so sorry. What happened?"

There was a heavy sigh over the line, and when Dylan went on, the grief in his voice was palpable. "I'm not sure. Someone caught up to him just as he was about to leave. G2 maybe. I don't know. He was shot in the back. Bled out."

The Magician winced. Mobile phone conversations, especially international calls, were monitored by automated systems that listened for certain words and phrases that might indicate criminal activity or a possible imminent terror threat. It was easy enough to evade the automated eavesdroppers with well-chosen doublespeak, but with his emotions running high, Dylan obviously wasn't thinking about doing that.

The Magician didn't know if *shot in the back* was one of those signal phrases, but using the words in the same sentence as *G2*—the commonly used name for the Cuban intelligence service—was a potential red flag. He needed to end the call as quickly as possible. There was just one piece of information the Magician needed from Dylan.

"And the package? What happened to it?"

"He saved your bleeding package," snarled Dylan. "Gave his life to do it."

The Magician breathed a relieved sigh. "You have my condolences, of course. Your brother was a true patriot. I promise his sacrifice will not be in vain."

"Do you, now?"

"Do I what?"

"Promise? Sean is dead. And now I've got a couple peelers here sniffing around, asking questions."

The Magician's breath caught in his throat. That Sean Fahey had run into trouble was unfortunate, but given what he had been sent to do, there had been a degree of risk involved. But what had put the police onto Fahey's people in Londonderry?

"What kind of questions?" he asked hesitantly.

"The kind we shouldn't be discussing over the phone," replied Dylan, finally showing a modicum of discretion. "But somebody put them onto us. So, I ask again, can you promise that Sean didn't die for nothing? That we're really going to be able to pull this off?"

"Is the package in your possession?"

"It's in transit now. I'll have it by this time tomorrow. Provided nothing else goes wrong."

"Then I promise," replied the Magician. "This will happen."

"What do you want me to do about the peelers?"

The Magician considered this for a moment. "Let me look into that. I'll get back to you shortly at your first alternate number. Do you understand?"

"Yeah, I understand" was the contemptuous reply. Then the line went dead.

The Magician let out his breath in a sigh, then quickly disassembled the disposable, removing the battery and the SIM card.

"Problem?" asked Sten warily.

"Maybe." The Magician handed him the now defunct mobile. "Destroy it. And make sure everyone is ready to move. Just in case."

Sten raised an eyebrow. "Do you think they're onto us?"

"That's what I intend to discover." He retrieved another disposable phone from a box in the corner of the room, powered it up, and composed a text message.

Two words.

Call me.

He did not have to wait long. Five minutes later, the phone vibrated with an incoming call. When the connection was established, an electronically distorted voice said, "This had better be important."

"Of course it's important," snapped the Magician. "Otherwise, I wouldn't have contacted you. I'm the one who established the emergency protocol, remember?"

"I'm listening." Though it was impossible to tell with the voice modulator, he thought he detected a note of contrition in the words.

"I've just heard from our friends in the north. They've received some unexpected attention."

"I'm not surprised. You left a couple of loose ends behind. Guess where they led."

The Magician was dismayed to hear that the *loose ends*—Colm Keaney and Ian Clewen—had already been exposed and, presumably, arrested. They didn't know anything that could lead back to the Magician, but they would certainly give the police a place to begin looking. "This is a problem."

"Yes, but it's not *my* problem. Look, our friends in the north were always going to take the blame. This just hastens things along."

"*That's* the problem. It's too soon. You've got to find a way to slow this down."

For the first time in the conversation, the person on the other end of the line hesitated before answering. "I'm afraid I can't do that."

"You'd better. You're the only one who can."

"No. There's too much risk."

"If our northern friends panic, the whole thing could fall apart."

"Then you do something. You are the bloody Magician, aren't you?"

The Magician frowned at the casual use of his nom de guerre. It was unlikely that the authorities were even aware of his existence, but it was the little details, like horseshoe nails, upon which everything depended. "What can I do?"

"Do what you always do. Create a distraction." There was a pause. "I have to go. Don't call me again."

The parting admonition was unnecessary. Unlike the Magician, the person on the other end of the line had just the one burner phone, and now that it had been used, any further contact would be impossible. He had wasted the call, though the outcome was hardly surprising. They were all taking a tremendous risk, but the person on the other end of the call had a lot farther to fall if the truth ever came out.

As he broke down the mobile, he considered the advice he'd just received. *You are the bloody Magician, aren't you? . . . Create a distraction.*

He had created a distraction when he'd employed Colm Keaney to double for the King. He had always intended that Keaney's association with the New IRA—which had never amounted to anything more than liking a few social media posts that were sympathetic to the Republican cause—would be discovered in due course, focusing the police inquiry on a resurgent NIRA. His mistake had been in thinking it would take the police at least a couple of days to single out Keaney and Clewen from the household staff at Balmoral Castle. Now he needed to distract the police from the distraction but only for a day or so. Just long enough to get everything back on schedule.

The Magician turned the problem over in his head. There was always a solution to be found; sometimes, it just required looking at the problem from a different perspective. He had always been good at lateral thinking.

"A couple peelers here sniffing around . . ."

He wanted the police sniffing around. He just didn't want them rolling up Dylan and the rest of the NIRA cell, not only preventing them from carrying out their part in the Magician's grand plan but also revealing the fact that the Irishmen knew fuck all about the King's abduction.

He could tell Fahey to go to ground, move the operation somewhere else, and carry on, but that might just spook the Irishman and make him abandon the operation altogether.

No, a quiet retreat wasn't the answer. Successful magic tricks relied on big distractions to misdirect the audience's attention away from what was really going on.

He knew just the thing.

He took out another disposable phone and entered Dylan Fahey's first alternate number. If the Irishman had followed his protocol, he would have destroyed the burner he had used in the earlier conversation and activated the one to which this number was assigned.

Dylan answered almost right away. "I hope you have some good news for me."

"That depends," replied the Magician. "Are both of the trucks fully operational?"

"Yeah. Just waiting on the package."

"I'm changing the plan. We don't need both trucks to deliver the package. One can do the job. Here's what I want you to do with the other."

Explaining his new plan in innocuous language that would not be flagged by any intelligence agencies proved to be a bit of a challenge, but Dylan had no trouble following along.

"Oh, I like this plan," he said when the Magician had finished.

"I thought you might."

TWENTY-SEVEN

Ross Sutherland peered through the windscreen, searching the area revealed in the Rover's headlamps and trying in vain to pierce the veil of darkness that lay beyond. The woods of St. Columb's Park, a playground for the residents of Londonderry during daylight, now seemed ominous and full of menace.

"I don't like this," he murmured, glancing over at Congreve.

Congreve hummed around the stem of his unlit pipe. "No. Nor do I. It's all a bit too melodramatic for my taste. But it can't be helped. Duggan chose this location for our meeting, and he's at much greater risk than you or I if he's found out. Besides, with you watching my back, I've nothing to fear."

Sutherland frowned. "And who's going to be watching my back?"

Congreve, pretending not to hear, opened the door and got out. The night air was cool but not uncomfortably so, and despite Sutherland's misgivings, the location wasn't nearly as secluded as it might have appeared at first glance. The park was situated on seventy acres, bordered to the west and north by the River Foyle and to the south and east by upscale homes and businesses in the Waterside section of the city. Like any urban park, St. Columb's saw its fair share of illicit and borderline-illegal activity after dark, but Congreve reckoned there was little to fear from the park's shadow dwellers. Moreover, unlike Bogside—or, for that matter, most of the rest of the city—Waterside was predominantly Protestant and Unionist and, therefore, somewhat more welcoming to two strangers who couldn't have looked more like policemen if they'd been wearing uniforms.

Still, Congreve wasn't going to take anything for granted. He absently patted the hard shape of his trusty .450 short-barreled Webley Metropolitan Police Revolver—the very same model of weapon carried by Holmes in *The Sign of the Four*. With the firearm presently tucked in the right front pocket of his greatcoat, he surreptitiously scanned the shadows, ready to react to any hint of trouble.

Sensing no peril, he set out across the green to the east of the car park, crossing to the start of the footpath that wove through the forested landscape, providing access to the park's many unique amenities, which included a ropes course and zip line park, numerous and varied sports pitches, and a disc golf course. Congreve, an avid golfer, had no earthly idea what disc golf was. The park also held the ruins of St. Brecan's Church. Built in the sixteenth century from the remains of a much older structure dating back to the twelfth century, the church was believed to be the oldest structure in Derry. It was also where Padraig Duggan had instructed Congreve to meet him.

With Sutherland trailing behind at a distance of about fifty yards and providing overwatch, Congreve made his way along a broad path lit by evenly spaced streetlights. The walkway cut across the green and hooked to the left around a section of woods that hid his destination from view. As he caught sight of the ruins in a small clearing, Congreve paused to stuff his Briar, using the moment to conduct a visual sweep of his surroundings before approaching the site of the old church.

The ruins consisted of not much more than two partially intact opposite-facing stone walls, each with a window opening, but it required only a little imagination to visualize the church as it might have looked five hundred years past. Congreve started forward, searching the shadows for the informant.

"That's close enough," hissed a voice from behind the wall.

Congreve halted. Evidently, this was not to be a face-to-face meeting.

"Are you sure you weren't followed?" asked the disembodied voice.

"We were careful," replied Congreve. "My associate is hanging back to ensure our privacy."

The other man, presumably Duggan, grunted. "That was right ballsy of you to walk into Seamus's place like that. What would you have done if I hadn't shown up when I did?"

"I imagine things would have gotten rather ugly," admitted Congreve. "However, it couldn't be helped. We are on a mission of some urgency. Time is a luxury we do not have. The Crown faces a dire threat, of which we know far too little. I hope you'll forgive me for using the direct approach. The fact that you requested this clandestine meeting suggests that my actions, however provocative, were warranted."

Duggan grunted again. "Well, you may be right about that. There's something going on all right, but no one's talking to me."

Congreve felt a twinge of foreboding at the vagueness of the answer but pressed on. "What *do* you know?"

"That's just it. They've shut me out. After you left, I started asking around. Asking why the police were suddenly taking an interest in our activities again when I knew we weren't up to nothing. Everyone denied knowing anything, but I could tell they weren't being straight with me."

Congreve contemplated this revelation. He'd been counting on Duggan to provide real information, not conjecture based merely on a suspicious reaction. "*Who* has shut you out? There must be a ringleader."

Duggan was silent for a long moment. "Aye. Could be Dylan."

"Dylan?"

"Dylan Fahey. Local boy. His father was one of my mates. Got killed near the end of the Troubles. Got caught out by a bunch of

Tartans and got his belly slit open. It was a struggle for the family after that. Dylan and his brother, Sean, had to grow up fast. They're good boys, though. Served in the Army. Sean was in the Paras. Now he works for one of those mercenary outfits."

Duggan paused again, and Congreve sensed the other man was trying to talk himself out of his suspicions. Rather than prompt him with more questions, Congreve simply waited, and at length, Duggan went on. "Make no mistake. Those boys carry a lot of anger, but I've never heard either of them condone violent action against anyone, least of all the Royal Family."

"But . . . ?"

"But . . ." Duggan echoed. "Dylan *is* a natural leader. The other boys all look up to him. If he decided to do something . . . well, there's a few who would follow."

Sensing that Duggan had nothing more to add, Congreve said, "Thank you for coming forward with this. You just may have prevented an unspeakable tragedy."

When Duggan did not respond, he went on. "I promise that we will be discreet in our investigation. If you learn anything more, please do not hesitate to contact me."

Congreve waited, hoping for some kind of acknowledgment, but there was only silence. "Duggan?"

Nothing.

His message delivered, Padraig Duggan had apparently melted away into the shadows.

The clandestine rendezvous had not yielded the sort of incontrovertible evidence Congreve had been hoping for, but at least he had a name.

Dylan Fahey.

That, along with Duggan's sense that something nefarious was in the works behind his back, had to mean something. But did it have anything to do with the abduction of King Charles? He wouldn't know that until he had a chance to speak with Fahey face-to-face and under conditions somewhat more favorable than the Bogside pub.

He dipped a hand into his pocket, pushing past the Webley, and found a small box of matches. His Briar was already packed and the short walk back to the Rover seemed like the perfect opportunity for a contemplative smoke. Turning away from the church ruins, he took out a wooden match and struck it.

At almost the same instant that the head of the match blazed into life, he heard an unusual noise from the woods behind him—the thud of an impact, as of something heavy hitting the ground, and the *oomph* of someone's breath going out in a rush.

It didn't take an investigator of Congreve's prodigious ability to realize that something bad was happening.

He flicked the match away and whirled back toward the ruins, searching the shadows for the source of the noise and the threat it represented. He groped in the pocket again, this time going after the revolver, but his fingers felt numb and unresponsive. The gun, which had slid into the pocket so easily earlier in the evening, now seemed to have become inextricably bound up in the fabric. Congreve's heart began pumping furiously in his chest, the rush of blood in his ears sounding like a waterfall. His pocket would not let go of the revolver.

"Ross!" he gasped.

Where's Ross?

The revolver abruptly broke free from the snare of the pocket. He brought it up in a two-handed grip and began sweeping it back and forth, looking for something to shoot, but all was still in the woods behind the church.

"Duggan?" he hissed. "Are you there, man?"

No answer.

There was not a doubt in Congreve's highly proficient mind that Padraig Duggan had met with some misfortune somewhere just beyond the edge of darkness, but he was not about to venture into the woods alone to investigate. Without looking away, Congreve cried out, "Ross! I need you!"

But Sutherland too gave no answer.

"Ross!"

Now fearing the worst, Congreve backed away from the woods, turning a full circle to check every avenue of approach. He searched the path back to the car park, but there was no sign of Sutherland or anyone else.

"Ross!"

Sutherland would not have abandoned him. If he was not there, it could only mean . . .

A voice reached out from the woods to his right. "Drop it, or I'll cut your friend."

Congreve turned toward the sound of the voice, aiming the revolver at the place from where he imagined it had come. He was not about to surrender his weapon, even with the threat to Sutherland's life, because he knew all too well that once he was disarmed, both of their lives would be forfeit.

"I said, 'Drop it!'" Movement accompanied the repetition of the threat, and a human shape emerged from the shadows, stepping into the fringe of illumination cast by the overhead lights.

It was Sutherland. Blood oozed from an abrasion above his left ear, and his eyes, while open, were unfocused. Harder to see in the darkness was the man standing right behind him, dressed all in black and wearing a three-hole balaclava with openings for his eyes and mouth. The man was mostly hidden behind Sutherland, revealing only a little bit of his right forearm and the hand that held a knife with the blade pressed up against the soft flesh under Sutherland's jaw.

"I will cut him," the man warned, his tone urgent and intentional.

"I believe you intend to do that anyway," replied Congreve, now strangely calm in the face of this ill turn. "To both of us. No, I think a better solution would be for you to put your weapon down before you do something that can't be undone."

Congreve did not really expect this appeal to reason to accomplish anything, but short of surrender, it was his only move.

Don't back down, he told himself. *Don't show fear.*

Despite the visceral nature of the threat to Sutherland, Congreve knew he had the upper hand because, as the old saying went, he had brought a gun to a knife fight. If Sutherland's captor attempted to make good on his threat, the DCI might be injured, but the odds of his survival with immediate medical attention were high, whereas Congreve's bullet, which would immediately follow such an attack, would prove far more decisive.

A standoff was a standoff only until someone blinked, and Ambrose Congreve was damned if he was going to blink.

"We can both walk away from this," he went on, "or you can be carried. It's your choice."

"Is that what you think, peeler?" answered the masked man with far more confidence than his position seemed to warrant. "Well, there's something you don't know. See, unlike you, I didn't come here alone."

There was more movement in the trees to either side of Sutherland's captor. Congreve moved the revolver left, then right, each time finding a new black-clad target to aim his weapon at—five in all—but unlike the man holding Sutherland, these men were armed with pistols.

Congreve's heart sank. It wasn't fear of imminent death that now suffused him, however, but rather a profound embarrassment. Perhaps because part of him had never really believed that the New IRA was responsible for the King's abduction, he had badly underestimated them and so had walked right into their trap. Worse, he'd taken Ross down with him.

The only reason he and Sutherland were not already dead was that the noise of a pistol shot would have brought a swift police response, but that would not hold them back indefinitely.

So, this is what checkmate feels like.

"Last time I'll say it, peeler," said the man holding Sutherland. "Drop it."

As loath as he was to give up his weapon, Congreve realized that surrender was now his only play—the only way to prolong his life, if even just for a few more minutes.

Just long enough to ensure that he did not die in ignorance.

"Wait," Congreve said, reversing his grip on the revolver, holding it by the frame with the barrel pointed skyward. "Which one of you is Dylan Fahey?"

The man holding Sutherland flinched at the sound of the name, but then his mouth broke into a broad grin. "Old Paddy told you about me, did he? Fat lot of good it will do you. Brian, get his rod."

One of the other masked men approached Congreve cautiously and snatched the Webley from Congreve's unresisting hand.

Now he was unarmed and in the hands of the enemy, but perhaps not completely defenseless. With the same calm voice he'd earlier used, he said, "Think, man. Do you know what sort of hell killing two investigators from Scotland Yard will bring down on you?"

Dylan's smile only broadened. "Oh, I think in the grand scheme of things, it won't make a lot of difference to anyone whether I kill you or let you live."

"What does that mean?" demanded Congreve.

Dylan ignored him, nodding instead to the man who had taken Congreve's weapon. "Do it."

Congreve, seeing his last chance for some clarity slipping away, blurted, "Do you have the King?"

Dylan's head tilted ever so slightly to the side, his lips forming a question that Congreve had no difficulty reading. *The King?*

He doesn't know, thought Congreve. *He's got nothing to do with it.*

Then something heavy crashed into the side of his head, and the darkness swept over him like the tide.

TWENTY-EIGHT

t was midafternoon when *Miss Maria* eased into a slip at the Conch Harbor Marina, and the mood aboard was grim. All throughout the hours spent crossing the Florida Straits, Stoke and Harry Brock had monitored the US Coast Guard frequency, hoping to hear of the successful interdiction of the narco sub carrying the Novichok nerve agent, but five hours after Brock had alerted his superiors at Langley to the threat, initiating the largest Coast Guard search operation in the Gulf of Mexico since Hurricane Katrina, there was no news.

Most narco subs were generally slow-moving autonomous submersibles built to operate at relatively shallow depths, which ought to have made them easy for Coast Guard aircraft to spot. That there had been no sightings meant either that the sub Sean Fahey and his co-conspirators were using to smuggle the nerve agent out of Cuban waters was exceptional in some way—running faster or deeper than most or cleverly camouflaged to avoid detection—or that Stoke's basic assumption that the smugglers would choose the shortest possible route to put their payload on American soil was mistaken, and rather than making the straight-line journey to Florida, the sub was taking a roundabout route to avoid detection.

There were, of course, other possibilities. The narco sub might have foundered in Cuban waters early on its journey, taking its deadly cargo to the bottom. It was even possible that there was no submersible and that the fire that had destroyed Fahey's boat had been just a freak accident, killing Fahey and his collaborators and burning up the No-vichok. But Stoke saw no advantage to countenancing such happy-horseshit explanations. As far as he was concerned, the nerve agent was on its way to America, and he wasn't going to rest until that threat was neutralized.

It was Stoke's intention to remain in port no longer than it took to gas up and restock the galley. Then he would head back out to begin scouting possible landing sites for the narco sub.

Since it could not just pull up to a Key West marina, the submersible would either have to rendezvous with a surface vessel or dock at a secret location where the cargo could be off-loaded. Unfortunately, because the Keys had hundreds of remote, uninhabited islands and were crisscrossed with unmapped coves and channels and dense, mazelike mangrove swamps, they were quite literally a smuggler's paradise.

Stoke knew that his search effort would be largely symbolic. The odds of him accomplishing what the combined resources of the United States Coast Guard's Seventh District could not were almost too overwhelming to consider.

But he couldn't just do nothing.

Then Harry threw him an unexpected lifeline. When Stoke returned from the marina store with a boxful of provisions, Brock was waving his phone, just as he had done that morning, albeit with considerably more enthusiasm now that he was no longer hungover. "I've got Jade Mitchell on the line."

"Who's Jade Mitchell?"

"She's in the DI . . . I mean, the DA . . . Directorate of Analysis. They keep changing the name. I can't keep up. Anyway, wait till you hear her talk. I've never met her, but if she's as sexy as she sounds—"

A sultry voice, low and husky, issued from the phone. "You know I can hear you, Harry. And unless you want to repeat the workplace sexual harassment training *again*, I strongly suggest that you, as the kids say these days, check yourself before you wreck yourself."

Stoke glanced over at Brock and mouthed the question, *Again?* Harry just shrugged.

He's not wrong about the voice, though, Stoke thought, visualizing Jade Mitchell as a voluptuous Viola Davis trapped in a sterile cubicle at CIA HQ in Langley, Virginia.

"Pleased to make your acquaintance, Miss Mitchell," Stoke began. "I'm Stokely Jones Jr."

"I know all about you, Mr. Stokely Jones Jr. You're quite the man of action. Fancha is a lucky woman."

Something about the intimate nature of the comment left Stoke feeling vaguely uncomfortable. "I think I'm the lucky one," he said, and he meant it.

"What I can't comprehend," Jade went on, ignoring his reply, "is why you would choose to associate with someone like Harry Brock?"

"Believe me, I wonder about that myself sometimes."

Brock clutched one hand to his chest as if wounded. Stoke ignored him. "So, what have you got to tell me, Miss Mitchell?"

"Well, I did a deep dive into the subject you identified in Cuba, one Sean Michael Fahey of Belfast, Northern Ireland."

"Harry already showed me his file."

"Harry gave you an egg. I done whipped you up a soufflé."

Stoke laughed despite himself and took a seat at the small chart table. "All right, let's hear it."

Much of what Jade had to say merely expanded on what Stoke already knew of Sean Fahey, particularly with respect to his early life and military service, but the inclusion of seemingly minor details provided a clearer picture of who Sean Fahey was.

The child of a former IRA dissident who had been killed in a street brawl with members of the Red Hand Commando, Sean and his older brother, Dylan, had risen above the penury of their fatherless childhood to find a measure of success in post-Troubles Northern Ireland. Both had served in the military with exemplary records—Dylan in the Army, Sean with the SBS. After leaving the Army, Dylan had returned to Northern Ireland, eventually settling in Derry, where he had become involved in dissident politics. Sean, however, had continued down the warrior's path, working as an independent contractor for the controversial South Africa–based private military outfit Strategic Vanguard Services. Because he was an independent contractor and not an employee, SVS did not keep any records of Fahey's activities on their behalf, but it was an easy thing for Jade to access his travel records and match them up with SVS contracts in order to create a road map of Fahey's paramilitary operations.

As impressive as Jade's efforts were, Stoke wasn't sure they warranted a comparison to gourmet food. But Jade had merely been laying the foundation for her most important discovery. "Before traveling to Cuba as Sean Farris, Fahey flew into the United States aboard the SVS private jet."

Stoke sat up a little straighter. "He's still working for them?"

"Looks that way," Jade confirmed. "Now, we don't know who SVS is working for, but when we figure out who their client is, we'll have a better idea of what they've got planned for the Novichok nerve agent."

"All right," Stoke said. "But that doesn't tell us where Fahey is right now."

"No, but remember that jet I told you about? It's sitting on the ground at a Dade County FBO."

Stoke sat bolt upright. "They're going to try to fly it out." It wasn't a question.

"Sure looks that way."

"We can stake out that jet," said Brock, catching on. "Even if he manages to make it ashore, we can intercept him when he tries to make it to that plane."

"Have they filed a flight plan?" asked Stoke.

"They have. Next destination is listed as Cork, Ireland."

"Ireland." Stoke turned this news over in his head. "From there, they could take it almost anywhere in Europe."

He made a mental note to call Alex Hawke and give him a heads-up.

"I'll alert the FBI and local law enforcement," Jade went on, "have them lock down that jet."

"No," said Stoke quickly. "If Fahey sees a police presence, he'll just walk away and then we'll be back to square one. Harry and me will take care of it."

"What if they try to take off before you get there?"

"I don't think they will. If I push *Miss Maria*, we can be in Key Biscayne in two and a half hours. I don't think Fahey will beat us there. If he does, you can have the FAA ground the plane, but I don't think we're going to need to do that."

He pushed away from the table and started for the cockpit. "Cast off, Harry. We're gonna nail that son of a bitch!"

Five hours later, Stoke and Harry were sitting in Stoke's classic black raspberry '65 GTO, parked in the lot outside the Miami Flight School hangar. They were peering through binoculars at the white Learjet 75 adorned with the ram's head logo of Strategic Vanguard Services. The plane was sitting idle on a hardstand just a couple hundred yards away. There was no sign of activity in or around the jet. No indication that it was ready for imminent departure. If the flight crew was aboard, they must have been bored out of their skulls, which was exactly how Stoke was starting to feel.

When they'd arrived two hours earlier, they had congratulated themselves on reaching the plane ahead of Fahey. Their hasty journey—first by boat, skirting the mainland shore with the engine throttle pushed to the max, and then by road from the Paradise Island marina where he'd traded *Miss Maria* for the GTO, which, to save time, he'd arranged to have Fancha bring over to the mainland—now seemed unnecessary.

Maybe Jade had misread the intel. Maybe Fahey had changed the plan after the encounter in Cuba. Or maybe he'd never intended to fly back on the SVS corporate jet. Maybe . . . Maybe . . . Maybe.

Maybe they just needed to be patient.

The only thing they knew for certain was that the Coast Guard had failed to locate the smugglers' submersible. Jade, who had been monitoring the search efforts on their behalf, confirmed that every time Harry made one of his increasingly frequent check-in calls.

Two more uneventful hours passed. The pink hues of twilight were ebbing from the sky to be replaced by the weird orange black of the urban night sky. The windows on the jet remained dark.

They eventually decided to take turns grabbing some shut-eye. The GTO was equipped with factory-standard bucket seats that did not recline, but the bench seat in the rear was flat and just big enough to allow Brock to curl up in a fetal ball for his two-hour power nap. Stoke didn't even bother trying to cram himself into the back seat, but simply rested with his head against the window. As a SEAL, he'd picked up the ability to switch off and sleep anytime, anywhere, waking fully refreshed and ready for action at the sound of a pin drop.

It was not a pin drop, however, that roused Stoke, but rather the hum of Brock's phone vibrating with an incoming call. His eyelids snapped open and he sat up, looking over at his companion expectantly.

"It's Jade."

"Well, answer it," urged Stoke.

Brock put the call on speaker. "Tell us some good news."

"Sorry," replied Jade, sounding utterly defeated. "I'm afraid the news is all bad."

Stoke felt his gut begin to churn. "What's happened?"

"I found Sean Fahey."

"Yeah? Where is he?"

"He's in a coffin that was just released to a mortuary service representative in Dublin, Ireland. The remains were flown out of Cuba on a commercial air carrier."

"He's dead?" asked Brock, incredulous. "Are you sure it's really him?"

"It's him," said Stoke. "I shot him, remember?"

"Cause of death was listed as cardiac arrest," said Jade.

"All that means is that Fahey's buddy from the boat found a doctor willing to sign a bogus death certificate so they could ship him back to Ireland." Jade's news added pieces to the puzzle that Stoke hadn't realized they were missing, and as he put them into place, he didn't like the picture that was revealed one bit. "You've got to stop them from releasing that body."

"You don't understand, Stokely. It's already gone. There's a five-hour time difference between here and there, so it happened in the middle of the night. The customs official rubber-stamped the paperwork and sent the coffin on its way. I didn't get the notification until he logged it into the computer, and by that time, the hearse was long gone."

"Then call the Irish FBI or whatever they call themselves. Send them to the funeral home. They've got to secure that coffin."

"I did that. They found the hearse abandoned on the side of the road a few miles from the airport. The coffin was gone."

"Damn it!" Stoke banged his fists down on the steering wheel.

"I don't understand," said Brock. "Why does the coffin matter? The nerve agent went out on the minisub."

"No, Harry. It didn't. That might have been their plan at the beginning, but when I killed Fahey, whoever he was working with changed the plan."

"You think they smuggled the nerve agent out in his coffin," Jade said, following Stoke's train of thought. "They would have put it through an X-ray machine before they released it."

"An X-ray wouldn't have shown anything. The nerve agent is a powder. Two different powders. Bags of powder don't show up on X-rays. And chemical sniffers wouldn't detect them until they're mixed and active."

Brock slumped in the passenger seat. "Then that's it. They beat us."

"Like hell they did," snarled Stoke. He stomped down on the clutch pedal, turned the key, and brought the engine roaring to life. "Jade, get us on the first thing smoking. We're going to Ireland."

TWENTY-NINE

BAVARIA

Once committed to the idea of escaping from Konigstahl's fairy-tale nightmare castle, Hawke and Pippa changed into attire more appropriate to making a hasty exit. Hawke chose a well-worn pair of blue jeans, a pair of Sebago Docksides, and his favorite T-shirt, emblazoned with the crest of the Royal Marine Sniper Troop and the quote "You can run, but you'll only die tired." Pippa returned to the outfit she had traveled in, which consisted of cotton slacks, a lightweight silk top, and trainers. Because Hawke's plan relied on staying light and moving fast, their luggage, including their dinner wear, would have to be left behind, much to Pippa's chagrin. After a final, longing appraisal, she stuffed her dress and heels into the garment bag and followed Hawke out onto the balcony. The only additional piece of clothing they took along was Hawke's tuxedo jacket, which Pippa once again donned as an added layer of protection against the night's chill. Even so, she began shivering almost immediately.

Rather than attempt to navigate the mazelike passages of the castle back to the main entrance, which Hawke did not doubt would be guarded by Klaus or some other ogre in Konigstahl's employ, they decided instead to take a more direct route—downclimbing from the balcony to the courtyard, and then heading straight out of the gate and down to the cable car station. Because mad King Ludwig had favored aesthetics over strategic considerations, the exterior walls were decorated with gargoyles, pillars, pilasters, and various other protrusions ideal for use as handholds, so climbing down to ground level was only slightly more difficult than descending a ladder, or rather it would have been had they been making the attempt during daylight hours. Schloss Wolkenheim possessed no exterior lights, so their egress was made with only the moon and stars to show the way. Fortunately, Hawke relied more on his sense of touch than on his vision, feeling his way down the wall, mapping the best route, and then advising Pippa where to find foot- and handholds. They moved in stages, descending from one balcony to the next until all that remained was a ten-foot free fall down onto the courtyard pavement. Hawke utilized the paratrooper landing technique of dropping flat and rolling to distribute the energy of the impact, and then he simply caught Pippa in his arms when she let go.

With solid ground underfoot once more, they headed for the gate. Hawke eyed the portcullis warily as they drew near, half expecting the spike-tipped iron lattice to come crashing down in front of them, but it remained fixed in place, permitting their exit. Now only one obstacle stood between them and freedom.

In the darkness, the cable car station seemed particularly exposed to the elements. A fierce, frigid wind whipped across the platform, rocking the idle cabin that dangled from the support cables overhead. Hawke did not venture out onto the platform, however, but instead moved to the adjacent structure, which he presumed housed the controls for the cable car. Navigating again more by feel than by sight, he located the access door.

"Locked," he murmured. It was the first thing he'd said aloud since leaving the courtyard.

"Can you pick it?" asked Pippa.

"Maybe if I had the right tools, which I do not."

"So how do we—"

A sharp crack, almost but not quite as loud as a pistol report, cut Pippa short, turning her question into a yelp. A second noise—the sound of the door, which Hawke had just opened with a mighty kick and slammed against the interior wall—followed a heartbeat later. Where the door had been a moment before, there was now only a rectangular void, like a passage into an alternate reality.

"A little warning next time," said Pippa when she could breathe again.

"Sorry," Hawke replied, unable to suppress a laugh.

"I don't see what you think is so funny. What if someone heard that?"

"If there's anyone around to hear it, then they already know we're here."

"What if there's an alarm?"

"Then we're in a fix. But I don't think there is one. Now come on, let's get inside." He found her arm and pulled her through the open doorway, closing it behind them before taking out his mobile phone, using the illuminated screen as a field-expedient torch. Its glow revealed the exposed machinery of the cable car, which looked both antiquated and ridiculously simple—just a series of large enmeshed gears and axles sprouting from a large electric motor. There was no control panel per se, just a power-cutoff switch for the motor, which, all appearances to the contrary, was in the on position, and a simple toggle switch, which controlled both speed and direction. There was a padlocked metal cage around the toggle and a small sign with a message in German, French, and English explaining that the switch was not to be used unless the primary motor controls, located at the main station, were locked out.

"Damn it," muttered Hawke. "I was afraid of something like that."

"Like what?"

"We can't operate the car from here."

Pippa received this news with a resigned sigh. "I hope you've got a plan B."

"Hmm. Not yet." He turned away from the motor and began shining the light around the structure's interior. "But let's have a look around. Maybe we'll find inspiration."

The rest of the structure appeared to serve as a maintenance shop, with a large workbench and several cabinets. These contained a variety of tools, bundles of rags, tubs of grease, and other equipment. One cabinet contained hard hats and heavy-duty nylon safety harnesses. Another held coils of eleven-millimeter static rope.

Pippa, evidently noticing Hawke's lingering interest in the latter discoveries, said, "If you're thinking about sliding down that cable, think again."

Hawke returned a grim smile. "You might prefer that to what I've got in mind."

"I'm afraid to ask."

"We're going to abseil down the mountain."

"Abseil down," Pippa echoed, sounding only mildly incredulous. "Why not? It's only three thousand feet straight down, and we won't be able to see a bloody thing."

Hawke had briefly considered the footpath Pippa's research had turned up in advance of their coming to the castle, but even if they knew where and how to access the old trail, the plain truth was that descending the mountain by foot would take too much bloody time.

Time that Hawke knew they did not have.

"I won't lie and tell you that it will be easy, but it's not going to be as bad as all that. The grade may be steep, but it isn't vertical. We won't even need to rope down all the way."

In the glow from the phone screen, Hawke could see the look of dread on her face, but to her credit, Pippa offered no further objections. He retrieved two of the safety harnesses from the cabinet, handed one to Pippa, and then demonstrated how to put it on correctly.

"Have you abseiled before?" Hawke asked as he safety-checked her buckles.

"I did a two-week training with the commandos. It's been a while, though."

"It will come back to you," he promised. "We won't be doing anything too fancy, mind you. Just a simple down rappel facing the mountain. I'll go first and then belay you from below."

He demonstrated how to use a carabiner clipped to the harness as a friction device and how to adjust speed either by holding the rope away from the body to decrease friction or by pressing it against the small of the back to stop completely. "This hand," he said, holding up his right hand, which was still gripping the rope, "doesn't leave the rope until you're off belay."

"What if I fall?"

"Don't. But if you should, just start screaming bloody murder. I'll take out the slack in the belay line and stop your fall."

After adding a hard hat and leather gloves to their respective ensembles, Hawke pulled out two coils of rope, joined them together with a double fisherman's knot, and tied off the other ends with stopper knots, then hefted the bundle onto his shoulder and headed for the door.

With Pippa holding the mobile to give him light, he rigged a releasable anchor, using one of the support struts from the platform, and then heaved the rope coils over the edge.

"We've got three hundred feet of rope," he explained, "so we're going to have to do this in several pitches. Don't try to rush. Remember your training. Trust your anchor and your equipment, and everything will be just fine. Got it?"

Pippa nodded and, in a small voice, said, "Got it."

Hawke clipped his carabiner onto the secured rappel line and, gripping it in one gloved hand, moved to the edge of the platform. "Wait for the line to go slack. That will be your signal to clip in. Going over this edge will probably be the hardest part because it's going to feel completely unnatural. All you have to do is just lean back, keep your knees locked, and let your harness do the work. Once you're over the lip, it's just a matter of walking backward down the slope. Do what I do, and you'll be down in no time."

With his feet on the edge, he began leaning back until the rope was taking all his weight. Then, with a single abrupt motion, he swung his body backward and surrendered to gravity. With his brake hand extended to reduce friction, he began descending like a spider paying out silk. The rope slid slowly but steadily through his loose grip, heating up the leather palm of his glove. Then, after he had dropped about thirty feet, his feet touched something solid, and he brought his brake hand back, slowing his descent almost to a full stop until he could plant the soles of his shoes against the mountain slope.

From there, it was a simple matter of walking backward down the mountain. He couldn't really see what lay below, but Hawke knew that there would be few obstacles this high up on the mountain. There were no trees to worry about—the slope was too steep for them to take root—and few protruding rock formations to get hung up on. It was difficult to gauge just how far he had come, but rather than risk running out the full length of his rope too soon, he began looking for a stopping place where he could rig the anchor for the next pitch. He found it in the form of a limestone outcropping about half the size of the Locomotive. Once he was sure of his footing, he hauled out several more feet of rope, creating enough slack in the line to send Pippa the signal that it was go time.

For a few minutes, nothing happened, but then he felt faint vibrations traveling down through the rope and knew that Pippa was now on rappel.

Time seemed to grind to a halt as he stood there on that wind-scoured nub, holding on to the belay line and gazing up into the darkness in hopes of catching even a glimpse of Pippa descending. Though he could not distinguish her visually, the constant movement of the belay line in his hand confirmed that she was on the move.

As he waited in the cold and dark, Hawke found himself admiring

Pippa's courage. After some initial and quite understandable reticence, she had embraced his plan for their escape despite knowing full well how demanding it would be. That she was intellectually formidable was never in doubt, but he never would have believed she possessed the physical aptitude for fieldwork.

He wondered now if he ought to have given her . . . given *them* more of a chance all those years ago. . . . And wondering that, he realized that he needed to think about something else.

Someone else.

Anastasia.

It occurred to him that he hadn't spared a thought for her since leaving London. That had nothing to do with Pippa, of course. He had just been so focused on the mission, so focused on finding the King. Thinking about what Anastasia and Alexei might be doing stirred up a stew of emotions in him: guilt at abandoning them, but also something almost like resentment at having been put in that position.

He recalled that last conversation with Anastasia.

"You must be the man you are, Alex. If you were someone else, I would not have fallen in love with you. I only wish you would stop lying to yourself about it."

She was right, of course. He had told himself a lie: not that he could be Alex Hawke, devoted husband and loving father, but rather that he could stop being who he really was—Hawke the spy. Hawke the warrior.

Can I be both? he wondered. Then came the harder question to answer. . . .

Do I even want to be?

Pippa's arrival afforded him a brief respite from this internal debate. When she was off belay, he hauled down on the other end of the joined ropes to release the anchor knot and then pulled them down to begin the process again.

It was a scene that would replay several times over the course of the night as they descended Wolkenheim one rope length at a time. Thankfully, the going got easier with each pitch, the sheer cliff face at the summit gradually giving way to slopes of just sixty and then forty-five degrees. Descending also kept the chill at bay as overall temperatures were warmer at lower altitudes.

When the descent brought them below the timberline, Hawke judged it safe to continue unroped, though he carried the coils slung across his chest like bandoliers just in case. The grade continued to flatten out as they neared the base of the mountain, and as it did and as predawn twilight illuminated the world around them, they were at last able to pick up their pace.

Overhead, the tram cables became visible through the forest canopy. The stark black parallel lines bisected the lightening sky and showed the way back to the car park where the Locomotive waited to bear them away. The cables were both an indicator of how far Pippa and Hawke had come and how far they still had to go—Hawke guessed at least two more miles—and a reminder of how quickly Konigstahl and his minions might be able to cut Hawke and Pippa off after figuring out how they had escaped.

Almost without warning, they happened upon the foundation of one of the stanchions supporting the cable car lines, the first such they had encountered. The structure, a tapering lattice of galvanized metal rising up through the forest canopy to a height of at least two hundred feet, was concealed by the trees surrounding it until they were practically on top of it.

The metal tower, however, wasn't the only thing hidden in the woods.

"I was beginning to wonder if you'd ever show up."

At the first syllable, Hawke's heart skipped a beat and then began to thunder with a rush of adrenaline. The voice, unmistakably that of Heinrich Prinz von Konigstahl, issued from the shadows just behind the base of the tower, and as Hawke and Pippa stood there, frozen in place like two deer caught in a spotlight, the Prince stepped out into the open.

The imperfect twilight showed him as more of a silhouette than a well-defined three-dimensional figure, but there was no mistaking the long rod that seemed to rise from just behind his right shoulder. It was the barrel of a large-caliber hunting rifle slung across his back.

If there had ever been any doubts regarding Konigstahl's ultimate intentions toward them, the presence of that weapon erased them all.

Hawke thought about going for the Glock in his waistband but decided to keep its existence secret just a little while longer. Instead, hiding his apprehension behind a facade of aplomb, he addressed the Prince. "Out for a hunt? A bit early in the year, isn't it?"

In the gloom, Hawke couldn't tell how Konigstahl regarded the show of bravado, but the Prince was ready with an answer. "It's exactly the right time for the sort of game I mean to hunt."

"Ah. So it's like that, is it? You intend to hunt the most dangerous game, just like in the story."

"I'll admit I wasn't sure that you would be worth the effort. I inquired about you, you know. You have the reputation of being a bit of a dandy. But when I discovered that you had successfully climbed down Wolkenheim in the dead of night? That was when I knew there was something special about you."

"Do you mean to say that if we'd just stayed the night like good little guests, you would have fed us breakfast and sent us on our way?"

That brought a great gush of laughter from Konigstahl. "My goodness, no. If you had done that, Klaus would have strangled you both in your sleep as I had originally intended. But I'm pleased that didn't happen. This will be so much more fun."

Oh, it certainly will, thought Hawke.

"Surely you can't imagine that there won't be questions asked when we don't turn up. I mean, people know that we're here visiting you. We're no threat to you. Wouldn't the smart play have been to simply let us leave as we came?"

"Ah, you sell yourself short, friend Alex. Don't you think I know what really brought you here? You as much as admitted to it last night. You think I took your pathetic King."

"Did you?"

"As it happens, no. And I've no idea who did or where he is."

Hawke hid his disappointment at this revelation. If Konigstahl was not even peripherally involved in the conspiracy, then he and Pippa were no closer to learning the truth about what had happened to Charles. And the clock was ticking down.

"Then why bother with us?" asked Hawke. "I mean, if you're above suspicion, why not leave well enough alone? The truth will out, as they say."

"Oh, I think we both know that I am hardly above suspicion. After all, you came here, didn't you? But the truth of the matter is, *you* want him restored to the throne, and I . . . I do not. That makes us enemies, don't you see?"

"Can't argue with you there."

"As to the lingering question of your *disappearance* . . . I will simply claim ignorance. In the near term, it will suffice, and in the long term, it won't matter."

"Because you think you'll be the King?"

"I *will* be King."

Hawke decided a change of topic was in order. "I'm curious about one thing," he said. "How did you get down here so quickly? We didn't hear the cable car being operated."

"As it happens, when I made the castle my summer residence, I added an alternate exit. A high-speed lift that runs from inside the castle and joins a four-mile-long access tunnel that lets out near the station. I do so hate having to wait on that antique tram."

"Ah," said Hawke with a sagacious nod, "all the comforts of home. So, you really mean to hunt us down, then?"

"Just you, friend Alex. There's no sport in hunting a woman. But you should thank me. She would only slow you down."

Pippa sucked in a breath, no doubt preparing to voice her objection to Konigstahl's overt sexism, but before she could express her righteous indignation, the Prince went on. "I mean to use her as leverage to ensure you give your best effort. The longer you stay alive, the longer she stays alive." He half turned in the direction of the stanchion and made a come-along gesture. "Klaus, take her."

The enormous shape of the ogre materialized from behind the metal tower and began lumbering toward Pippa. Hawke sidestepped to put himself between Klaus and Pippa.

"Were I you," remarked Konigstahl as he slipped the rifle's sling from his shoulder, "I'd start running."

"What, no head start? Not very sporting."

The Prince shrugged. "I'll give you one minute. Starting now."

"And if I win," pressed Hawke, "you'll let us both go?"

"Oh, Alex," said Konigstahl, laughing, "you aren't going to win."

THIRTY

Ambrose!"

The shout penetrated the darkness in which Congreve drifted, raising him almost to a state of full awareness, but it brought with it a spike of pain that made him want to shrink back into oblivion.

"Ambrose! For God's sake, wake up!"

The urgency of the appeal supplied the necessary motivation to push through the pain and claw his way fully back to consciousness. Yet, as he opened his eyes and began taking in the details of his unfamiliar environment, the sudden rush of sensory inputs left him momentarily paralyzed.

"Ambrose!"

That's Ross, Congreve thought, wrestling one bit of coherent information from the hash of stimuli. Sensation and memory now warred for his attention. He thought he must be lying on his side, for there was tremendous pressure against the right side of his body, and his right cheek was pressing against a hard, unyielding surface.

I was in a park . . . St. Columb's . . . meeting with Padraig Duggan. And then . . .

There was a dull, persistent humming sound, not quite loud enough to drown out the sound of Sutherland's voice but too loud for polite conversation. It vibrated through him, a flat, atonal drone that was somehow familiar.

Someone got the jump on us.... Fahey. Dylan Fahey. That's the fellow's name.

His vision gradually began to clear, and the world gained focus by degrees. For a moment, everything appeared to be doubled, as if his eyes weren't aligned correctly, but with effort, he brought the crooked halves of the world together. This reconciliation did not immediately bring clarity, however, for nothing he beheld made sense.

"Ambrose? Can you hear me?"

"I hear you, Ross," he managed to mumble. The effort sent fresh waves of pain through his skull, but he sucked in a breath and tried again. "I'm here, Ross. Half a minute."

Sutherland's sigh of relief was audible even over the droning noise. "Thank God. I feared you were dead."

"Not yet, though I'm wondering if that might not be preferable to the way I'm bloody feeling." Congreve tried to extend his hand in order to raise himself into a seated position, but his arms wouldn't respond. He tried again and could feel his muscles tensing with the effort, but something restricted their movement. "Someone's tied me up."

"Both of us," confirmed Sutherland. "I only just woke up myself a few minutes ago. We seem to be in the back of a lorry."

Sutherland's assessment supplied the necessary context for Congreve to finally assemble the sensory puzzle into a coherent picture. The low hum, the slight sway and vibration, even the hard surface pressing against him—all of them were consistent with being in the cargo area of a moving vehicle. There was only a little bit of light filtering into the interior, but it was enough to add more detail to the emerging picture. He lay on a scuffed wooden platform with metal dropsides and a tailgate and a high canvas canopy, like a military transport. Right beside him, and presumably separating him from Sutherland, were two wooden pallets, arranged one ahead of the other, loaded with fifty-five-gallon metal drums banded together with nylon ratchet straps.

Congreve squirmed and wriggled into a position where he was, with no small effort, able to sit up without using his hands or feet, which he had discovered were also bound together at the ankles with several wraps of gaffer tape. The effort to sit up not only left him somewhat spent but raised the throb of pain in his skull to near blinding intensity. When the sensation receded to merely a dull ache, he began scooting up the length of the platform until he could see around the drums.

"Ross!" he exclaimed when he finally caught sight of Sutherland. Just seeing the other man gave him a measure of hope. He saw a similar emotion reflected in Sutherland's visage. The meeting with Duggan might have ended badly, but at least they were still alive. And while there was life, there was hope.

"Any luck slipping your bonds?" asked Congreve.

"Not yet. I had a knife on my belt, but if it's still there, I can't bloody reach it."

Congreve thought it unlikely that their captors would have overlooked something like that, but the possibility was worth exploring. "I'll try to scoot over there," he said, and immediately began doing so. "Maybe I can reach it."

"Worth a try." Sutherland began shuffling as well, shortening the distance Congreve would have to travel. They met in the middle, directly in front of the pallet, whereupon Ross turned sideways, thrusting his hip toward Congreve.

Congreve could see a leather sheath right next to the holster for Sutherland's pistol. Both were empty.

"It's gone."

"Well, it was a long shot anyway," said Sutherland. "I don't suppose you've got one."

"I did," said Congreve. "But if they searched you, they probably searched me as well."

"All right, what else can we try?"

Congreve began looking around for inspiration. The rough wood edge of the pallet seemed like it might be sharp enough to saw through their bonds, but that would take a while.

"Do you have a lighter?" Sutherland asked. "Maybe we can melt the tape."

"That sounds like a singularly bad idea. But to answer your question, no, I don't have a lighter. I do have matches. Or at least I did. Front pocket."

He shifted around to put the pocket of his greatcoat within Sutherland's reach. Sutherland also turned away and then groped blindly until he got one hand into the big pocket. "I've got something," he said after a moment. "Doesn't feel like a box of matches, though. Maybe the stem of your pipe?"

The possibility that his favorite Briar was still with him raised Congreve's spirits. He had no memory of putting the pipe into his coat pocket.

"No, it's not a pipe," Sutherland went on, dashing Congreve's burgeoning hopes. "Feels more like a penknife. I've almost got it."

"I don't possess a penknife— Oh, goodness. It's my pipe tool."

Congreve's Laguiole pipe tool did indeed resemble a common penknife, at least at first glance, but a closer examination would have revealed it to be anything but common. Handcrafted by Forge de Laguiole in Laguiole, France, the polished and engraved brierwood-and-steel handle halves concealed a folding scraper blade and a hinged pin for shaping the tobacco mix, along with a flat miter cap on one end for tamping the mix in the bowl. The hand-filed spring top and spine were engraved with traditional symbols—a shepherd's cross and a honeybee. It was a functional work of art and, after his pipes, one of Congreve's most treasured possessions.

"Will it work to cut through this tape?" asked Sutherland.

"The scraper blade might do the trick, though it's not very sharp."

"I'll give it a try." Sutherland fumbled with the pipe tool for a moment. "How does it open?"

"There's a spring release at the top in the shape of a bee."

"I can't see the bloody thing, Ambrose."

"Yes, yes. Just press down on the ends. One of them will release the blade."

"Half a second." A faint *snick* signaled success. "Got it."

"All right. Now, see if it will cut through." Congreve could feel Sutherland's bound hands moving over his own, feeling the thick wrapping of gaffer tape, locating the small hollow between his wrists, and gently . . . gently inserting the flat blade.

The scraper was intended for removing carbon residue from the pipe bowl and was not meant for precision cutting, but it did have a bit of an edge. Working slowly at first, with careful, deliberate strokes, Sutherland started to saw back and forth.

Congreve began to despair of any progress being made, but then, without any warning, the tape came apart, separating like a torn seam. Congreve's arms felt like balloons full of water, hanging from his aching shoulders, but with his release, circulation was restored, and sensation quickly returned. After taking a moment to massage away the pins and needles, he took the pipe tool from Sutherland and went to work sawing at the tape holding the DCI's wrists together. Despite having the full use of his hands, more or less, Congreve's technique left something to be desired, but at length, the scraper blade finally cut a notch in the tape binding that, once started, quickly yielded to his efforts.

"Thank God," Sutherland sighed as he began stretching and flexing his arms. Then, using just his fingernails, he found the end of the tape wrapped around his ankles and began ripping at it.

Congreve was still working on his own leg bindings when he heard Sutherland groan. "Oh, dear God."

Congreve raised his head and saw Sutherland on his feet but hunched over due to the high canvas canopy. He was glancing down at the metal drums with a look of horror. "What is it, Ross?"

Before the other could reply, Congreve pulled himself upright for a better look and immediately got his answer.

There were eight drums in all, each painted blue but with no markings to indicate their contents. No markings were necessary. The tangle of wires sprouting from the tops of the drums and coming together in the middle, where they disappeared through a hole bored in the side of a plastic toolbox, provided all the information Congreve needed to determine what the drums contained.

"Oh," said Congreve, and then unnecessarily added, "A bomb."

Though he had no formal training in dealing with explosive devices, as a veteran police inspector, he had seen more than his share of them. Most had been only in photographs and videos taken by bomb-disposal experts shortly before the devices were destroyed in controlled detonations—the safest way to disarm them—but once or twice, during the course of his investigations, he'd come upon devices in various stages of construction. There had seldom been any sort of uniformity in their designs, but somehow, they had all shared characteristics that made them easy to identify.

Congreve surmised that the drums likely contained a mixture of ammonium nitrate and diesel fuel oil—commonly referred to as ANFO—that was perhaps enhanced with a bit of powdered aluminum. ANFO had long been a favorite of terrorists everywhere, owing to the fact that its dual-use ingredients were fairly easy to obtain—ammonium nitrate, despite its explosive reputation, remained one of the most commonly used agricultural fertilizers, and anyone could buy diesel at a filling station. During the Troubles, both the IRA and the Ulster loyalists had used ANFO bombs to deadly effect, but perhaps the most infamous use of the chemical compound had been the 1995 bombing of a United States federal building in Oklahoma City, when a pair of anti-government terrorists had exploded a truck bomb containing forty-eight hundred pounds of an ANFO variant, killing 168 people.

Congreve's lightning-quick brain began calculating the yield of this device. Assuming that the drums were filled and contained a ratio of about twenty to one—and not including any other enhancements like TNT or gelignite to boost the detonation—each of the drums might conceivably contain eight hundred pounds of the mixture, for a total of sixty-four hundred pounds.

Sutherland finally broke the spell of silence cast upon them by the discovery. "I hope that brilliant mind of yours has some kind of plan to get us out of this mess."

Congreve felt completely out of his depth. This was the sort of thing Alex usually dealt with. He, Congreve, preferred more cerebral challenges. And yet what was this if not a puzzle to be solved?

"Holmes would call this a three-pipe problem," he muttered. "Alas, I shall have to make do without."

He sat down and resumed sawing at the tape around his ankles, but as he did, he began thinking aloud. "We must assume the device is armed and outfitted with some sort of anti-tamper trigger."

Sutherland nodded. "There are fine copper wires in the tape they used to secure the detonator wires. Probably rigged to an open relay switch. Break any one of these connections, and the whole thing goes up."

"Hmm," agreed Congreve. "Rather reckless of them to put us back here with it, but perhaps they did not anticipate that we would be able to shed our bonds."

"Or they just don't care if we blow ourselves up."

Congreve shook his head, then grimaced as a fresh wave of pain throbbed through his skull. "I'll warrant the driver cares. Besides, one doesn't go to the trouble of building a device like this just to vaporize a couple coppers. We seem to be in motion. It follows that our captors are transporting this device to a predetermined location where they mean to detonate it, killing us in the process."

Sutherland nodded and then, as if inspired, began making his way toward the rear of the platform. Without a word of explanation, he loosened the straps holding the backflap of the canvas cargo cover in place and lifted a corner. Daylight flooded the compartment, along with a rush of wind, sucked in by the lorry's slipstream.

It's morning already, thought Congreve. *No telling how long we were unconscious.*

Sutherland gazed out at the passing landscape for several seconds, then turned and made his way back to Congreve. "We're on the M2 traveling south. Just passed a turnoff to Glengormley."

"Glengormley," murmured Congreve. They had driven past the suburb on the way to Derry. "We're nearly to Belfast."

"I would say so. Ten minutes, give or take."

"Take would be my preference." Congreve gave his bonds a hard pull, and this time, they yielded. "Ah, much better. Belfast, you say. No shortage of targets there. We must find a way to prevent them from reaching their ultimate destination."

Sutherland gazed back at him, clearly looking to him for guidance. For his part, Congreve tried to imagine what Alex might do in the same circumstances. The solution—that is to say, the solution he imagined his friend would devise—was straightforward enough but by no means simple.

"We must wrest control of this vehicle from our captors," he declared.

Sutherland narrowed his gaze. "How are we going to do that? We don't have any weapons."

"We shall have to prevail through main force. I propose that we make our way along the exterior of the cargo area, enter through the nearside door . . . or, if it's locked, smash through the window. Subdue the passenger, if there is one, then force the driver to pull to the side. I fear attempting to go in on the driver's side could cause him to lose control."

Sutherland gaped at him. "You mean to do this while we're moving?"

"I don't see that we have a choice. The villains may not stop until they reach their ultimate destination, by which time it may be too late to prevent the device from being detonated. We must make the attempt before we reach a populated area."

"Let me just make sure I understand you correctly." The tinge of sarcasm in Sutherland's voice suggested that he understood all too well, but Congreve let him speak. "We're going to climb around outside this lorry, like Indiana bloody Jones in that movie, while it's moving down the motorway at sixty miles per hour. Smash through the window using . . . What? Our fists?"

Congreve, recalling how Alex had used his wristwatch for a similar purpose back at Balmoral, held up the pipe tool. "This should do the trick."

"And the blokes inside will be so amazed at our audacity that they'll forget to shoot us in our faces. Have I got that right?"

"The plan is not without risk," admitted Congreve. "But I would aver that it has a higher probability of success, to say nothing of survival, than allowing our captors to reach their destination."

This rationale did not appear to mollify Sutherland, so Congreve went on. "At any rate, this is probably best done one at a time." He clapped his hands against his thighs. "If I should fall, it will be up to you—"

"Oh, do shut up, Ambrose," Sutherland cut in with a heavy sigh. "You're in no shape for this. I'll go."

Congreve knew he ought to protest, for chivalry's sake if nothing else, but he was a rational creature and knew that his colleague was not wrong. So, instead, he simply handed the pipe tool to Sutherland. "Godspeed, Ross."

THIRTY-ONE

From his earliest memories, Ross Sutherland had felt—to borrow a phrase from a certain American film—the need for speed. He'd chased that thrill throughout his adolescent years in fast cars and faster racing bikes, and then had gone on to become a Royal Navy aviator, either flying or copiloting a number of different supersonic fighter aircraft. After he had left military service, his search for new ways to go fast and live dangerously had led him to rally racing in his beloved Mini Cooper—a hobby that, while not nearly as exciting as hurtling through the sky at five times the speed of sound, was plenty risky enough, especially for someone with a wife and young child waiting at home.

In all his years of chasing the thrill, however, no experience, not even the ill-fated sortie he'd flown with Alex Hawke over the skies of Iraq, had brought him so vividly face-to-face with his mortality as what he was now attempting.

I've got to be out of my bloody mind, he thought as he stuck his left foot through the opening he'd cut in the canvas covering near the front of the cargo area. It had quickly become apparent that attempting to shinny along the exterior of the cargo bay would be a hopeless endeavor. There simply wasn't anything to hold on to. By exiting from the front, he would have to traverse only a couple of feet to reach the passenger's-side door on the left, where he would have a stable platform to stand on—the running board—and lots of things to hold on to. Thankfully, because the lorry was traveling in the inside lane, he wouldn't have to worry about cars whizzing past his back. All the same, that first step, with the wind whipping at his trouser leg, sent his heart rate soaring.

Don't think about it, he told himself. *Just do it.*

He swung his other leg out, then twisted around so that he was facing inside with both legs dangling down and the top of the side rail pressing into his abdomen. He extended his left foot forward, sliding it in the direction of the door while steadily lowering himself down until his outstretched foot came to rest on the running board. He quickly lowered himself the rest of the way, fighting the wind to bring his other foot forward onto the running board. Speed was of paramount importance. If the driver happened to glance at his side mirror, Sutherland would lose the element of surprise and quite possibly his life.

With three points of contact—two feet on the running board and one hand clutching the side rail—he stretched out his left hand and grasped the door handle. As soon as he had a firm grasp on it, he let go with his right hand and hauled himself forward, grasping the door handle with his right hand and simultaneously letting go with his left and moving it to the mirror frame.

Although he now had an unrestricted view of the interior of the cab, he wasn't looking. Instead, his attention was almost completely given to the parallel tasks of holding on for dear life and working the door lever. Nevertheless, it did not escape his notice that the cab had only one occupant.

Just the driver, he thought. *This just might work.*

The door was unlocked, the latch releasing when he worked the lever. He opened it just enough to reach inside and grasp the doorframe, then let go of the mirror and swung his body back toward the rear of the cab, giving himself enough room to pull the door open.

He imagined the driver, now fully aware of the attempted intrusion

and overcoming his initial shock, would be reaching for a pistol in order to repel the attack, but there was nothing to be done about it.

Fighting the pressure of the wind against the door, he forced it
open wide enough to slip through and pulled himself into the cab, his
left hand raised in preparation to deflect the driver's weapon.

Only there wasn't a weapon. The driver hadn't moved, hadn't reacted to the intrusion. He just continued to stare straight ahead, seemingly oblivious to Sutherland's presence.

"Pull over!" commanded Sutherland. "Right bloody now!"

The man gave no indication that he had heard.

Sutherland was about to repeat the demand, but before he could, he
realized two things. The first was the identity of the man in the driver's seat—it was Padraig Duggan.

The second was that Duggan wasn't, in fact, actually driving the
lorry because, unless Sutherland was very much mistaken, Padraig
Duggan was stone-dead.

Just to be sure, Sutherland pressed two fingers to the man's neck,
searching in vain for a pulse. Duggan's pallid flesh was cool to the
touch.

"Poor sod," Sutherland muttered. Evidently, the same goons who
had taken him and Congreve had caught Duggan as well and, likely
branding him a traitor to the cause, had summarily disposed of him
rather than merely tying him up to be another victim of the bomb
blast. "If you're dead, who's driving the bloody lorry?"

For the first time since gaining the cab, Sutherland took a moment
to inspect the interior. The dashboard panel was a flat-screen, the
gauges and indicators virtual rather than mechanical, displaying a
range of visual and textual information beyond just the current speed
of the vehicle. One of the displays was a real-time GPS map, with the
lorry marked as a blue dot following an ever-shortening route also
marked in blue. At the top of the screen, in bright red letters, was the
message "Autonomous Drive Mode—On."

Even just a few years earlier, this revelation would have beggared belief, but Sutherland knew that robotic vehicles were no longer the stuff of science fiction. He supposed it was inevitable terrorists would see their potential for use as land-based strike drones.

That explains why they weren't worried we might set the bomb off.

Relieved that he would not have to fight for control of the lorry, Sutherland set about maneuvering Duggan's body out of the driver's seat. The deceased man's limbs were stiff with rigor mortis, which actually made the task a little easier, though Sutherland still had to perform a contortion act in order to climb over the body and insert himself in the driver's seat. Once stationed there, he immediately grasped the steering wheel and began applying the brake pedal. Either of these actions should have immediately kicked the vehicle out of autonomous mode, but the brake pedal remained unyielding, as did the steering wheel. Frowning, he tried tapping the notification on the display screen, but it too remained unchanged.

Sutherland experienced a sinking feeling in his gut. He tried the brake again, tried hauling on the steering wheel with all his might, and even tried the parking brake and motor shutoff button. None of those efforts worked. The controls were utterly unresponsive. The lorry rolled onward.

Through the front windscreen, he could see the urban skyline of Belfast coming into view. In a few minutes, they would pass through the heart of the city.

On the display, the right indicator began flashing, and a few seconds later, the steering wheel moved in Sutherland's hands as the lorry eased into the middle lane and then, when the way was clear, moved over one more. The reason for the lane change became apparent when the motorway split in two directions. An overhead sign revealed that the leftmost lanes turned west into Belfast, while the right lanes, where the lorry now was, continued east, becoming the M3 motorway.

"East," Sutherland murmured. "Where are you going anyway?"

He consulted the GPS map on the display and saw that the blue line continued along the M3, across the River Lagan, heading in the direction of the airport, at which point the line vanished off the edge of the map. He brought a tentative finger to the screen, hoping to zoom out and see the ultimate destination, but the map, like all the other controls, remained locked.

Below the map, the miles remaining and the estimated time of arrival provided the only clues to what that destination might be.

Six miles. Nine minutes.

He started as the passenger door opened, filling the cab with a rush of wind, and then a flushed-looking Congreve pulled himself awkwardly inside.

"Ambrose!" Sutherland exclaimed. "What the devil?"

Congreve, breathing rapidly and clutching the armrest as if holding on for dear life, took a moment to answer. "When we didn't stop, I feared the worst."

He glanced down at the corpse occupying the space between them, and his forehead creased in a look of confusion.

"It's Duggan," Sutherland explained. "He's dead. I mean, he was already dead when I found him."

"Then where's the driver?"

"There isn't one. This is an autonomous vehicle, and unfortunately, I haven't worked out how to take over the controls."

"Autonomous, you say." Congreve cast a jaundiced eye over the high-tech display screen. "Horrible idea, letting robots drive us around."

Sutherland eyed the map again. "Yes, well, you'll only have to put up with it for another eight minutes. That's how long we've got if we can't figure out how to shut it down."

"Eight minutes." Congreve glanced at the map, then began looking about the cab. "There must be a panel somewhere. A fuse or some wires we can pull."

"I'm sure there are. They're just not in here with us."

Congreve continued his futile search a moment longer, then brought his attention back to the map. Sutherland noted that they were down to seven minutes. "We aren't going to figure it out in time," he said gravely.

Congreve seemed not to have heard. "We're approaching a turn-around," he said.

Sutherland looked down again and saw that Congreve was correct. The blue line showing their route made an abrupt U-turn near the airport, turning south onto a series of connected local roads—Holywood Road, Hawthornden Way, Knock Road, Upper Knockbreda, Belvoir, and more—all of which composed the A55, a ring route that almost completely encircled Belfast proper. Sutherland recalled that he and Congreve had taken the same route when making the two-mile commute from the airport to . . .

"Police headquarters," he said with a heavy groan. "That's the target, Ambrose. They mean to blow up the police service."

THIRTY-TWO

Alex Hawke didn't run. Not right away at least.

Instead, he whipped the Glock from its holster at the small of his back, brought it up, and put a bullet between Klaus's eyes.

He would have preferred to take Konigstahl with the shot, but the ogre had put himself in the way, making him the more immediate threat.

The woods rang with the report, but before the sound could echo, even before the ejected spent shell casing could hit the ground, Hawke was moving, sidestepping the mortally wounded man, to put the front sights of his weapon on Konigstahl, and as Klaus toppled like a felled tree, Hawke pulled the trigger again.

But Konigstahl was also moving, overcoming his surprise and retreating behind the base of the tower, and even though Hawke tried to lead him, the second shot missed, sparking off the metal framework.

Hawke resisted the impulse to give chase. Konigstahl would almost certainly be waiting for him, ready to take a killing shot with the rifle the instant Hawke rounded the corner. Konigstahl was a hunter, not a fighter, and hunters played the waiting game. That gave Hawke an opening.

Now it is time to bloody run.

Hawke grabbed Pippa's arm and dragged her along, fleeing into the woods, moving perpendicular to the cable car line. The trees would provide immediate, if imperfect, cover from the Prince's long rifle.

At least until Konigstahl decided to start tracking them.

The irony of the slogan on his T-shirt was not lost on Hawke. He was accustomed to being the hunter, not the hunted, and the idea of behaving like prey galled him to no end. Though he was not often given to reflecting on his own mortality, at some level, he understood and accepted that dying of old age was probably not in the cards for him; nor, truth be told, was doing so something he even desired. His would be a warrior's death, charging *into* battle, weapon in hand, when the Valkyries came to welcome him into Valhalla.

But not today, Hawke told himself as he sprinted. *Not yet.*

There were also practical arguments against running. There was a reason that self-defense trainers advised their students to charge a gun, flee a knife. It wasn't that bullets became less lethal the closer you got, but rather that trying to take a gunman's weapon away, while most likely a suicidal endeavor, stood a far better chance of success than showing him your back.

And if you failed, then at least you died fighting.

Cue the Valkyries.

But, like all good advice, there were situations where that timeless wisdom simply didn't apply. This, Hawke judged, was one of them.

Hawke knew that in the classic short story "The Most Dangerous Game" by Richard Connell—which both Konigstahl and Pippa had referenced the previous evening—a mad Cossack general named Zaroff turned a Caribbean jungle island into a private hunting reserve where he stalked and killed human prey. A big-game hunter named Rainsford, inadvertently marooned on the island, became Zaroff's most challenging foe, turning the tables on the Cossack, rigging traps and ambushes, exchanging the roles of hunter and hunted, and ultimately defeating Zaroff.

No doubt that was the sort of challenge Konigstahl envisioned for Hawke.

That, however, would require Hawke to play along, something he had no intention whatsoever of doing.

No, Hawke wasn't going to play Konigstahl's game. He wasn't going to lurk in the woods, stalking Konigstahl in turn or lying in ambush, wasting precious time waiting for the Prince to come to him. As appealing as that course of action might have been, his priority was the mission.

Must find Charles, Hawke reminded himself, his legs and lungs burning as he continued to run, dodging trees and branches as he went.

Even if Konigstahl wasn't, as he claimed, involved in the plot to abduct King Charles, the man knew of it, and an investigation into his phone or internet activity might reveal how he had come by that knowledge. And that was a thread that just might lead back to the kidnappers. Therefore, it was imperative that Hawke and Pippa escape the Wolkenheim Forest as quickly as possible. And so, as bad as Alex wanted to kill Konigstahl and put an end to the man, Hawke had no choice but to run.

As soon as the clearing with the tower was a good hundred yards behind them, Hawke veered north, trying to orient himself in the direction of the car park where the Locomotive—and freedom—waited.

Konigstahl would eventually, if he had not already, realize that this was their goal and would almost certainly try to reach the station ahead of them, which meant there was no time to waste. Because Hawke was moving at a near run, as fast as conditions would allow, there was no chance to explain any of this to Pippa, but he sensed she needed no explanation. She had pulled free of his grasp but matched his stride and was actually moving through the woods far more gracefully than he.

Hawke had estimated the distance to the car park to be about two miles—about half an hour at their current pace. The going would get easier in full daylight, but that would also work against them, increasing their visibility.

From somewhere behind them, he heard the roar of a small engine—likely a motorcycle or some other off-road vehicle. The pitch of the engine immediately began to change as the source began moving away—Konigstahl, no doubt, was racing along an access road or game trail to reach the cable car station ahead of them. In the story, Zaroff had cheated by using dogs to track Rainsford, as well as arming himself with a pistol while allowing Rainsford only a hunting knife.

Here Konigstahl was cheating with technology.

"He's going to get there ahead of us," breathed Pippa.

"Nothing for it," answered Hawke. "We'll just have to deal with it once we get there. At least we know where he is for the moment."

That moment lasted only about ten minutes. During that time, the engine noise continued to recede until it was a barely audible whine, but then it cut out altogether.

Hawke came to a full stop, head cocked, listening for the sound to come again. "He's reached the car park. Now he'll set up a shooting position somewhere and try to pick us off when we come out of the woods."

"I know he thinks he can get away with murder" was Pippa's skeptical reply. "But shooting us in cold blood and in broad daylight?"

"He'll make sure there's nobody around to see it."

"Then how do we make it past him?"

Hawke did not have a good answer to that question. No matter how clever their approach, they would, in the end, have to cross open ground—at least a hundred yards from the edge of the woods surrounding the cable car station to where the Locomotive waited.

From his military training, Hawke knew that sometimes there was no good alternative to crossing open ground to reach an objective. Infantrymen were taught techniques for movement under fire, but the odds always favored the enemy in a fixed location. The longer you were in the open, the more chances that enemy would have to shoot you dead.

"If only we could shorten that distance somehow," he mused aloud.

"Or move faster," said Pippa. She cocked her head to the side. "He had a motorbike stashed out there. Maybe there's another one for Klaus to use."

"Pip, that's bloody brilliant." Unprepared for such high praise, Pippa broke into a broad smile. Hawke, however, wasn't finished. "We'll have to backtrack to the tower. And if there isn't a second motorbike, it will be a wasted trip."

"I say we take the chance. Anything that might give us an advantage."

Hawke regarded her for a moment and then, recalling Sir David's parting words, nodded. "You're the boss, Miss Guinness."

———————

There wasn't a second motorcycle.

When they reached the base of the stanchion, Hawke took a moment to turn out a very dead Klaus's pockets, an effort that produced nothing useful, after which they began searching the surrounding area, quickly locating a concrete structure about the size of a single-car garage. It was secured with a heavy-duty metal roll-up door.

"This must be Konigstahl's back door," said Hawke, inspecting an electronic keypad that presumably restricted access to the interior of the structure. "If there is another motorbike, it's on the wrong side of it."

"There must be some way to open it."

Hawke shook his head. "I don't think we're going to kick our way through this one."

Pippa sagged. "That's it, then. This was all a waste of time, and we're still going to have to run the gauntlet."

Hawke looked up at the tower framework, searching for inspiration. The tower was now completely visible, stark against the cloudless sky;

it loomed over them like the exposed skeleton of a colossal iron giant holding up the cables with its upraised arms. The only part of it that looked even remotely human in scale was the metal maintenance ladder that rose up through the middle of the lattice. "Maybe not," he said slowly.

Pippa, following his gaze, looked up as well. "What are you thinking?"

"We try your other idea."

"My other idea?"

Hawke's smile was without humor. "We do what even eagles didn't dare."

THIRTY-THREE

Her earlier objection notwithstanding, Pippa received Hawke's plan with, if not exactly enthusiasm, then at least a sort of weary resignation. Hawke guessed that their earlier abseil had inured her to the sort of gut-clenching fear typically engendered by activities where one's feet weren't on solid ground. Or perhaps the certain knowledge that death was waiting for them to walk out of the woods gave her the courage to embrace daring alternatives.

The ascent of the maintenance ladder raised them above the treetops, rewarding them with an unobstructed view of the valley below and the cable car station, a postage-stamp-sized clearing. From the ladder, it did not look all that far away, but Hawke knew that would change once they reached the platform at the top.

The platform, like the tower, had been engineered to flex and sway with the wind. While structurally sound, this design feature created the impression of instability—much like standing up in a rowboat—which only exacerbated the sense of vertigo Hawke felt as he crawled on hands and knees across the exposed platform to the outrigger that supported the cable car's forty-eight-millimeter fixed suspension line and the twenty-six-millimeter haul rope. Despite the sheer insanity of what he was about to do next, he felt a profound sense of relief when he successfully clipped the carabiner on the front of his safety harness to the haul line. Once Pippa was clipped in behind him, and after reviewing some basic but critical aspects of the plan, he took a deep breath and then flung himself from the platform.

He fell hardly at all, the carabiner and harness arresting his motion and redistributing the potential energy of the fall along the slope of the cable. After that, a lot of things began to happen very quickly.

While Hawke's plan owed much in the way of inspiration to the exploits of cinematic action heroes, he understood that depictions of silver-screen action figures like James Bond rarely took into account physical realities. Hawke was neither a physicist nor an engineer, but as a former combat aviator, he had a better-than-average understanding of Newtonian physics. He knew, for instance, that a body in free fall accelerated at a rate of about ten meters per second squared, reaching terminal velocity—the rate at which atmospheric drag canceled out acceleration—of about 120 miles per hour in twelve to fourteen seconds. He also knew that the rudimentary form of zip-lining that he and Pippa were attempting would greatly reduce both the rate of acceleration and terminal velocity. The exact numbers were beyond his ability to calculate, but he estimated acceleration at roughly half of free fall and a terminal velocity of no more than forty miles per hour. That would get them to the bottom in about three minutes, though the sudden stop at the end of the journey would be roughly equivalent to getting hit by a wrecking ball. That was cause for concern, but it was not the most immediate challenge posed by his rapid acceleration.

Another core principle of physics was that energy never went away; it only changed forms over time. The energy required to climb the tower, fighting gravity, was called potential energy. The leap from the tower, surrendering to the acceleration of gravity, transformed potential energy into kinetic energy, which, absent any means of arresting the fall, like a bungee cord, would have reached its full potential in the catastrophic impact with the ground. Zip-lining down the cable slowed the rate of acceleration through friction braking and lengthened both the time and the distance of the fall considerably, but in so doing, it changed some of the kinetic energy into thermal energy.

Heat.

In a matter of seconds, the friction of the steel clip rubbing against the steel cable created a hot spot that almost immediately began throwing off bright yellow sparks and a visible haze of rust-colored smoke that hovered around the clip and cable like an aura. The conductive properties of the metal rapidly distributed the heat, quickly raising the overall temperature of the carabiner, making it too hot to touch, even with gloves.

Not that Hawke was going to put his fingers anywhere near either the cable or the carabiner.

The sparks, he knew, were actually tiny particles of metal oxidizing as they scraped away from both the cable and the clip. While the heat generated by friction was nowhere near hot enough to melt through steel, the cable would, over a long enough distance, effectively saw through the carabiner. Anything less durable than steel—say, for example, flesh and bone—would offer roughly the same amount of resistance as soft cheese.

The heat radiating off the carabiner, which was already hot enough that Hawke could feel it on his face, was concerning for another reason. While there was little risk of the clip failing in the near term, the nylon fabric of the safety harness was another matter. As a way of mitigating the heat effect, he had taken the precaution of stuffing a strip of leather—which he'd cut from dead Klaus's belt using his reliable old Victorinox Swiss Army knife—between the carabiners and the D ring connection point on their harnesses. He could only hope that it would provide enough insulation to keep the harness from melting through.

Thirty seconds and more than three hundred yards into the descent, with the carabiner shrieking like a banshee above him, the smell of hot metal and scorched leather in his nose, and his heart pounding like a jackhammer, Hawke put his fears aside, leaned back in his harness, and allowed himself to enjoy the ride. He glanced back up the line just in time to see Pippa take the leap.

Although Hawke was traveling at a frenetic rate, the cable car station at the base of the mountain remained maddeningly distant. After another full minute, Hawke felt like he had barely traversed a quarter of the distance while above him, the carabiner continued to shriek and smoke, scattering sparks as if it might, at any moment, disintegrate completely, leaving him to plummet into the forest canopy a hundred feet below.

When he reached the halfway point in the journey, however, his perception of time elapsed and distance traveled flipped. The station no longer looked quite so distant. In the car park beside it, the Locomotive and two other vehicles occupying the mostly empty square of asphalt now looked less like toys in a shoebox diorama. The end of the journey seemed to be approaching with alarming rapidity. His somewhat irrational fears of mechanical failure took a back seat to the very real problem of slowing down in time to avoid a sudden stop at the end. Fortunately, he had given this some consideration ahead of time and prepared accordingly.

Just as a car's brake shoes added friction to fight not only a vehicle's inertia but also its motive force from the drive train, he would need something to supply additional friction to his descent system—something he and Pippa could use as a brake shoe. His solution was to use an actual shoe—not his own but rather one of the sturdy oversized brogues that had been worn by Konigstahl's ogre servant, Klaus.

Carefully, keeping his hands well clear of the cable as the carabiner raced along it, he placed the heel of the shoe against the cable and pressed hard. The shoe immediately began to smoke, adding the smell of burning rubber to the miasma trailing Hawke down the mountainside, but the shoe's effectiveness in reducing the speed of his descent seemed negligible.

The cable car station loomed ahead of him, rising quickly.

Too quickly.

He pressed harder with the shoe, feeling the rising heat through layers of leather. He half expected the shoe to burst into flames, like a meteor burning up in the atmosphere.

This isn't working, he thought. *I waited too long.*

But no, it *was* working. He *was* slowing down. He could feel the effects of steady deceleration, his body swinging forward just a little as its inertia warred against the added friction slowing the carabiner.

At the platform below, he could now see the waiting cable car attached to the line down which he was sliding. Five hundred yards to go? Four hundred?

And he was moving at . . . What? Fifteen miles per hour? Twenty?

Maybe faster?

Hitting the cable car at that speed would be like running at a full sprint into a brick wall.

Suddenly, the sound of a gunshot tore through the persistent high-frequency shriek coming off the cable, reminding Hawke that crashing to a stop wasn't the only deadly peril he faced.

Konigstahl. The bastard saw us.

Hawke peered into the clearing below, hoping to fix Konigstahl's location. He knew the sound of the report would not travel as fast as a rifle bullet, which meant that Konigstahl had already missed with the first shot—or missed *him* at any rate. A glance back up the line showed, to Hawke's immense relief, Pippa furiously pressing Klaus's other shoe against the cable.

Missed us both.

That wasn't a surprise. Hitting a moving target was an exceedingly difficult skill to master and not one that Konigstahl—a hunter, not a fighter—was likely to have bothered with. But shooting them would get easier the closer they got, the slower they were moving.

"Come on," Hawke whispered, scanning the clearing again. "Take another shot. Show me where you are."

Konigstahl obliged, and a heartbeat later, a faint flash of an orange-yellow flame and a puff of smoke issued from the vicinity of Hawke's Bentley.

The bastard's shooting from behind my own bloody car!

This time Hawke both heard and felt the bullet sizzle through the air, mere inches from his head. The report followed almost simultaneously.

Hawke considered drawing his Glock and returning fire, if only to give the Prince something to worry about, but decided against it. He was only ten or fifteen seconds from reaching the station and the cover it would afford. Once down, he would deal with Konigstahl.

Tossing aside the smoking remnants of the shoe, Hawke let gravity accelerate him forward once more. The platform rose up under him like the waiting deck of an aircraft carrier. He soared above it, arrowing toward the roof of the waiting cable car. At the last instant, he brought his legs up, then extended his feet toward the front exterior wall of the cabin, and . . .

Contact!

The sudden stop was jarring, sending jolts of pain up his legs, but he allowed himself to fold up like an accordion, dissipating some of the energy from the collision. As soon as the initial shock passed, he flopped forward onto the roof of the cabin, which was now rocking back and forth crazily from the impact, and he rolled over in preparation for Pippa's arrival.

Like Hawke, she had managed to reduce her rate of descent considerably, so it seemed to take forever for her to close the distance—an eternity in which Hawke felt particularly vulnerable. Konigstahl was nearby, out in the car park, not even fifty yards away.

Come on, Pip.

Then she was there, coming at him like she'd been shot from a cannon. With impeccable timing, he threw an arm around her hips, hugging her against his body, cushioning her impact. Searing pain blossomed along his upper arm as he made glancing contact with the carabiner attached to her harness, but he endured it until the cabin's violent rocking subsided. Then he drew out his Swiss Army knife, opened it, and, with two quick cuts, sliced through first his own harness at the D ring connection point and then Pippa's.

As he made the second cut, a bullet from Konigstahl's rifle tore into the roof of the cabin, showering them with toothpick-sized splinters.

"Get down," he urged. "Find cover."

Pippa did not need to be told twice. She rolled from the roof of the cabin, flopping down on the far side of the platform, keeping the cabin between her and the car park. Hawke dropped down beside her, coming up in a crouch behind the painted wooden side panels with his Glock at the ready.

"Stay here," he cautioned, and then rolled out from behind the cabin, bounded up, and ran for the nearby station house. Another report cracked in the air, another miss, and then Hawke was behind the building.

He didn't linger there, however, but instead continued along the back of the structure at a dead run, rounding the far corner to move along the side of the building toward the car park.

Now that he'd again made it to cover, Hawke was done running.

It's time to fight.

He spied the Locomotive sitting exactly where he'd left it, and saw Konigstahl kneeling near the back corner of it, peering through his rifle scope, looking, or so it seemed, directly at him.

He threw himself flat onto his belly just as Konigstahl pulled the rifle's trigger, again loosing a round that passed through the air above Hawke, right where he'd been standing a moment before. Hawke, now in the prone position, brought the Glock up in a two-handed grip and returned fire. Konigstahl, however, was already falling back, shrinking behind the rear end of the Locomotive. Hawke bolted to his feet and sprinted ahead, the Glock leading the way.

He hadn't gotten a good look at the Prince's rifle, but based on Konigstahl's pattern of fire, he surmised that it was most likely a bolt-action hunting rifle and not a semiautomatic assault-type rifle. That meant that with each shot fired, the Prince would have to manually work the bolt to eject the spent cartridge and advance a round from the internal magazine. Most hunting rifle magazines held five rounds—the exact number Konigstahl had fired. That did not necessarily mean that Konigstahl's rifle was out of bullets—he could have been reloading as he went—nor did it preclude the possibility that he possessed a sidearm. Nevertheless, Hawke was willing to take the chance.

He did not slow as he emerged from beside the station house but moved toward the Locomotive, advancing in a tactical shooter's stance, holding the Glock out in front of him with both hands, slightly hunched over to reduce his profile. When he reached the Bentley, he checked both ways, then continued around it in a clockwise fashion without slowing. As he rounded the back end of the coupe, he checked the two vehicles in the lot—a silver Mercedes S-class sedan and a white BMW i8 coupe, both of which, he recalled, had been in the lot when they'd arrived the previous night.

Konigstahl's toys, no doubt.

He glimpsed movement off to his left, shifted toward it, and saw the Prince running flat out across the car park in the direction of the mountain. Hawke snapped off a reflex shot but Konigstahl was already beyond the effective range of the pistol, and before Hawke could take better aim, the Prince disappeared into the wood line.

Hawke started off in pursuit but then just as quickly pulled up short. As much as he wanted to wipe Heinrich Konigstahl from the face of the earth, he had more urgent priorities. He'd beaten Konigstahl, escaped Wolkenheim Mountain, and survived the hunt, and that would have to suffice.

At least for now, he told himself.

Without lowering the Glock, he called out, "Pip! All clear. Time to go."

After a quick check to ensure that the car had not been booby-trapped or otherwise tampered with, Hawke and Pippa boarded the Locomotive and charged away from Wolkenheim Mountain.

Although they were exhausted from the ordeal of escaping Konig-stahl's mountaintop fortress, rest was the last thing on Hawke's mind as they raced down the two-lane mountain road leading out of the Ammergau Alps. Now that the ordeal was behind them, he felt increasingly anxious to share what they had learned, and even more so with respect to what would happen next.

The Prime Minister's deadline was fast approaching. Charles was still out there, presumably still a captive. And all Hawke and Pippa had to show for their efforts was a gossamer thread of evidence that might lead nowhere.

Hopefully Ambrose is having better luck, he thought.

His anxiety translated into a heavy foot. The Bentley roared down the highway, well in excess of the posted speed limit. Hawke was oblivious to the magnificent scenery passing by outside and barely even aware of the slower-moving vehicles around which he wove like a downhill slalom skier. Sitting beside him, Pippa was wholly focused on the screen of her mobile phone, which, like the proverbial watched kettle that never boiled, had yet to acquire a signal.

A roadside sign alerted him to an upcoming curve, along with a recommended speed of forty kilometers per hour—about twenty-five miles per hour. Hawke grudgingly tapped the brake and downshifted, but knowing the Bentley's capabilities, he brought it down to only forty *miles* per hour entering the turn.

"Finally!" cried Pippa, waving her phone triumphantly.

Hawke kept his eyes on the road but heard the buzz of his own mobile vibrating on the seat beside him as a day's worth of pending notifications began pouring in. Curious despite himself, he picked it up and glanced at the list of missed calls and texts, hoping to see Congreve's name.

Congreve had not called or texted. Nor, he realized belatedly, had Anastasia, and it bothered him that it didn't bother him more. There were, however, several missed calls from Stokely Jones Jr.

Stoke, what the devil are you up to?

The curve proved to be just one of several serpentine undulations weaving to and fro along the flank of a rocky hillside. To the left, the loose terrain was held back by a chain-link mesh. To the right, a guardrail provided a visual warning of the drop-off beyond. Despite his faith in both himself and his machine, Hawke was obliged to ride the brake into each turn, if only to avoid flinging Pippa about like a pebble in a tin can.

"Damn," said Pippa. "Lost it again."

At that very moment, Hawke glimpsed in the rearview mirror a vehicle approaching fast.

Much too fast for his liking.

"What's this bloody fool on about?" he murmured, keeping one eye on the mirror until the curve took the other vehicle out of view. He let off the brake and was just beginning to accelerate out of the turn when the car hove into view once more, much closer now than it had been, practically right on top of the Locomotive.

Hawke reacted more by reflex than by conscious thought, pressing the accelerator harder, but even as the Bentley began to pull away, the other driver whipped his car into the opposing lane, charged up alongside him, and then, inexplicably, slowed to match his speed.

Hawke's irritation flashed to anger as he recognized the vehicle—it was the Mercedes S-class he'd last seen in the car park at the cable car station.

Konigstahl's Mercedes.

But when the driver turned to look over at him, he realized that it wasn't Konigstahl sitting behind the wheel.

"It's Tildy!" cried Pippa.

As if this identification were the permission she'd been waiting for, the unsmiling, formerly obsequious maid turned her gaze forward, and then the sedan began pulling ahead.

Hawke had no clue what the woman was doing, and his inability to fathom her intent set alarm bells ringing in his head. She was Konigstahl's creature, so her presence could only mean that the hunt was not finished after all.

He brought his foot to the brake, intending to further cut his speed and let the Mercedes pull ahead, but before he could, the sedan swerved to the right.

Hawke stomped down on the brake pedal, but it was already too late. The Mercedes collided with the front end of the Locomotive, shoving it to the right. Hawke hauled the steering wheel over, trying to keep the Bentley on the road, but to no avail. In the blink of an eye, both vehicles, locked together in a deadly embrace, veered off the pavement, smashed through the guardrail, and hurtled down the embankment.

Two minutes later, a white BMW i8 coupe arrived at the line of cars backed up along the highway. The driver, whom some locals might have recognized as Prince Heinrich Konigstahl von Bayern, got out and joined the growing throng of morbidly curious onlookers who had similarly left their cars behind to bear witness to the aftermath of the horrifying accident that had only just occurred.

The hillside below bore the scars of the event. Huge swaths of disrupted earth and destroyed vegetation showed the path of destruction left by the doomed vehicles, but it was the smoking wreckage more than a hundred feet below that gave the most accurate testimony to what had happened.

"Hat jemand einen Krankenwagen gerufen?" asked one bystander.

Did someone call an ambulance?

"Besser gleich einen Leichenwagen," replied another. *"Das hätte niemand überleben können."*

Better to get a hearse. Nobody could have survived that.

Several others signaled their agreement with this sentiment.

A highway patrol motorcycle trooper arrived a few minutes later, threading the narrow gap between the stalled lanes. His first task was to disperse the crowd, ordering the onlookers to return to their vehicles so that the traffic jam could be cleared in order to open a lane for emergency responders. Konigstahl took one last satisfied look at the wreckage below, then headed back to his car.

Tildy had performed spectacularly, a testament to the effectiveness of his training, and while he felt a small measure of regret at the necessity of having to sacrifice her, he was eager to begin training her replacement.

But first, he had a throne to win.

THIRTY-FOUR

The lorry slowed, nearly coming to a full stop as it rounded the interchange onto Holywood Road. Had they been so inclined, Congreve and Sutherland could have simply opened the doors and leapt clear, but escaping fiery destruction was not their immediate concern. In seven minutes' time, when the lorry reached its preprogrammed destination—the headquarters of the Police Service of Northern Ireland, the spiritual successor to the hated Royal Ulster Constabulary—the detonation of the two-and-a-half-ton high-explosive mixture of ammonium nitrate and fuel oil would wreak immeasurable harm, not only to the police officers and support personnel who would be injured or killed in the blast but also to the quarter-century-long peace that had endured, if somewhat uneasily, in Northern Ireland.

Seven minutes.

That was how long Congreve and Sutherland had to prevent the bomb from reaching its target.

"There has to be an override switch somewhere," said Sutherland as the lorry began accelerating again. He tapped at random spots on the touch-screen dash console, then leaned down into the footwell to search beneath the console. In an ordinary vehicle, there would have been exposed wiring and a fuse box, but the lorry's electronic inner workings were concealed beneath a molded plastic covering.

"If I can just get this panel off," Sutherland said, trying to work his fingernails into a hair-thin seam.

"Try the pipe tool," urged Congreve.

Sutherland fished the folding tool from his pocket, flipped it open, and tried to jam the scraper blade into the seam. It skittered away, leaving a long gouge on the plastic but otherwise yielding little result. He tried again and, after working it back and forth, finally succeeded in opening a small crack near the seam, but the rest of the panel remained maddeningly intact.

"It's no good, Ross," said Congreve, eyeing the revised ETA on the GPS map. Six minutes. "We're not going to stop it in time."

"We can't just give up, Ambrose."

"I concur. We must redirect our efforts to better effect."

"The bomb?"

"Exactly. If we can defuse it, stopping the lorry becomes a moot issue."

Sutherland sagged back in his seat. "It's tamperproof. If we try to defuse it, we'll just set it off prematurely."

Congreve glanced out at the passing scenery. The section of road through which they were passing was semirural, with woodland to the left and low-density development well away from the road to the right. From their earlier travels, Congreve knew that would change the closer they got to PSNI headquarters. A more immediate concern, however, was road traffic. There were easily a dozen or more vehicles within a hundred yards of the lorry at any given moment.

"Then we must be exceedingly cautious," Congreve advised. "But if it must go off, better that it be out here than at police headquarters."

Sutherland stared back at him as if aghast at the cold calculation his colleague was making but then sagged in defeat. "You're right, of course." He regarded Congreve a moment longer. "Best let me go first."

Congreve, who was still feeling jittery after having made the traverse from the back of the lorry to the cab, just nodded and did his best to get out of Sutherland's way. The younger police inspector moved quickly to the left-side door, opened it, stepped out onto the running board, and then, without any hesitation, pulled himself up into the lorry's cargo area. Congreve gave the GPS one last look, noting that they were down to four minutes, and then moved to follow.

Having successfully made the transit in the opposite direction, he was marginally more confident making the second attempt. *Just like climbing a ladder,* he told himself, though as a general rule, he preferred to avoid any activities that required him to do that.

With both feet on the running board, he reached up and took hold of the side rail where Sutherland had created the opening in the tarpaulin. Congreve realized only then that returning to the rear cargo area would be fundamentally more difficult than leaving it. Getting to the cab had been merely a question of stepping down onto the running board, but getting back up would require him to both leap up and pull himself the rest of the way, using only his upper body strength.

Nothing for it, he told himself. *Just make it happen.*

As he clung there, trying to summon up the courage to commit, he realized that he was now the object of much attention from other drivers. He heard their honking horns and saw their pointing fingers and looks of amazement.

If only there were some way to communicate with them, he thought. *Warn them to evacuate the police headquarters.*

But even if there had been some way to do that, there simply wasn't time for an evacuation. Defusing the bomb was their only hope.

He flexed his knees experimentally in preparation for the leap and then, after an audible three count, heaved himself onto the side rail. The leap took him farther than he had dared hope, and he was able to pull himself up so that his abdomen was folded across the side rail. But without anything to brace his feet against, he was unable to go any farther. He kicked his legs as if swimming, but all this did was make him feel like he was slipping.

"Ross! Lend a hand, old boy!"

Sutherland, who had been hunched over the fuel barrels, staring down at the web of detonator wires, looked over and, seeing Congreve's struggle, hurried over to assist. He gripped Congreve's forearms but then, instead of pulling him the rest of the way in, just held him there. "How long do we have?" he asked.

"Three minutes," grunted Congreve. "Maybe less."

Sutherland looked past him, gazing through the opening and out at the road passing by. "How fast do you think we're going? Thirty kph? Forty?"

"I've no bloody idea. Help me up."

"It's no good, Ambrose," sighed Sutherland, forlorn. "Anything I do will just set it off."

"Better to die trying. Now, help me up."

Sutherland shook his head. "No reason both of us should die."

"What? That's rubbish, Ross. Pull me up. We'll do this together."

But Sutherland just gave a grim smile, slid his hands down to Congreve's wrists, and then, in a single fluid motion, broke Congreve's grip on the side rail and thrust him away.

Congreve barely had time to cry out in alarm as he fell backward away from the lorry, arms flailing. Then he hit the macadam, and his cry was silenced as the breath was knocked out of him.

Sutherland watched anxiously as Congreve tumbled and skidded along in the lorry's wake, finally coming to rest, arms and legs splayed out like those of a sacrificial offering. Thankfully, the cars trailing behind the lorry stopped well short of him, blocking traffic so that there would be no chance of anyone running him over. Sutherland kept watching just long enough to see one of the drivers get out and run over to offer aid to Congreve. Then he looked away and returned to the bomb.

He did not regret shoving his old friend off the lorry. There was a very real possibility that Congreve would sustain serious injuries from being ejected from the lorry at that speed, but he *would* live.

Sutherland leaned his elbows on the top of one of the fuel drums and peered at the wires sprouting from its filler cap. From what he knew of such devices, the wires would connect the power source in the plastic toolbox to blasting caps—small explosive charges—inside the drums. In addition to a power source, the box would hold some sort of trigger device—a timer, a GPS device, or even a mobile phone—that, once initiated, would set off the blasting caps, which would, in turn, detonate the ANFO mixture. Defusing the bomb was conceivably as simple as cutting the blasting caps off from the power supply, which was why bomb makers sometimes added tamper triggers so that any attempt to cut the power supply would instantly trigger the device. Sutherland had seen evidence of just such a countermeasure during his initial inspection of the bomb and knew that there was no easy way to beat it. The strips of tape holding the detonator wires in place also contained fine copper wires conducting a low-level current that, unless he was mistaken, supplied power to an electromagnetic relay. Removing the tape or breaking the wires would interrupt the circuit and close the relay, which would, in turn, trigger the bomb.

He had not overstated the problem when he'd told Congreve that anything he might attempt would set the bomb off.

But Congreve had not been wrong in his determination that it was better to die trying.

There was a chance, a very slim chance, that if he was able to rip all the wires loose from the power supply in a single pull, the blasting caps would be rendered inert. If he got it wrong, he would die, along with everyone else in a hundred-yard radius, but as Congreve had also said, better to detonate the bomb on the road than in the car park outside police headquarters.

He moved back over to the open corner of the canvas cover, looked out, and saw trees flashing past.

If I'm going to do this, he thought, *it has to be now.*

He moved back over to the bomb, gripping the power supply with one hand and the bundle of wires in the other.

"God save the King," he murmured, and then pulled.

THIRTY-FIVE

UNKNOWN LOCATION

The Magician watched the news reports coming out of Belfast with rapt fascination. While things had not gone quite according to plan, with the truck bomb detonating nearly a mile away from the designated target, injuring several but, at last report, killing only two, it had nevertheless ignited a fire in Northern Ireland, a fire that was quickly spreading.

Ulster Protestants were flooding social media sites with demands for a swift military reprisal and a return to martial law. Republican dissidents had been slower to react, initially denying any involvement, but their message had quickly evolved. Quite a few of the more conspiracy-minded influencers, finding it suspicious that the bomb attack had failed to destroy its target, began accusing Unionists of conducting a false flag operation. Best of all, at least to the Magician's way of thinking, mainstream news outlets were beginning to question the seeming ambivalence from Buckingham Palace. The heir to the throne, Prince William, had made an appearance, giving a strongly worded but politically cautious statement urging patience, calm, and unity, but the King?

Where was the King?

As distractions went, it was very nearly perfect. The attention of the authorities was focused on Northern Ireland. Eventually, they would widen the scope of their investigation, but by then, it wouldn't matter.

Dylan Fahey was less pleased with the outcome.

"Bloody hell," he raged, storming into the control room where the Magician and Mr. Sten were watching a Sky News live stream.

The Magician looked up but did not rise. "Ah. You've arrived."

"This is a fucking disaster. I can't believe I let you talk me into this."

The Magician fought the urge to respond in kind. Fahey's reaction was maddening but not altogether unexpected. The Irishman was eager for violence, but then, when things didn't go exactly to plan, he panicked. "Calm down. Now is not the time to overreact."

"Like hell it isn't. One of the peelers survived. He knows my name."

"Now that you're here, it doesn't matter."

"It was a mistake," Dylan raged through gritted teeth. "Now they'll be looking at us. At me."

"Of course they will. That was the point. It was never your intention to fight from the shadows." Before Dylan could offer further complaint, the Magician took a more conciliatory tone. "This isn't a failure. You've gained us what we needed most. Time. The police will be looking for you in Belfast, expecting you to strike again there."

Dylan gazed back at him through narrowed eyes for a moment but offered no rebuttal. The Magician decided to press on to more important matters. "You have the package?"

"Aye. We were to lay my little brother to rest alongside our da today. But now?" He shook his head. "I don't know if we'll ever be able to lay him in consecrated ground."

"My condolences," interjected Mr. Sten. "I worked with Sean on several operations. He was a good man."

Dylan appeared somewhat mollified by the man's comments. The Magician seized on this, laying a hand on Dylan's shoulder as if offering a benediction. "After tomorrow, you'll be free to give your brother a hero's funeral."

The Irishman appeared to weigh this promise. "Do you really think it will work? I mean, *really* work?"

"Do I really think we can destroy the British monarchy and end the United Kingdom with one stroke?" The Magician smiled. "Let me show you something."

———————

The King heard the sound of his cell door open, heard the footsteps of one of his jailers approaching, but he did not raise his head. He would not give them the satisfaction of seeing just how low they had brought him.

"Majesty." The electronically modulated voice could belong only to Mr. Sten. "Have we given you sufficient time to reconsider our demands? Or do you perhaps require another demonstration of our resolve?"

The none too thinly veiled threat chilled the King. Did they have another hostage?

He didn't answer, didn't look up.

An electronic warble assaulted his ears—Sten laughing. "Relax, Majesty. There will be no need to repeat that unpleasantness. You see, when it became apparent that you would not relinquish your throne voluntarily, we realized that there were other ways you might prove useful. The good news for you is that your time with us will soon be at an end."

This disclosure almost prompted the King to look up, but sensing that the words concealed a fresh trap, the King refused to take the bait.

"The government has negotiated your release," Sten went on. "To-morrow, you'll be taken to Westminster."

Sten's words rang in his ears.

"The government has negotiated. . . . You'll be taken to Westminster."

Why Westminster?

He could think of only one good reason. The Palace of Westminster, on the north bank of the Thames, was where the members of the Houses of Parliament met and, therefore, the true center of the government of the United Kingdom. Although the King was the head of state and the Prime Minister led the government in the King's name, it was understood that true political power rested with the Ministers of Parliament, and with enough votes, they could, if they so chose, end the monarchy altogether.

Were those the terms of his release? Had his captors made a deal with the Prime Minister or some faction of Parliament to further reduce the power of the monarchy or perhaps end it altogether as a condition for his release?

Or was this merely another torment?

The click of the door latch engaging did what Sten's taunts could not. It aroused the King's curiosity sufficiently for him to raise his head. Sten had left the cell. Charles was alone once more.

———————

"Bloody hell," gasped Dylan as the hostage's face finally appeared on the screen showing the feed from the camera in the cell. "That's really *him*. You've got the bloody King."

"I do," replied the Magician.

"So that's what the peeler was on about. He asked me . . . asked me if I had the King. Couldn't make sense of the question, but now I understand. How did you pull it off?"

"With a great deal of planning and forethought. And of course, some help from your brother's organization."

"That must have cost you *something*," said Dylan.

"A king's ransom," said the Magician with a sly smile. "But worth every penny."

"What do you mean to do with him?"

"Just what he was told. Tomorrow, he goes to Westminster Palace."

"You negotiated his release?"

"Ah, no. That part was . . . a slight exaggeration."

Dylan was incredulous. "Then you're just letting him go?"

The Magician's smile broadened. "Not exactly. You see, we are going to send a message to Parliament. A message they will not be able to ignore. And the King, well, he will be our messenger."

THIRTY-SIX

Stokely Jones Jr. looked at the screen of his vibrating phone and frowned when he saw an unfamiliar number, along with the words *Munich, Germany.* "Who the hell do I know in Germany?"

It was a rhetorical question.

In truth, Stoke actually knew several people in Germany. Most were operators from the GSG 9, the elite counterterrorism service of the Federal Police with whom Stoke had run joint operations back when he'd led SEAL Team Six. Moreover, because Tactics International was . . . well, international, there were any number of German government officials and businessmen who might have had good reason to call him. All the same, he considered letting the call go to voicemail. He had a lot on his plate right now.

But . . . then again, it might be important.

He took the call. "Stokely Jones Jr. here."

"Stoke, old chap, it's Alex."

"Alex!" Stoke's disposition immediately improved by several degrees. "I didn't recognize the number. What are you doing in Germany?"

"New phone. Lost the old one and haven't had a chance to set the new one up with my number. And I'm not in Germany anymore. I'm in the air on my way back to London."

"Man, I've been trying like crazy to reach you. Hold on a sec. Let me put you on speaker." He did so and placed the phone on the tabletop before continuing. "I'm here with Ambrose and Harry."

"Where exactly is *here*, Stoke?" said Hawke. "And what the devil is Ambrose doing there with you? Last I heard, he was in Northern Ireland."

"He is. I mean, we are."

"Hullo, Alex," added Congreve desultorily.

"Ambrose, good to hear your voice."

Stoke heard in Hawke's reply an uncharacteristic weariness.

"Stoke," Hawke went on, "I know why Ambrose is there, but what on earth brought you and Harry over?"

"Long story, boss, and I'm going to tell you all about it, but first, there's something you should know." He glanced across the table at Congreve, who sat stiffly in his chair as much from grief as from the scrapes and bruises he'd sustained earlier that day. "Maybe you should tell him."

"Tell me what?" asked Hawke impatiently. "Would somebody bloody well—"

"Ross is dead, Alex." Congreve's grave tone silenced Hawke for a long moment.

"I'm sorry, brother," said Stoke. "I know you were close."

"Close," echoed Hawke quietly.

Stoke knew Hawke's history with Ross Sutherland. Their bond went beyond mere friendship. The two men had flown together in the Royal Navy, and many years back, when their fighter jet had been shot down, resulting in their capture by the enemy, Hawke had orchestrated their escape and literally carried Sutherland across the desert to freedom. It was a life debt that had been at least partially repaid when Sutherland helped Stoke track down and kill the Cuban sniper who had assassinated Hawke's wife, Victoria Sweet, on the steps of the church mere moments after the pronouncement of their union.

"What happened?" Hawke finally asked, his tone grief-stricken.

Congreve, who had been staring down at the tabletop, sighed heavily. "He gave his life to save others," he said. Then he added, "He saved my life as well."

Haltingly at first but then with more ease as he went along, he recounted the events that had led up to Sutherland's noble sacrifice. It was only at the end of the account, as he began to describe how Sutherland "threw me off the bloody lorry," that he began to choke up.

"I can't say for certain what happened next," he admitted. "I took a fair tumble and was barely hanging on to consciousness, but a few seconds later—" The words caught in his throat. He took a breath and tried again. "He must have tried to"—his throat constricted again, but he pushed through it, grunting out the last few words—"defuse the bloody thing. Or maybe when he realized he couldn't, he just . . . to keep it from . . ."

"That's all right, Ambrose," said Hawke. "I understand. Were you injured?"

"A bit bruised and battered," admitted Congreve.

"Yes, well, I know that feeling." Hawke paused a beat. "Ambrose, I have to ask. Is there a connection between these New IRA hooligans and . . . ah, the matter you and I have been investigating?"

"Ambrose read us in, Alex," intoned Stokely.

"Ah, good. That will save time. All the same, this may not be a secure line, so I think a measure of discretion is called for."

"Read you loud and clear, boss."

"To answer your question, Alex," said Congreve, "I'm afraid the truth is, we just don't know. I asked the leader of the group, a man named Dylan Fahey, if he knew anything about the . . . erm, matter at hand and got the distinct impression that he did not. I fear that Ross and I may have stumbled across an entirely unrelated plot. Our timing proved fortuitous, though I hesitate to call it serendipity, given the outcome. And from what Mr. Jones and Mr. Brock have told me, this attempted bombing may just be the tip of the iceberg."

"You're going to have to spell it out for me, Ambrose."

Stoke fielded the question. "Harry and I have been tracking about a hundred pounds of Novichok nerve agent that was stolen in Cuba and smuggled out in the coffin carrying Dylan Fahey's brother, Sean."

"I'm sure there's a story there," replied Hawke. "Smuggled to where?"

"Here."

"Dublin, actually," Congreve corrected. "But that may have only been a destination of convenience. The nerve agent could be anywhere in the isles by now."

"That's why I've been trying to reach you," added Stoke. "It's on your turf now."

"Ambrose," Hawke said slowly, the gears turning in his head, "are you certain that there isn't a connection here?"

Congreve raised his head, looking mildly interested. "Why do you ask?"

"I don't like coincidences. We found a connection to the New IRA, and it led you to this Fahey chap. Now we're to believe that these incidents are unrelated?"

"Fahey didn't know about what happened . . . erm . . . in Scotland."

"Maybe because he's not the mastermind of the plot, just a useful tool, a pawn in somebody else's game."

"The left hand doesn't know what the right is doing. Is that it?" Congreve appeared to consider this for a moment. "But even if what you suggest is true, how does it help us?"

"As it happens, I also have a lead."

Congreve jolted in his chair as if waking from a nap. "What's that? Do tell me, old boy."

"I've just come from a rather unpleasant meeting with a chap in Bavaria—Prince Heinrich Konigstahl—who as much as admitted that he knew about what had happened. He denied having any direct involvement, but the fact that he knows about it at all is suspicious, especially given the blanket of secrecy the PM has cast over this."

"You think he may be in direct contact with the . . . ah, miscreants we're looking for?" Congreve steepled his fingers together under his chin. "And how does this information benefit us?"

"We've plucked two threads, Ambrose. Dylan Fahey and Heinrich Konigstahl. Let's see if we can tie them together."

"How do you propose to do that?"

"I was thinking we'd start with a keyword search of ECHELON intercepts."

ECHELON, Stoke knew, was the National Security Agency's worst-kept secret—a massive eavesdropping program that literally recorded and monitored every phone call, text message, and email sent by anyone, anywhere on the planet. The sheer volume of data was enormous. A single day's intercepts—the estimated number was about 1.7 billion—would have required hundreds of millions of man-hours to review—but the NSA had a secret weapon, namely a network of supercomputers that passively monitored the data, looking for keywords and patterns that might indicate, say, a terror attack in the offing. While ECHELON was an American asset, under the terms of the Five Eyes agreement of 1941, the US actively shared and exchanged signal intercepts with other Western nations, including the UK.

"If we can pinpoint when and where the information was passed along," Hawke went on, "it should be fairly easy to trace it back to the sender."

Congreve seemed skeptical. "Electronic intercepts are a bit outside my bailiwick, but wouldn't these villains have employed some means to obfuscate their signal trail? Disposable phones and whatnot?"

Harry Brock leaned in close to the table. "No, hold on now. Alex might be onto something. Ah, hey, Alex, it's Harry. Long time, am I right?"

"Yes, Harry," replied Hawke with just a touch of impatience. "You were saying."

"Oh, yeah. So, if they used burner phones or cloned email accounts, we wouldn't necessarily be able to get an ID, but the metadata would contain geographical information."

"So we would know *where* they are," said Congreve, "but not necessarily *who* they are. Have I got that right?"

"Pretty much. Honestly, I don't know much about how it works either, but I know someone who might."

Stoke found himself nodding. "Jade."

"I know it's a long shot," said Hawke. "But right now it just might be our *only* shot."

"I'll get right on it," Harry declared, eager to be part of the solution.

"Ah, Alex, a moment," said Congreve. "There's the matter of confidentiality. I don't think the PM will be at all pleased to hear that we've brought the CIA into her 'security bubble.'"

"We'll stick to the story we've been using. We're investigating a threat against the Royal Family. We can . . . What was the word you used? Obfuscate our true objective by broadening the scope of our keyword search. Include a few red herrings to muddy the waters, so to speak."

Congreve raised a dubious eyebrow. "Well, I'm not at all certain how to feel about relying on computers to solve crimes."

"Come now, Constable," chided Alex. "You've got to embrace the future. Besides, the computers are just tools to speed us on our way."

Congreve harrumphed. "We shall see."

———————

Much of what happened over the course of the next few hours sailed well over Congreve's head. He had a basic understanding of what Harry Brock had proposed—wiretaps and other forms of electronic eavesdropping had been around far longer than he himself had been a copper, and he knew, or at least thought he knew, how that technology had evolved in the digital age, but the ways in which Brock's CIA associate squeezed the raw data until it gradually began to yield up useful information frankly astounded him.

He nevertheless made an effort to keep up with what was happening, if only to keep his mind from replaying that last horrible moment— lying in a heap on the macadam with cars screeching to a halt all around in order to avoid running him over and then, just as the daze began to clear and before he even started to feel the pain of the injuries he'd sustained in the fall, he looked down the road at the lorry and saw it disappear in a flash of light.

Ross!

Ross Sutherland, who had so much of his life yet to live, had willingly given the remainder that others might go on living. But would that be of any comfort to his wife or to his daughter, who was too young to understand why Daddy would never be coming home?

Focusing on the investigation, even if he couldn't really grasp what was going on in some distant computer room on the other side of the planet, gave him something positive to think about.

We will find him, Ross, he promised. *We'll bring him back. I swear it.*

But as the hours ticked by with no apparent progress, Congreve's natural skepticism began to stir. After all, it had been digital detective work that had put them on the trail of the NIRA, and where had that gotten them?

He knew that argument was disingenuous. While the jury was still out on whether there was a connection between the NIRA and the King's abductors, following that trail had not been a complete waste of time. Nevertheless, in his heart, he believed that it would be old-fashioned police work that would root out the villains and bring the King home safely.

He took himself back to the beginning, to Balmoral and the original deed—the abduction of King Charles. He recalled his interview with Tommy Fairbairn-Sykes and his discussion with Alex about the motive being of more import than the method. *Why* had led him to *how*, and that had led him to Colm Keaney and Ian Clewen, members of the household staff. Inside men but clearly only relatively minor pawns in the villain's employ.

Upon deeper reflection, though, Congreve found it hard to imagine that the two men could, by themselves, have made the elaborate preparations necessary to carry out the plot.

A realization hit Congreve like the proverbial ton of bricks.

There's another inside man. And we stopped looking.

But maybe it wasn't too late.

"Stokely!" he called out. "I have an idea."

Stoke, who was on the phone with Brock's CIA contact, held up a hand to silence him. "Incredible work, Jade. We'll take it from here."

He ended the call and then faced Congreve. "Whatever it is, it will have to wait. We found them!"

THIRTY-SEVEN

SCOTLAND

A Royal Navy AW101 Merlin medium-lift helicopter on loan to Special Branch, its rotors spinning overhead, ready for a quick takeoff, waited for Hawke on the tarmac at the Aberdeen airport. This time, he would fly the rest of the way to Balmoral. This time, expediency was a higher priority than security.

As he boarded the aircraft, Hawke could not help but think about Ross Sutherland, whom he had met up with only days ago, not far from the very same spot. He would never have imagined that his last meeting with Sutherland, just before they embarked on their respective missions, would, in fact, be their *last* meeting.

No chance to say goodbye, he thought. *But how could I have known?*

Of course, he could not have. He inhabited a violent, dangerous world, and losing friends, brothers-in-arms, and even family without warning, without a chance to say that final goodbye, simply went with the territory.

This was not the first time he'd lost a close friend; nor would it be the last—barring, of course, the possibility that the next fall of the scythe might touch him.

Today, it almost had.

If he had died at the bottom of a ravine in Bavaria, it would have been him leaving behind things unsaid. His parting from Anastasia and Alexei in Bermuda would have been the last time they ever saw him.

"Three knocks, remember."

The words arose unbidden from the depths of his memory. Not his own words, but rather the last thing his father had said to him. Hawke could not recall what he had said to Alexei before hastening off to Scotland. Probably some benign pablum.

"Love you . . . Back soon . . . Listen to your mum."

If he had died at the bottom of that ravine in Bavaria, those banal words, whatever they were, would have been seared into Alexei's memory.

He had survived this time, but one day his luck would run out. When it did, he would leave behind a widow and a fatherless child.

Unless . . .

Unless he kept his promise to Anastasia.

Unless he took a step back from the precipice, stopped playing dice with the devil, and instead became the husband Asia deserved and the father Alexei needed.

Unless he did the right thing.

But can I do it? Can I really turn my back on this life?

"Life was so much simpler when I was just living it for myself," he murmured with a sigh.

———

Twenty minutes later, the Merlin delivered him to the lawn south of Balmoral Castle. It was now early evening, and aside from the portable landing lights and a scattering of illuminated windows, the castle was dark, appearing almost uninhabited.

Hawke found Stoke and Congreve waiting outside the carriage porch. The former embraced him in a bear hug that elicited more than just a wince of pain. The latter regarded him with a shocked expression.

"Good heavens, Alex. You look like . . ." He paused as if unable to think of an adequate simile, then said simply, "Well, like me. And I fell out of a moving lorry. What on earth happened to you?"

"Ambrose is right, my man. You look like shit," supplied Stoke. "Are you okay?"

"Much better off than the other guy," Hawke assured them.

What he did not say was that the other *guy*—Konigstahl's creature, Tildy—had been taken away from the accident scene in a body bag. Hawke and Pippa had been luckier.

When Tildy had run the Locomotive off the road and sent it plummeting down the embankment, he had managed to maintain control for part of the descent, keeping all four wheels more or less in contact with the ground, even as the Mercedes sedan turned cartwheels in front of him, leaving pieces of itself strewn across the landscape. For a few seconds, the old Bentley had glissaded down the slope, surfing a wave of debris and loose rocks, staying upright and even responding somewhat to his attempts to steer.

Then their luck had turned. The front end rammed against a protruding boulder, and the coupe began flipping arse over teakettle.

Everything after that was a blur.

When his ability to think clearly returned, Hawke found himself hanging upside down, suspended from the aftermarket safety belts he'd installed in the Locomotive—seat belts had not been a standard feature in the 1950s. The restraints had almost certainly saved his life. Without them, he would have been forcefully ejected and probably crushed under the two-ton vehicle. As it was, he could detect no serious injury to himself—just scrapes and bruises.

Pippa had not been so lucky. She was still beside him, likewise inverted, but it was not just her seat belt that held her where she was. A section of the frame had crumpled inward, collapsing onto her legs and pinning her in place. That was not the worst of her injuries. She was unconscious and bleeding profusely from numerous gashes.

After freeing himself, Hawke immediately went to work trying to pry her loose and, failing that, did what he could to manage the bleeding. Given the circumstances, he didn't think she would survive, so once he'd done all he could, he simply took her hand and started talking. If asked, he wouldn't have been able to recount what he had talked about. He just hoped that the sound of his voice would be a lifeline for her to hold on to until the rescuers arrived.

It must have worked, because she was still alive when the first responders succeeded in cutting away the wreckage to free her, and she was still alive when the air ambulance delivered her to the Hospital of the Technical University of Munich. At last report, she was still in surgery. The odds of her surviving were good. The odds that she would be able to walk again were a coin toss.

Because he was not in extremis, Hawke had not ridden with her but had instead been taken by ground transport to the nearby Garmisch-Partenkirchen Medical Center. There, as his minor injuries were attended to, he fielded questions from the local accident investigators. He kept his story simple—a crazy driver had tried to pass him in a curve, cut him off, and caused the wreck. He did not admit to knowing the identity of the other driver; nor did he make mention of her motive for running him off the road or point the finger at Prince Heinrich Konigstahl. The clock was still ticking; he could not afford to get bogged down in a criminal investigation, especially not one that would pit him against local royalty.

It was the urgency of the mission that prompted him to arrange transportation back to the Munich airport, where he boarded his G800 and told the pilots to fly him home. He felt dreadful leaving Pippa in the care of strangers, but he would have been no good to her or anyone sitting in the surgery waiting room. His one concession was to contact the British consulate general in Munich to have someone look after her.

"It's a long story, Constable," Hawke continued, "and one that I shall gladly tell over a dark 'n' stormy when this is all behind us. Right now we've got more immediate concerns."

Congreve gave a thoughtful hum. "Yes, quite."

"In your last call, you indicated that you've narrowed down the King's location?"

"Well, that's what we're hoping," replied Stoke, opening the door to the carriage porch. "It will all make sense in a minute."

"Where, Stoke?" Hawke insisted.

Stoke hesitated just a moment. "A place called Dunnottar Castle."

"Never heard of it," admitted Hawke.

"It's an old ruin on the coast, about twenty miles south of Aberdeen."

"Then what the bloody hell are we doing here?"

"Just come inside. It will all make sense."

Biting back his questions, Hawke followed Stoke and Congreve into the castle and through the corridors to the security office, where he'd met with Congreve not three days previously. There were two more individuals waiting there—Harry Brock and Tommy Fairbairn-Sykes.

Congreve took the lead. "Alex, you remember Chief Superintendent Fairbairn-Sykes?"

"Of His Majesty's protection detail," said Hawke, dutifully accepting the other man's handclasp.

"In the interest of preserving the PM's security bubble," Congreve went on, "I've brought the chief superintendent into the fold."

This explanation raised more questions than it answered, but Hawke, knowing that all would be explained, simply added those to the pile.

"Stokely has already supplied you with the target location," Congreve continued, gesturing to a large plasma screen on the wall that displayed a satellite view showing a bulbous promontory jutting out from a green shore and, upon it, the too perfect straight lines that could have only been the artifice of human engineers. "Dunnottar Castle. However, I think a little background is in order to explain how we arrived at this location. Mr. Brock, I yield to you."

After a moment's hesitation, as if uncertain whether he ought to stand or remain seated, Brock chose the former. "Uh, yeah. So . . . ah . . ."

"Go on, Harry," prompted Alex.

"Yeah, so we used your idea of looking at the data intercepts for Dylan Fahey and that German prince, but that didn't tell us anything. There was nothing even remotely suspicious in the signal traffic, which really isn't that surprising since we already figured they would be too smart to use their own accounts. So, instead, we took a big-picture approach. We knew where those two men were, geographically speaking. So, we began looking at all the data transmissions to and from those locations, focusing on unique sources."

"Unique sources?"

"New mobile accounts that were used only once or twice and then went dormant."

Hawke nodded in understanding. "Which might indicate that the devices used were burner phones."

"Most ordinary people tend to make use of their mobile devices once activated," supplied Congreve. "Only those with something to hide would use a device once and then deactivate it permanently."

"Long story short," said Brock, "we found the smoking gun. Phone conversations between Dylan Fahey and someone using an electronic voice modulator. In one of them, Fahey talks about his brother's death and something they referred to as 'the package.'"

Stoke broke in. "That's almost certainly a reference to the Novichok nerve agent Sean Fahey was trying to smuggle out of Cuba."

"In another," continued Harry, "sent from a different account just a few minutes later, the unknown subject tells Fahey to send one of the 'trucks' to make a 'special delivery' to Knock Road." Harry made air quotes with his fingers as he spoke.

"HQ of the Police Service," supplied Congreve.

Hawke frowned. "That only confirms what we already knew. It doesn't give us anything related to the King's abduction."

Brock, looking only a little chagrined, nodded. "You're right. There's nothing in any of their exchanges to back up that assumption. But we hit pay dirt with the other search."

"Konigstahl," said Hawke.

Brock made a little finger gun and pointed it at Hawke, wiggling his thumb. "Bingo. When we looked at the unique sources in the same geolocation as Prince Heinrich's personal phone, we found a text message with an image attachment."

He circled around the table and bent over the laptop. A moment later, the satellite image of the Dunnottar promontory was replaced by a still photo of a man sitting on a mattress on the floor, looking forlornly into the camera's eye.

"Charles," breathed Hawke. "He's alive. Thank God."

"At least he was when this was taken. Unfortunately, whoever sent that pic scrubbed the metadata, so we can't use it to get a location, but it's a definite connection between Prince Heinrich and the King's kidnappers."

"But you weren't able to identify the sender?"

"No. Or I should say, not yet. He used a VPN to cover his tracks. That's a virtual private network. Basically, a way to completely anonymize your online activity. Same with the calls to Fahey, which means it's a pretty good bet that they're the same person. Without a rough idea of where to look, trying to pinpoint the location of the sender would be like looking for a needle in a field of haystacks. The NSA has the computing power to do that, but it will take time."

Hawke narrowed his gaze at Harry. "And yet, somehow, you arrived at the conclusion that the King is in this old Scottish ruin. How did you manage that?"

Brock broke into a broad smile. "Because the King told us so."

"In the other message," explained Congreve, "the one where he directed Dylan Fahey to send a truck bomb to the Police Service headquarters, he instructed Fahey to—and I'm quoting—'Bring the other, along with the package, to my castle.' And then he sent the location. Dunnottar Castle."

Hawke gaped in disbelief. "He just sent it? In the open?"

"What is it you're always saying?" said Stoke. "When your enemy is making a mistake, get the hell out of his way."

"The villain likely believed that his precautions were sufficient to keep the authorities from picking up his scent," said Congreve.

"How do we know this isn't a ruse?" Hawke asked.

"Once we knew where to look, we were able to confirm it as the location of the messages to both Fahey and Prince Heinrich.

"This morning, a CCTV camera at the ferry terminal in Cairnryan captured an image of someone believed to be Dylan Fahey behind the wheel of a hybrid electric lorry disembarking the ferry, so we may safely assume that Fahey has completed the journey and delivered the package to Dunnottar Castle."

Hawke stiffened. "Then why are we sitting here? For God's sake, it might already be too late. There's no telling what he's got planned for that nerve agent."

Stoke made a patting gesture. "Alex, just hold your horses. We're already working on it."

From anybody else, the platitude would have earned a corrosive reply from Hawke, but Stokely Jones Jr. was a seasoned counterterrorism operator trained in hostage rescue. If anyone could develop a plan to assault Dunnottar Castle, neutralize the nerve agent, and rescue the King, it was Stoke.

At a nod from Hawke, Stoke moved over to the plasma screen and took center stage. "Harry, put the sat photo back up."

With the image of the promontory once more displayed, Stoke launched into his briefing. "You wouldn't know it today, but Dunnottar Castle was once a pretty happening place. The Scottish crown jewels were kept there for a while during the Wars of the Three Kingdoms. Later on, the lord of the castle, the tenth Earl Marischal, had to forfeit his title when he supported the Jacobite rebellion."

Hawke wondered what Pippa would have made of that bit of trivia. Was there some deeper significance to the selection of Dunnottar Castle as the villain's secret lair?

"As you can see from the sat photo, it's mostly in ruins right now, but there are a few structures still intact. It's presently owned by

Dunecht Estate, who maintain it as a tourist destination and occasionally lease it out as a shooting location for a few movies and television shows. In fact, according to them, that's what it's being used for right now, so it's temporarily closed to the public. Only the production company that's supposedly filming there is a shell corporation."

"Clever of them. They can come and go as they please, and no one is the wiser."

"There's one other thing," continued Stoke. "That shell company also hired Strategic Vanguard Services to provide security for the site. SVS also happens to be the outfit Dylan Fahey's brother worked for."

"Strategic Vanguard Services," murmured Hawke. "Mercenaries. A rather unscrupulous lot, as I recall."

"They say they'll fight for anyone, anywhere, as long as the price is right."

"As I recall, didn't they end up fighting on both sides during the Syrian civil war?"

"Wouldn't surprise me," said Stoke with a chuckle. "But listen, if these guys are providing security, then we're gonna have a fight on our hands."

Now Hawke understood why Stoke had decided to proceed cautiously. "What are our assets?"

"Special Branch is providing logistics and air support," said Congreve. "Weapons and equipment. Drone recce and rear security. But the PM insists we maintain the security bubble. That means limiting the rescue team to those who are already in the know."

"Right now that's me, you, Harry, Ambrose if he's up for it. And him." Stoke gestured to Fairbairn-Sykes.

"Me and the rest of the lads. Six of us."

Hawke gazed back at the King's chief bodyguard. "This is a job for trained counterterrorism operators, not police officers."

"We've trained for hostage rescue," Fairbairn-Sykes assured him. "I'm a former commando. So are some of my mates." He paused a beat, and then his tone lowered almost to a whisper. "Please, Lord Hawke.

His Majesty was lost on my watch. Give us a chance to redeem ourselves."

Hawke was moved by the man's conviction, but it in no way lessened the gravity of the situation. He turned back to Stoke. "Six of them and four of us. That's ten men going up against God alone knows how many hostiles occupying a literal fortress and holding on to a VIP hostage and a deadly nerve agent." He shook his head wearily. "I don't suppose there's any way to get T and L in on this."

"I gave 'em a call," replied Stoke. "Unfortunately, they're on another assignment somewhere in Eastern Europe. Even if they could get away from it to help us out, it would be another twelve hours before they could get here."

"Twelve hours we don't have." Hawke sighed. "All right, Stoke. Let's hear your plan."

And as his old friend began laying out in detail how the assault on Dunnottar Castle would proceed, Hawke couldn't help but feel that somewhere in the universe—heaven or Valhalla—his ancestors were looking down on him and smiling.

THIRTY-EIGHT

DUNNOTTAR CASTLE, SCOTLAND

They came from the east, flying low, almost skimming the North Sea wave tops. The Merlin was not a stealth aircraft per se, but its three General Electric CT7 turboshaft engines—optimized for lower rotation speed—and advanced composite BERP rotor blades made it significantly quieter than most other helicopters. And because the Merlin was staying low, well below the summit of the headland, what noise it did create would be deflected away from any listening ears in the castle, giving the ad hoc hostage rescue team a brief but critical window of opportunity in which to launch their assault.

That was the theory at least. Hawke and the rest of the men riding along in the Merlin's cargo bay were about to put that theory to the test.

With the headland now less than a mile away, Hawke keyed the push-to-talk on his Bowman C4I tactical radio set.

"Stoke, it's Alex," he said. It was a small operation, and they were transmitting on an encrypted channel, so there was no need for fancy quasi-military call signs, which Hawke found rather tedious under the best of circumstances. "Do you copy?"

"Read you loud and clear, boss."

"Are you in position?"

"Sitting pretty," replied Stoke.

"We're approaching the go/no-go line. How does it look there?"

"We've got eyes on two tangos posted up on the tower house."

The tower house, sometimes called the keep, was a large structure positioned on the westmost section of the headland, right behind the ruins of the original gate, which guarded the narrow landward approach to the headland. While there wasn't much left of the tower house now, it was still the ideal place to post a lookout because the footpath from the mainland was the only way to reach the castle.

Unless, of course, one had a helicopter.

"No indication of increased activity?" pressed Hawke.

"Quiet as a hooker in church," Stoke assured him.

"Then we're good to go. ETA, one minute." He then caught the eye of the helicopter's crew chief and flashed an upraised thumb.

Thirty seconds later, with the headland almost within spitting distance, the pilot increased the collective pitch and hauled back on the cyclic. Hawke felt his stomach drop as the helicopter gained seventy-five vertical feet in the blink of an eye, coming level with the top of the promontory and nosing forward over the open green space at the southeast corner.

Hawke took a second—exactly one second—to survey the surrounding terrain, which even at two a.m. looked bright as day if rather colorless in the blue-tinged monochromatic display of his XACT nv33 binocular NOD (night optical device).

The aches and pains of the injuries he'd sustained in the wreck seemed to vanish miraculously—not healed but masked by the adrenaline pumping in his veins. He felt positively electric. Superhuman almost.

The crew chief pointed to the door, giving the prearranged signal, and Hawke shouted, "Go! Go! Go!" Then he was moving, bounding from the helicopter, his SIG MPX-SD, equipped with a Trijicon RMR aiming device, at the high ready. He was mindful to keep his head down as he moved out under the sweep of the Merlin's rotors.

Hawke hadn't gone three steps when he spotted movement ahead and to his left. Fifty yards away, a black-clad figure emerged from behind a low stone wall—the roofless remains of a structure known as Waterton's Lodging—and aimed a weapon in the direction of the helicopter.

"Contact, ten o'clock!" Hawke shouted, even as he calmly put the sighting dot of his reflex optics on the figure and squeezed the trigger. The report, already nearly whisper quiet thanks to the SIG's integrated suppressor, was so completely drowned out by the roar of the helicopter that Hawke wasn't sure that the weapon had actually discharged until he saw the target slump to the ground.

But even as the man went down, two more took his place, and unlike their fallen comrade, they had the sense to stay behind cover. Tongues of white fire, supernova brilliant in the NOD display, lashed out from their rifles, the reports cracking through the disturbed air. Hawke kept moving, targeting the muzzle flashes, loosing controlled pairs. Behind him, the Merlin's turbines roared, and the downdraft intensified as the helicopter lifted off, backing away from the battle.

Stoke's voice sounded in Hawke's ear. "You got trouble heading your way."

"It's already here, Stoke!" he replied.

Across the lawn, more gunmen were joining the fray, prudently keeping their heads down but firing blindly on full auto—spraying and praying.

Hawke heard an agonized cry of "I'm hit!" and, from the corner of his eye, saw one of his teammates stagger back, clutching his chest. Like Hawke, the man was wearing body armor—a military-issue Virtus Scalable Tactical Vest, with heavy armor plates that could stop just about anything short of a .50-cal round—so the odds were good that he wasn't mortally wounded, but the impact would still have felt like taking a sledgehammer to the chest, taking him, if only momentarily, out of the fight. Hawke didn't stop to check on the man, didn't slow, but kept advancing, kept firing until his magazine was spent, then switched it out without missing a step and resumed firing.

He kept going because, with every second that passed, the chances of finding the King alive diminished exponentially.

He kept going because *this* was who he was—a man naturally good at war.

The Warlord.

———————

The Magician awakened to a distinctive *pop-pop* echoing throughout the castle ruins. He had never served in the military and never fought in a war, but he knew the sound of gunfire when he heard it.

His blood went cold in his veins.

No.

No. No. No!

His denials, no matter how fast and furious they flooded his mind, had no effect whatsoever on reality. He rose from the cot, his only bed these past few days, and started for the Drawing Room—the best-preserved room in the old palace, which had become the nerve center of his operation.

No sooner was he through the door than Sten appeared in front of him, a pistol in hand. "We're under attack!"

"Who?"

"Who do you think?"

He'd asked the wrong question. What he really wanted to know was *How?*

How did they find us?

But he doubted Sten had any more idea than he did.

He found his gaze drawn to the gun in Sten's hand, a symbol of the violence that, while always a distinct possibility, had caught him unawares. He forced himself to look the man in the eye. "You have to hold them off. At least a few minutes more!"

"We will," growled the mercenary, "or die trying."

Sten pushed past the Magician, heading for the exit door. When it opened, the noise of the battle intensified, and the sulfurous smell of gun smoke wafted in. Then the door closed, muffling the reports once more.

The Magician continued to the Drawing Room. With his computer in sleep mode, the monitor screens were all dark. He tapped the keyboard, and the screens hummed to life. One of them showed a grainy video feed of an empty cell. He ignored it, focusing instead on a screen that showed a real-time GPS map of Great Britain.

His heart stuttered again when a figure burst into the room behind him. *Not yet! I need more time.*

"What the hell is going on?"

The Magician went weak in the knees with relief. The intruder was Dylan Fahey.

"What do you think?" he said, not looking away from the screen, his fingers moving on the keys. "They found us."

"How in the hell did that happen?"

"If I had to guess, they probably followed *you.*"

"Not a chance. It's your lot that must have fucked up."

The Magician ignored the Irishman's complaints, focusing his attention instead on verifying the destination coordinates displayed on the monitor screen.

And enter.

The next prompt was for the command to initiate.

Not just yet. Must wait a bit. He made a quick calculation to determine the amount of delay necessary to achieve optimal results.

"Well, what are we supposed to do?" asked Fahey, strident with rising panic.

The Magician had almost forgotten the other man was still there. He updated a new start time, and then, with one final keystroke, it was done.

He glanced back at Fahey. "It doesn't matter. They're too late to stop us."

"It matters to me. I'm getting the bloody hell out of here." Fahey didn't wait to see how this decision would be received but promptly turned on his heel and fled the room.

The Magician merely shrugged. Fahey's ultimate fate interested him not at all. The Irishman had already served his purpose.

He logged out and then, for good measure, smashed the computer against the stone floor just to be sure that no one, not even the cleverest technician, could undo what he had set in motion.

It wasn't quite how he had imagined his final victory unfolding, but it would suffice.

Time for one last trick.

———

Perched on a cliff top a hundred feet above and two hundred yards southwest of the headland, Stokely Jones Jr. had an unrestricted view of the castle grounds, but it was the MAXIKITE 2 6X-magnification night scope mounted to his AWM L11513A Long Range Rifle that allowed him to get up close and personal with the combatants.

On the headland below, Hawke and the team of royal bodyguards led by Tommy Fairbairn-Sykes were clearing by fire, engaging targets as they made their way toward the castle ruins, where, if all went according to plan, they would locate and secure the objectives—King Charles and the Novichok nerve agent. It was Stoke's job, with a little help from Harry Brock and Ambrose Congreve, to make sure Hawke's team had a level playing field.

While Hawke and the others had been rehearsing in a crude mock-up of the castle grounds on an unused runway at the Aberdeen airport, Stoke, Harry, and Ambrose had rolled out with a squad from Special Branch who had been tasked with establishing a cordon around the landward approach to the headland. Stoke's party then moved in on foot, setting up their present overwatch position in order to provide cover for the arrival of the helicopter bearing the assault team.

So far, the operation was going like clockwork. Stoke didn't have a clear shot at the group of shooters Hawke was presently engaging, but with Brock acting as his spotter, he had already tapped the two men stationed atop the tower house and bagged two more who, on their way to join the fight, had come out of the building known as the Silver House. Now Stoke was just moving the rifle back and forth on its bipod mount, searching for a new target.

"Hey, got a squirter," announced Brock.

In the parlance of special operations, a squirter was anyone who attempted to flee the scene of a raid or hostage rescue. The word was usually applied to a tango—a bad guy—making a run for it, but there was always the possibility that the person might be an escaping hostage or an innocent bystander running from the sound of gunfire.

"Where?" Stoke asked, resisting the reflex urge to begin searching with the scope. With its six-power magnification, it was great for detail work but was next to useless for getting the big picture.

"On the path, heading back to the mainland. He's really booking too."

Stoke would not have expected any of the SVS mercs, given their reputation, to hoof it out the back door, but the possibility that one of them might have experienced a momentary episode of cowardice did not concern him. His job was to suppress the enemy actively engaging the assault team, not kill everything moving.

"Let him go," he advised, not bothering to put glass on the squirter. "The Special Branch guys can roll him up when he hits the perimeter."

"It's Dylan Fahey," murmured Congreve.

That prompted Stoke to look up from the scope. Both Congreve and Brock were looking through their respective optical devices. Brock's Nightforce TS-82 spotting scope and Congreve's pair of L3Harris F5032 lightweight night vision binoculars were oriented toward the path leading away from the headland.

"Let me see your scope, Harry."

Brock passed the glass to Stoke, who was quickly able to find a lone figure moving along the footpath, nervously glancing over his shoulder with every few steps. Although it was impossible to tell his hair color in the monochrome display, the man's resemblance to Sean Fahey was uncanny.

Congreve lowered his binoculars. "Gentlemen, I fancy a chat with Mr. Fahey."

"Just hold your horses, Ambrose. You can talk to him tomorrow when he's in custody. He's not getting away."

Stoke expected some sort of protest from Congreve, but what he got was silence. "Ambrose, you hear me, man?" He lowered the scope and turned to look the former policeman in the eye.

Congreve wasn't there.

"He's gone, Stoke," said Brock belatedly.

Stoke brought the scope back to his eye, swept the surrounding area, and found Congreve's retreating back, now already thirty yards from their position.

"Damn it, Ambrose."

———————

When he was within twenty-five yards of the enemy position, Hawke took a stun grenade from his vest, prepped it, and shouted, "Flash out!" Then he pitched it over the stone wall behind which the gunmen were hiding.

He looked down to make sure that the objective lenses of his NODs wouldn't be overwhelmed by the resulting flash, and waited for the bang. In the open air, the 175-decibel report probably wasn't quite as debilitating as it would have been in an enclosed space, where the grenades were typically employed, but the seven-million-candela flash would be positively blinding for the enemies—especially if, as Hawke suspected, they were also equipped with NODs.

As soon as he heard the boom, Hawke was moving again, not walking now but running to close the gap with the enemy position and seize whatever advantage the stun grenade had created.

He rounded the wall with his MPX at the ready. Three men writhed on the ground in front of him, struggling to bring their weapons to bear, discarded night vision devices beside them.

Hawke moved through them with brutal efficiency, giving one man after another after another double-tap head shots, just in case they were wearing body armor. When he was certain that the immediate threat was neutralized, he hooked right, heading north across the bowling green toward the palace.

The castle was laid out with most of the palace and other residences occupying the northeast quarter of the castle mount, while a smaller complex—which included the tower house, the stables, and the old smithy—curled around to the southwest. The latter structures were roofless, which tended to rule them out as likely locations for holding hostages, but they still posed a problem tactically as they formed a maze of low walls and niches where hostile gunmen could strike from. Further complicating things, Hawke's force was already down two men. One of the RaSP officers had taken a round in the neck and would almost certainly bleed out despite the ministrations of another, who had himself been shot in the leg.

The smart move would have been to clear the southwest quarter first and then to sweep around to the partially intact palace ruins, which was where they expected to find the King and the bulk of the hostile element, but doing so would have delayed the King's rescue, potentially giving his captors time to consider killing their hostage as a last resort. To reduce that likelihood, Hawke's plan was to hit the palace hard and fast, leaving it to Stoke and Brock to cover their six.

He gathered what was left of his team—five men, counting Hawke—at the door to the Silver House. There were two bodies sprawled out on the ground nearby—Stoke's handiwork, no doubt—but no sign of activity inside. The team lined up behind Hawke and then, on his signal and just as they had rehearsed, swept inside.

Evidently, the mercenaries had been using the Silver House as a bivouac. Half a dozen military-surplus cots were arranged in close order on the floor. Otherwise, the house was empty.

"Clear," Hawke shouted. "Move out."

They filed out as quickly as they had entered and then immediately moved into the fifty-yard-long corridor of connected roofless rooms known as the West Range. The dividing walls separating the rooms created a series of blind corners, which Hawke and the team had to negotiate tactically one by one. Each time, Hawke expected to walk into a storm of bullets, and instead of being relieved each time it didn't happen, he felt his apprehension for the next one intensify.

They reached the seventh and last room, turned right into the North Range, and approached the entrance to the best-preserved part of the old palace—the Marischal Suite. As before and just as they had rehearsed, the men lined up behind Hawke and prepared to make a dynamic entry.

That was when all bloody hell suddenly broke loose.

THIRTY-NINE

One of Hawke's assaulters—the man tasked with providing rear security—noticed movement from behind them and started to cry out in alarm, but his warning was swept away as fire and thunder filled the small enclosure. Stacked for entry beside the door to the Drawing Room, the team formed a single-mass target, impossible to miss.

Hawke, caught with one hand outstretched to open the door and his back to the ambush, tried to pivot but then felt the one-two punch of rounds striking his vest, driving him against the wall, and knocking the breath from his lungs. A third round, almost unnoticed, plucked at his thigh, feeling more like a hard slap than a penetration. Stunned, he slid down the wall, collapsing into a sitting position amidst a haze of smoke and dust.

Fluid, stretched out like soft taffy, Hawke in a single moment beheld the rest of his team sprawled out like a scattering of broken toy soldiers. Then, from out of the swirling smoke, a veritable angel of death emerged to stand over the fallen men. One of them—Hawke saw that it was Tommy Fairbairn-Sykes—fought through his pain and made a grab for his weapon, but before he could bring it up, the ghastly specter extended his hand, which held not the reaper's scythe, but a pistol. Then he fired twice into the fallen man's face. Without a pause to regard his handiwork, the shooter shifted to the next man in line, coldly took aim, and fired twice again.

One man, thought Hawke as he cursed himself for falling into the trap.

One man had done this to them. He had been lying in wait outside the West Range gallery, hiding while they passed by and then striking from behind when their attention was focused forward. He had emptied the magazine of an assault rifle on full auto into their midst, and now that they were down—stunned, wounded—he was going to finish them off one by one.

Hawke realized in that instant that his own weapon was half underneath him and that in order to make use of it, he would have to roll to one side or the other, a motion that would immediately draw the killer's attention.

But what choice did he have?

In another second or two, he would be dead anyway.

Unless . . .

Two more shots thundered in the small enclosure, and another man died.

For Hawke, it was like the sound of a starter pistol.

He rolled off the MPX, but instead of trying to pick it up, he rolled again, *toward* the gunman. The effort sent waves of pain radiating through him—not just from his latest wounds, but from every quarter. Muscle and bone screamed in protest, rebelling at this fresh insult. He felt as though he were trying to swim through quicksand. And yet it was rage that propelled him forward—the kind of white-hot rage Hawke had not felt since his final interaction with a man named Smith more than a year prior.

The killer's pistol swung in his direction, but before the man could pull the trigger, Hawke unleashed a powerful kick that swept the man's legs out from under him. The man was taken completely by surprise; his arms and legs flew up even as the rest of him went down, landing flat on his back on the hard, blood-slick stone.

Hawke pounced, heaving himself across the man's torso, pinning down the hand that held the pistol with one arm and striking a cross-body punch to the shooter's jaw with the other. But even as the blow landed, he felt the man bunching beneath him, gathering his energy for an eruption that would hurl his attacker away. Hawke was as skilled in unarmed combat as he was in the use of firearms, but in his present state, he wasn't at all certain that he could survive a prolonged fight. He had to end this quickly and decisively.

Still fiercely gripping the arm that held the pistol, Hawke collapsed against the man's chest, and when, as expected, the man tried to buck him off, Hawke shot his free hand up and grabbed the man by the throat. Sinking his fingers deep into the man's neck—nails penetrating flesh in such a way that no doubt compromised the trachea, leaving the other man unable to speak or breathe—Hawke, with all the force he could muster, violently slammed the man's head down onto the stone pavement. A hollow *thunk* rang out like a cantaloupe being dropped on the floor.

The impact vibrated up Hawke's arm, the intensity of it surely enough to render the man unconscious, if not already dead. Hawke, however, needed to be certain of victory. With his fingers still clamped like a vise about the man's neck, Hawke raised him up and then drove down for another blow. And then another.

Blood and tissue erupted from the man's every orifice. Hawke could feel the man's skull come apart, fragments of bone grinding together with each meaty impact, but he did not relent . . . would not relent.

Then, just as Hawke was gathering his energy for one more blow, a bootheel came down squarely in the middle of the man's already ruined face, smashing it flat.

Hawke looked up and saw that the boot belonged to one of the RaSP officers—a young man he knew only as Ned. Ned stood a little unsteadily above the combatants but nevertheless ground his heel back and forth.

"That's for the chief, you shite!"

Because his face was destroyed beyond recognition, it would be nearly two weeks before DNA tests would identify the dead man as a South African national named Pieter van der Berg, better known to his royal hostage as Mr. Sten.

―――――――

Though he was not the fittest physical specimen, Ambrose Congreve could move surprisingly quickly when sufficiently motivated. He gritted his teeth through the first few steps, but impelled by the urgency of the situation, he pushed through the pain until his body, realizing that he wasn't going to yield to its demands, stopped protesting.

Anticipating that his quarry would make for the car park a quarter mile from the castle gate, Congreve made a beeline for the same, which took him over a low split-rail fence—another feat for which he was not well-endowed—and across a field of spring barley. Thankfully, the field was flat, allowing him to move with swift sure-footedness he had not exhibited when descending from the cliffside perch where Stokely Jones and Harry Brock had established their overwatch position. With the terrain now working in his favor, he moved at a near jog, or what Alex Hawke might have called a fast waddle, reaching the far side of the barley field and clambering over another fence a stone's throw from the car park.

Even so, he was almost too late.

The car park was mostly empty. Just a couple of panel vans, an SUV, and a lonely-looking sedan, all of which probably belonged to the mercenaries who had taken the King hostage. Something about the scene nagged at Congreve's subconscious, but before he could puzzle it out, he glimpsed movement from the entrance to the footpath at the opposite end of the lot. Like Hawke's assault team, he was wearing night vision goggles. The man squinting into the darkness some twenty yards away was not.

Congreve pulled up short and drew his weapon, a rather ordinary Glock 26 that he'd taken from the Special Branch armory to replace his lost Webley. The cross-country race had left him more than a little winded, so resting his hands on his knees, he took a couple of deep breaths before venturing into the open. Aiming his pistol at the unsuspecting man, he gave a stentorian shout. "Police! Stop right where you are."

The Irishman's head snapped toward him, his hand reflexively moving toward his waistband and the weapon that was, no doubt, concealed there.

"Don't," warned Congreve, bracing the Glock in a two-handed grip aimed at Fahey's chest. "I will shoot you dead right where you bloody stand."

Fahey's hands froze and then slowly came up. His head turned this way and that, presumably searching for Congreve. In the display of Congreve's NODs, the pupils of Fahey's eyes appeared as coin-sized white spots.

"Ah, ya caught me, Constable," Fahey said, affecting an almost playful tone. "What's the penalty for sleeping rough round here anyway?"

"I know you, Dylan Fahey. And you know me."

Fahey stiffened, his eyes narrowing as they searched the darkness. "Ah, so it's like that, then. And now I suppose I'll be shot resisting arrest."

"You *are* under arrest," replied Congreve evenly, "for the attempted bombing of police headquarters—and for the murder of a police officer, a good man with a family."

"We're all good men with families, Constable. We're just on different sides of this war."

Congreve watched Fahey closely, the trigger of the Glock already pulled halfway back to disengage the internal safety system. "Your war ended twenty-five years ago. You're not a soldier. You're a terrorist. A criminal."

"The war didn't end back then, peeler. Not for us. But today?" His lips curled into a triumphant smile. "Today, it will."

"Why? What happens today?" Even as he asked the question, Congreve knew the answer, and then the thing that had been worrying at his subconscious emerged from its cocoon.

Where's the lorry?

Fahey began slowly lowering his outstretched hands.

"Don't," warned Congreve. "I will shoot."

"I know you will," said Fahey, and then went for his gun.

There was no time to mourn the dead. Hawke—with a pressure bandage wrapped around his thigh binding the only notable wound he'd sustained, and with Ned, the only other survivor of the ambush, backing him up—pushed through the door to the Drawing Room, ready for a fight. But the room beyond the door was empty.

The Drawing Room had not only survived the passage of time but been lovingly restored to an approximation of how it might have looked in the days when the Earl Marischal of Scotland had hidden the royal regalia from Cromwell's Roundheads. Its most noteworthy feature was an elaborately paneled oak ceiling. In that setting, the broken pieces and trailing wires of a shattered computer were completely anachronistic. The presence of technology indicated that the hostage takers had made use of the Drawing Room, but there was no evidence that the King had been kept there. Hawke cautiously stepped over the debris, wary of possible booby traps, and continued to the door at the opposite end of the room.

Beyond the Drawing Room, the palace was mostly a ruin with crumbling stairwells and passages that no longer went anywhere but that still might be used as a prison cell for a king—or a fighting position for any remaining mercenaries. Hawke and Ned cleared each one before moving on.

From his earlier studies of the castle plan, Hawke knew the search was leading them to the Whigs' Vault, an ancient cellar that had, in 1685, been used as a temporary prison for a large group of Covenanters— anti-royalist Presbyterian Whigs who refused to swear loyalty to King

James VII and II, the man who would himself, just a few years later, have his throne pulled out from under him. If the King's abductors had any sense of historic irony, the Whigs' Vault would be where they kept their hostage.

And where the last of them might be waiting to make their final stand.

The entrance to the Whigs' Vault was blocked, not with an ancient portcullis but a crudely constructed plywood door with a simple gravity latch. Hawke gave Ned a three count and then opened the latch and threw the door wide, ready to meet fire with fire.

But the vault beyond held no threats. Just a lone miserable figure seated on a mattress who looked up at the noisy intrusion, searching the darkness with eyes wide.

It was *not* the King.

But the face staring up at him was someone Hawke recognized immediately—the other abductee, Balmoral's head gamekeeper, Roderick McClanahan.

"Roddy!" Hawke cried out.

McClanahan's head bobbed this way and that. "Who's there?"

"It's Alex. Alex Hawke."

"Lord Hawke! I remember you. What on earth are you doing here?"

"Looking for His Majesty, Roddy. Is he here?"

"I don't know, m'lord." McClanahan's head continued to move back and forth, reminding Hawke that while he could see in the dark thanks to his NODs, the gamekeeper could not. "I've not seen him since early yesterday. They played a most cruel trick on him. Pretended to kill me right in front of him. I've not seen him since."

The flame of hope that had begun to burn in Hawke's head with the discovery of one of the hostages now guttered. "Steady on," he advised. "Let's get you out of here. Cover your eyes a moment. I'm going to light a torch."

McClanahan did as directed, whereupon Hawke switched off his NODs and then, closing his own eyes to avoid being blinded, toggled the switch on the SureFire tactical torch clipped to his vest. Even through closed eyelids, Hawke felt the sting of the intensely bright light.

When his eyes had adjusted enough to tolerate the brilliance, he opened them and regarded McClanahan, who stared up at him with wide-eyed disbelief. Hawke realized his appearance must have shocked McClanahan, who knew him only as one of the King's noble friends and occasional hunting partners, not a hard-bitten, blood-soaked counterterrorism operator.

He extended a hand to the gamekeeper. "On your feet, Roddy."

McClanahan accepted the offer of assistance and stood unsteadily beside Hawke.

"You must tell me everything you remember," Hawke said as they made their way back up to the Drawing Room. "Did they say anything about what they might have planned?"

"They were quite keen on having His Majesty give up the throne. He refused, of course. Said he'd rather die than sign their paper."

There's a lot of fight left in the old boy, thought Hawke.

"That sounds like Charles. Anything else? Any talk of moving him elsewhere?"

The gamekeeper shook his head. "Can't recall any talk like that, but I've heard naught at all since yesterday."

Hawke felt the flame go out entirely. They had waited too long, been too cautious, and so had missed their last, best chance to rescue the King.

FORTY

While Hawke was calling for the helicopter to return in order to medevac the casualties, Ned tended to the wounded out on the green, where they had initially deployed. Sadly, the number of fatalities far outstripped the number of wounded. McClanahan took upon himself the grim task of gathering the dead on the bowling green outside the palace. He laid them out on the lawn side by side, faces shrouded with Mylar space blankets taken from their first aid kits.

When the helicopter was on its way back, Hawke called Stoke to give him an update.

"No joy," he reported. "We were too bloody late."

Hawke had expected words of commiseration from his old friend, but Stoke seemed barely to have heard. "We've got bigger problems than that, boss. We're on our way to you. I'll let Ambrose tell you when we get there."

Hawke had an idea what Congreve would have to say, but he did not press Stoke for more details over the radio. Nevertheless, the fact that so many brave men had fallen with nothing to show for their sacrifice put him in a dark humor, so when his friends arrived just a few minutes later, Hawke faced Congreve impatiently.

"Well, Ambrose, let's have it."

Congreve, however, looked past him, regarding McClanahan with unconcealed surprise. "I see your rescue attempt wasn't *entirely* unsuccessful," he remarked.

"Ah, where are my manners?" said Hawke with irritation. "Ambrose, this is Roddy McClanahan, head gamekeeper at Balmoral. You may recall that he was also taken hostage along with His Majesty. Roddy, this is Detective Chief Inspector Congreve. And now can we bloody well get on with it, Ambrose?"

Congreve's gaze lingered on McClanahan a moment longer; then he turned to Hawke. "The lorry that Dylan Fahey brought over from Ireland."

"Yes, what about it?"

"It's not here."

That was more or less what Hawke had been expecting. "Nor is the King," he replied. "I don't think it requires a Holmesian genius to deduce that these facts are related."

"Alex, I'm not certain you grasp the significance of this, old boy. That lorry is a near duplicate of the one that Dylan Fahey sent to destroy PSNI headquarters."

"You think it's another bomb. And this time, it's the King who's going along for the ride."

"I do. There is a certain symmetry at play here. The attempt in Belfast was merely a prelude."

"Only the main event is going to be a hell of a lot worse than the warm-up act," said Stoke, "because this time, that bomb is also going to spread Novichok nerve agent."

"I spoke with Dylan Fahey a few moments ago," Congreve went on. "He's dead now, but before his recent and most timely demise, he intimated that this scheme will come to fruition today. Sadly, he did not reveal the target or the exact time."

"Bright and early, no doubt," said Hawke as he folded his arms across his chest. "And on the day of the Scottish referendum."

"It's no coincidence," agreed Congreve.

As they spoke, McClanahan followed the conversation, his eyes flitting back and forth like a spectator at Wimbledon watching an epic rally. "Are you sayin' that all of this has to do with the independence vote?"

Congreve gazed back at the gamekeeper, his head cocked to the side as if appraising the man. "It would seem so."

McClanahan shook his head. "Madness."

"Hmm. Quite." Congreve returned his attention to Hawke. "But we've strayed from the point, dear boy. Fahey said, 'Today.' There's a reason these villains haven't already carried out their attack. For maximum effect, it must happen during daylight hours."

"Meaning?" prompted Hawke.

"Meaning, we have time to stop it."

Congreve, ever the pragmatist, was not given to flights of rosily optimistic fancy, so Hawke took this statement as a sign that the investigator was already thinking several steps ahead. "Go on, Ambrose. Lay it out for me, will you?" His patience was running thin.

"Among Dylan Fahey's personal effects were the keys to a sedan hired from an agency in Aberdeen late yesterday afternoon. That vehicle is presently in the car park just down the way, and Mr. Fahey did us the favor of leaving the contract in the glove compartment. We know that Fahey brought the lorry to Scotland on the ferry to Cairnryan, and I believe we may safely assume that he drove it to Aberdeen, where he picked up the hire car. A review of CCTV footage from the area around the car provider should not only confirm the lorry's presence but give us a plate number that we can track."

Hawke felt his mood lift, if only slightly. "Ambrose, that's bloody brilliant!"

Congreve nodded. "I believe we may eventually discover that the lorry was never actually brought here and that, in all likelihood, His Majesty was transported from the castle to the lorry early yesterday evening. Quite probably before our search yielded up this location."

"Then why did they come back here?" asked Harry Brock.

Hawke glanced over at the CIA officer, mildly surprised at his astute question.

"If I were to guess," replied Congreve, "I would surmise that this is the nerve center of their operation." He pointed to the roof of the Drawing Room, directing everyone's attention to a small satellite dish that Hawke had not earlier noticed. "They likely planned to monitor the situation remotely."

"Well, we shut this place down," said Brock. "Doesn't that mean we stopped 'em?"

Congreve gave a thoughtful hum. "It's possible. It would depend on whether the destination has already been uploaded and the command to execute given."

Hawke recalled the shattered computer parts on the floor of the Drawing Room. "I suspect that ship may have already sailed."

"In any event," Congreve went on, "it is imperative that we locate the lorry with all haste, if only to ensure the King's safety."

"Then what are we hanging around here for?" asked Brock.

"Quite right. Sooner the better, and all that. There is, ah . . . a matter of some importance that we should attend to first."

Hawke raised an eyebrow. "And what might that be, Constable?"

Congreve looked down and began patting his pockets. "Lost my favorite Briar," he muttered. "Damnable luck."

After another few seconds of fruitless searching, he raised his eyes and looked around, finally settling his gaze on the gamekeeper. "Mr. McClanahan, this may be something you can help with . . . as the only actual witness to the King's abduction."

McClanahan returned a surprised look. "I'm afraid I don't recall much. They doped us both up pretty good."

"I'm actually more interested in examining the antecedents."

The statement drew a blank look from McClanahan and a frown from Hawke. He was familiar with Congreve's investigative techniques and understood that the detective was trying to get at something important, but his timing left more to be desired. "Are you quite certain this is the time, Ambrose?"

"Quite certain," Congreve echoed. "You see, something has been nagging at me since the start of this whole affair. A feeling like I'm seeing only half the picture."

"Rubbish," countered Hawke. "You've been ten steps ahead of the rest of us the whole time."

"Hmm. And yet the villain . . . the mastermind of this plot has been several steps ahead of *me*. Consider. We've been led to believe that two relatively minor members of the household staff were able to intercept His Majesty and Mr. McClanahan here, drug them, and then assume their identities while their confederates, disguised as outside vendors, removed the hostages from the grounds. I ask you, does that make logical sense?" Without waiting for an answer, he turned to McClanahan again. "What is the last thing you remember before waking up here?"

McClanahan recoiled a little at the intensity of the question. "I—uh, well, I was waiting for His Majesty just inside the carriage porch. Then Colm—that's Colm Keaney, one of the groundskeepers—came up and told me that the King had asked for me."

"And you didn't find that unusual? A groundskeeper running errands for His Majesty inside the residence?"

"I . . . uh . . ." McClanahan shot a glance in Hawke's direction, a silent plea for help.

"What, then?" demanded Congreve. "Think, man."

"I went with him to the . . . to the kitchen. Come to think of it, that was odd. There was no reason for the King to be hanging about there." He shook his head. "That's all I remember."

"Did you see anyone else?"

The gamekeeper's eyes darted back and forth as he searched his memory. "Clewen. Ian Clewen. He was there."

"Clewen?" pressed Congreve.

"Another groundskeeper."

"And is it customary for groundskeepers to have the run of the palace?"

"Now that I think on it, no, it is not. It's damned strange, is what it is."

"Just those two? Nobody else?"

McClanahan's eyebrows came together in a look of consternation, but then he shook his head.

Hawke followed the exchange with growing interest. "I can see you've got a bone in your teeth, Ambrose. But where is this going?"

"We've been operating from the premise that this plot was conceived by someone on the outside. The New IRA. Scottish separatists. Foreign agents. Or some diabolical union of them all. But we overlooked something . . . well, something rather obvious."

"And what would that be?"

"Quite simply, there had to be another insider. Someone much closer to the King than these groundskeepers. A confidant. Someone His Majesty trusted enough to follow into the trap that had been set for him."

McClanahan let out an audible gasp at the revelation.

"It goes without saying," Congreve went on, "that while this deceiver remains at large, he will attempt to thwart our efforts to rescue the King."

"Who?" McClanahan wondered, his voice barely louder than a whisper. "Who would do such a thing?"

Congreve turned on him. "Why ask *who*, Mr. McClanahan, when you already know the answer?"

The gamekeeper registered confusion. "I don't know what you're talking about."

"Enough playacting," Congreve snapped. "Your mistake was in pointing the finger at Clewen and Keaney, two men who you knew were already dead. What you forgot was that both of those men had been assigned the task of body doubles for the King and yourself. The preparation for those roles was no small endeavor. They had to be ready to immediately take the place of their doppelgängers. Ergo they could not have been the ones sent to lead the King into the trap. No, McClanahan, it was *you* whom the King trusted. You who led him into a trap of your own devising. You are the betrayer. Do you deny it?"

"Holy shit," muttered Harry Brock. "He's the guy."

"Yeah, Harry," said Stoke. "Try to keep up."

"Of course I deny it," retorted McClanahan. "I've never heard such a load of—"

Suddenly, McClanahan was moving, diving toward the nearest of the covered bodies, throwing back the Mylar blanket, seizing the dead man's MPX. He whirled and raised the machine pistol, finger seeking the trigger.

Before the man could fire, a quiet burst from Hawke's weapon stitched across his chest, knocking him back across the body of the slain officer. Stoke and Harry both had their weapons at the ready as well, but there was no need for additional firepower.

"Cut that rather close, didn't you?" said Congreve reprovingly.

"Not at all," replied Hawke. In truth, he'd been watching McClanahan closely after Congreve's accusation and read in the man's body language not only his guilt, but his intention to attempt violence. He strode over to the fallen gamekeeper, taking the unfired weapon from the man's nerveless fingers.

McClanahan was still alive for the moment, but Hawke knew that he didn't have long. Blood burbled from his lips and he was struggling to breathe. Hawke knelt beside him, as if to take the gamekeeper's final confession, which in a way was exactly what he intended.

"Why, Roddy? Charles loved you."

McClanahan's face twisted into something like a sneer. Hawke couldn't tell if it was a pain response or an expression of utter contempt, though he suspected the latter.

"Loved?" gasped McClanahan. "Not worthy of—" A spasm of pain cut him off, a froth of blood and spittle filling his mouth.

Hawke's curiosity regarding the man's motives burned within him, but he knew McClanahan's time was short, so he asked the only question that really mattered. "The King, Roddy, where is he?"

Now something like a smile touched the gamekeeper's lips. "Too late. Never fi—"

Agony gripped him again, causing his whole body to go rigid. Desperate, Hawke gripped his shoulder. "Don't end it like this, Roddy," Alex pleaded. "You can still fix this. Tell me where to find Charles, Roddy. Tell me how to stop the bloody bomb!"

McClanahan's eyes started to roll back in their sockets, but then they snapped forward again, meeting Hawke's stare, and through clenched teeth, as the life drained from his body, he managed to speak three final words. "One last trick."

Then he was gone.

FORTY-ONE

velyn "Evie" Sinclair slid her favorite mug under the Nespresso
machine, selected a classic espresso capsule, and pressed the start
button.

The mug—which was white with a small chip along the rim and
had been a birthday gift from her younger sister—was adorned with
the words that had become her personal mantra, "Keep Calm and
Crunch Data."

For Evie, crunching data *was* what kept her calm. A technician at the
National Traffic Operations Centre, Evie was that rare individual who
actually enjoyed coming to work. Analyzing traffic information, identifying patterns, and solving complex problems gave her a much-needed
sense of control in a world that was so chaotic. She especially enjoyed
working the night shift because it gave her the perfect excuse for ducking out of awkward social engagements with girlfriends who felt it was
their mission in life to help her find a partner to settle down with.

When the coffee machine finished hissing and spitting, she retrieved her mug and quickly made her way back to her workstation.
One of the three monitor screens on her desk was cycling through
recorded feeds from traffic cameras on the major motorways, while an-

other display pinpointed the location of each feed by projecting a blue pin on a map of Great Britain's highway system. One of her ongoing tasks at the NTOC was to compare real-world data with the computer models used to predict the traffic outcomes in order to refine those models. It was an extension of the work she had done as a student of computer science at the University of Glasgow, and while it was, like most quotidian jobs, an assignment that could never truly be finished, she found a measure of satisfaction every time reality provided her with some new way to improve the algorithm.

There were far worse ways to make one's way in the world—and worse ways to spend a night.

Plus, there's coffee, she thought, taking a sip.

It was at that moment, just as she was savoring her favorite blend of Colombian coffee mixed with notes of cocoa and rich praline, that she spied the flashing light on her desk phone indicating that a voicemail message was waiting in her inbox. She hardly ever received calls so late in her shift or, for that matter, ever, since most of her colleagues preferred to communicate using emails and text messages. Curious, she played the message while midsip and felt a little thrill of delight as she recognized the voice.

"Ah, Miss Sinclair. Ambrose Congreve here. You may remember we spoke earlier this evening."

Evie broke into a grin as she set her mug down. "Of course I remember, silly," she said aloud. "It was only four hours ago."

This was only partially true. The actual reason why that earlier conversation had been so memorable was that it had given her a chance to demonstrate her unique talents in a way that she found far more exciting and rewarding than simply modeling traffic patterns, namely by assisting law enforcement agencies in identifying and tracking suspect vehicles. Whenever, as sometimes happened, she was asked to comb through hours of traffic-camera footage to find one particular vehicle, it always made her feel like Sherlock Holmes.

Cumberbatch. Not the old one with the funny hat.

She had also found Congreve's polite, self-effacing manner rather charming.

Almost as a reflex, she used her mouse to open the tab on her computer desktop, where the image file Congreve had earlier requested was still displayed. The picture showed the front end of a Tevva lorry, with both the number plate—T7X-2024—and the face of the driver, a bearded, red-haired man who bore more than a passing resemblance to a certain actor. Evie couldn't recall the actor's name, only that he died in almost every movie he appeared in. A quick pass through facial recognition software had yielded up the driver's name—Dylan Fahey of Londonderry—along with a copy of his driving license, which, she had noted at the time, did not include the C1 provisional endorsement required to operate a commercial lorry.

She had no earthly idea why this particular lorry was so important to Congreve, but she knew better than to ask. Still, her mind raced with the possibilities. Was Fahey a smuggler? Was the lorry carrying narcotics or perhaps even human cargo?

She took another sip of coffee as she listened to the rest of the message.

"I'd be most grateful if you could ring me back," Congreve went on, and then supplied his mobile number. Evie ended the playback and immediately dialed the number.

Congreve picked up almost right away. "Congreve here."

"Mr. Congreve, it's Evie Sinclair at NTOC. You rang me?"

"Ah, yes, Miss Sinclair. Thank you so much for getting back to me. It seems I am once again in need of your expertise."

"Always happy to be of assistance," replied Evie cheerily. "How can I help?"

"It concerns the matter you helped with earlier. That business with the lorry?"

She glanced at her monitor screen that still displayed the photo of Dylan Fahey, and grinned. "Yes, I remember."

"Well, I was wondering if you might be able to determine its present location."

This was actually a rather big ask. She would have to review camera footage from all the motorways in the general vicinity of Cairnryan, starting from the time stamp on the original sighting, and then employ a predictive algorithm to anticipate the lorry's movements over a period of almost twenty-four hours, which was enough time for it to go literally anywhere in the United Kingdom. But this was exactly the sort of challenge that Evie thrived on.

"Certainly," she replied, "though I may need to brew another mug of coffee."

"I may be able to narrow down the search a little," Congreve went on. "I have reason to believe that the vehicle in question was in Aberdeen at approximately 1900 last evening, possibly in the general vicinity of a hire car provider on Great Northern Road."

"That will help," Evie agreed. A quick map search gave her the specified location and allowed her to access archived footage from all the cameras in an area roughly one mile in diameter. Just to be on the safe side, she rolled back the start time to 1830, entered the lorry's number plate, then launched the search. "Okay, this should take only a moment."

A new image popped up on the screen, clearly showing the lorry on the A96 motorway, traveling east.

"Here we go. I've got your lorry passing the camera at Cairnfield Crescent at 1837 yesterday evening."

"Excellent. Now can you use that information to determine its present location?"

"That may take a little longer," Evie cautioned. "Can I ring you back?"

"How much longer?" asked Congreve. There was an edge to his voice that she had not heard before. "It's really quite urgent that we locate this vehicle rather quickly."

She was tempted to give him her standard answer—*It will take as long as it takes*—but then she realized that there was probably a very good reason for his uncharacteristic abruptness.

What's in that lorry? she wondered.

"I'll be honest with you, Mr. Congreve. I can't tell the computer to look at every camera in the kingdom in real time. We have to start with the last-known time and location and then follow the trail, moving forward in time as we go. Now, we can compress the time quite a bit, but it's still going to take a while. Maybe a few hours."

There was a disappointed humming sound on the line. "Hours. Hmm. Well, can't be helped, I suppose. Can you at least determine if the lorry moved on from *that* location?"

"Give me a moment." She resumed the search, cycling through multiple camera feeds until, almost five minutes later—five minutes in which the only words spoken over the open line were her plaintive updates, "Still looking"—a new image appeared on her screen.

"Good news," she announced. "I have your lorry on the A92, heading south at 2223."

"That's a gap of nearly four hours," remarked Congreve. "South, you say?"

"Mm-hmm." Evie added a new set of parameters, instructing the computer to search the feed from all nearby cameras, report each hit, and display them as connected dots. It quickly became apparent that the dots were following the course of the A92 motorway south out of Aberdeen, heading toward Dundee.

Congreve, who had been listening patiently, now spoke up. "If you were to venture a guess, where would you say he's headed?"

"Well, from Dundee, he could continue on to Edinburgh or Glasgow. Any of a number of places, really."

"Hmm. London?"

Evie opened a new screen and created a route from Dundee to London. "Yes. It would take a little over eight hours." She checked the clock on the desktop—it was a little after four o'clock a.m. "If he drove through the night, he'd be nearly there."

Congreve hummed again. "Best not to get ahead of ourselves, I suppose. Please, continue the search."

"Are you sure you don't want me to ring you back?"

"Quite certain. As they say, I have nowhere else to be just now."

At her workstation, Evie just shrugged. "Me neither."

―――――――――

Congreve remained on the line with Evie for another two hours as the lorry's relentless journey was reproduced, one traffic camera at a time. The vehicle passed through Dundee, turned east on the A90, bypassed the turnoff at Craigend that would have led to Edinburgh and instead continued toward Glasgow. Evie dutifully updated Congreve not only on the route but also on the time stamp for each hit. They were catching up, at least in a temporal sense, but there were still many hours to go.

Shortly after midnight, the lorry had reached the outskirts of Glasgow but then veered away, heading south on the M74.

"London, then," Congreve observed.

Evie did not bother with her earlier caveat. While there were any number of major cities that could have been reached along that route—Manchester, Liverpool, Birmingham—never mind the hundreds of smaller towns, London remained the principal destination for travelers on the M74. "Looks that way."

"Hmm. Please, continue."

Every subsequent contact seemed to confirm Congreve's prediction. Evie chased the lorry, in a manner of speaking, as it headed relentlessly southward, leaving Scotland behind, following the M74 as it transitioned into the M6. Slowly but surely, she was shrinking the time gap. Evie thought it a little ironic that the lorry had passed to the east of Birmingham, less than ten miles from the NTOC building, only about an hour earlier.

"If he continues on this course," she told Congreve, "he'll reach London about ninety minutes from now."

"Shortly after eight a.m.," Congreve said gravely.

Evie checked the clock on her desktop and was surprised to see that it was already 0630. She'd been so consumed with the search that she'd worked past the end of her shift.

"Miss Sinclair," Congreve went on, "I cannot stress how critical it is that we find that lorry *before* it reaches London. Is there anything at all that you can do to expedite the search?"

The despair in his tone was so palpable that for the second time since the phone conversation had begun, Evie resisted the impulse to remind Congreve that the search could not be rushed. Instead, she did something that she almost never did.

She took a shortcut.

Using her algorithm, she leapt ahead of the ongoing search to predict where the lorry would be five minutes into the future if it continued on the M1 without turning off or slowing down, and then instructed the number-plate-scanning program to start actively watching the feed from the next camera along the way. The danger in taking this approach was that it depended on the assumption that the lorry was going to stay on that route and not turn off on any of the dozens of junctions along the way.

"All right," she said resignedly, "based on the model, he should be approaching the junction to Luton sometime in the next five minutes."

"Luton," murmured Congreve. "That's only thirty miles from London."

"That's correct. If he's still on the M1, that's where he'll be. If he's already turned off, then we'll have wasted five minutes looking in the wrong place."

"Very well. Please, proceed."

Even though it was impossible for her to read the number plates of the vehicles as they flashed by, Evie nevertheless watched the live feed from the camera at Junction 11 with the rapt intensity normally reserved for a sporting event. And when a new screen suddenly appeared, showing a captured frame with the lorry and its number plate clearly visible, she let out a cheer worthy of a winning goal at a football match.

"We got him!"

"Thank goodness," said Congreve. Then in a muffled voice, she heard him say, "Alex, we have a confirmed location. He's on the M1, just past Luton. . . . One moment . . . Miss Sinclair, are you still there?"

"Still here. You'd have to drag me away."

"Ah, very good. We have a helicopter in the area attempting to establish visual contact. Could you send me the GPS coordinates of that camera?"

She gave Congreve that information and then listened as he relayed it to the man he called Alex.

"He'll be a couple miles further along by now," she said. "Let me give you the coordinates of the next camera in line so that you can be there waiting for him." She rattled off the digits, and then, a few minutes later, when another captured still image popped up, she cried, "He's there."

"Thank you, Miss Sinclair. We have him. Your help has been invaluable."

"It was my pleasure." Aglow with satisfaction, she leaned back in her chair and stared at the image on her screen.

"What have you got in there that's so important, Dylan Fahey?" she murmured. Overcome by a sudden inexplicable impulse, she zoomed in to get another look at the driver's face. The resolution was grainy but sufficient for her to see that the man sitting behind the steering wheel of the lorry was not the redhead she'd identified earlier. Nevertheless, there was something familiar about him. It took her a few seconds to figure it out.

"Blimey," she muttered, "he looks just like the King!"

FORTY-TWO

Hawke gazed out the open rear door of the Merlin as it flew above the motorway, matching the speed of the vehicle below. The morning sun was flashing off the lorry's windscreen and right into his eyes, denying him a look at the person in the driver's seat. But if Congreve's last message was correct, this was the lorry transporting the bomb with the nerve agent and quite likely King Charles as well.

When Congreve had first shared with Hawke, Stoke, and Harry his belief that the lorry was on its way to London, all of them had boarded the Merlin and made the ninety-minute flight to London. After a brief stop to top off the Merlin's tanks, Hawke, Stoke, and Harry had gone aloft once more—Congreve would remain on the ground to coordinate with the traffic center—and begun flying along the motorway in an admittedly desperate attempt to pick the lorry out from among the river of traffic rushing toward the island's most populous city. With the sun already in the sky, even the unflinchingly optimistic Hawke began to worry that Congreve had guessed wrong and that the lorry was bound for some other corner of the kingdom. Fortunately, Congreve had been right as usual, and when he'd called again to report a positive sighting, they were, as luck would have it, just two minutes away from the location.

"Can you get any lower?" Hawke called over the internal comms. "And pull alongside it. I need to see the driver's face."

In the front seat, the pilot shook his head. "It's against regulations."

"Damn the bloody regulations," Hawke snapped. "I'll take full responsibility."

Although they had not been fully briefed on every aspect of the crisis—notably the identity of the VIP hostage Hawke and the others were trying to rescue—the crew of the helicopter understood that the stakes were very high and that if there were ever a time to throw caution to the wind, it was now.

The pilot nodded and then began reducing the collective pitch while easing forward on the cyclic. The aircraft eased downward and fell back just a little until it was flying barely higher than the lighting stanchions that lined the motorway and moving parallel to the lorry. Over the intercom, Hawke could hear the clamor of automated warning systems advising the pilot that he was perilously close to the terrain and needed to pull up.

Hawke leaned forward, as far as his safety harness would allow, peering down at the figure seated behind the lorry's steering wheel.

"Lower!"

"This is as low as I can get!" the pilot shouted back.

Hawke muttered a curse under his breath, then turned to one of his fellow passengers. "Stoke! Give me a hand here," he shouted, and then unbuckled his harness so that he could lean out even farther.

"Whoa!" cried Stoke, realizing almost too late what Hawke was asking of him. He shot out a hand and grasped the back of Hawke's combat vest even as Hawke began leaning out into nothingness.

A few seconds later, Hawke flashed a thumbs-up, and Stoke pulled him back inside. Hawke fell back into his seat but did not buckle in. "It's him, Stoke. Charles is in that lorry."

"Is he . . . you know . . . ?"

"Alive? Yes. He looked me dead in the eyes."

"Well, all right, then," said Harry Brock. "Mission accomplished."

"Not quite, Harry. We still have to get him away from the bloody thing."

Stoke nodded gravely. "Looks like it's time for plan A."

A few hours earlier, when it had become apparent that Charles was likely aboard the doomed vehicle, Hawke's mind had begun turning over the problem of how to, first, rescue Charles and, second, prevent the bomb from detonating. A repeat of Ross Sutherland's noble sacrifice wasn't even something to consider as a last resort because this time there was the added complication of the Novichok nerve agent. A detonation, even in an unpopulated area, would have still created a deadly plume of the toxin that might have been carried on the wind. So, while Congreve set about trying to pinpoint the lorry's location and ultimate destination, Hawke considered what they would do once they found the damned thing.

He didn't have a solution for the second problem, but the first seemed fairly straightforward. They had a helicopter at their disposal after all. He would just fast-rope from the helicopter down to the vehicle, force his way inside, and effect an expedient rescue of the King by the safest means possible.

Problem one solved.

Pushing back on said plan, Stoke had called him crazy and said that they could surely come up with a better rescue than that. However, hours of brainstorming hadn't found a way to get around the basic problem of how to transfer onto a moving vehicle. Stoke's best suggestion was to make the attempt from another vehicle, moving parallel to the lorry, but this plan, aside from not really being any safer, had another very significant drawback. The lorry's autonomous drive mode would cause it to automatically move away from any vehicle attempting to get close enough for a transfer, either by changing lanes, slowing down, or speeding up.

"It's self-driving, right?" Brock had put in at one point. "Those things are programmed to follow the rules of the road and avoid collisions. Just block the road, and it will stop."

"That could work," said Stoke, shooting a hopeful glance at Hawke.

But Hawke just shook his head. "The bomb they tried to use in Belfast was tamperproofed. They might have rigged it to detonate automatically if it stops for too long. We can't take that chance."

Given the time constraints upon them, there simply wasn't a better alternative to plan A, and even Stoke knew it.

Hawke was not indifferent to the risks inherent in what he was about to attempt. He would be sliding down a rope while traveling forward at about fifty miles per hour, with the wind buffeting him as he tried to establish some kind of stable position on the lorry.

Another concern, and one that he had mostly managed to conceal from his friends, was his own physical condition. His body had been through the wringer. He couldn't remember the last time he'd gotten any sleep. His joints were stiff, his muscles aching. He had bruises all over, including two new ones on his back where he'd been shot during the raid on Dunnottar Castle. His body armor had saved his life, but it hadn't rendered him invulnerable to the impact of being struck by a pair of objects moving at nearly the speed of sound. The bullet wound in his thigh, though only a graze, still throbbed. The medic who had sealed it with surgical glue advised him to stay off the leg for a week or two to let it heal. Hawke would have liked nothing better, but he wasn't the sort to sit out when there was rough work to be done. He'd already survived so much, gone through hell just to make it this far, that the idea of letting someone else finish the mission was simply unthinkable. He had thanked the medic for his concern and promised to take it easy.

After this is finished. He didn't say the words aloud.

With a signal to the crew chief that they were ready to make the attempt, Stoke kicked the coil of forty-millimeter rope off the deck, letting it unspool in the air below. The rope, which was about the same diameter as a can of Red Bull energy drink, was heavy enough that it didn't whip about in the wind, but it did curl away to dangle like a prehensile tail. With guidance from the crew chief, the pilot jockeyed the helicopter over the roadway until the end of the rope was trailing about ten feet above the roof of the lorry's cargo bay.

Hawke, with a balaclava and ballistic goggles, both to protect his eyes and to conceal his identity from hundreds of motorists who would doubtless be recording his exploits with their mobile phones, clipped a twelve-millimeter belay line to his belt as an added safety measure and then, with Stoke giving him a helping hand, carefully lowered himself over the edge, gripping the big rope, first between the soles of his boots and then with gloved hands.

"On rope!" he shouted.

"Wait for it," warned Stoke, looking at the motorway below. Hawke just hung there, breathing slowly to quiet his racing heart as the wind whipped at his back.

A few seconds later, the end of the rope grazed the top of an over-roadway sensor installation—one of the metal structures that arched over the lanes at varying intervals, and upon which were mounted informational signs, sensors, and the traffic cameras that had enabled Hawke and the others to pinpoint the lorry's location. These arches and other obstructions like roadway overpasses were a dangerous wrinkle in Hawke's plan. Once committed, he would have only the length of time it took for the lorry to move from one obstacle to the next to make his descent and go off the rope.

As soon as the rope cleared the arch, the helicopter nosed down, bringing the end of the line in contact with the lorry's roof.

"Go!" shouted Stoke.

Hawke pushed away from the aircraft and began sliding down the rope like a fireman sliding down a brass pole in a station house.

The heat of the thick rope sliding through the padded leather palms of his gloves called to his mind the crazy descent from Wolkenheim Mountain, and that recollection triggered a cascade of memories. He found himself thinking about Pippa and wondering if she had survived the night.

Then, almost before he knew it, his feet came off the rope and grazed the lorry's roof. He absorbed the impact with bent knees and tightened his grip on the rope, using it to steady himself against the onslaught of the wind. Then he lowered himself to a prone position, let go of the big rope, and clung to the top of the cargo bay like a gecko climbing a wall. His MPX, its sling attached to his tactical vest, thumped loudly against the translucent fiberglass roof. Although he had not anticipated a hostile reception, he'd cited the Boy Scout motto and brought the weapon along, just in case.

He was still attached to the helicopter by the belay line, and if he lost his hold, it would arrest his fall, but now that he was down, the belay line was as much a liability as it was a safeguard. He quickly unclipped the carabiner connected to the belay rope from his belt and thrust it away, shouting, "I'm down," into his radio mic mere seconds before the lorry passed under another over-roadway installation.

Hawke's daring descent had not gone unnoticed by the other motorists on the road. Thankfully, those closest to the lorry had slowed down, though it was impossible to say whether they had done so to give him plenty of room in which to operate or to get themselves better angles for recording the spectacle with their mobile phones. With arms and legs splayed out to maximize contact surface, he pushed forward, then slid off the cargo bay and onto the roof of the cab. He carefully leaned over the left door, and using the butt of his MPX like a hammer, he smashed through the side window. Then, reversing position so that his feet were leading, he lowered himself over the edge and through the window opening, dropping into the empty passenger seat opposite the wide-eyed man behind the wheel.

Hawke whipped off his balaclava and goggles and then inclined his head in an almost irreverent bow. "Good morning, Your Majesty."

FORTY-THREE

The King blinked, but whether in disbelief or because of the wind swirling about the interior of the cab, Hawke couldn't say. "Alex? Good heavens, it is you! Alex, how the devil did you get here?"

"No time to get into that just now," said Hawke. "We need to get you out of here."

"I fear that may be easier said than done." Charles nodded his head toward the steering wheel, to which, Hawke now saw, his hands had been secured with a heavy wrap of gaffer tape. "All appearances to the contrary, I'm not really driving this bloody thing."

"Never fear." Hawke retrieved his Victorinox from a pocket and used its large blade to slice through the layers of tape.

Charles pulled his hands away from the steering wheel, peeling the adhesive from his skin with a deep sigh of relief. "Much better," he said as he began stretching and flexing his cramped muscles. "I've been stuck sitting like this for hours."

"Are you injured?"

Charles shook his head. "No. Just a bit stiff. And I desperately need to use the lavatory."

"Then you're not at all going to like what happens next," said Hawke with a grimace. He delved into a cargo pocket and produced a lightweight climbing harness, which he passed over to Charles. "Do you remember your training with the commandos?"

Though it was not widely known, a much younger Prince Charles, during his military service as an officer in the Royal Navy and a helicopter aviator, had undergone a thirteen-week commando training course with the Royal Marines.

The King, however, regarded the harness as if it were a poisonous snake. "That was fifty years ago."

"Like riding a bike," Hawke promised.

But the King remained dubious. "I'm not a young man anymore, Alex. Maybe you're immune to the ravages of time, but I most certainly am not."

"Charles," said Hawke soberly, "here's the situation. We haven't worked out a way to stop this lorry yet. It is quite likely carrying a very large explosive device that will detonate when it reaches its destination."

The King's eyes widened. "Westminster! That's where it's going. That bastard Sten told me as much."

Hawke decided this was information worth passing along. He keyed his radio mic. "Stoke, it's Alex. I'm with the King. We'll be ready for the extraction in a moment, but you need to pass something along for me. Tell Ambrose the target is Westminster Palace."

Stoke's voice sounded in his ear. "Westminster? That's your version of the Capitol, isn't it?"

"Right you are, Stoke. Tell Ambrose. He'll know what to do."

"Whatever it is, he's not going to have much time to do it."

"I'm aware. Hawke out." He turned back to the King. "As I was saying, this vehicle is carrying a rather large bomb, and while we're working on a way to stop it, I need to get you away, and this is the only way to do it. It's perfectly safe, but we need to do this now."

With some hesitation Charles accepted the harness and then proceeded to thread his feet through the fixed belt and leg loops with the familiarity of someone donning a pair of pants.

Hawke keyed the mic again. "We'll be ready in a minute, Stoke. Start looking for the best place to do this."

There was a long delay—*Too long,* thought Hawke—before Stoke's voice came over the line. "All right, you're about to come up on a series of road overpasses. Three of them. Then, after that, you're clear for about half a mile."

"Half a mile? That's cutting it close. All right, we'll be ready." Hawke turned to the King. "Here's what we're going to do. In a few seconds, my friend Stokely Jones Jr.—I believe you've met him—Stoke is going to lower a belay line down to us. You're going to clip in and then jump."

"Coming up on the first overpass," Stoke called out.

Hawke looked forward and saw the structure ahead. He turned back to Charles. "You won't hit the macadam, because Stoke is going to pull you right up. It should be no more of a shock than what you would feel in a parachute jump."

The overpass flashed overhead. Another loomed only a couple hundred yards farther along.

"Why do I think it's not going to be as simple as that?" said Charles.

"Well, we'll only have about thirty seconds to snag the belay, get you clipped in, and make the leap. If you're just clipping in when we reach an overpass . . . well, it won't be pleasant."

Charles gave a sober nod just as the lorry passed under the second overpass. The third one was just a hundred yards away.

"We're right above you and matching your speed," Stoke called. "Watch for the end of the line."

As the lorry raced under the third overpass, Hawke began looking in vain for the trailing end of the rope. After a few seconds, he leaned out through the empty window frame and gazed up at the helicopter. He could just make out the rope whipping back and forth behind the aircraft. "Stoke, it's not working."

"Ah, the wind is blowing it all over the place. It's not heavy enough. We're going to have to weight it."

"There's no time, Stoke."

"I know. Hang on."

A few seconds later, another overpass appeared in the distance.

"Okay, you're coming up on several more overpasses, but the good news is that once you're clear of them, we'll have about a mile to play with."

"That's not going to do us much good if you can't get that rope to me."

"I'm working on it. Just hold your horses!"

Frustrated by the delay, Hawke turned to look at the large display console. "Where the devil are we anyway?"

"Edgware," replied Charles, tapping the GPS map.

The name wasn't familiar to Hawke, but a look at the map supplied the answer to the question he hadn't asked.

Distance to destination—13 miles.
Time remaining—31 minutes.

Thirty-one minutes, thought Hawke. He knew better than anyone how plastic time could be in crisis. *Too much and never enough.*

He dug into another cargo pocket and took out a device that looked like an ordinary mobile phone except for a strip of two-sided adhesive tape on its back. When he powered up the device, a single word appeared on the otherwise dark screen:

Searching . . .

He stripped the backing off the tape and then pressed the device against the lorry's console. The affixed device continued to flash its singular message.

"What's that?" asked the King.

"A gift from the tech boys over at Vauxhall Cross. It's a mobile phone cloning device, but they tell me it should be able to duplicate this lorry's auto-drive computer and hopefully reprogram the route."

Hawke didn't add that the technician, who at C's behest had delivered the device to him during the refueling stop, had expressed grave doubts about whether they would be able to crack the encryption in time to reroute the lorry. It was, as the Americans would say, a Hail Mary play, but absent any better solutions, it was one that had to be attempted.

After a few seconds, a new message flashed on the screen.

Device found.
Cloning . . .

A progress bar appeared below the words, along with the percentage of the operation completed. The numbers were still in the single digits and increasing at a glacial pace.

Hawke brought his attention back to the more immediate problem of evacuating the King. He noted that traffic on the motorway had diminished to almost nothing. There were no vehicles moving to pass, and the road ahead was clearing out fast. Evidently, some well-meaning traffic controller or police superintendent, no doubt responding to reports about what was transpiring on the motorway, had closed the on-ramps. While prudent from a public-safety standpoint, clearing the roads meant that the lorry would reach its destination that much sooner.

Another series of overpasses came and went. Seeing a stretch of open road ahead, Hawke keyed his radio. "Stoke, what's going on up there?"

"We're still having trouble weighting the damn line," growled Stoke.

Hawke knew that his friend was doing everything possible and needed no urging, but his own frustration was mounting. He shot a glance at the console. The minutes were slipping away, and the Palace of Westminster was growing ever closer. The GPS map showed the route as a bright blue line following the M1 toward the heart of London. That gave him an idea.

Hawke keyed his mic again. "Stoke, can you pass on another message to Ambrose?"

"Kind of got my hands full right now."

"Then have Harry do it."

Brock's voice now came over the line. "I'm here, Alex."

Hawke took a moment to consider how to phrase his request. "You gave me an idea, Harry, when you said these self-driving vehicles follow the rules of the road. But they're also always looking for the shortest, quickest route to their destination. If Ambrose can get his contact at the traffic center to start closing roads, the AI should automatically change to the next-best route. Do you follow?"

"Yeah, I think so. You think if we close off all the roads, maybe it will just pull over?"

"I don't want to close off all the roads. But if we can control the route, it will give us some options."

"I'll pass it along," said Brock.

Stoke broke in. "Alex, we're ready up here. You've got a clear stretch coming up in about twenty seconds. Be ready because we're only going to get one chance at this."

Hawke glanced forward and saw another overpass approaching. "Understood, Stoke." He turned to Charles. "Ready, Majesty?"

The King managed a grim nod.

As the lorry emerged on the other side of the overpass, Hawke leaned out the window again, gazing up at the helicopter, which was still matching the lorry's speed about seventy-five feet above the road surface. He was looking for the rope end, expecting to see it hanging down with some sort of heavy weight attached. Instead, what he saw was an enormous figure—someone about the size of your average armoire—leap from the helicopter's open door to hurtle downward like an incoming meteor.

For a terrifying moment, Stoke appeared to be in free fall, but then, when he was about thirty feet above the macadam, his descent slowed almost to a full stop. Hawke realized then that his American friend was tied onto the belay line and that he'd used himself to weight the end.

Stoke dangled there for a few more seconds as the helicopter maneuvered to bring him in closer to the lorry and then he dropped the rest of the way. He landed on the cab with such force that the rooftop buckled, sending spiderweb fractures across the windscreen, and the lorry started bouncing on its suspension.

A moment later, Stoke appeared just outside the left-side window, seeming to float above the roadside as he hung at the end of his belay line, dangling from the outside mirror with one hand. "Let's go!" he shouted urgently, waving with the other. "Let's go!"

Hawke realized then what Stoke had in mind, but there was no time to explain it to Charles. The next overpass was already approaching.

Fifteen seconds . . . maybe less.

Without a word of explanation, he grabbed Charles by the arms and heaved him across the interior of the cab, thrusting him headfirst through the window opening and into Stoke's waiting arms.

Stoke bear-hugged Charles to his chest and kicked away from the lorry, swinging like a pendulum beneath the beating rotors of the helicopter. Then both men were whisked out of Hawke's view, just as the lorry rolled under another overpass.

"Did you get him?" Hawke shouted into his radio. "Stoke! Talk to me. Is Charles safe?"

After a pause that felt like an eternity, Stoke's breathless voice sounded in Hawke's ear. "I got him, Alex. He's safe."

Hawke sagged in relief. After so much pain and sacrifice, they had done the impossible.

They had saved the King, but there was still work to do.

Now, to save Westminster.

FORTY-FOUR

Distance to destination—9 miles.
Time remaining—22 minutes.
Cloning . . . 54%.

Alex Hawke's entire world was now reduced to three sets of numbers—the first two counting down to oblivion, the third steadily increasing but of uncertain value. There was no guarantee that the cloning device would be able to give the hackers at MI6 the ability to change the lorry's destination or disengage the auto-drive, and even if they could, there would still be the problem of the bomb. Would diverting the lorry from its original destination trigger an immediate detonation?

Hawke keyed his mic again. "Stoke, take Charles to Ambrose and stay there with them. I'm counting on you to keep him safe."

"I'm not leaving you down there, Alex."

"I'm not coming with you, Stoke. One way or another, I'm going to see this through to the end."

"Alex—"

"No arguments, Stoke. Time to move. I'm going to see what I can do about that bomb, but keep me updated."

Stoke gave a heavy sigh. "All right. But you'd better come back. Anastasia'll have my ass if I let you get yourself killed."

Anastasia.

A wave of guilt suddenly washed over Hawke, not so much at the thought of leaving Asia widowed before they were even wed . . . or leaving Alexei half orphaned. No, the real guilt stemmed from the fact that Hawke—who had once again gotten caught up in saving the bloody world—hadn't taken much time to think about Anastasia, let alone to consider how his actions might impact her.

Now's not the time, he told himself.

There was precious little time left, and none whatsoever to waste.

"Wouldn't dream of it, old chap," he finally said with forced aplomb. "Hawke out."

Pushing the unwelcome feelings away, he worked the door handle and then carefully climbed out onto the running board.

Emptied as it was of all traffic, the motorway seemed like something from a postapocalyptic nightmare. Hawke tried to put this ominous association out of his mind as he sidled along the running board, the wind whipping at his back. He worked the flush-mounted latch on the side door—unlocked, thankfully—then pulled the door open and climbed inside.

The bomb was almost exactly as he'd expected based on Congreve's description—eight large drums and a tangle of fuse wires held in place by strips of anti-tamper tape—but there was one significant difference. Resting atop the drums, like a scattering of throw pillows on a bed, were eight gallon-sized zip-seal plastic bags filled with an ultrafine powder that could only be the Novichok nerve agent.

The idea that only a thin barrier of polyethylene stood between him and enough toxin to kill thousands of people did not give Hawke the "warm and fuzzies," as Harry Brock might have said.

He made a cautious circuit around the device, visually inspecting it for any vulnerabilities that a bomb-defusing expert might have been able to exploit. The twenty-odd minutes remaining weren't time enough for an explosive ordnance–disposal technician to be put aboard

the lorry, but it might be sufficient for Hawke, guided remotely by such
an expert, to pull the plug. It was certainly more time than had been
given to Ross Sutherland.

After his quick appraisal, he returned to the side door and transitioned back to the cab partly because he was a little leery of using his
radio in close proximity to the bomb, on the off chance that it might
have an RF detonator, but mostly to make another check of both the
GPS and the cloning device. While he had been occupied in the cargo
bay, the lorry had reached the end of the M1 where it joined with the
North Circular Road, and was now heading east toward the junction
with Hendon Way, where, according to the GPS route, it would turn
south. Soon, it would leave behind the major traffic arteries and enter
the web of lesser streets with traffic signals and reduced speed limits,
but also with homes and businesses and innocent bystanders who had
no idea that a carriage of death was speeding through their midst.

Distance to destination—8 miles.
Time remaining—19 minutes.

Hawke was somewhat heartened by the fact that the cloning device
appeared to have finished creating its virtual copy and now flashed alternating messages.

Enter password.
Log-in information incorrect.
Enter password.

The techs from Six had explained that they would be making a
brute-force attack on the lorry's autonomous driving module—a trial-
and-error method of testing randomly created log-in credentials in the
hopes of breaking through the device's safeguards. When techs were
given enough time and computing power, it was a reliable method for

gaining access to an encrypted device, but while there was plenty of the latter at the disposal of the kingdom's intelligence service, there was very little of the former.

That matter, however, was completely out of Hawke's hands. His sole focus for the next nineteen minutes was the bomb.

Hawke keyed his radio again. "Stoke, do you read?"

"Loud and clear, boss. We're still inbound, but we passed your message on to Ambrose. They're going to try closing some of the roads between you and Westminster. If it works like they think it will, you should automatically be routed east pretty soon."

"That's fine, Stoke. But what I really want is for you to tell me more about this nerve agent."

"Harry's the expert."

"I'm here, Alex," Brock broke in. "What do you want to know?"

"There are several bags of white powder arranged around the bomb."

"Yeah, that would be the Novichok agent. What kind of bags are we talking about?"

"Ordinary zip seals. One-gallon capacity."

"Hmm. Any markings or labels?"

"None that I've noticed. Harry, it's my understanding that the Novichok is a binary composition, with two separate ingredients that have to mix together to become lethal."

"That's right."

"Is there a way to tell if the ingredients have already been combined?"

"Good question. I don't really know. But I'd say if they put the stuff in Ziploc baggies, then they weren't too concerned about exposure, so my guess would be that they didn't premix it. They were probably counting on the explosion to do that for them."

"And if they aren't combined, the ingredients are more or less harmless by themselves?"

"I don't know if I'd say *harmless*. But definitely *less* harmful."

"What does that mean, Harry? We don't have much time."

"The precursors are organophosphates. Same stuff that's in weed killer, similar composition. You don't want to get any on you, but it probably won't kill you if you do. Not right away at least. I think they can cause cancer, but only in California."

"Is that a joke, Harry?"

"Hell if I know."

Hawke felt his ire rising. Harry Brock often had that effect on him. "What I need to know, Harry, is what will happen if I empty these bags out the back of this lorry, scatter the powder along the road. Will it hurt anyone?"

"If they're not already mixed, it probably won't do much. Maybe kill some weeds along the roadside."

Hawke cast a glance out the window. With the departure of the helicopter, the ordinary traffic pattern seemed to be reasserting itself. The lorry had reached the ramp and was beginning the turn that would bring it to the looping interchange known as the Brent Cross Flyover, and in a moment, it would be heading toward the heart of London.

Not exactly an ideal place to scatter the components of a deadly nerve agent, even if in their unmixed state, they were *less harmful.*

"What would happen if it mixed with water?" asked Hawke.

"Depends on how much water."

"A river's worth."

"I'm told it breaks down pretty quickly in water."

"Hmm. All right. Contact Ambrose and see if he can figure out a way to route me across Waterloo Bridge."

"Waterloo Bridge? Got it."

Hawke leaned back in the seat and checked the console again. The cloning device was still battering against the auto-drive computer's security gates—no telling when or if it would succeed. The GPS map now showed six miles and seventeen minutes remaining.

Then the display changed. The numbers disappeared and a message appeared across the map.

Rerouting.

"Ambrose, you bloody genius," Hawke whispered.
The numbers returned but this time they read:

Distance to destination—8 miles.
Time remaining—23 minutes.

Hawke had never felt so happy to have an extra six minutes.

He climbed back outside and into the cargo bay, where he bypassed the bomb and instead went to the rear roll-down door and threw it open. Air rushed in, swirling around the cargo bay and creating a miniature vortex. Outside, the city blocks seemed to be in retreat, shrinking away to the vanishing point.

In truth, Hawke did not think of himself as a Londoner. He felt much more at home at Teakettle Cottage than anywhere else, and he could not recall having spent more than a few weeks cumulatively at his Mayfair abode. Yet despite the fact that he could not have said with any certainty that he had ever before driven down this particular stretch of road, there was something intensely familiar about the tree-lined avenue and the redbrick houses. He knew, without quite knowing how, that he was very close to the heart of the city.

He made his way back to the bomb, this time focusing his attention primarily on the plastic bags containing the nerve agent. He saw nothing to indicate that any sort of anti-tamper mechanism had been used. The bags appeared to have been simply deposited there haphazardly as a matter of expedience. Nevertheless, it was with great care that Hawke lifted one of the bags, slowly rolling it off the top of the fuel drum, all the while looking for any sort of pressure plate or trigger wire. Finding none, he moved the bag closer to the rear, set it down a few feet from the open doorway, and then went back to the bomb and repeated the process.

As he was depositing the fourth bag of nerve agent, he felt the lorry slowing. A glance outside revealed that he was moving through a neighborhood consisting mostly of blocks of upscale flats. The vehicle had already reduced its speed down to about twenty miles per hour, but now it seemed to be slowing even more, almost to a full stop. Then Hawke felt a shift in his center of gravity as the lorry made a left-hand turn. A sign posted on a brick wall in front of a block of flats gave him a concrete clue to his location.

PRINCE ALBERT ROAD

Now Hawke knew exactly where he was. The densely wooded area off to the lorry's right was the Regent's Park. Beyond it, about three miles to the south, lay the lorry's final destination and the target of Dylan Fahey's bomb: the Palace of Westminster.

Though the setup and the threat scenario were different, this was not the first time someone had attempted an attack on the Houses of Parliament. Several years back, a British-born Muslim radical had driven a hired vehicle across Westminster Bridge, intentionally ramming several pedestrians before crashing into the palace gates, where he then fatally attacked a constable before he was himself put down by armed police officers. But that recent incident was not nearly as well remembered as the one that had taken place on the fifth of November 1605, when a group of English Catholics had conspired to place barrels of gunpowder in the cellar beneath the House of Lords, with the intention of blowing up the palace and assassinating the first King James. With his rolling lorry bomb, Fahey was attempting to finish the undertaking of Guy Fawkes and his fellow conspirators.

Acutely aware of just how little time was left to him, he returned to his labors, moving the bags of nerve agent away from the bomb while the lorry continued along the north edge of the Regent's Park and then turned south on Albany Street. If Congreve failed to close the direct route, Hawke would have no choice but to start dumping the bags out onto the street, scattering the powder along the route. He'd have to hope and pray that a broad dispersal would prevent the precursors from mixing together. If he couldn't prevent the bomb from detonating, he could at least eliminate the danger from the nerve agent.

The lorry continued along Albany Street, then slowed to negotiate a series of diversions that culminated in a left turn onto Euston Road, part of London's Inner Ring Road.

The eastward deviation was a hopeful sign that Congreve was having success in redirecting traffic. The most direct route to Westminster would have meant a right turn and then a left onto Portland Place, through Marylebone, past Soho and Mayfair, through Piccadilly Circus, past Trafalgar Square and Nelson's Column, and then south down Parliament Street to the palace. It was also possible, however, that the lorry's computer had simply determined that another route would be faster. In the West End, all roads led to Trafalgar Square.

Hawke held his breath in anticipation of another quick change of direction. If the lorry turned south at the Hampstead Road signal, he would commence dumping out the nerve agent components.

Instead, he breathed a sigh of relief when the lorry did not turn, and as it passed through the intersection, Hawke finally saw why. A police car, lights flashing, was parked across the lanes to the south.

Hawke shook his head in disbelief. When Congreve had promised to try to close the roads for him, Hawke had assumed he would accomplish this simply by having someone at the traffic center push a few buttons on a computer. It hadn't occurred to him that it would be necessary to send police officers out to physically block the roads. The enormity of what that entailed was mind-boggling. It was as if Congreve were playing chess, with the streets of London as his board and the Metropolitan Police as his pawns.

One wrong move and the lorry might slip through his defenses and make the final run to the objective.

A few minutes later, the lorry and the surrounding traffic came to a full stop. Hawke leaned out the side door and saw that the vehicle had come to a traffic signal and that it was in the lane to make a right turn onto Upper Woburn Place.

Hawke did not possess a cab driver's knowledge of London streets, but he knew his way around the landmarks. Woburn led through Bloomsbury to the Inns of Court and the Strand, another of the many spokes radiating out from Trafalgar Square. But the street also continued on to Waterloo Bridge.

As the lorry continued down the narrow two-lane, past Tavistock Square, Russell Square, and historic Southampton Row, Hawke saw police vehicles blocking every street to the west, no matter how insignificant. Nevertheless, it wasn't until he saw two more police cars blocking westward access to the Strand that he finally allowed himself to believe his gambit might succeed.

The lorry was now committed to crossing Waterloo Bridge.

Like most of the more than thirty bridges spanning the Thames in London, there was nothing particularly remarkable about Waterloo Bridge, aside from its location, which commanded a spectacular and unrestricted view of the city's iconic skyline. The bridge was eighty feet across, with just two lanes for vehicle traffic running down the center, and wide pedestrian and bicycle lanes to the outside. The only thing between the sidewalk and the empty air above the Thames was an elbow-high safety rail. It was this lack of architectural embellishments that made the span ideal for Hawke's purposes.

When he was certain that the lorry was out over the water, he selected one of the bags of Novichok, gripped the doorframe with his right hand, and heaved the bag with all his might. Each bag weighed only five or so pounds, but Hawke's awkward position, not to mention the fact that he was throwing left-handed, left no room for error. Nevertheless, when he released the bag, it soared through the air and over the pedestrian lanes, cleared the guardrail with room to spare, and disappeared from view.

If his estimation of the durability of the zip-seal bag was correct, it would almost certainly burst on impact, allowing the chemical powder inside to quickly dissolve in the water. Even if the bag did not burst, it would surely sink to the bottom, disappearing forever in the silty depths.

Buoyed by this success, Hawke continued hurling the bags out into the Thames, disposing of the last one mere moments before the lorry arrived on the other side of the river.

The exertion, coupled with a sense of satisfaction at having thwarted at least this small part of Dylan Fahey's plot, left Hawke feeling drained. Exhausted to his very bones, he wanted nothing more than to sag against the wall of the cargo bay and rest, maybe forever. But it was not in his nature to leave a task unfinished.

There was a bomb on its way to Westminster Palace, and he was the only person on earth who could stop it.

Once over land, the bridge gradually descended onto the streets of the South Bank and fed into an enormous traffic circle that curled around the immense glass structure that housed the BFI IMAX cinema. Halfway through the circle's orbit, the lorry came to another full stop.

Hawke dragged himself forward, looking out the side door to see the reason for the stoppage—a traffic signal showing red.

Red light, stop. Green light, go.

The words, like something remembered from a childhood chant, entered unbidden into his mind. Only now it was the red light telling him he needed to *Go!*

Before the light could change, he leapt down from the idling lorry, and in that instant, he was presented with a choice. He could turn away, save his own skin, and leave the doomed vehicle, about which there was little he could do anyway. Or he could climb aboard, remain at the wheel until the bitter end, and go down with the figurative ship or perhaps even make the same calculation Ross Sutherland had made—one life to save many. If, as Sutherland had done, he initiated the anti-tamper triggers, perhaps while crossing Westminster Bridge, there would be significant damage to the span, but comparatively few lives lost.

Or . . . I can find a better answer.

Without quite knowing why, he keyed his mic. "Stoke, are you there?"

The voice that sounded in his ear did not belong to Stokely Jones Jr. "Alex? It's Ambrose. Stokely is here with me. Along with Harry and His Majesty. Where are you?"

"Don't you know?" Hawke had expected Congreve to be following him in real time.

"I'm afraid I haven't been able to keep up. A lot of balls in the air, as it were."

"I'm sure there are. I'm on the South Bank, near Waterloo Station."

"Then the traffic diversion worked?"

"It did. And the nerve agent has been neutralized. I'll probably get a fine for pollution, but at least we don't have that to worry about anymore."

"Thank God. Alex, you've done all you can. Get off that lorry at the next opportunity."

"There's still a bomb on its way to Westminster, Ambrose."

"I'm aware. The police have evacuated the palace and are trying to clear the exterior as we speak."

"*Trying?* There's a bloody bomb on its way there!"

"They're trying to avoid causing a panic."

"If there was ever a reason to panic, I think this would be it."

"A stampede could cause more injury than the explosion. Trust me, they're doing all they can to keep casualties to a minimum."

"What's a minimum, Ambrose?"

When Congreve didn't answer, Hawke pressed on. "Have you heard from C? Are the tech boys at all close to cracking the code?"

"Sir David is here with me as well, Alex."

C's voice replaced Congreve's in Hawke's ear. "I'm here, Alex. But I'm sorry to say, there's simply no way to tell if we're close. There are millions of possible combinations, and only one that's correct. We won't know until the door opens, so to speak. I'm afraid it's all down to luck."

Hawke saw the signal from the intersecting street change to yellow. It was time for his decision.

"Luck. Well, I guess I'd rather be lucky than good."

"What's that?"

"Tell them to keep trying," Hawke said, and as the signal changed to red, he opened the lorry's door and climbed in.

FORTY-FIVE

Distance to destination—1 mile.

Time remaining—5 minutes.

On the GPS map, the blue line, which showed the lorry's route, snaked down through the South Bank and around the Park Plaza Hotel. Then it crossed Westminster Bridge and turned left into Parliament Square. Midway down Abingdon Street, directly between the palace and Westminster Abbey, it stopped.

End of the line, thought Hawke.

When the bomb detonated, it would destroy St. Stephen's Hall, the west entrance to the House of Commons, and decimate the historic Henry VII Chapel, which was west of the abbey and was where the remains of Henry; his wife, Elizabeth; and King James I were interred. It would also likely injure or kill dozens, perhaps even hundreds of visitors.

That can't happen.

Alex Hawke wasn't going to let it happen.

He keyed the radio again. "Tell Ambrose to have the police stop all traffic heading east onto Westminster Bridge."

"Alex, I hope you're not thinking of doing anything rash," said C.

"Well, I suppose that rather depends on your definition of *rash*, now, doesn't it, Trulove?"

"Alex . . ."

"Sorry. Can't talk. Hands are bloody full at the moment." Hawke removed his radio headset and tossed it aside, then slid over into the driver's seat. Even though he knew it would be futile, he tried moving the steering wheel and pressing the brakes. Nothing happened. On the console, the cloning device continued flashing its messages of failure.

The lorry was moving again, getting up to speed and heading down York Road. Waterloo Station passed by to Hawke's left. The Park Plaza Hotel building appeared ahead of him, and then it was sliding to his right as the lorry followed the curve of the road. When the vehicle came around and made the turn onto Westminster Bridge Road, Hawke could see the Elizabeth Tower—rechristened in honor of the former Queen's diamond jubilee but still commonly but inaccurately referred to as Big Ben—rising in the distance like a lighthouse on a distant shore.

Less than a mile now, Hawke noted, *and only minutes left.*

Though he had an idea of how he was going to stop the lorry from reaching its destination without sacrificing himself to do it, Hawke wasn't altogether certain that it would work. His plan was to wait until the lorry was about midway across the span, then to step out onto the running board and fire a burst from his MPX into the left-front tire. The resulting blowout would cause the vehicle to veer to the left and send it crashing through the barrier, off the bridge, and into the river, giving Hawke time to leap clear. When the lorry hit the water, some thirty feet below the bridge, the fuel drums containing the explosives would be tossed around the cargo bay like nuts in a can, and this would almost certainly trigger the anti-tamper measures and cause the bomb to detonate, but if all went according to plan, the water and the underside of the bridge would absorb or deflect most of the energy of the blast.

The one wrinkle in the plan was the vehicle's autonomous drive computer.

If it was programmed to respond to a blowout by steering in the opposite direction, as a human driver would do, the lorry would stay on course, limping along until it reached its destination. If that happened . . .

Hawke would have no recourse but to trigger the device himself, just as Ross Sutherland had done.

It'll work, Hawke told himself. *It has to bloody work.*

The lorry passed County Hall and the South Bank Lion, and then it was on the bridge, rolling relentlessly toward its final destination on the opposite bank of the river. Ahead lay the quintessential icon of London, the Palace of Westminster, stretched out along the North Bank of the Thames. The large clockface on the Elizabeth Tower, visible even from half a mile away, showed the time—eight fifty-six a.m.

Four minutes until Big Ben rings the hour.

Hawke hoped he'd still be alive to hear it.

It'll work, he told himself again.

As the lorry neared the midpoint of the bridge, Hawke took a breath, bracing himself for what would follow. He would get only one chance at this, and if he hesitated, even for only a moment, all might be lost.

He slid over to the left-side seat and was just reaching for the door handle when a strange chiming sound emanated from the console. Hawke glanced over and saw the cause of it. On the cloning device, a different message was showing: **Access granted.**

And on the large display screen, a new update read: **Autonomous Drive Mode—Off.**

"They're in!" cheered Hawke, who suddenly found himself armed with a new appreciation for the sage wisdom of Lefty Gomez. The brute-force attack of the tech gurus at MI6 had finally blasted through the cyber gates of the drive computer, and not a moment too soon.

Hawke's elation was short-lived, however. No sooner had he slipped back into the driver's seat than a black box flashed up on the console.

Route will terminate in 30 seconds. Reengage autonomous drive mode to continue to your destination.

And a second later, the two digits in the message changed to **29**.
Then **28**.

Hawke gripped the wheel, squeezing until his knuckles were white.

Route will terminate . . .

What the hell does that mean?

If the bomb was wired into the GPS and keyed to detonate when it reached its destination, then, logically speaking, terminating the route could only do one of two things—it would either effectively disarm the device . . . or it would instantly set it off.

At best, it was a coin flip.

This is why I hate leaving things to luck, thought Hawke, knowing it was a chance he couldn't afford to take, not with countless lives on the line.

The countdown on the display screen was already down to **24** when he glanced at it again. With no foot on the accelerator pedal, the vehicle had coasted almost to a full stop. That wouldn't do for what Hawke had in mind, so he stomped the pedal in an effort to bring the engine back to life. The lorry started picking up speed, the digital speedometer ticking up even as the countdown clock ticked down.

20 m.p.h.

Route will terminate in 20 seconds.

"Get on with it!" yelled Hawke, pushing the pedal harder into the floor, desperate to increase the lorry's speed. In any ordinary vehicle, doing so would have resulted in a surge of power, but the lorry, with its electronic drive system, didn't respond the way a petrol-powered engine might. No matter how much force he used to smash the pedal into the floorboard, the lorry continued accelerating at a slow but smooth and constant rate of about five miles per hour per second. That would have been fine except for one little detail—he was running out of bridge.

Forty will have to do, he thought, and cut the wheel to the left.

As the front end of the lorry swung toward the bridge rail, Hawke saw a group of camera-toting tourists directly in front of him, frozen like statues, staring at the vehicle in absolute disbelief as it swerved right at them.

Hawke uttered the harshest oath he knew as he wrenched the wheel back to the right, changing the angle of his approach just enough to avoid hitting the group and, in so doing, sacrificed a precious second that he had been counting on to make his escape.

As the lorry smashed through two of the steel bollards separating the traffic lane from the pedestrian sidewalk, it shuddered and shed a little of its momentum but not nearly enough to stop it in its tracks. As the tires hit the sidewalk curb, bouncing the lorry on its frame, Hawke worked the door handle and flung himself out of the cab. In the fraction of a second it took for him to fall, the lorry crashed into the concrete guardrail, smashed through, and kept going.

Hawke tucked into a paratrooper roll just before hitting the pavement, a decision that spared him serious injury but did not stop his own momentum from carrying him forward. A heartbeat later, he slammed into the rail just a few feet to the right of the newly created breach. The impact knocked the wind out of him just as the world below him shook violently from the massive explosion as the bomb, now just beneath the surface of the water, finally detonated.

FORTY-SIX

Twenty-two miles away, at the Lippitts Hill Air Support Unit base, the five men watching the live feed from a CCTV camera trained on Westminster Bridge let out a collective gasp as the Tevva lorry that had just crashed through the guardrail hit the river and then vanished in a flash of light and a rapidly expanding cloud of gas and water vapor. The explosion shook the bridge but, miraculously, did not breach it. A fraction of a second later, the force of the explosion raised a plume of water that splashed over the bridge, soaking the unsuspecting nearby souls who were strewn about the sidewalk, stunned by the initial blast.

"Where is he?" demanded Stokely Jones Jr. "Did he make it off that thing before it blew?"

"Of course he did," Congreve declared with far more confidence than he actually felt. "Alex fights like a dog, but the man has more lives than a cat."

"True," replied Stoke, "but he's already used a bunch of 'em."

"I'm certain that I saw him leap from the lorry just before it went over," declared Sir David Trulove. Then he stabbed a finger at the monitor. "There he is. Look!"

Congreve squinted his eyes, focusing on the bedraggled but familiar figure sprawled out in the puddle of river water slowly draining away from the bridge. The blast had hurled Hawke twenty feet from the sidewalk, depositing him in the traffic lanes, which fortunately were empty of moving vehicles.

"Is he alive?" wondered Harry Brock. "He's not moving."

"Shut up, Harry," growled Stoke.

Congreve recognized the helplessness that lay behind the big man's gruff manner, for he shared it. Hawke had once more thrown himself into harm's way, heedless of the peril, and now, when he needed his friends the most, they were miles away, watching him face that danger alone.

It was only seconds, but waiting for any sign of life felt like an eternity.

Just as Ambrose let himself think the worst, Hawke slowly rolled over and gently pushed up onto hands and knees, shook his head, and began looking around.

The five men broke out into a rowdy cheer. None of them were more effusive than the man whose life Hawke had so recently saved. "Thank God," declared the King. "I feared the bloody worst."

He then turned to Stoke. "Sir Stokely, I'm afraid in all the hullabaloo, I failed to convey my gratitude to you."

Stoke, who rarely heard anyone use the title that had been bestowed upon him by Queen Elizabeth following the earlier incident at Balmoral Castle, beamed. It had been explained to Stoke that because he was not a citizen of the UK, the investiture was honorary, so the fact that the King himself had used that form of address for him was deeply meaningful. "Thank you, Your Majesty," Stoke replied with a bow. "It was an honor to be of service."

Charles then turned to Congreve. "Ambrose, I must know. Who in the bloody hell did all this? And why? Why go to such elaborate lengths to snatch me up and put all of this in motion?"

It was not a question Congreve had expected to hear. "You don't know, Majesty?"

Charles shook his head. "I was kept in isolation. The only one of my captors who spoke to me called himself Mr. Sten, but aside from demanding that I abdicate, he never said a word about his motivations or allegiances. It makes no damned sense."

Congreve hummed. "Well, Majesty, we don't have the full picture just yet, but we believe the chief aim of this plot was to sow discord in advance of the Scottish referendum."

"My goodness, that's today, isn't it?"

"It is. We know that elements of the New Irish Republican Army were involved in the attempted bombing, but they were not responsible for your abduction."

"Then who was?"

"You really don't know? He didn't reveal himself to you?"

"Who?" pressed the King.

Congreve took a breath. "It was your gamekeeper, Roderick Mc-Clanahan."

Charles was taken aback. "No. That's not possible. Roddy stayed with me until . . . until they murdered him right in front of me."

"That was a bit of theater. McClanahan was the mastermind. His guilt is beyond question."

"It cannot be. It just can't. Where is he? I must speak with him."

"He's dead, Majesty." Congreve didn't elaborate further.

"Roddy?" The King shook his head, still incredulous. "Why on earth would he betray me?"

"It seems he harbored some deep-seated resentment toward you. But there's more going on here than meets the eye. The execution of this plot would have required substantial resources, far beyond Mr. McClanahan's means. We're already digging into his background. I assure you we'll get to the bottom of it as quickly as possible."

Charles stared back at him for a long moment, then nodded his head. "Then I shall leave it in your capable hands." He paused, then turned to Trulove. "Sir David, because you are the senior representative of the government present here, I wish you to act as my agent in this matter."

"Whatever you require, Majesty," replied Trulove.

"Please make arrangements for transportation to Westminster and inform the Prime Minister that I wish to address the nation."

"Sir, may I suggest a different venue? It will be bedlam in Westminster."

"Exactly why it *must* be there," said the King, "and with all haste. See to it."

Trulove inclined his head. "As you wish, Majesty."

Not half an hour later, the Merlin set down in Parliament Square Garden, at the northwest corner of the Palace of Westminster. The area had already been cordoned off by the police, so there were few witnesses to the unscheduled arrival of the King. A sizable contingent of uniformed members of the Royalty and Specialist Protection division was on hand to escort the King and his guests—Congreve, Trulove, Stoke, and Brock—across the street and into the palace via the Sovereign's Entrance at the base of the Victoria Tower in the southwest corner of the palace. From there, they were ushered by one of the King's valets into the monarch's suite of rooms, whereupon Charles excused himself to prepare for his impending address to the nation.

Another of the King's attendants showed the four guests to a well-appointed but seldom used guest room where they were invited to refresh themselves after their long journey. Congreve took this to mean that they should clean up, which was wholly appropriate since, aside from Sir David, they were all still attired in military fatigues and had not had so much as a chance to wash their hands since the raid on Dunnottar Castle.

Stoke, however, had other concerns. "Where's Alex?"

Trulove rephrased the question for the uncomprehending retainer. "Would you please inquire regarding the whereabouts of Lord Hawke?"

"Right away, sir."

"I'll come with you," Stoke said, following the man out the door. "Come on, Harry. This place is too classy for you anyway."

The retainer shot a questioning glance at Trulove, who just nodded in return. "Do try to stay out of trouble," he told Stoke.

No sooner had they departed than there was a knock on the door, and another attendant entered. "Sirs, the Prime Minister wishes to see you," he said, and then showed Livia Steele into the room.

After a somewhat formal exchange of greetings, Steele got right to business, addressing Congreve. "Excellent work, Sir Ambrose. And in the nick of time."

"Thank you, Prime Minister, though Lord Hawke deserves the lion's share of the credit."

Steele nodded but seemed to dismiss the subject. "I know that the investigation is ongoing, but are you able to shed any light on the identity of the perpetrators? Was this solely the action of the New IRA?"

"I don't believe so," admitted Congreve, "but at present, there is a dearth of evidence to point the finger elsewhere."

"A replay of the Troubles is the last thing any of us wants." Steele sighed. "Do you have any idea what the King intends to say?"

"None whatsoever, though I imagine he will address the matter of the Scottish vote."

"Hmm. I do wish he would have given us some idea of what to expect, but he *is* the King after all." She gazed off into the distance for a moment, then returned her attention to Congreve. "Thank you again, Sir Ambrose. I'm sure we'll continue this discussion later."

Stoke and Brock found Hawke in an examination room in the emergency department of St. Thomas' Hospital, on the opposite side of the river from the palace. Hawke, along with everyone else requiring medical attention following the explosion on the bridge, had been taken there for evaluation and treatment.

Alex, who felt he needed neither, greeted his friends from his hospital bed like saviors come to rescue him. "Ah, Stoke! Harry! Thank God you're here."

Stoke approached the bed cautiously, appraising Hawke, who, in addition to his hospital gown, wore several wraps of gauze about his head and arms. "Boss, you okay, man?"

"I'm fine," said Alex with a dismissive gesture. "Nothing a tot of Goslings Black Seal won't set right."

"A bit early in the day, isn't it?" said Stoke.

"I'm sure the sun is over the yardarm somewhere in the Empire. I'd have left already, but these medieval-torture specialists insist on subjecting me to further testing, and as they seem to have taken my clothes, I'm bloody stuck here."

"Good luck finding a place that's open at this hour," said Brock. He flopped down in a corner chair. Then he noticed the television set mounted on the wall opposite Hawke's bed, and pointed to it. "Hey, if we're not going anywhere, can we watch the news? The King's planning to give a speech."

"Is he, now?" asked Hawke, taking an interest in the subject. He took up the bedside remote, which served as both a call button and a TV control device, and activated the latter. The set came to life, and because it had been tuned to BBC News by the last person to use it, the first thing that appeared on the screen was a shot of a stained glass window in a large, seemingly empty hall. Hawke knew the place immediately, even without the caption, which identified the location as Westminster Hall. The message in the chyron crawling across the bottom of the screen read: King Charles to address the nation in the wake of devastating terror attack.

The broadcast jumped between the live shot and footage of the lorry crashing through the guardrail and exploding, with various talking heads offering very little substance in between. There was speculation about the identity of the perpetrators but even more about what the King might say in his address. One pundit, identified as a Labour supporter, remarked that it was quite unusual for the King to be speaking out on the matter, as it was the constitutional role of the monarch to support the decisions of the democratically elected government and not to propose or promote policy. Unfortunately for him—but fortunately for viewers—the man's attempted monologue was cut short when the anchor broke in and, in a solemn voice, said, "We go now live to Westminster Hall, where His Majesty King Charles is about to speak."

The camera at Westminster Hall now zoomed in on a lectern that had been set up on the landing just below the magnificent stained glass window. A moment later, Prime Minister Livia Steele approached the lectern and spoke into the microphone.

"Ladies and gentlemen of the press and all of you watching on television, it is my honor to present His Majesty King Charles III."

Tentative applause filled the room as she stepped away and Charles came forward. Though obviously a bit thinner than in his last publicity photo, he looked considerably more robust than he had just a couple hours earlier when Stoke had plucked him off the doomed lorry. A bespoke charcoal-gray suit had replaced his tired hunting outfit.

When the applause and flashing of cameras subsided, Charles began to speak.

"My fellow citizens of the United Kingdom," he began, somehow putting emphasis on each and every word, "as you are no doubt aware, yesterday a terrorist bomb detonated in Belfast, taking the life of a senior police official. Earlier this morning, a second explosive device damaged a part of Westminster Bridge. These incidents are under investigation by the Metropolitan Police, in whom I have the utmost faith. I can say with certainty that neither attack succeeded in reaching its designated target and that thanks to the efforts of a few brave individuals—most notably Detective Chief Inspector Ross Sutherland, God rest his soul—catastrophic loss of life was prevented. It is not my place to speculate regarding the perpetrators of these vile actions, but I can assure you all that the threat has been neutralized. That is all I have to say on that subject. Instead, let us turn our attention to a matter of even greater import.

"Today, we stand at a crossroads—a momentous decision that will shape our nation's destiny. The question of Scottish independence looms large, and I urge each of you to vote with your conscience.

"Scotland, with its rich history, vibrant culture, and fierce pride, has always been an integral part of our kingdom. Its landscapes have inspired poets. Its people have contributed to science, art, and governance. But today we face a choice—a choice that transcends borders and flags.

"As monarch, I respect the democratic process. I have always believed in an enlightened monarchy. It is not the role of the King to rule but rather to lead, and I pray you will follow me through this present darkness and into the future.

"The right to self-determination is a fundamental principle, and I encourage all Scots to engage in this debate with open hearts and open minds. Consider the implications, weigh the pros and cons, and cast your vote knowing that your voice matters.

"But let us not forget our shared heritage—the battles fought side by side, the victories celebrated together, the challenges overcome as one. Our Union has weathered storms, and it has flourished. It is a tapestry woven with threads of loyalty, sacrifice, and mutual respect.

"And so, as we approach this historic referendum, I ask you to reflect on what it means to be British. Our identity is not confined to geographical boundaries; it transcends them. It is a spirit that binds us—a spirit of unity, resilience, and compassion.

"As for Northern Ireland, let me offer a glimpse into the future—a future where dialogue replaces division, where bridges are built across the divide. While I cannot predict the path ahead, I hold hope that someday the people of Northern Ireland will have their say—a say in their destiny, their sovereignty.

"But for now, let us focus on Scotland. Let us engage in respectful discourse, listen to one another, and honor the democratic process. Whatever the outcome, let it be a reflection of our collective will—a testament to our shared values.

"May our choices be guided by wisdom, empathy, and a vision of a united kingdom that stands strong, not in spite of its diversity but because of it.

"God bless and save the United Kingdom."

Thunderous applause filled the hall.

Congreve, standing with Sir David amidst a crowd of reporters, MPs, and government officials, shouted and clapped along with everyone else. It was, he thought, one of the finest speeches a monarch had ever delivered and at just the perfect moment, no less.

More than once, Congreve had very nearly been brought to tears by the King's entreaty. He did not pretend to know how the referendum vote would turn out, but he felt quite certain that whether or not Scotland remained a part of the United Kingdom, Charles would remain their King.

As the King stepped away from the lectern and the crowd began to disperse, Congreve took out his new mobile phone to see who had been trying so incessantly to reach him during the address. The phone, set to vibrate, had buzzed like a hive of angry bees in his pocket almost from the moment the King began to speak. All the calls were from the same number, one he called earlier that morning while also trying to track down the lorry. The number was an exchange at New Scotland Yard and it belonged to Mary Havilick, the researcher who had, just a few days earlier, uncovered Colm Keaney's relationship with the New IRA. Congreve had given her the task of performing a deep dive into Roderick McClanahan's background in hopes of identifying his co-conspirators.

"Sir David," he said, "if you'll excuse me, I need to make a call."

A moment later, the last piece of the puzzle finally fell into place.

FORTY-SEVEN

t was, all things considered, perhaps the most famous front door in the world. Certainly in the United Kingdom. Black, like the color of the brick building to which it allowed access, and adorned with a black iron knocker in the shape of a lion's head, a brass mail slot engraved with the words "First Lord of the Treasury," and two digits in white that announced the street address.

Number 10 Downing Street.

One might be forgiven for thinking, based solely on the ubiquitous photographs of that iconic front door, that the residence and offices of the Prime Minister of the United Kingdom were situated in a modest townhome or block of flats. In truth, behind that iconic black door was a mansion comprising more than a hundred rooms—offices and conference, reception, sitting, and dining rooms where the Prime Minister and civil servants performed their day-to-day duties and where government ministers, national leaders, and foreign dignitaries were met and hosted. And, of course, there was a private residence for the Prime Minister on the third floor.

This was not the first time Ambrose Congreve had paid a call to Number 10. He had visited it on many prior occasions and with many different householders, so he felt no sense of awe as he and Sir David Trulove were escorted through the building to a conference room just down the hall from the PM's private office.

A few minutes later, the Prime Minister, looking rather harried, swept into the room. Her gaze lingered for a moment on Trulove, then shifted to Congreve. "Sir Ambrose, I neglected to comment on it earlier, but I couldn't help but notice that you rather flagrantly ignored my direction to keep the matter of the King's abduction a closely held secret. You had no right to bring the SIS into this affair."

Congreve coolly returned her stare. "In point of fact, Prime Minister, the Secret Intelligence Service's role in the affair was limited to stopping the bomb plot. And might I add, without their assistance, we might be having a very different conversation just now."

Steele sniffed. "Well, I suppose it doesn't matter. All's well that ends well."

"Quite, except we're not just yet at the end of the road, so to speak."

Steele took a seat at the table. "Yes, you mentioned that you've made significant progress in the investigation?"

"That is correct."

"Well, let's have it, then."

Congreve folded his hands on the tabletop. "We now know that the mastermind behind the King's abduction was Balmoral's head gamekeeper, Roderick McClanahan."

"McClanahan?" asked Steele. She shook her head. "Wait. I thought he was also a hostage."

"Yes, well, you see, we were meant to believe that when, in fact, it was McClanahan who delivered the King into the hands of his associates at Balmoral while arranging for doubles of both himself and His Majesty to create the very illusion that initially hampered our investigation. We believe he had been developing anti-royalist sentiments for quite some time, and this led him to an alliance with members of the New Irish Republican Army."

"Where is McClanahan now?"

"Dead."

Steele appeared to reflect on this for a moment. "Well, while I hate to say this aloud, that's probably for the best."

Congreve cocked his head to the side. "Why do you say that?"

"Isn't it obvious? The man clearly must have had some sort of radical agenda. Had he been taken alive, we would have been obliged to give him his day in court and so provide a forum for him in which to spread his poison."

"Hmm. Yes, I take your meaning. Unfortunately, now we may never know for certain what that agenda actually was."

"Seems obvious enough to me."

There's that word again, thought Congreve. Obvious.

And it was. He just hadn't seen it.

"Assassinate the King," Steele continued, "blow up Parliament. Strike a blow against the kingdom, and on the eve of this Scottish vote no less. Thank goodness you were there to stop him." Steele placed her palms flat on the table as if preparing to push herself to her feet. "So that's it, then? Case closed?"

"Not quite. You see, while McClanahan orchestrated the King's abduction, it seems quite unlikely that he was able to carry out this plot without significant assistance from some other entity. We know, for instance, that he was receiving logistical support from a South African private military contractor. That sort of help doesn't come cheaply. Then there's the matter of the two lorries that were meant to deliver the bombs to their intended targets. Those vehicles were brand-new and quite expensive. What's more, the auto-drive technology they employed is not factory standard. The modifications would have been quite costly. All of it was paid for by a shell company, the same shell company used to pay for the use of Dunnottar Castle, the location where the King was kept for a time."

"Are you able to discover who's behind that shell company?"

Congreve gave an equivocal shrug. "We shall make every effort, but I think it unlikely. I do have my suspicions, though."

Steele raised an eyebrow. "Would you care to share them?"

"Perhaps in a moment," replied Congreve. "We've had somewhat better luck looking into McClanahan's background."

Steele settled back into her chair. "Is that right?"

"Quite so. It seems that he was not the loyal retainer he appeared to be. He has a history of anti-royal sentiment going back more than thirty years. It seems that when he was at university, he briefly attended meetings of the Republicans Club and was known to express rather colorful opinions regarding the then Prince Charles and his personal life."

"Aren't members of the household staff subjected to extensive background checks?"

"Indeed, they are. And aside from that brief episode, which somehow slipped through the cracks, McClanahan subsequently hid his true sympathies quite well. One can only conclude that he realized he could do more damage to the Royal Family by remaining on the inside, using his family's long history of service to get close to His Majesty, biding his time and waiting for the perfect opportunity to strike."

"To plot something so nefariously diabolical . . . nurturing such hatred while outwardly professing love and loyalty, it's like something from Dumas."

"Hmm, indeed. One wonders what sort of incentive was offered to set him on that path."

Steele crooked her head sideways. "Incentive? I don't follow."

"Oh, I think it's quite self-explanatory. A young man full of anger and passion . . . a man like that isn't patient. Doesn't even think about playing the long game. No, someone put the idea in his head."

"Who?"

"Isn't it *obvious*, Prime Minister?" Congreve stared at her for a long moment before answering. "It was you."

Steele recoiled. "I beg your pardon!"

"Come now," admonished Congreve. "You attended uni with McClanahan. Your relationship was no secret. You were lovers. For the better part of a year. Do you deny it?"

"Do I . . . Of course I deny it! Until this whole affair, I'd never even heard of Roderick McClanahan. And I certainly would know who my . . ." She trailed off, her eyes darting back and forth as if searching for a memory. "Oh. Oh, my. You don't mean . . . Rick." She found Congreve's gaze again, her eyes pleading. "He was my boyfriend, only I never knew him as Roderick. Only ever Rick. I had no idea."

Trulove cleared his throat. "Let's dispense with the charade, Prime Minister. Ambrose here rather likes the sound of his own voice, but I prefer to cut to the chase. You are guilty. Thirty years ago, you recruited Roderick McClanahan. You turned him, as we say in the business. You seized on his disaffection toward the royals and gave him a purpose. I'm sure the offer of your bed didn't hurt. You made him your weapon. A sleeper agent inside the household staff, close to the Family. And now, at this opportune moment, you unleashed him against the King."

Steele was on her feet. "This is preposterous. You've both gone bloody mad! I don't have to listen to this—"

"Sit down!" barked Trulove. The forcefulness of the command extinguished every last flicker of defiance. "This is not an accusation that you will have an opportunity to refute or deny, but a statement of the facts already in evidence. And this is just what we have learned in a few hours. When we have peeled away the layers of your life and laid bare your every secret, it will only confirm what we all know to be true. You are caught. The only thing you should be concerned with now is saving your own skin."

Steele glared at him, her nostrils flaring, but said nothing.

"Understand this," Trulove went on. "There will be no trial. No . . . How did you put it? No forum for you to spread your poison. The Prime Minister conspiring to assassinate the King and destroy Parliament? That is a scandal that must never be brought into the light of day. There will be no arrest, no criminal charges, no trial."

Steele found her voice. "You would just . . . kill me?"

"It's what I do, Prime Minister. I *kill* the enemies of the kingdom. And I would have not the slightest compunction in ordering your death."

Steele's tongue darted out, licking her lips. "This is madness. I'm the Prime Minister. You can't just come in here and threaten me."

"I don't make threats. I present choices. A quick, painless death is one choice I put before you. Here's the other.

"You will resign immediately, citing a health emergency. You will then retire from public life, move to a little cottage in the country, and enjoy the rest of your life, however long that might be."

"Retire?"

"House arrest, if you prefer. You would, of course, be under constant supervision. This choice does come with a price, however. Your cooperation."

Steele blinked furiously. "This is . . . madness," she said again. "Get out. Get out before I have you thrown out." She stabbed a finger in the direction of the door. "I'll have *your* resignation."

"And who will you call, Prime Minister? The ax is already descending upon your neck." Trulove glanced over at Congreve. "It seems we have our answer, Sir Ambrose."

"It does at that, Sir David. Tell me, how will it happen?"

"A previously undiagnosed heart problem, I should think. These things happen." He pushed away from the table. "Well, that's that, as they say."

Congreve also started to rise.

"Wait!" cried Steele. "Just wait a bloody minute!"

Congreve and Trulove exchanged a glance. "Is there something you wish to share?" asked Congreve, assuming the role of good cop to Trulove's bad cop.

Steele leaned against the table, her eyes flashing like those of a cornered feral cat. "I . . . I need . . . I need to think."

"There's nothing to think about," snapped Trulove. "You've made your choice."

"Now, now, Sir David, I'm sure this is a lot to process." Congreve turned to Steele. "But I'm sure if you think about it, you'll realize that cooperation is really your only choice."

"Cooperation." Steele breathed the word as if tasting an unfamiliar dish.

"Let's start with who you're really working for. We'll find out eventually, of course, but it would go a long way as a show of good faith."

"There's no one else," she said, just a little too quickly. "Rick and I made the plan."

"Come now," chided Congreve. "I think we both know better."

"This is a waste of time," sneered Trulove. "She tried to murder the King and blow up Parliament. She doesn't deserve leniency."

"That was never supposed to be the plan," wailed Steele.

"What's that?"

"We weren't going to hurt him. Just hold him until after the election and then let him go."

For the first time since the audience began, Congreve sensed the woman was telling the truth. And she had as much as admitted to everything. "What *was* the plan?"

"Just what I said. We were going to let him go when the vote was done."

"And you would have us believe that you and McClanahan acted alone? The truth now! Who are you working for?"

"I don't . . ." She hesitated, took a breath, and then went on. "It started when we were at uni. My sociology professor. He . . ." Her eyes flashed to Trulove. "He *turned* me, as you would say. At first, I thought we were just a . . . a direct-action network. It wasn't until later that I realized who we were really working for."

"And who was that?"

She swallowed and then, in a small voice, said, "Russia. The SVR."

"I thought as much," murmured Congreve.

"By the time I realized it, there was no getting away from it."

"The long game," said Trulove. "Putin excels at it."

"And they have been running you all these years?" pressed Trulove. "Helping you politically, I imagine, in order to put their asset in the highest office in the land."

Steele just nodded.

"Why attempt to sway the outcome of the election?" asked Congreve. "How does Russia benefit from a broken Union?"

Steele shrugged. "They just want to create chaos. Anything that weakens the NATO partnership."

"Imagine the chaos regicide would create," remarked Trulove. "You really expect us to believe that you intended the King no permanent harm."

"I swear it's true." Tears were now streaming down Steele's cheeks. "Whatever else I am, I'm still British. I could never . . ." She choked up, unable to finish the sentence.

"Whether it was your intention or not," said Congreve gravely, "your plot caused the death of one of the finest men I have ever had the pleasure of knowing."

Steele hung her head.

Trulove shared another look with Congreve. "Well, if it's not the truth, we'll get at it eventually."

He reached into a pocket, took something out, and placed it on the table in front of her. It was a small capsule such as might hold a dose of medicine. "Take this. With or without food, it hardly matters."

Steele swallowed nervously. "What is it?"

"It is your lifeline," said Trulove. Then he added, "It's an emetic compound. An hour . . . maybe forty-five minutes after you take it, you will experience stomach pain and nausea. You'll be taken to the hospital, where a physician will diagnose you with an ulcer. Stress of the job. You already know what to do afterward."

Steele stared at the capsule. "And that's it? You'll let me . . . live."

"Under house arrest."

"For how long?"

"Why . . . for the rest of your life."

Steele swallowed again. "And how long will that be?"

Trulove smiled, but it didn't reach his eyes. "As long as you have something to tell us, I should think."

FORTY-EIGHT

Prince Heinrich Konigstahl rarely showed emotion. One could never tell just by merely looking at him whether he was happy, sad, angered, or aroused. His range of facial expressions was limited to a slightly sardonic smile and a frown of mild disapproval.

When he got out of his BMW i8, breathing in the crisp Alpine air for the first time in days, his countenance was an undecipherable tableau, as mysterious as the Voynich Manuscript or the Rongorongo tablets of Easter Island. Behind that impassive mask, however, a storm raged.

Charles Windsor was still alive, and that meant the bastard was still the uncontested monarch of the United Kingdom.

The Magician, Konigstahl's mysterious benefactor, had utterly failed to deliver on the promise of a kingdom.

Someone will pay, he decided, and the thought of precisely how he might exact that price brought just a hint of the sardonic smile to his face. *But who?*

The Magician had gone silent, and if the rumors circulating around the swamp of the dark web were correct, he'd been killed in a bloody firefight in Scotland.

If not him, then whom?

Ewan MacAlpin, that human slime mold from the Stewards of Alba Party, would be a good place to start, if only because he'd been the one to get Konigstahl's hopes up in the first place.

Yes, that one will squeal.

Still, as irritatingly ineffectual as MacAlpin was, he could hardly be blamed for thwarting the Magician's scheme. Although a clear picture of the events that had transpired two days earlier had yet to emerge and likely never would, one name kept bobbing to the surface of the swamp.

Alexander Hawke.

"Highness?"

Konigstahl raised his eyes to the pair of figures approaching from the edge of the parking lot where a Bombardier Maverick R side-by-side all-terrain vehicle was parked. The shorter of the two was his private secretary, Rudolf. The other, a tall, physically imposing character with close-cropped blond hair, he did not recognize.

Rudolf halted within a few steps and inclined his head in a modest bow. "Highness, it is good to have you back with us. I am sorry that things did not go as planned in Scotland."

"Let's not speak of it," said Konigstahl, a touch more sharply than he intended.

"Of course," Rudolf said with another bow. He turned and gestured to the stranger. "Highness, this is Gunnar Lundqvist. I've brought him on to replace Klaus. He's a former commando from the Swedish Special Forces and comes highly recommended, both for his prowess and his discretion."

Konigstahl gave Lundqvist an appraising glance, noting his ice-blue eyes, which stared straight ahead unwaveringly, as well as his impressive physique and rigid, military bearing. He certainly looked capable enough, but discretion was the trait Konigstahl valued most, and that wasn't something that could be determined from physical appearance. "Well, if Rudolf says you'll do, then you'll do. Has he explained your duties?"

"He has, Your Highness," replied the Swede, still looking forward in the position of attention.

"Excellent." Konigstahl turned to Rudolf. "That still leaves us with a vacancy to fill. I think a visit to Anatoly is in order."

"Of course, Highness. When would you like to make the trip?"

"Hmm. Since I'm still packed for travel, let's go today. But later. This afternoon. Right now I feel the urge to hunt."

"I thought you might, Highness. I've left your rifle and a change of clothing in the boot room. The game cameras picked up a small herd of red deer moving about a mile to the north earlier this morning, and there has been a lynx sighting on the south slope of the mountain."

"Lynx?" Konigstahl allowed himself a smile. He enjoyed hunting predators most of all. "Yes, that will do nicely."

That thought brought Alex Hawke back to the forefront of his mind. He'd badly underestimated the English lord. Dismissed him as a dandy and anticipated an easy kill, even after his clever escape from the castle. When Konigstahl had learned that Hawke had survived the crash, his first reaction had been outrage—he'd sacrificed Tildy for nothing—but after further contemplation, he realized that he'd been given the opportunity for a grand hunt, one not limited to a specific geographical context.

The globe itself would be his stalking ground. He would hunt Alexander Hawke to the ends of the earth.

And if the rumors held even a shred of truth . . . if Hawke was some sort of commando warrior working for the British government, then all the better.

He gave Lundqvist another look. The man's military experience might prove invaluable in the hunt if he had the stomach for it. "Gunnar, is it?"

"Yes, Highness?"

"Do you hunt?"

"I used to. Hunt animals, that is. Now I hunt only *men*, Highness."

"Is that a fact? Hmm. Are you any good at it?"

"Yes, Highness," the man answered without a trace of braggadocio. "Very."

"That's excellent. Come with me. We'll discuss this further." He turned and began walking toward the Maverick. Rudolf, understanding that Konigstahl no longer needed him, turned on his heel and marched toward the cable car station.

With Lundqvist in the driver's seat, the side-by-side, which looked a little like a cross between a sports car and a dune buggy, zipped down the narrow service road that ran from the parking lot to Konigstahl's private entrance near the base of the cable car support tower. As they rolled along, Konigstahl's anticipation of the Great Hunt quietly intensified. Perhaps he would postpone the trip to Minsk. As pleasurable as the process of selecting and training a new slave was, the thought of stalking Hawke and coldly putting a bullet in his skull surpassed it by an order of magnitude.

A moment later, a concrete block structure appeared through the trees, and Konigstahl's daydreams were rudely interrupted by the realization that the roll-down door had been left open. "Stop!" he commanded.

Lundqvist brought the Maverick to a sudden halt a hundred feet short of the structure. "Yes, Highness?"

"The door has been left open."

Lundqvist looked, then shook his head. "It was closed when we left. I saw Rudolf close it."

This statement sent a tingle of apprehension down Konigstahl's spine.

I don't like this.

"That door is never left open. Check it out."

"Yes, Highness." Lundqvist drew a matte black Glock 19 from a holster concealed under his jacket and got out, immediately assuming a shooting stance as he began sweeping the woods, looking for a possible threat.

Konigstahl got out as well. A person was never more vulnerable than when sitting in an idle vehicle.

Lundqvist quickly cleared the surrounding area, then approached the open entrance. Beyond the roll-down door was a small garage where the side-by-side and Konigstahl's motorcycle were kept. Just past that was the boot room—or rather a small apartment where Konigstahl could clean up after a hunt—and past that was the tunnel with a high-speed electric trolley and, at its terminus, a high-speed elevator that went directly to the castle atop the mountain. If an intruder had breached the secure gate, then they could be anywhere.

And if there is an intruder, thought Konigstahl, *then they've made a fatal mistake coming here.*

Lundqvist performed a quick visual inspection of the garage but did not go in. Instead, he stepped back and then moved up to the side of the structure, clearing the area; then he continued around behind it.

Konigstahl felt violated. Wolkenheim was, literally, his very own castle. His sanctuary. This invasion was an indignity beyond measure.

Who?

But, of course, he knew the answer. It was Hawke.

Always Alexander bloody Hawke.

No doubt Hawke had implicated him in the accident and turned the attention of the police investigators toward him.

But the police would never show our family such disrespect.

It occurred to him that Lundqvist had been gone an awfully long time. "Gunnar!"

There was no answer. Had the Swede found something suspicious? Perhaps he was stalking his prey, ready to pounce?

Konigstahl advanced toward the structure, following Gunnar's route around the side, calling out every few steps. He rounded the corner, but there was no sign of the man. Turning, he gazed into the surrounding woods, looking for some indication as to where the Swede had gone.

"Gunnar! Where are you?"

Once again, there was no answer, but as he called out, Konigstahl spied something in the grass nearby. He knelt down to get a better look and saw that the object was a strip of black-dyed leather secured into a loop with a small heart-shaped padlock.

It was a slave collar.

Tildy's slave collar.

Konigstahl's blood ran cold.

That was when he noticed that the grass around the collar had been trampled down, and leading away from the spot into the woods were parallel lines of similarly trampled vegetation.

With his heart beating like a jackhammer, Konigstahl followed the trail. He found Gunnar twenty yards from the structure, hidden behind a large tree trunk. The big man was sprawled out on the ground, unmoving.

It's him. He's come for me.

"Show yourself!" he cried out, unable to keep a quaver of fear from his voice. "I know you're here, Hawke. Are you afraid to face me? Like a man?"

"Like a man?" came a voice far too close for comfort. "And what would you know about that?"

Konigstahl whirled to find his nemesis standing just out of reach. Hawke's face was a map of bruises and abrasions, but none of that softened the deadly steel of the gaze he now fixed on the Prince. Konigstahl did not fail to notice the long barrel of a hunting rifle—*his* hunting rifle—slung over Hawke's shoulder.

"What do you want?" Konigstahl demanded.

"Well, I should think it's bloody obvious. Smart chap like you, I'm sure you've already figured it out."

"You mean to hunt me, then? Is that it?"

"Why, isn't this what you live for? The thrill of the hunt, yes? Well, if it's a game you wanted, then you've bloody got it. First round to you, *friend Heinrich.* You wrecked my favorite car. But now it's my turn at the crease."

"Alex, we can settle this like gentlemen."

Hawke laughed aloud at that.

He means to do it. He means to hunt me down like some wild animal.

"Please, Alex," begged Konigstahl. "Name your price. Anything you want. I broke your car. . . . I can give you ten just like it. Girls? I can give you a harem of slaves who will—"

"Is that what you think your life is worth?" Hawke shook his head. "There's only one thing I want from you."

Looking death in the eye, Konigstahl discovered an untapped vein of courage. "Are you so certain? I hunted you. Now you want to hunt me. We're alike, Alex. Kindred souls."

"We're nothing alike," Hawke replied coldly. "You hunt for sport. I'm putting down a rabid dog." He unslung the rifle and moved his finger to the trigger. "Were I you, I'd start running."

FORTY-NINE

P ippa Guinness was ready to go home. Unfortunately for her, Herr
Doktor didn't agree.

"You just survived major surgery," he told her, his clipped
manner and accent making the words sound more like his native German than English. "It's too soon for you to be on an airplane."

"What if I take the train?" She wasn't sure why a twelve-hour train
journey would be less harrowing than a two-hour flight, but it seemed
a reasonable compromise.

"Tomorrow, we see," replied the doctor. "If there is no infection,
we see."

And so she was forced to endure another day in a hospital bed more
than five hundred miles from home.

At least she had the television to keep her company. Between the
still undetermined outcome of the Scottish vote, the attempted bomb-
ings in Belfast and London, and the unexpected resignation of the PM
due to a sudden illness, the latest news from home was more engaging
than any scripted program. But nobody was reporting the biggest story,
the abduction of King Charles. He was no longer a hostage, as evi-
denced by the fact that he had been able to present his historic address

to the nation, but how that had been accomplished, Pippa could only guess.

No doubt Alex had something to do with it, she thought.

"Visitor for you," announced her nurse, Greta, from the doorway.

"Visitor? Who would . . . ?" Her heart skipped a beat. *Could it be . . . ?*

"A gentleman," purred Greta. "A *very* handsome gentleman."

Over the nurse's shoulder, Hawke's face floated into view. "Hullo, Pip!"

Disappointment and joy struggled briefly in Pippa's heart, but the joy won out. "Alex!"

Hawke pushed past the nurse and entered the room. In his hands was a vase filled with white roses and baby's breath. When he reached the bedside, he looked down at the flowers uncertainly, then held them out to her. "I wasn't sure which ones to get, but the florist said you can never go wrong with roses."

Pippa rewarded him with a smile, then gestured to the side table. "Put them there, won't you?"

He set the vase down as instructed. "I'm sorry I wasn't here for you."

"Alex, I understand. You've been busy. I've seen the news."

The comment elicited a faint smile from Hawke.

"And look at you," she went on. "You look like you should be in here with me." Then, realizing how that sounded, she quickly amended, "In the hospital, I mean."

"They tried that," Hawke said with a laugh. "I escaped."

"You must tell me how. I feel like a prisoner here myself."

They shared a moment of laughter, and then Hawke became serious. "Are you . . . all right? I mean, are you going to be all right?"

Her smile faded just a bit. "The doctors say I will be. It will take some time, but eventually, I'll be good as new."

"Better than new."

The assurance, empty though it was, brought back her smile. "I gather you found . . . him."

"It was a close thing, but yes, we did. All God's children are safe at home, and all is right with the world."

"I want to hear all about it. Pull a chair over. I'm not going anywhere."

Hawke looked around nervously. "I'm not sure this is the place. Everything's hush-hush, you know."

Pippa's smile turned into a pout. "Oh, you're probably right. Then let's talk about something else. I'm so bored here, Alex."

Hawke shifted nervously but then reached for a chair. As he did, Greta called out from the door, "Look who is Miss Popular today. You have another visitor."

Pippa's eyes widened in alarm.

Not now.

But it was Sir David Trulove who entered the room. "Ah, Miss Guinness, good to see you still among the living."

Greta spoke up, addressing Pippa. "Is this too much for you? You need your rest."

Relieved, Pippa shook her head. "No, no, it's fine, Greta. Thank you."

Trulove moved closer until he was standing next to Hawke. "Is there anything I can do for you, my dear? Anything you need?"

"What I *need* more than anything is to be home."

"I'll see what I can do about that." He then turned to acknowledge Hawke. "Ah, Alex, I'm a bit surprised to find you here."

"Well, I had to check on Pippa, didn't I? I was in a bit of a hurry when I left here."

Trulove looked skeptical. "First chance you got, you came down here—is that it?"

"Something like that. I also had to come collect the Locomotive. It got rather smashed up. I'm making arrangements for it to be shipped to Hawkesmoor. Young Ian promises me he'll have it fixed up good as new."

"Better than new," murmured Pippa.

"I see. Say, Alex," said Trulove with a side-eye glance, "you wouldn't happen to know anything about what happened to Prince Heinrich, now, would you?"

"Not a thing," said Hawke, feigning surprise. "Something's happened to him?"

"Yes, he's dead. A hunting accident. That's what they're saying at any rate."

"Hunting," Hawke tsked. "A dangerous hobby."

"Mmm, quite. Well, from what I've heard of the fellow, the world's a better place." He stared at Hawke a moment longer before going on. "Alex, I wonder if you could give Miss Guinness and me a moment. Alone."

A look of relief came over Hawke, but then he affected a suspicious expression. "Going to talk about me?"

"Of course not," rumbled Trulove. "We have far more interesting matters to discuss."

"Well, as it happens, I really do need to see about getting the Loco home." He turned to Pippa again. "Do get better soon."

"I will, Alex."

He seemed to want to say more but, not finding the words, simply turned and left.

When he had gone, Trulove turned to Pippa again and took her hand. "We're going to take care of you, Gwendolyn. You may depend upon that. We'll bring in the best surgeons. A live-in nurse. Whatever you need."

The outpouring brought tears to her eyes. "Thank you, Sir David. But just now there's only one thing I need."

Trulove patted her hand. "I thought you might feel that way. She's in the waiting room."

"She's here?" Pippa's eyes went wide. "Does Alex . . . know?"

"It's not my place to tell him."

Pippa let out her breath in a long sigh. "Good."

EPILOGUE

I t was Christmas Eve. It was also his birthday.

And it all felt like déjà vu.

Lord Alexander Hawke was standing before his dressing room mirror, humming.

Not the whole song, mind you, just a few bars of the chorus to his favorite holiday carol.

He hummed as he brushed his hair and finished donning his white tie and tails. Tonight, he, Anastasia, and Alexei were off to attend a very fancy Christmas Eve feast.

This festive event—which was hosted every year by Lady Diana Mars and her husband, Ambrose Congreve, at their home, Brixden House—had not originally been on the agenda for Lord Hawke. He had intended, rather than partaking in a splendid black-tie affair, to spend his first-ever Christmas Eve with Anastasia and Alexei together in private, most likely in Bermuda, at Teakettle Cottage. But this year, it was much more than a holiday feast. In fact, it was a prewedding celebration for Alex and his soon-to-be wife.

The grand gesture was both thoughtful and, if he was being honest, a tad intrusive. Congreve, his longest and dearest friend in all of the world, should have known that Alex would have much preferred a quiet, more intimate setting for his newly reunited family.

Plus, Hawke did not like having to dress like a penguin.

As a boy, Hawke had loved Christmas, and even now, despite everything, he found his mood to be cheerier than he would have first thought. It helped that Alexei, who was brushing his hair next to him, was smiling ear to ear, singing along as Hawke hummed the chorus.

"May your days be merry and bright . . . and may all of your Christmases . . ."

The room fell silent.

"Why did you stop, Papa?"

"Does this remind you of anything, Alexei?"

"Do you mean your outfit?"

Hawke smiled at his son. "Well, yes. That too. Come here, won't you?" Hawke sat his hairbrush down, then hoisted Alexei into his arms. "Do you remember this very night just three years ago?"

Alex watched the gears turn behind his son's eyes as he desperately searched for any memory of three years prior. Then they came to a stop. "I don't remember, Papa."

"Oh, my boy, it was just this night several years back now when you and I stood in this very place, readying for the same party we'll soon be off to at Uncle Ambrose's house. You asked me something about the meaning of a white Christmas, and then we took off across the snow-covered streets to celebrate with many, many important people. Ambrose was only engaged at the time and hadn't yet made an honest woman out of Lady Diana, though he did remedy that problem the very next day."

Hawke made a mental note to wish his friend a happy anniversary, then continued. "I believe you made a wisecrack about their wedding, in fact."

"I did?"

Hawke nodded. "Hmm, indeed. It was both funny and spot-on, I might add."

"I still don't remember," said Alexei, frowning. "But we can make new memories, Papa!"

"I intended to do just that, my boy," he said with a nod. Hawke sat Alexei down and turned his attention back to his dressing mirror as he began fussing with his white tie.

Always a chore to tie the damn thing.

Usually, Pelham was right there to help him. But since Hawke, Anastasia, and Alexei were off for a few nights' stay to enjoy the holidays together, Hawke had thought it best to give the dear fellow two weeks off to visit with family in Wales and enjoy some much-needed time away.

Odd, thought Hawke. *I do believe Pelham was also off to visit family three years ago.*

Déjà vu struck Alex again, freezing him—hands on his tie, still wrestling the damned thing into place—in his tracks.

Then Anastasia walked in.

"Let me help you, dear," she said.

Anastasia stepped in front of Hawke. She wore a snug white silk dress that hugged her hips and backside, accentuating her hourglass figure. As she reached up and delicately manipulated Hawke's tie into place, Alex couldn't help but think about how she was the only birthday present he wanted to unwrap this Christmas Eve.

Anastasia smoothed his tie, then ran her hand down Hawke's chiseled chest, letting it linger just long enough to suggest that he might get his wish upon returning home from the party.

"There now, all fixed. You do look dashing, dear. Very handsome indeed."

"Thank you," said Hawke. "You look more radiant than ever, Anastasia. How lucky I feel knowing I will have you on my arm tonight."

"What about me, Mother?"

Alexei turned now to face his parents. Dressed like his father, the small boy beamed with pride for having graduated to the adult-looking attire. It was, Hawke noted, a seriously far cry from the dark blue vel-

vet suit, short pants with knee socks, and patent leather shoes that he
had worn those few years ago.

"You, sweet boy," said Anastasia, "will be the most handsome young
man there tonight." She very carefully dropped to a knee, then tightened Alexei's tie and, just as she had done with Hawke, smoothed it
into place. She made doing so look effortless. "Come, Alexei. Time to
leave."

"Beat you to the car!"

Hawke was the last to exit the room. As he did, he turned to flip the
light switch and caught his reflection in the frosted window. Only, it
wasn't *his* reflection.

At least, not his current reflection.

No, instead, Hawke saw himself and Alexei. Next to his son was the
boy's puppy, and Alexei had his arms wrapped tightly around the dog's
neck. Hawke stared for a moment at the ghosts of his past, unable to
move.

"Did you and Mama ever get married?"

"In our hearts, we did."

"What's that mean?"

*"We couldn't get married. Some very bad people took your mother and you
away from me, and—for a very long time, I thought she was in heaven. With you."*

"She's in Russia."

"I know."

*"Why don't you go there and marry her, Papa, so you can spend your whole
life with her?"*

*"You know what, darling? Maybe someday, when you're older, I will do just
that. You and I will go there together. And we won't leave Russia until she agrees
to come home with us."*

"And then get married to us forever."

"And then get married to us forever."

"Papa! Are you coming?" Alexei called up the stairs.

Hawke blinked the memory away.

Forever.

Something resembling a shiver ran up Hawke's spine.

He flipped the switch and walked out of the room.

The backcountry roads were icy that night, but Hawke's BMW X5 trekked through the fresh powder with relative ease. They arrived at Brixden House and took a right turn through the grand gates at two minutes before seven that evening. Theirs was to be the wedding of the season, and though both he and Anastasia wanted a much quieter gathering, Hawke nonetheless expected tout le monde would turn up for the affair. Just as they had three years prior for Ambrose and Lady Diana's big day, assorted royals, in addition to everyone who was considered a part of the upper echelons of London society, not to mention members of the press and the media, had shown up dressed to the nines.

"It looks like a winter wonderland, Papa!" said Alexei. He had his face pressed to the glass of the window and was looking down at the sight that was Brixden House and the surrounding gardens, all of which were decorated immaculately for Christmas.

"It's gorgeous, Alex. Are you seeing this, my love?"

"Yes, yes. A lovely winter wonderland. Rather enchanting, don't you think?"

Alex parked the car and stepped out into the cold night's air. Fresh, thick snowflakes dusted his jacket in no time, but he didn't mind. Hawke had always loved the snow. In fact, as a boy, he used to pray that the snowstorms would never stop.

Hawke walked hand in hand with Anastasia and Alexei. He stole a look at the great evergreen trees lining the long drive, all strung with countless fairy lights, leading from the gate, through the woods, and all the way up to the house's main entrance.

Three years ago, the sight of such splendor had been not merely breathtaking but joyful. At the time, Hawke had been unsure if he'd ever find such happiness again.

And yet now he had.

Hadn't he?

The receiving line snaked up the grand staircase and all the way to the Grand Ballroom on the second floor. It was, thought Hawke, just as he remembered it from the last time.

Inside the house, it was yet again a glittering affair. Flaming candles and Christmas decor of every description stretched as far as the eye could see.

"Any of this ringing a bell yet, my boy?"

Alexei's eyes lit up. "I remember this, Papa. I do!" Hawke watched his son turn in search of something. "There!" he said, extending a chubby finger toward a door. "We went that way last time, remember?"

"Right you are, Alexei," said Hawke, guiding their party of three toward the door Alexei had pointed at. Alex knew the large oak door led into an empty reception room off the Great Hall. It was how they had snuck in last time rather than wait their turn in line.

"When the coast is clear, let's make a break for it."

"Are you sure this is okay, my love?"

Real concern registered on Anastasia's face, causing Hawke to laugh.

"I should think so. We are the honored guests after all, are we not?"

A moment later, the trio made a break for it.

Inside, everything was nearly exactly as Hawke remembered it. Just as it had been before, the Grand Ballroom was packed to the gills: a sea of fashionable men in formal attire and women in glittering costumes and perfectly coiffed and festooned with diamonds that rivaled the long row of majestic crystal chandeliers above. In the center of it all was an extravagant forty-foot Christmas tree, and to the side of the room, a stage had been erected. Hawke thought he remembered a full orchestra playing Christmas carols last time, but he couldn't be certain.

He'd been in many great rooms over his lifetime, and the music—live or otherwise—was never his favorite part of it all.

"What in the bloody hell are you doing out here?"

Hawke turned and smiled at his old friend.

"Merry Christmas, Uncle Ambrose!"

"Merry Christmas, Alexei. Hullo to you all." Congreve spoke fast as if the politeness was nothing more than a formality, something he had to say in order to get on with whatever message he had come to deliver.

"Merry Ch—"

"Now, what in the devil are you doing out *here*?" Congreve repeated, cutting Hawke off. "You're the guests of honor, for bloody sake. You cannot be *here* until you're announced. Come right this way. And do hurry before Lady Diana thinks the big surprise has been ruined."

———

Ambrose Congreve led Hawke, Anastasia, and Alexei up the grand stairway and turned right. When they reached the library—which Hawke thought to be the most beautiful in Britain—Congreve shouldered his way into the room and flicked on the lights.

"Wait here until you're called, Alex. It won't be long now."

"What about me?" asked Alexei, looking from Hawke to Congreve.

"Ah, now, you can come along, dear boy. Let me show you around, maybe have a glass of whisky or two. You do like whisky, yes?"

"Ambrose," said Hawke.

"I'm kidding. Tonight is a night of celebration, of course." He winked at Alexei. "We're only serving champagne."

Hawke let out a chuckle. "If you serve a boy champagne, I will be the least of your worries, Ambrose. He'll be yours until morning or until"—he looked at Anastasia—"mother bear strings you up like an ornament on that very large Christmas tree you have downstairs."

They all had a laugh. And then Ambrose Congreve and Alexei

went back downstairs, leaving Hawke and Anastasia alone in the library.

———

They were alone, just the two of them, but to Hawke, the library felt more empty than it should have. It had been that way since he returned home several months back, battered and bruised. Those wounds had healed, but there was still something *off*—something he couldn't quite place.

A sudden heat came over him, and Alex tugged at his tie.

That's odd. I remember this very room being quite cold three years ago.

"Are you all right, Alex?"

"Think I just need to cool myself off for a moment, if I'm being completely honest." He walked quickly toward the small doorway that gave way to the balcony. A moment later, the heat wave subsided, replaced by the cool chill of the winter wonderland raging outside.

Hawke stepped onto the balcony and leaned over the railing. The grounds really were immaculate, replete with pristine decor and holiday cheer.

What in the hell is wrong with me?

"Alex?"

Hawke felt Anastasia behind him. She slipped an arm around the back of his neck, then moved in beside him, her head tilted back to look at him.

"I'm sorry. I just need a moment."

"What's the matter, Alex? Tonight is supposed to be spectacular and full of bliss, is it not? Talk to me. Is it the birthday blues?"

"No, nothing like that." Hawke had never been one to make a big deal of his birthday. Nor had anyone else, for that matter. But that was only because pulling off a birthday party is next to impossible when such a day falls on Christmas Eve.

"Then tell me what's troubling you."

"Well, that's just it, isn't it?"

Anastasia eyed him suspiciously.

Letting out a sigh, Hawke turned and placed both arms around her, resting his chin delicately on the top of her head.

"Is this love, Anastasia?" Hawke whispered.

"I do love you, Alex. I always have. Don't you know that by now?" She arched back enough to look him in the face. "Do *you* think this is love?"

Hawke was silent for a long while as he searched for the right words. Finally, he looked up, staring her right in the eyes, and said, "I'm no longer sure I even know what love is, to be bloody honest with you."

Anastasia let go of him.

"What are you saying, Alex?" Her voice was trembling.

"I will always love you, Anastasia. Always. I just don't know . . ." Hawke took a long, deep breath, letting the cold air fill his lungs. For the first time in a long while, he craved a cigarette.

"I loved you fiercely before," Hawke went on. "But then I lost you."

"But you didn't *lose* me, my love. I was always here."

"No," Hawke said softly. He knew that Anastasia was referring to the couple of years when Hawke thought her to be dead. "I mean, when I went to Russia, my heart bursting at the seams to see you, take you in my arms, and bring you home. You and our boy, our *beautiful* boy. But . . ." A tear slipped from Hawke's eye and slowly wound its way down his face. "But when you chose to stay in Russia, damn it, Anastasia, part of my heart stayed with you, and I don't think I've ever gotten the bloody thing back."

"But I *am* back, Alex. Is your heart not full again?" Her eyes were pleading.

"Not yet, darling." Hawke kissed her cheek. "Not yet."

For nearly ten minutes, the only sounds that could be heard were muffled voices from the party taking shape below and the soft cries of Anastasia, who pressed her face into Hawke's chest as she wept.

"I'm so sorry, Alex," she finally said, "for not returning with you and our son. I should have, and I wish more than anything that I could go back and make it right." Reaching up on her tiptoes, she kissed him deeply. "Will you ever forgive me?"

"Of course," said Hawke quickly. In truth, he didn't want to hurt her. "I just ... I just ..."

"You need time, my love."

Hawke nodded.

"Then, Alex, I shall wait for you. As long as it takes."

"Will you still stay with Alexei and me? I want to be a family, Anastasia, more than anything. And Alexei, the poor boy deserves it. Do you know that three years ago, on this very night, he and I were here for the celebration for Ambrose and Lady Diana? They were married the next morning. I don't quite know why they chose Christmas Day of all days for their wedding, but that night, before we left the house, Alexei asked me if you and I had ever married."

"Sweet boy."

"Indeed, he is. I told him then that in our hearts, we had married. And he asked me if we could go to Russia and marry you so you'd be with us forever. Please don't leave us—*him*—because of me. I can hardly bear the thought. He's had such a hard life already, you know."

"I wouldn't dream of leaving. I want to be with you and him both. I'll do whatever you need, Alex. But do take some time, and I will be here when you're ready."

"Thank you for understanding."

"I think," said Anastasia, "that's what love is. Understanding."

Maybe she's right. And maybe I don't deserve her at all.

"I quite like that. *Understanding*," Hawke said.

"Alex, can I be frank with you?"

"I would expect nothing less."

"I own very much the way I handled things in our past, and I will forever regret my own actions, but, darling, have you ever considered that there are other forces at play here—things that go back much, *much* further than our time together?"

"I don't know that I'm following you," Hawke said truthfully.

"I know that I hurt you, my love. But your pain runs far deeper than whatever I've done, does it not? Maybe, Alex, you finally have everything you've ever wanted, and that scares you because either you're afraid it won't last or you simply don't know *how* to be happy."

She'd hit the nail on the head, saying the very things that had been concerning Hawke the most since he'd returned from his latest globe-trotting, England-saving escapades.

My parents, Victoria Sweet, Nell Spooner . . . why does everyone I love have to bloody die?

"I will learn, Anastasia. I promise you."

"Like I said, dear, you just need time. Take it, Alex. I won't go anywhere. Now, come, let's go back inside. You're going freezing cold and wet. I'm afraid you'll catch death if you stay out here any longer."

The cold hadn't bothered Hawke, nor had he realized how much snow had collected on his head and shoulders. "When I was a boy, I used to pray that the snowstorms would never end. Did I ever tell you that? Wonder what that says about me," he said.

"The storm is all you know, Alex. . . . It's where you thrive. Not in warm shelter but in the chaos of elements you cannot control. That's where you most come alive. You don't need to weather the storm. You *are* the storm. Don't you ever forget that, my love."

Hawke nodded, his mind racing. While simple, Anastasia's words had a profound impact on him.

"It's where you thrive . . . in the chaos of elements you cannot control. . . . You are *the storm."*

Suddenly, it was as if the puzzle pieces were finally falling into place.

"Let's go inside. I may fancy the storm, but you look positively frozen."

"Before we do, there is one more question we need to answer. What to do about tonight?"

"Tonight? Ah, yes, *tonight.*"

"There are many people gathered here to celebrate our . . . well . . ."

"Wedding." Hawke rubbed the back of his head, embarrassed by the timing of it all.

Why didn't I tell her this before we came?

"I certainly picked a bloody great time to drop this bomb, didn't I?" They both smiled at each other.

"Quick," she said. "You grab Alexei, and the three of us can make a break for it and be back on the road in a few minutes. We can say one of us fell ill. We'll figure it out."

A knock at the door startled Hawke, who spun on his heel and walked back into the library.

"Too late," he said over his shoulder.

Hawke had expected either Congreve or Lady Diana to retrieve them when it was time, and he found it hard to stifle his surprise when Sir David Trulove walked through the door.

"Trulove?"

"Alex," said Sir David, "forgive me for so rudely interrupting. However, I am afraid this matter just couldn't wait a moment longer. You see, Charles, the King, well, though he is immensely grateful for all that you did to ensure his safe return home, uh, he requires our help at once. You see . . ." Trulove's eyes flicked toward Anastasia, then back to Hawke. "Is there anywhere we could speak in private for a moment?"

Anastasia brushed the snow from her shoulders and strode in from the balcony right past Hawke and Sir David. "You can speak in private here. I was just on my way out, Sir David."

"Where are you going?" asked Hawke.

"To find Alexei, of course."

"Hold on! David, my apologies. Give me just a moment, please."

Hawke hurried past Trulove and followed Anastasia into the hallway, catching her at the top of the stairs. "Anastasia!"

She stopped, turning to face Alex. "It's okay, my love." A weak smile formed across her face. "This is your get-out-of-jail-free card."

Hawke didn't understand.

"My . . . my *what*?"

"Clearly, Lord Hawke, the King himself once again needs you . . . rather tragically, I might add, on the very eve we are to celebrate our forthcoming wedding, which, by the way, must no doubt be postponed until you're back from whatever assignment MI6 is sending you on."

The message was clear. She was giving him an out—one that everyone would damn well believe too, Hawke knew, because of how long he'd been married to the job.

The irony wasn't lost on Alex.

Hawke took Anastasia back in his arms. "Are you sure about this?"

"Take whatever time you need, Alex. I will be waiting for you when you get back."

"I don't even know what the assignment is or what—"

"Shhhh," said Anastasia, holding a finger to Alex's lips. "In my heart, I am already married to you forever. We'll figure out the rest later on." Removing her finger, she replaced it with her lips and again kissed Hawke. When she finally pulled away, she said, "Now, go. I'll find Alexei and explain to Ambrose and Lady Diana that the King himself has summoned Lord Hawke, and beg their forgiveness for ruining this perfect night."

"Thank you," whispered Alex.

He stood there as Anastasia walked down the stairs, eventually disappearing from sight into the sea of people that had spilled out from the Grand Ballroom. He sensed someone at his side and turned to find Sir David standing next to him.

"It would appear that there's a Warmonger, Alex, a bloody, fucking nasty man causing all kinds of ruckus around the world, primarily in Turkey and Russia. We don't know much about him, to be quite frank, but you see, he's making demands of the King, and, well, Charles trusts nobody but you to handle this."

Another mission, thought Hawke. *A new storm . . .*

"A Warmonger, you say? Hmm. Well, Trulove, then it does sound like we had better get moving rather quickly, don't you think?"

Sir David patted Hawke on the back. "I do regret the timing of it all, but I must say, it's good to have you back, Alex."

Hawke nodded his thanks. "Now tell me everything you know about this Warmonger fellow, and I want to know what demands he's making of Charles."

"He's waiting to tell you himself."

"Who is? Charles?"

"Like I said, the King requests your presence immediately, I'm afraid."

"Well, let's not keep the old boy waiting, then, Trulove."

And with that, Hawke descended the stairs, found Anastasia and Alexei, and walked back into the cold night.

The radar showed that heavy snow would soon cover most of England, and as thick, wet flakes fell rapidly all around them, Alex Hawke secretly thanked God for the storm. . . .

And he prayed that it would never, ever stop.

For Ted.

ACKNOWLEDGMENTS

Writing *Monarch* was, and I mean this quite seriously, the hardest thing I've ever done. It's daunting enough to step into the shoes of a legend, but even more so when that legend is someone you loved dearly and owe so much to.

Ted Bell, for those who don't know, was more than a friend to me. He was a mentor and, at many times, my greatest champion. I would playfully call him "Teddy B" whenever he'd ring me, and I can still hear that big, loud voice he spoke with in my head. "Buddy!" he would always say by way of greeting before launching into a story of some sort. Once, I remember quite vividly, Ted called very excited, having just learned the true origins of the dark 'n' stormy, a drink that you, dear reader, likely know Alex Hawke became quite fond of. So did Hawke's creator.

Another time, during the early days of COVID-19, Ted called and told me he was thinking of chartering a yacht and taking to the ocean for a few months. "Come with me," he said. "We can talk about the next book!" Having worked with Ted behind the scenes for nearly a decade, I knew he was kidding, but only partially. "Ted," I replied, "if I leave my wife and six kids at the height of a pandemic to go cruise around the ocean without her, I'll return home to find out my wife left me and has filed for divorce." He laughed hard. Ted had a big, infectious laugh that was contagious and healing. "Yeah," he shot back, "but it'll only be your *first* divorce, so it doesn't count!" We both laughed. We always laughed.

Yes, Ted Bell meant a lot to me. When I was coming up as a young writer, he championed me. He played a large part in helping to shape the story idea for my debut novel, *Fields of Fire*, and was always confident that I would become published. He spoke about it often, motivating me. He always said, "When your book comes out . . ." and never "*If* your book comes out . . ." I loved him for that too. But never—and I mean this sincerely—*never* did I think that I would one day be writing books in his series.

So, first, I would like to thank my friend Ted. I wouldn't be here without him. And yes, writing *Monarch* was so hard because, well, I loved him so much that I didn't want to let him down. That added pressure was suffocating at times—I won't pretend it wasn't—but through it all, I found comfort in hanging out with Alex Hawke, Ambrose Congreve, and, of course, Stokely Jones. The first chapter I wrote of this book is the one where Hawke is in Teakettle Cottage, waiting for Anastasia and Alexei to return home. You will notice subtle nods and references to Ted (who actually was the Writer in Residence at Cambridge for a time) in that chapter, including Alex reading, as you might have guessed, *Tsar*, by none other than Ted Bell, which was his favorite Hawke book.

The weight of filling in for Ted hit me while I wrote that scene, and when I typed that first quotation mark, signaling that Lord Hawke was about to speak, I realized that until that very moment, nobody had written Alex's voice but Ted. I sat at my keyboard and wept so hard my wife came in to check on me. Then I called my new dear friend, the lovely and amazing Byrdie Bell.

Byrdie, thank you so much for trusting me to find Hawke's voice and for allowing me the awesome opportunity to write this book. I am so incredibly thankful for you, our friendship, and your support every step of the way. As you know, writing *Monarch* was a labor of love, and as much as I want your dad's fans to love this book, you were the person I thought of every day while sitting at my desk and chipping away at this story. I know how much you miss your dad, and I hope that, in some small way, this book helps and comforts you.

Anyone who knew Ted knew that he loved his daughter, or as he affectionately referred to her, "My kid, Byrdie," and let me tell you, Byrdie is the real deal. My friend, your dad would be so proud of all the work you've done to keep his characters alive, and every time we talk about Hawke, the books, and story ideas, I just know he's smiling down, laughing right along with us.

To John Talbot, my agent, thank you. I remember where I was and what I was doing the very moment John called me to say that Penguin Random House was considering continuing the Hawke books, and that I might be considered to take over. I was outside, sitting on my swing, playing with my rottweiler, Rubble. It was sunny and warm and still early in the afternoon. Then my phone rang, and I knew instantly that something big was going on because I heard the genuine excitement in John's voice. John, I know how much you did to make this happen, and I'll never forget it.

Even with John and Byrdie on board, it takes support from the publisher to make a book deal happen. For this one, it was Tom Colgan, editor extraordinaire, who believed in the story and bringing back Alex Hawke. Moreover, Tom—a giant in our industry who has worked on everything from Tom Clancy's books to Mark Greaney's Gray Man series—believed that I was capable of finding Hawke's voice, which in turn made me believe I was capable of doing so. Tom, what a joy it is to work with you. Thank you so much, not only for this opportunity but for all of your sage advice and help along the way.

My father, James Steck, is a voracious reader. In fact, he reads more than me, and I do it for a living! His favorite author? Ted Bell. My dad has always loved Ted's books, and for *Monarch*, he was my first reader. Knowing that my dad, a Hawke and Ted fan through and through (he's got a special place in his heart for Stoke and his GTO), enjoyed this book meant a lot to me. My mother, Rhonda Steck, listened to me read pages aloud, usually when I was worried that the characters didn't sound British enough, and on many occasions watched our kids or took them out so that I could work. Mom and Dad, I love you both so much. Thank you for everything.

Alex Hawke has a very specific and unique way of talking. There's a cadence and rhythm to his sentences, and his word choice is distinct and deliberate. He's proper, but he's also whimsical and sarcastic at times, and the timing of that needs to be just right. Getting Hawke's voice down was no easy feat and would have been impossible without John Shea, Ted's longtime narrator and friend. For six months straight, I constantly played Ted's audiobooks when I was writing, driving, sitting in my office, taking a walk, and, yes, even while falling asleep. Hearing John perform Hawke helped me while writing dialogue for Alex, and to be frank, I don't know that I could have done this without his masterful work on the audiobooks.

To Ryan White, a fan of Ted's, thank you for your willingness to talk about the books and lend your perspective on the characters and series as a whole. Ryan was one of the very first people I told after signing my contract to write *Monarch*, and his enthusiasm meant a great deal to me.

Writing a book is just the beginning. Once it's done, it falls to people like Loren Jaggers to tell the world about it. Loren, a longtime friend, is the assistant director of publicity at Berkley and one of the best publicists in the business. To that end, everyone at Berkley has been amazing. From the copyeditors to everyone in the art department to marketing and beyond, thank you so much for all your hard work on this book.

I referenced my beautiful wife, Melissa Steck, above. Thank heavens I never boarded that yacht or left her during COVID, because she has never left me. My best friend, the mother to my children, and the one person who knows me better than I know myself, Melissa kept me going while in the dog days of wrapping up *Monarch*. She was by my side every step of the way, encouraging me and supporting me in whatever way was needed at exactly the right time. Babe, thank you for always believing in me and being there for me. I love you beyond words.

And finally, to you, the readers. If you've made it this far, then that means that you took a chance on me and read *Monarch*. Thank you. I wrote this book out of love, and I hope you felt that on each and every page. I also wanted it to be a fun, entertaining entry in Ted Bell's bestselling series, so I sincerely hope that you enjoyed this adventure. If you did—then good news! Lord Alex Hawke will set sail again. Remember that pesky Warmonger I mentioned in the epilogue? Well, next year, you will see him square off with Hawke as the Warlord goes toe-to-toe with the bloody Warmonger, and I promise it's even bigger and more action-packed than *Monarch*.

Oh, and don't worry. Hawke will soon commission the building of a new superyacht to replace the *Sea Hawke*. I won't spoil it here, but I do believe I've come up with the perfect name. I can't wait to share that and more with you next year.